DAUGHTER OF WAR
BLADE OF TRAESHA BOOK I

KELLY COLE

KCB

Kelly Cole Books ISBN 979-8-9853212-0-3

kellycolebooks.com

Cover Design by Ellen Kenneda

Instagram @comicoffii

For the four who have always been there: Allison, Charlie, Ben, and Anna. Thanks for letting me have all the creative genes. (Just kidding. Love you!)

CONTENTS

CHAPTER 1

"Remember your breathing," my father said, words muffled by his scarf and the whistling wind.

"Remember *your* breathing," I muttered into my own scarf. The air was damp and musty where it caught in the thick fabric, but warm. We'd been out here for hours and my father's instructions were getting more nit-picky by the second. Half because he knew it annoyed me, half because he was worried.

He huffed a laugh at my tone, stepping back out of my space. I adjusted my grip on the mid gun I held, ignoring my father when he clicked his tongue at the habit. He hated fidgeting with weapons. In seconds he was going to open his mouth to admonish me.

We'd lost our target minutes ago, but I clung to our game. "I've lost visual."

My father reached for an imaginary earpiece. "Commander Larson speaking. We've lost sight of the target." He squinted, pretending to listen to a response. "Continue north. Copy. Will remain on high alert. Target armed and dangerous. Three patrols have already fallen under its attack."

I snorted. We were crouched behind one of the many boulders creating a makeshift, rolling wall around the city of Vichi. Here we were out of the biting wind and the threat of more snow it carried on its scent. My fingers were stiff with cold inside my gloves.

I wanted to stay out here forever.

My father made a few quick motions with his hands. Bellovian signals every child was taught in their first weeks of school. *Keep low. Move forward two units of cover. Stay together.*

With a nod, I did my best to stay serious and play along. Keeping as low as possible, I dove into an exaggerated roll, gun barrel pointed to the side so I didn't accidentally shoot myself. I straightened and backed against the next boulder quickly. I turned in time to see my father roll over his shoulder, snow flying and limbs flailing more than necessary. I stifled the laugh he was working so hard to draw out of me. He had to roll twice to cover the distance I did. When he straightened, he was so snow-covered he had obtained the perfect camouflage.

I dropped to my stomach and crawled on my forearms to the next cover, body slithering on the ground behind me. Snow made its way into every gap in my clothing and nearly blinded me, stinging the bit of skin still exposed on my cheeks. No doubt we were both completely covered with it now. I looked back and my father shook his head at me, unwilling to commit so much to our game. The snow started melting into my inner layers and I couldn't blame him. He crawled on hands and knees to join me. It might have been an even more hilarious sight than his somersaults.

Slightly breathless, he pushed me out of the way so we were both hidden again. When he turned, the sight of snow clinging to his eyebrows and eyelashes did me in. I fell to laughter and he lunged to cover my mouth. "Not so loud, Larson!"

I could barely breathe between his hand and my scarf. The mouse we'd been "hunting" was long gone. I tucked the gun into my waistband and grabbed his arm. Using the movements he'd taught me, I removed his hand and twisted out of reach. Challenge sparked in my father's dark eyes. Snow flying, boots slipping on the rocks and snow, we moved into sparring. Soon I tugged my scarf away from my mouth to breathe as the exercise warmed me. My father taught me everything I knew about fighting and shooting and warfare. He taught me the Bellovian way of life. On top of my schooling, he gave me lessons to keep me safe and hidden. To keep me from falling for the commander propaganda. I hated the war because my father taught me how pointless it was. How harmful.

I trained for the war because there was no other place for me.

I spun into a kick and knew as soon as I shifted my weight it would be too quick. I softened the blow before I hit my father's arm and his layers protected him from damage, but it was too late. He'd marked my speed. The shift in his demeanor reminded me how cold it was out here.

"Finley."

"I know." I looked away from the disappointment in his eyes. The fear it masked. "I was too fast."

He pinched the bridge of his nose. I don't know if he picked the habit up from my mother or if she picked it up from him, but they both did it when I had uniquely disappointed them. They never pinched their noses for my brother. He never made them worry.

"You can't volunteer. You aren't ready. It's too risky, not just for you but also—"

"I am ready! I just got caught up."

"No. Fin, it's too dangerous."

"So what am I supposed to do? Clean Command Hall to earn my keep? Shovel the streets? Go live in the Squalor with the rest of us who can't find work? At this point I've done too well in school not to volunteer. It'll be suspicious and put focus on you and Mom. *That's* risky. There are no jobs. I'm not good at anything else. We know this. It's why we've been training."

"Finley, if you can't conceal your Trish blood, your speed or how light you are, or even the urge you have to speak Trish like you did just now because you're getting upset, you won't have a life at all."

I fumed silently, collecting my argument amounts the fears and frustration built in my mind. "I don't have a choice, Dad. And I will hide it. That's the first time I've slipped up in months and it only happened because I'm worried about leaving. I don't want to go, but once I'm there, that will be all I have to focus on. It'll be okay. I'll be okay."

He sighed, deflating. In the Bellovian school system, they looked for the fighters early. I'd singled myself out in second year when I punched Dani Carns for speaking ill of my brother. Since then, I'd been placed in all the classes that encouraged aggression and battle strategies. Anyone could volunteer for war. Most people in Bellovi served at least four years if for no reason than the guaranteed meals. Kids in my classes, especially kids who did as well as I did, were expected to go to war and do well.

I hated that I excelled. I knew it was my father's Bellovian blood that gave me the instincts that had gotten me so much attention from the teachers. I wished I was more like my gentle Trish mother or even my brother, who graduated school only to fall into the background playing the piano at important events.

All eyes were on me. My class was one of the most promising and today we were expected to put our names down to leave on the next train for base.

From there I would learn truly to fight and embrace my inner Bellovian. I would learn to kill and rise in the ranks without drawing attention to the advantages my mother's Trish blood gave me. And when I got high enough, I would learn how to destroy the people who had overtaken my mother's homeland of Traesha, killed and enslaved her people all to fund a war against the Florians. A war that had been in stalemate so long most people barely remembered or cared how it started anymore.

I was going to end that war.

THE SUN WAS HIGH OVERHEAD. I was determined to volunteer, but still found myself hoping my father wouldn't notice the time and we would stay out here too long to make it to the meeting.

Of course he noticed. "We should go. I have to speak today. Commander Adkins has been on my case, saying I need to give a report."

"It's bad, isn't it?"

My father didn't respond, only began trudging through the snow back to our cycle. He was head accountant for the

Bellovian commanders and knew better than anyone how war was bringing poverty to our midst.

The worst example of it was the Squalor surrounding Vichi. In the heart of Bellovi, a land of cold, sparse land-scape, our city was nestled inside the ring of boulders where my father and I escaped to train. Next was a ring of manmade disrepair and starvation, a ring of middle-class apartments, a ring of houses for the rich, then City Center, the hub of the commanders' offices, schools, city resources, and war technology.

One could barely see Command Hall where we stood. It was made of the metals our small country mined before the war consumed our workforce. Now we only spared enough able bodies to dig for coal in our need for warmth. The metal was a matte steel that matched the materials of the gun in my hand. The Command Hall sucked in the sunlight and drew the gray from the clouds suspended above. I hated that building. It swallowed my father's time and energy and housed the men and women who worked ceaselessly to continue Bellovi's war against the Florians. Who orchestrated the attack on Traesha, my mother's homeland, and robbed the northern country of its resources and enslaved its people not for the betterment of Bellovi's poor, but only to finance the war efforts further.

One day I would be a commander. All I had to do was keep my enhanced abilities a secret so they wouldn't know I wasn't fully Bellovian. So they wouldn't send me and my mother back to Traesha. Or worse. In time, with work, I would be welcomed into those cold halls and have access to the information that would bring that building down.

My father let me drive the cycle back to City Center, where the war meeting would take place and I would be given the opportunity to volunteer. Going through the

Squalor always left me with a bitter taste in the back of my throat. It was early enough in the day that most of those who lived here were still huddled inside the now sagging, cracked, and crumbling structures that passed for buildings and houses out here. The streets were scattered with treacherous holes and piles of garbage and ruin that took most of my concentration, yet I still felt the eyes that peered out at me through dirty windows at the sound of our passing. My father's cycle was a commander's cycle, so most knew better than to approach, but my neck hair prickled with potential danger. There were rumors of a black market and unruly rebellion in the Squalor. Black market guns and stolen technology. Rumors likely spread to create a greater rift between those living here and those living in greater comfort near City Center. My father told me the people here were only doing what they needed to survive.

Despite these assurances, the stories that circulated at school had me gripping the handlebars and constantly scanning our surroundings.

In a small square, the street was in good enough condition that I could look up. I locked eyes with a girl around my age, hollow-cheeked and hungry-eyed, standing at the base of a broken statue. I nearly swerved our cycle when rather than looking down and scurrying away at the sight of the commander's stripes on my father's uniform, a slow smile spread across her lips and she dropped a wink in my direction. My father shifted behind me and I thought I heard something fall, my sharp hearing picking up the thud over the engine's roar, but my father's impatient grunt stopped me from looking back.

We passed through the rest of the Squalor and the apartments without further incident, if making eye contact with the smiling Squalor girl could be called an incident, and soon had parked in front of the low gray brick building where war meetings were held.

People streamed inside, shouting at each other to be heard through their scarves and hats. I winced at their loud, barking voices and booming laughs. I wanted to be back in the calm outside Vichi. Once the cycle was parked and stowed properly, my father only gave me a brief nod before rushing in to get to his place in front. I hung back until the crowd was only a trickle, nerves slicking my hands inside my gloves. It was really happening. I was about to seal my fate.

With a sigh, I followed a man leading four young children inside.

I slipped into the last row and unwound my scarf. I spotted my brother Nico up front, playing mindlessly on the piano no one paid any attention to. He went through the Bellovian national anthem twice without anyone noticing. He caught my eye and sent me a wink, the corner of his mouth lifted in the slightest smile as he went at it for the third time. I returned his smile for just a breath, and with practiced ease, we both slipped back into our neutral stares. The less the Bellovians around us knew what we were thinking, the better. Seeing Nico was the only good part of war update meetings, especially since my mother refused to attend them anymore.

The little girl next to me looked old enough to be in second phase at school. She frowned at my expensive leather boots and the new sweater I wore. Her own were scuffed and patched multiple times over. Likely they had previously belonged to her older sister sitting next to her. She arched an eyebrow and turned her attention to the front of the room, angling her shoulders away from me. I held in another sigh.

The tall girl in front of me turned around, face twisting into a sneer. I was truly regretting my choice of seat.

"Larson," she said.

"Carns."

"Your father better have some positive updates. I'm tired of him cutting my mother's salary."

"I'll file a complaint for you." I knew my blank stare unnerved her, so I kept my voice flat and my features mild.

She frowned in confusion, trying to decide if my words were sarcastic when I'd said them with so little inflection. "You—"

The piano music stopped and Dani's mother elbowed her side. She turned back around but lifted the hand opposite her mother in an inappropriate gesture. The girl next to me giggled. When I looked down, she gave me the same vulgar hand signal. Bellovians were not known for their creativity.

Commander Adkins stood and walked to stand behind the podium. He began in his drawling voice, carrying on about shifts at the Front, some new training technology, and the high number of volunteers they were expecting. Being one of those volunteers, I came to attention.

"I look out at all our children, ready to take up the call, and I feel lucky to be Lead Commander in Vichi. This year's class is predicted to be among our finest batches of volunteers. Now is the time to add your name to the list. Please stand if you are ready to join our fight against our oppressors and free our nation once and for all!"

I swallowed. I looked around Dani Carns, now on her feet, over the rows of pews to my father and brother at the front of the room. Nico's eyes were sad. My father shook his head, just slightly.

But I was doing this for them. To free them, too.

I stood. Back straight, head high, I didn't let the Bellovians see what crumbled inside as my name was taken and I made the promise to go to war. I had to let go of what little Trish nature my mother had passed to me. Had to let go of fantasies of queens and gods and green fields.

The time had come to embrace the half of myself that screamed for vengeance and violence. The people around me had killed those dreams long before this moment. It was time to fight back.

"Excellent! The train is scheduled to leave this Secondday morning, weather permitting." My stomach dropped. I knew we'd be summoned soon, but the day after tomorrow wasn't nearly enough time. "Make our city proud in the week of training to follow and the war ahead."

Everyone cheered, so happy to send their children off to battle. Although, the children were cheering too. I forced out a whoop of my own when I felt the eyes of the girl next to me.

Our names were taken and the cheering died down. Most of the other volunteers received slaps on the back or handshakes as they settled back into their seats. The lead commander gestured to my father and he stood next. He kept his speech short, yet it was still enough to bring down the celebratory mood. Another budget cut was imminent due to dwindling resources from Traesha. His words caused a stir and earned me a glare from Dani. I almost frowned. I hated that the Bellovians relied so much on my mother's homeland, stealing its resources and labor, but I didn't like knowing the production was falling either. What did this decline mean? Were the people, enslaved and overworked already, unable to keep up with demand? Was my mother's land dying? Was the magic she claimed existed there fading? After eighteen years without a queen and its balance disrupted, this wasn't so hard to imagine. My mother's beliefs consisted of three gods representing the royal family, the land, and the people. The bonds that tied them were what allowed her people to flourish. The Bellovians cut that bond when they planted a bomb in the throne room. If the land was dying, were the gods? I believed in the gods enough to send prayers out of habit, but this development gave me pause.

I pulled my coat closer. I hastily prayed to Mags it wasn't too late. That by stopping the Bellovian rot one day, I could save them.

My father sat down and Commander Adkins retook the stage. I went so far as to close my eyes to ignore him as he carried on about changes to the third phase curriculum. A sudden yelp made them fly open again. A few rows ahead of me, I saw Mayze Hale climbing back into her seat, glaring at her cousin. Oken was coughing aggressively into his arm in a way I knew meant he was barely containing his laugh. Even from here I could see how pink Mayze's ears were. Everyone refocused their attention to the front with a few unhappy mutters. Oken mimed jabbing her side again and Mayze punched him solidly in the shoulder. Their play was such a nice distraction, I had to fight off a smile from the sight. His curls of black hair shook as he struggled to control his laughter. His aunt scowled at him until he finally stilled.

Even this view of the back of his head made it harder to breathe. He was tall enough that I could see his shoulders, his gray sweater looking soft and worn. He stretched and the view of his back got even better as the muscles pulled taunt. I forced my eyes to the podium, swallowing in an attempt to settle my fluttering stomach. I tried to remember if they had stood when Adkins called for volunteers.

The meeting finally droned to a conclusion. People began talking, mostly in excitement over a forward shift in the southern reaches of the Front and the fresh volunteers. I stood quickly, thinking I would find Nico and squeeze in a few words before I went home. I craved my mother's company, though I dreaded telling her I'd given my name.

I made my way to the hall that would take me to the front of the room. It was usually empty as most preferred to stay in the seating area to mingle after the meeting. Yet as I walked, I heard heavy footsteps following me. No one was in front of me to see my eyes roll. When I rounded the corner, I pressed against the near wall. This was the second time Dani had attempted to corner me in this hall. The last time we were interrupted by the arrival of some commanders. This time we might have a chance to fight. I was determined to get the upper hand.

I was already going to war, what was the point of trying to keep the peace at this point?

I tensed to jump her. She was much taller than me, so I planned to go low, trip her up, and gain control on the ground.

"Dani!"

I hated that I recognized his voice so easily. Dani stopped just before turning the corner and Oken was quick to catch up with her.

"What do you need, Sars?"

"We're training early tomorrow. Fallen's Gym. Want to join?"

"Sure."

There was a pause. "What are you doing down here?"

The question sounded strangely rehearsed. I longed to look around the corner.

"I was going to have a talk with Larson. Little thing thinks she has what it takes to go to war. I thought maybe I should give her a taste of what to expect. She's probably up with the commanders now, though."

"Shame," Oken said. I glared at the floor and swallowed the pang of hurt. Of course Oken felt the same about me as all the Bellovians did. Only my family was any good.

They retreated down the hall and the tension in my shoulders relaxed. I opened my fists and turned just as my father, brother, and our family friend, Commander Gale, appeared. They all wore uncharacteristic frowns as they muttered with their heads bent together. "—basement cells. I've heard them referred to as 'trainees' but I don't know why—" Commander Gale cut off when she spotted me. Their faces shifted into forced smiles.

"Finley! Congratulations!" Commander Gale wrapped me in a hug, her one arm strong and familiar. She had lost the other at the Front but insisted she remain in the fight. My father said her determination was the reason she'd made it to three-stripe commander. I thought it was the insanity she showed in the heat of action if the war stories she's told around the table when we invited her to dinner were any indication.

"Thanks, Commander."

She gave me a sad smile. It looked like a goodbye as she ruffled my hair once more and continued on her way.

"I have to go to Commander Adkins' to play for his son's birthday celebration," Nico said by way of greeting.

"So you won't be at dinner?"

He shook his head.

"Maybe I'll swing by in the morning," I said as noncommittal as I could. Nico's apartment was near Fallen's Gym. I might see Oken on the way to school if I left from there. It was too hard to resist the excuse to see him before I had to leave. He might be a Bellovian, but I could enjoy the view of his smile one last time.

Nico pulled on my braid and hurried on his way. I turned to my father.

"I have to go to the office for a bit," he said.

I narrowed my eyes at him. "You hardly ever work on Seventhday."

My father gave me a tired smile. "The finances are a mess, Finley. I have to work today so I can have tomorrow night off." My last night at home. I reluctantly nodded.

"Can I at least take the cycle then?"

He tossed me the keys. "Give your mother my love. I'll come home as soon as I can."

I rolled my eyes at his answer, knowing that could be anytime between dinner and nightfall. With no one around to see, he gave me a quick hug and we parted ways. I practically ran to the cycle, already knowing my mother wouldn't be happy with me. Even more so now that I had to tell her my father was putting in extra hours today and Nico wouldn't be around for dinner.

CHAPTER 2

I parked the cycle in our garage and stepped into the kitchen. Like most of the wealthy homes on our street bordering City Center, it was warm inside. The color scheme was not very different from the dreary winter world outside. I removed my boots to the smell of garlic in the soup simmering on the stove and bread baking in the oven. I took my time shedding the rest of my winter layers, my stomach in knots.

With a steadying breath, I went in search of my mother. She was upstairs in bed under layers of blankets and napping with a small dial timer and empty tea mug on the nightstand beside her. I stopped at the doorway and looked my fill.

I'd inherited some of my father's height, but not much. My mother looked tiny bundled under the covers. Her hair was dyed black, same as mine. The same color hair as the Bellovian people. I realized we'd have to dye mine a couple of days earlier than usual before I left for war. Our black hair was our best disguise. This and the expensive clothing we wore was usually enough for Bellovians to decide we weren't worth their interest even with our light-colored eyes and darker skin.

Above my parents' bed rested a slim, unsheathed sword on a pair of hooks. The blade faced me, etched with delicate vines.

My mother told me it used to belong to her mother, who was a high-ranking member of the Trish royal guard. The *magsai*. I never failed to stare at the beautiful weapon and wish it could be used for more than decoration. Many of my fantasies growing up featured me wielding the sword at the Front, using it successfully despite the guns fired all around me. Like a *magsai* warrior brought back to life.

Yet all the sword did was gather dust or hide in the back of the closet when company came by. Once, when I was little, I reached up to feel the cool silver of the blade and received a nasty cut in the process. I rubbed the first two fingers of my right hand against my thumb and felt the ridge of the scar on the pads of my fingertips. I now knew enough about knives and weapons to see the wicked sharpness of the blade even from here.

Listening to my mother's stories about Traesha, the ones about the *magsai* were always my favorite. I used to ask my mother about them and the Trish princess nightly, until I felt childish dreaming of any of their survival. I knew now all the *magsai* guards were killed during the invasion. I had accepted the death of the Trish princess. It was as difficult to believe she had survived as it was to think a girl wielding a sword would make any difference in this war.

I sighed and went fully into the room, sliding under the blankets on my father's side of the bed. My mother was quick to turn and pull me into her warmth. I knew she was at least slightly awake. But I couldn't ruin this moment of peace with her. I let her hold me, knowing there would be nothing close to this once I stepped onto the train headed for the training base.

In little time, sleep claimed me as well and I fell into a familiar dream.

I never knew where I was here. It wasn't Vichi. A big part of me wanted to believe this was Traesha. That somehow my mother's stories had brought the land to life in my dreams.

It was peaceful here. Quiet. Once I appeared, the girl next to me sighed, her shoulders relaxing as if relieved that I showed up. I could never really see her, just a silhouette on my periphery, but I was as familiar with her presence as I was with Nico's.

I wondered if these dreams would follow me to war. I reclined backward, tilting my head to look up at the canopy of leaves above us. I'd never seen trees in my real life. Well, an occasional sparse pine in the boulders didn't count. But when I came here, there was always green. I was always warm.

I started to hum and the girl settled back into the grass too. If she were real, our arms would be pressed together. I called her my dream shadow. Sometimes I worried I'd conjured up her presence because of the loneliness of my childhood. A make-believe friend to keep me company at night. She kept showing up more and more in my dreams lately. Right as it was time I outgrew childhood fantasies.

A sharp crack sounded in the bushes behind us. I flipped over to look, rising onto my knees. My dreams weren't usually disturbed by sounds like that. By other presences. I squinted into the trees, but I couldn't see anything. I was surprised to find myself worried for the made-up girl next to me. I could leave, wake up, before something charged out of the bushes to threaten us, but what would happen to her?

When nothing appeared, I reasoned my daytime anxiety had seeped into the dream. My thoughts returned to war. The peace I found here shattered.

I woke with a start, my mother's arms no longer there to comfort me. I heard her and my father downstairs, readying the dinner table. My relief that work hadn't held him up was short-lived. Would he tell my mother I volunteered before I had a chance too? My mother likely knew what was coming, she always seemed to, yet I still put off the moment as long as I could, breathing in the comforting scent of my parents and staring at my grandmother's sword. I was looking for the strength I usually found in the sight of it. Today, there was only a chill in the air.

No help for it. I threw off the blankets and went downstairs for dinner.

As I entered the kitchen, my eyes went immediately to the stove. I nearly didn't see my father step from behind the doorway and reach for my wrist. He used to get me all the time, grabbing it, spinning me, and pinning my arm high on my back, never where it hurt. Now I danced out of reach with an easy laugh.

"How was the nap?" he asked, ruffling the hair on top of my head. Even contained in a braid, sleep had made it messy.

"Really good. I'll m—" I almost said "miss your bed" but remembered my mother's presence just in time. That wasn't how I wanted her to learn I was going to war the day after tomorrow.

My father caught my meaning and his eyes dimmed, the deep brown almost black. I'd never understand how my mother's light-blue eyes managed to make their way onto my face, competing with such a dark shade. My older brother, a full Bellovian from my father's first marriage, had inherited those dark eyes down to the way they betrayed every emotion if you knew how to read them.

18

My mother said my father's eyes were the only reason she trusted him enough to follow him out of Traesha.

She turned from the table and ordered us to sit. Her hands fluttered in the air, betraying her worry the same way my father's eyes gave away his. She knew the volunteering was today, but the glimmer of hope in her expression told me my father hadn't said anything. I swallowed the hard lump in my throat and sat.

A few probing glances from my father were the urging I needed to speak. "Mom, I volunteered today."

She dropped the ladle into the soup pot, not even noticing how it splashed the table. Her eyes had gone distant. "I thought you might. Tell me again why you think this is a good idea?"

"I don't have any other options."

"You could play piano like Nico."

"Nico only gets jobs because he uses a fake name and looks like everyone else. Only a few people actually remember Dad is his dad." No one liked our wealthy family, but Nico had a far easier time blending in by using his mother's name on school documents, and being so calm and always collected, he faded into the background.

But kids at school had always known there was something different about me. The fights it caused brought on far too much attention. Fading from notice had never been an option.

Also, I was a terrible piano player. There was no need to remind my mother of the fact.

"You could have waited. Finished school at least."

"Everyone volunteers when they turn seventeen."

"Finley, you are so smart. I know you didn't take specific classes for other skills, but you could be anything. I don't understand why you have to go!"

I dropped my eyes to the table. The tears at the edge of my mother's voice were almost enough to make me question myself. But I was doing this for her. For my family.

"It's because she's angry, Elise. Isn't it, Finley?"

My father's words surprised me into looking up. I shouldn't have been shocked, though. He had probably seen it all throughout our years of training. Each time I came home with a split lip or a black eye from school, he'd taken every hit I needed to get out after and taught me more and more difficult combinations, only stopping us when I tapped into my Trish speed and accidentally outmatched him.

"I *am* angry." My voice came out a whisper. "I want them to pay for what they did to Traesha. I want to stop the commanders before they hurt more people. Before they hurt you guys."

"By going to fight in their war?" my mother checked. I couldn't read the look on her face, something that rarely happened.

"Yes. I'm good enough to become a commander. When I'm among their ranks, I'll learn what I need to do to stop them."

"You understand your father is a commander?"

"He's an accountant now, though. He doesn't have access to things like weapons development or movements along the Front."

"What about Gale? We trust her, don't we, Teo?"

"Not that much, Elise. Finley shouldn't approach anyone but us with these treasonous thoughts."

There was a moment of silence.

"You want to get revenge for Traesha. All on your own?"

"I'm the only one who can do it, Mom. Maybe with the rebellion, but I've only ever heard rumors they exist. I can't wait any longer. Something has to be done and with my abilities and Dad's training, I'll quickly rise in the ranks."

"They'll find out what you are, then you'll be as likely to be killed by friendly fire as the Florians'. Either way, it's too dangerous. With the Florians' abilities, you won't make it past the Front!"

"I don't care about the Florians or their abilities. We don't even know if they still have them! They haven't used anything besides guns at the Front in ten years. All I care about is stopping the commanders."

My parents were looking at each other now, a conversation dancing between their eyes. Finally, my mother's shoulders slumped. "It's too late to change anything now."

"When you get there, you need to make sure no one suspects you have Trish in you." My father went on to tell me to stay at the top of my class, but not the very top. In some respects, I could excel without causing suspicion, but I was too small to justify being stronger and faster than some of my fellow volunteers. He talked me through the tests he could remember from his time at the training base. My mother remained silent until he ran out of cautions.

"Finley, you are at an age where those blessed with stronger Trish abilities grow into their full strength. You need to be extra careful that you don't skip. It runs in our family." Skipping was the Trish word for their bursts of lightning-fast speed. I'd only seen my mother do it a handful of times.

"I doubt I'll have the ability, Mom. I'm not in Traesha and I'm not full Trish. I'll be fine."

She frowned at the table. In the quiet that followed, a heavy exhaustion fell over the table. My father was the first to rise, kissing the top of both our heads after he cleared most of the table. My parents shared one of their loving looks before he left us, and my heart tugged.

The meal I usually loved grew tasteless and hard to swallow the more I thought about leaving. With my father gone, I gave up and set my spoon down. Guilt twisted my knotted stomach further when I thought of all those starving in the Squalor while we left our meals uneaten.

"I'll save it for tomorrow. Don't worry." My mother smiled tightly, reading my thoughts as only she could. "It's cold enough outside to leave the pot in the garage."

I nodded, my throat tight just looking at her. I'd been preparing for this week my whole life, but the reality of my departure still hit hard. How could I leave my mother? She was the only other Trish person I would ever know. She taught me everything about our people. We shared something my father and brother could never understand. They didn't partake in the hair dying, the fearful and deliberate slowing of our movements to match the Bellovians, the insults the people around us threw without thought about our weak, conquered people.

I would find nothing like her in the years to come. No gentleness. No soft whispering tones of Trish. No hugs and forehead kisses and worried smiles. No stories of the *magsai* or Trish ships. No songs about love, forests, and queens of old with their white hair and golden throne.

"You look tired, Finley." No one could even say my name the way my mother did, like a word taken out of a song's chorus. "Head to bed, my love."

I hugged her tightly before going to my room. Sleep after my nap was long in coming, but I was still relieved to burrow under my blankets. For all our hugs and loving gestures, my mother and I preferred to cry alone, and tonight we did.

CHAPTER 3

My father moving on the stairs woke me. I sat up, eyes bleary and swollen. A glance at the clock confirmed that if I hurried, I would still have time to visit my brother. I jumped out of bed to ready for the day.

My father was in the hall when I left my room. He gave me a tight, fleeting hug.

"Have a good la—day at school, Finny," he said. We both winced a bit when he stopped himself from saying last.

"I'll do my best. You'll be home tonight, right?"

"I wouldn't miss it if it meant ending this war." We let out a laugh. Ridiculous was my father's favorite brand of humor.

He lingered at the top of the stairs long enough to give me another smile before he turned and left for work. I watched him go, feeling hollow.

In the bathroom I took a quick shower and dried my hair as well as I could so it wouldn't freeze in the cold outside. I braided it straight down my back as school and

Bellovian tradition required. I dipped my chin to check my roots. We'd dyed it a bit over a week ago, but my mother and I would be doing it again tonight to be safe. After that, I'd have to figure out when to sneak to the bathrooms to dye it myself at base. The thought swirled anxiety in my core.

I'd only ever seen the slightest tinge of silver at the roots before my mother determined it was time to color it. The most telling Trish features I had were my high, prominent cheekbones, my narrow nose that curved upwards, my sky-blue eyes, and slightly darker skin tone my mother warned me would be more noticeable after time spent under the sun. These features might be a problem at base, but I had no way to change them. I looked Trish. But I knew how to be a Bellovian.

It would have to be enough.

The anxiety churned harder. I swallowed and turned from my reflection.

The bathroom grew chilly. I pulled on my thick leggings, sweater, and padded socks. Ready for my last day. When I entered the kitchen, my mother was sitting with a cup of steaming tea clutched in her hands, clinging to its heat. She did this every morning in the same way she soaked in the warmth coming from the fireplace at night.

"I'm going to stop by Nico's on my way to school," I said, crossing the room to the coats hanging by the door, stopping just long enough to grab a slice of bread from the counter.

She gave me a small smile. Worry tightened the corners of her eyes. "Send him my love."

I pulled on my leather coat, red knitted scarf and matching hat, boots, and the new white gloves I had received for my birthday.

"Until I see you next." This was the closest phrase the Trish had for goodbye.

"Unless I see you first," she replied. Her worry and distraction were tangible in the air. I itched not to be surrounded by the tension a second longer, yet at the same time wanted to relish every minute I had left with her.

"Finley, wait."

I paused with a hand on the door.

"It's not just the Bellovian in you."

"What do you mean?"

"Your desire to fight back. I can tell it makes you uncomfortable. But it's not just the Bellovian. I'm angry too."

I considered her words. "But it's... this violence. This pull I feel toward the Front. I ache to be there. It's not right, Mom. I hate them."

"You don't hate them all. You love your father and Nico. You have some friends at school—" she ignored my snort "—and you feel for the people in the Squalor."

"Yes. It only makes me hate the commanders more."

"But not Bellovians. Just remember not all of them destroyed Traesha. That many of them reaped the benefits, but they didn't take part. I couldn't let your father hold me if I held onto an anger like that. He and Nico aren't the only gentle Bellovians. Commander Gale isn't the only one not caught up in bloodlust. It's what they are taught, it doesn't mean it's who they all are. I just don't want you to feel ashamed of your instincts. I want you to listen to them. Your heart will lead you true."

She didn't know. Not really. How much I wanted to fight back, to show my speed just once and put people like Dani Carns in their place. To prove to the world I was strong and powerful. There was anger and there was

25

Bellovian bloodthirst. I gave my mother a small smile and left, opening and closing the door quickly so I didn't let the heat out of the kitchen.

It was still dark and the streetlight set the white snow to sparkling. The new layer was just a dusting, but the wind picked up as I walked, sharp and cruel. I tucked my face into my scarf and stayed close to the edge of the road in case a cycle or transport made its way past.

More snow was not far in coming. I could smell the crisp tension of it building in the clouds. People I passed risked the cold just briefly to tilt their heads from their scarves and look at the sky. I wondered how they would transport the volunteers if it fell too heavily to move the train and remembered Commander Adkins's words: *weather permitting.* I forced down the hope I might be given more time and refused to join those around me in checking the clouds.

I passed several groups of students just leaving their homes for training before school. None of them was Oken. Those who couldn't afford the membership at a training facility were running through the streets in too little clothing. Two people, muddy and out of breath, exchanged blows in a yard outside an apartment building. Their angry expressions made it difficult to distinguish if they were practicing or in an actual fight. Both were equally likely to occur on these streets, though it was early still for a true argument in my opinion.

As I wound further into the cluttered block of apartments, more people filled the streets. By the time I reached my brother's building, I was walking against a crowd trudging into City Center for work. Weapon developers, sanitation workers, communication experts, and the like were all tired and overworked at jobs I still sometimes longed for.

I ran up the stairs to Nico's apartment on the tenth floor and jiggled my key enough times in the knob to force it open. My brother's rooms were old, but clean. I walked in and stepped over a small pile of mail for Hapton Travs. All invitations to play piano at upcoming events. I frowned at the letters bearing his fake name. Nico claimed he used it so no one assumed our high-ranking father bought him the success. I suspected he did it because our family name garnered too much hatred and Nico worried it would lose him jobs.

In the center of the room, Nico's well-loved piano took up the majority of the space.

"Nico?" There was no answer, but I heard water running in the bathroom. I prayed to the gods he heard me and would come out covered. I went to the window. From the back of the apartment, one could barely see the ruins of the Squalor surrounding the city. The beginnings of sunrise illuminated all the wisping smoke trails rising from the fires people there lit in a desperate attempt to stay warm. Nico always glanced that direction when he played sad ballads from Traesha.

I grew cold standing so close to the frosted glass and moved to sit down at the piano bench. I positioned my fingers on the worn keys and played a Trish song, singing quietly.

They hunt with quiet laugher
The deer follow the sound
They kill them with their beauty
They skin their gentle hides
They cry for their company
They sing the forest song

The trees whisper along
I am the deer and proud trees
I take and don't return
Cover and build, arrow and sword
Consume and burn
I love and protect
I take but never give
The forest is my song.

I missed the second to last key and finished the song awkwardly, my voice carrying when the piano abruptly ended on the wrong note.

"You should really leave the playing to me. *I* respect *you* enough not to sing," Nico said from behind me. The steam from his shower touched my face now that the door was open. Thank the gods he was fully clothed.

I stuck out my tongue and he laughed. "I should take back my spare key," he said, pulling my braid and walking to the counter to make some toast for breakfast.

"It's not like I'll be using it much longer." I tried to keep my voice light. We both ignored how I failed. "You'll be there tonight, right?"

"Of course I'll be there, Fin." He sat down next to me on the small bench, our shoulders touching. We had sat like this countless times before. Him playing. Me singing. The music flowing out like it was desperate to be released. "Don't go acting like this is some big goodbye. We all know you've trained enough to stay away from the Front. You'll be promoted to commander in no time, and then you'll be visiting Vichi between missions and barging in here whenever you please like you never left." Nico bumped me with his shoulder, trying to make me smile.

I half-heartedly played a couple of notes from the song. I hated the thought of leaving Nico. Like me, he'd had few friends in school and retained none of them. There used to be men he'd talk to or about, but even that stopped in the last year. As far as I could tell, he was entirely focused on his music. Background noise to the rest of the city.

We'd always just had each other. I leaned my head against his shoulder.

"I'm going to be a commander. I have to get high in the ranks to make any difference. What will I have to do to get there?" Nico stayed silent, sensing more was coming. "And I heard Mom and Dad talking. He said the Florians have been getting more aggressive since that team got to Helsa and killed the Florian queen. Mom's worried they'll stop holding back, that they'll use their abilities. I might have Trish gifts, but what will they do against that? If Mom's stories about what they can do are true—"

"Stop worrying! They may be more aggressive, but they still aren't moving on the offensive. Just reinforcing some of the lines. Trust me, I've heard plenty of commanders groaning about wanting more action." I could tell from his tone Nico rolled his eyes. "You just play it smart. Keeping a cool head will get you further than being successful in battle."

I hit a key a little too forcefully and ignored Nico's answering cringe. "I just wish I had a better idea what to expect. Besides the training and all that, I mean. I wish I knew where they will put me. And what I'll have to do not to be found out. How best to keep you guys safe here." What kind of monster the war would turn me into.

"Hey now, we're the last thing you need to worry about! You'll figure it out." Nico put his arm around my shoulder and pulled me close. I ached knowing how much I'd miss speaking in Trish and his easy affection. I might only be leaving behind few people in Vichi, but each loss was tearing at me. I would desperately miss my family.

The sun cast the room in an orange glow as it rose. "I should head to school," I said.

"Okay. Try to relax. I'll see you tonight."

Nico hugged me at the door. Going down the stairs, my feet felt twenty pounds heavier than they were when I first arrived. Leaving my brother, I truly regretted volunteering for the first time.

I kept to the side of the road again and the untouched snow was clean enough to keep me squinting as it reflected the new sun. There was a point in my life when I'd owned a pair of goggles that blocked light. But around the time they broke, the wealth Bellovi experienced after overtaking Traesha began to dwindle and my father had to impose a budget cut that hurt even his salary.

That act also ensured even fellow wealthy Bellovians hated my family.

The students who were training until now were just getting out. My heart skipped at the sight of them. I couldn't help but look for Oken in the crowd. We traveled in the direction of the three schools at the edge of City Center, breaking into groups based on our ages as we got closer. Those still warm from training wore their coats unbuttoned and loose to cool themselves. The students my age were laughing and boisterous, the call for volunteers the main topic of conversation. Even if they hadn't volunteered, school was nearly finished for all of us.

Despite my planning, I couldn't believe my luck when Mayze Hale caught my eye and spared me a quick smile. I could almost call her a friend, but we weren't close. Mostly we just worked on projects together. She occasionally let me in on some big gossip. Last week we talked about how our recent birthdays made us eligible to volunteer. We'd probably be on the train together tomorrow.

Mayze also happened to be close with her cousin.

There he was, walking by her side. Oken didn't look my way, yet still I tucked my suddenly burning cheeks deeper in my scarf. His black hair curled loosely and flopped on his head with his bouncing steps, his energy undaunted by the training he'd just put in. He spoke quickly and made big gestures, his leather jacket flapping on his arm where he'd draped it as though the cold had no effect on him. He smiled so big his light-brown, almost golden, eyes squinted. I'd shared classes with him my whole life and still the sight of him never failed to make my heart flutter. His expressive face and unrestrained laugh brightened the gray stones of the apartment buildings.

He could ruin me with that laugh.

Oken was a mechanic and worked after school. Even from here I could see a dark tinge on his fingers left from the motors. He likely hadn't felt pressure to volunteer because of his trade. He already worked on army vehicles and would be allowed to stay behind to continue contributing to the war in this way. I didn't need to worry about him distracting me once I left Vichi.

With this thought, I lifted my head and let myself look my fill. It might be my last chance.

His group stopped while Mayze checked for something in her bag. I slowed my pace just a few steps behind them and Oken happened to glance over at me mid-sentence. Our eyes caught, but he wasn't the only one to notice me.

"What are you looking at, Larson?" Dani asked, spitting out my last name. She crossed her arms, lips curling into a sneer. Oken trailed off whatever he'd been saying.

I straightened my shoulders and kept my face void of

expression. "You. I won't have many chances left before they send you to the Front." The words came out without a thought.

She actually growled. I dodged the wild punch she threw my way with ease. "You better watch your back! The Florians will be the least of your worries."

I backed away. Oken was staring at me. His eyebrows pinched. Seeing his expression, I regretted my words. Still, I turned and met Dani's glare long enough to show her I wasn't intimidated. When she scoffed and looked away, I ducked into the crowd, moving quickly, but not too quickly. If Dani looked back, she would be the first person to turn me in for any Trish traits she spotted.

It took until I reached my seat in the back row of the classroom for my heart rate to calm. Oken and his friends followed not long after and took their usual place in the front. I picked at a loose string on the sleeve of my black sweater, telling myself I didn't need, or want, to look at him again.

Teacher Reddings followed the last of the students in and shut the large wooden door, pulling none too gently against the old hinges. He began his lesson, droning on about scope equations and drawing angles and proportions on the board. I could feel my eyes glaze over almost instantly. With all resources going to the war, few students in my class had likely ever held a real gun before. Most lessons about them were done with broken, useless ones and mechanics written on the board. At least I would be gone before we were tested on any of this. When boredom urged me, I broke my resolve and chanced a glance at Oken. I almost laughed to find him slumped back in his seat, mouth hung open as he slept. Teacher Reddings either didn't notice or didn't care.

We jumped in our seats when there was a knock on the door. Especially Oken, who let out an abrupt snore upon jerking awake. The door squealed when the low-ranking commander forced it open and walked in.

"Due to the coming storm, the train carrying volunteers to base is scheduled to leave within the hour," she began. Everyone straightened. My throat closed even as my brain rejected the meaning of her words. "I need Hetta Busha, Dani Carns, Mayze Hale, Matten Holm, Finley Larson, Oken Sars, and Rody Tills to come with me now."

CHAPTER 4

Dani jumped up with a whoop. The commander nodded to Teacher Reddings and turned for the hall. I was numb. Detached. The world shifted to a dull roar. I pushed back my chair, stood, and followed the commander out. In the narrow corridor, volunteers were led from every upper grade classroom, most smiling or rubbing their hands together. Only a few looked upset about the loss of goodbyes.

I thought about the night I would miss. Nico and my mother would have played the piano, me standing behind them singing. I loved to sing, but it was only a Trish custom. Bellovians were capable of using their voices only to bark commands, complain, or boast of achievements. The Trish sang of love, loss, ancient magic, nature, and happiness. I knew all the words by heart. My father would smile from where he watched on the couch. When we finished our songs for the night, he would claim we were the best thing he'd done with his life, but he was still waiting anxiously to hear the piece we'd been writing about him. My mother would assure him it was in the works and let him wrap his arms around her. She would snuggle in closer, always clinging to warmth. She looked years younger when she relaxed in my father's arms.

Eventually she'd go on her tiptoes, seeking a kiss. Nico would cover my eyes and beg them to stop, making everyone laugh. At the end of the night, before he left for his apartment, he would pull me in for a hug and compliment my singing, always too sweet to be a Bellovian, too sweet for war. I would love every moment with my family of secrets.

I hated the commanders even more for taking away my last night with them.

Word spread of the early departure and Bellovians flooded the streets. People cheered and congratulated us as we were paraded deeper into the city.

"Stay strong!"

"Kill the Florians!"

"Victory for Bellovi!"

"March steady!"

Snow began to fall.

Students eagerly accepted stiff handshakes and pats on the back, the extent of Bellovian affection. I kept my face neutral and lifted my chin. I shook the hands jutted in my direction and joined the cheering. I tried to prepare myself for what was to come.

Time moved more quickly than I ever dreamed it could. I found myself at the base of the stairs to the train platform.

"Finley! Fin!" I halted at the sound of Nico's voice, my sharp hearing picking it up over the cheering. I pushed away from the line of students to the edge of the crowd where he was shoving a path for himself. He threw a canvas bag into my hands. I slipped the strap over my head without thought, settling it at my hip.

"I heard while I was playing this morning," he panted.

"I love you, Nico." I knew he couldn't hear me as well as I heard him, but he read my lips with ease.

"We all love you too, Fin." He lowered his voice to speak in Trish. "Until I see you next."

I stood frozen. I wasn't ready for this. We held eyes. Our breath fogged the air between us. I saw Nico's chin quiver, but even he couldn't give into tears now. I opened my mouth to respond, to tell him I'd see him first, but a surge in the crowd separated us.

I stumbled back and strained to look over the others and return his wave. To maybe catch sight of my parents. Were they out there? My mother was too short to be seen over the Bellovians surrounding her. Likely my father wouldn't be able to leave his desk, but still, I desperately searched the crowd until a hand on my bicep turned me to take the stairs. Oken was watching me. I froze and felt my face instinctively drain of any expression. Had he heard Nico speak Trish? Did he suspect? My heart hammered. I was pushed up the platform steps and into a train car before I could decipher the look on Oken's face.

Inside the walls were completely gray, the seats a minimally cracked, black leather. The white tile floor was smeared with a path of muddy footprints. It smelled of new paint and an underlying tang of discharged bullets.

I found a seat in an unoccupied row and clutched the bag Nico brought me to my chest. Air puffed out and briefly the smell of home—lavender and fresh baked bread— assailed me. I closed my eyes and tried to ignore the sounds of celebration.

From this point forward I would embrace the Bellovian soldier inside of me. The brute. The unfeeling. I could not be weak. Weak people were sent to the Front to buy time while the commanders planned ways to end the never-ending war.

Bellovi had been at war so long most of us didn't know how it started. I suspected my father knew, but he hated talking about it. Home was his sanctuary away from all that. All I knew was the defeat of Traesha and the assassination of the Florian queen were the only notable accomplishments the Bellovian people claimed in living memory. The current stalemate at the Front was decades old, but rumor had it things were changing since the Florian queen was killed almost a year ago. They were sending in more people.

The train jerked into motion. Someone sat heavily to my right and my eyes flew open, betraying my surprise. It wasn't good for my neutral expression to have cracked so soon, but my emotions were running high. Mayze Hale gave me a bright smile that I returned with some effort. I wouldn't have expected her to find me on the train to share in her excitement. If I were her, I'd be sitting next to Oken with the loud group in the back of the car. As if the thought conjured the noise, his contagious laugh sounded behind me. Why did he even volunteer?

"I hate that we didn't get to say goodbye, but it's finally happening! A chance to prove ourselves!"

"I know it'll be us who end this war! I can just feel it, can't you?" It was so easy to speak Common Tongue like the Bellovians did. All hard stops and starts and rough noises I felt in the back of my throat. Harsh words I didn't mean.

"Yes! I do! You didn't really train with us, but people like Oken, Dani, and Rody are going to make all the difference. You did train some, right? At least with running?"

"My father trained me. He's a commander. I don't know

how I compare to other people, but I think I can hold my own."

"Oh. Of course. Must have been nice." Her voice softened and I recalled the day she'd been pulled from class to be informed her father hadn't survived the Front. She was red eyes and sniffling the rest of the school day. She cleared her throat and pressed on, upbeat once more. "Well, we can train together once we get to base and maybe have more moves to teach each other that way."

We fell quiet, watching out the window as the crowd disappeared from view. The train moved down the tracks, pulling me steadily away from my family. Picking up speed, we passed through the Squalor. The view was different from the train car than it was speeding through on the cycle with my father. More people came out to watch, cheeks gaunt and eyes hollow. Some made crude gestures at us. Others just looked empty. It was easy to spot the kids on the train who had grown up here on the outskirts of Vichi. Sickly and underfed. Scrawny things like them would likely be at the Front within minutes of training week ending. They sat huddled in their seats now under layers of grime, completely out of place on the expensive, shining train. I wondered how they even stayed warm enough to survive in their layers of thin, torn clothing.

The Squalor gave way to the treacherous rock formations that surrounded and protected the city. My stomach clenched with memories of the time spent there with my father. The train continued on, through the windblown plains and two more small mining towns where we stopped to pick up what children had turned seventeen since the last round of volunteers. Dry sandwiches were handed out at some point in the day. The tracks pulled us north. The snow melted into shades of tan and sagebrush.

Gradually night fell and the car grew quiet. When Mayze's breath evened out, I unzipped the bag Nico gave me and examined the pieces of home it contained in the moonlight.

My favorite navy sweater was stuffed on top. I pulled it out first to press my nose into its soft warmth. A note fell out of its folds, written hastily in Nico's hand:

Your heart will lead you true—Stisha colm.

Frustration flooded me, unexpected in its force. The second reminder today only made the directive sound more impossible. How was I supposed to listen to my heart while fighting to get to the position of commander? Participating in the war as much as any other Bellovian until the time was right? If I truly followed my heart, I'd be off the train and running back to my family in Vichi. But we all knew who was punished when Bellovian soldiers deserted. I wouldn't put my family in danger.

And *stisha colm*? The Trish signoff had me wracking my memory for the meaning of the phrase. When it finally came to me, I was even more confused. If I remembered correctly, it was what Trish people used to say when greeting their queen. There wasn't a Common Tongue translation for it, but the feeling behind the words praised that which was sacred in Traesha—the three gods and the gifts they left us, especially the royal family. It was an acknowledgment of the queen's power and authority. Such words held no meaning on a Bellovian train racing to war.

I frowned and tore up the note. In my head the Trish words were too much of a risk to hold on to, even though the other contents of the bag were equally incriminating.

Under the sweater were three bars of my favorite soap, a brush, and ten containers of the hair dye my mother and I used. It seemed like so much, but still I worried how long the dye would last as I ran my fingers over the jars. We hadn't had a chance to touch up my roots. I swallowed. Surrounded by Bellovians, for the first time I really considered how difficult it might be getting alone long enough to cover my hair in dye and let it set. I did the math quickly and rubbed my sweaty palms on my pants. I had two weeks, three tops to figure it out.

~

A CRASH SOUNDED. *Fear washed over me with freezing force. Blurred figures in black uniforms flooded the small room. Wood walls and sparse furniture. It didn't feel like a home. A man with light gray hair was closest to the kicked-in door. He stood with a shout. He was thrown into the wall. Shock made him appear to fly slowly through the air. The thud was sickening. His body went still. Dread curled in my stomach. My dream shadow was completely still, turned in the direction of the body. I was stuck myself, unable to help her no matter how much I struggled to move. Even when the attackers turned their attention to her. She was yanked toward the door, away from the body. Only then did she react. She screamed, the sound piercing enough I had to remind myself it was a dream. Was this a projection of my feelings about being taken to war? My vision in the dream blurred. My shadow's scream rang in my ears as the scene faded away...*

An alarm blared, startling me awake and nearly sending me over the edge of our triple-stacked bunk bed. It took me a moment to remember I was at the Bellovian training base. The dream replayed in my consciousness, every blurred detail. The sound of the man's body hitting the wall. The screaming. I shivered. My mother used to struggle to wake me from my dreams. I slipped away with my shadow and spent the nights trying to communicate; the more I failed, the more I resisted waking. No one in my family understood when I explained. They didn't know when they were dreaming. They even had control over what happened sometimes. The *luxury*.

When I could breathe normally again and the strange nightmare faded into a hazy terror-filled memory, I sat up to grab my uniform from the cubby in the wall. It was black and folded stiffly next to the bag Nico gave me. I tucked it under my arm and climbed down to change. The pants were a sturdy material and baggy. The matching shirt fit loosely too. I went to work tucking it in, cinching the black belt to the furthest hole, and rolling up the pant legs and sleeves. I realized looking around it was all simply too big for me. The size was tailored for the average Bellovian girl's frame and fit most of those readying around me.

I caught a few smirks from girls who knew me from school and wished I inherited less of my mother's slim build. When my feet slid into the boots too easily, I put them away and opted for my old, worn ones. The black was similar, so I hoped no one would notice. Before leaving the space between the bunks, I twisted my hair into its usual braid.

Mayze had slept in the bed below mine and waited for me to finish getting ready, quiet and droopy eyed. We followed the other soldiers outside and to mess hall. There was still fog in the air, rolling off the nearby mountains and forest trees. It was strange to walk on the paved path and not a muddy street. The commanders spared no money maintaining this base.

We reached the mess hall and were swept through the serving line. Surrounded by fellow volunteers, I noticed I wasn't the only person whose clothing fit poorly. Most of the others who were too small for the black uniform were marked by the pale skinniness of the Squalor. Dani's muscles strained against the seams in her uniform, her pant legs just brushing the tops of her boots. I focused on how uncomfortable she looked in the restraining clothes, rather than how intimidating.

The older soldiers chose their seats and began eating without ceremony. Mayze and I looked at each other, shrugged, and sat down at the nearest empty table. I barely smoothed my expression when Oken sat down next to Mayze. Several other kids from school followed him. Although Hetta shot me an icy look, the others didn't bother to glance my way.

"Morning, Spacy Mayze," Oken sang the rhyme and playfully tugged on her braid.

"Morning, Oaks. What do you think about this place so far?" Their familiarity made me miss Nico. Seeing them together up close I found some subtle family resemblances in their sharp chins and lifted, amber-colored eyes.

"Everything I dreamed," he said. He caught my eye and added a wink, making my foolish heart skip a beat. I looked away quickly.

Talk around the table turned to anticipation for the day's training. Everyone wanted to catch the eyes of the higher-ups. I couldn't help but hope to do the same, despite my father's urging me not to draw too much attention. Nerves slicked my palms with sweat and I discreetly wiped them on my loose pants.

I could do this. I had it down. I just needed to remember my training at all times. *Always focus.* I took a deep breath and concentrated on the lukewarm, stiffening oatmeal in front of me.

Focused. Not thinking about silly winks.

In little time we were escorted to the training field and

told to line up in alphabetical rows in front of the commander waiting between a climbing wall and what looked like an oversized seesaw. The four red stripes on the shoulder of his black uniform marked his high rank.

The commander was a bulky man who stood impossibly straight and proud. His dark cropped hair was peppered with gray. He watched us file into line, bumping into each other and making sure we were in the correct order by asking each other's last names multiple times. His raised eyebrow told me he was not impressed.

Standing under his scrutiny, everyone exchanged uneasy glances. I accidentally caught Mayze's eye and she gave me a not-so-subtle thumbs up, looking ridiculous in the line of serious, want-to-be soldiers. I looked away and fought off the unexpected smile that threatened.

"Listen up, children. I'm Commander Silken. Some of you may already know each other but get used to referring to each other by last name only. Say yes, sir—"

"Yes, sir!" we repeated.

"Okay... now, answer with that when I get to your name." He shook his head and looked at the clipboard in his large hand. We slowly realized he hadn't been finished with his sentence and jumped the gun with our "Yes, sir!" I held back another smile and someone turned a laugh into a cough behind me to the right. I'd heard Oken do this in class enough times to know it was him immediately.

"Arka."

"Yes, sir!"

"Badnit."

Commander Silken made his way down the list, pausing only when he reached my name. "Larson."

"Yes, sir!"

"Any relation to Teo Larson?"

"My father, sir." The rows of kids bristled. My rich father yet again giving me an advantage.

"I fought with him during his service. Good man, good soldier. Great accountant. You inherit any of that?"

"I guess we'll find out." I stiffened. I hadn't meant for such informal words to slip out. Relief flooded me when Commander Silken chuckled.

"You got his humble humor too, I see. That man could always make us laugh." I smiled a bit at that. The commander studied me a beat longer before continuing down the list. He recognized a few other names, but none as fondly as mine.

"Let's see what I'm working with," Commander Silken said when he finished. "Run until I say otherwise." He pointed to the track and stepped out of our way.

I started off in pace with the others, but when they separated, I put myself in third. I was painfully conscious of everyone's eyes and debated falling further back. But with their glares came the desire to distance myself from them. Being a good runner didn't mean I was Trish. I kept my face blank and tried to relax into my strides. I listened close to the girl's footfalls behind me so I didn't pull too far ahead. I held my pace in the top four and found myself just behind Oken, watching his long legs eat up the distance. His black hair blew wild in the wind.

When I heard Oken struggling for breath I tried to mirror the sound. The girl behind me dropped back and Oken began to do the same, so I slowed my pace. A few people stumbled in their new, stiff boots. Squalor kids fell to their knees and pushed on, bent over and barely moving faster than a walk. They didn't even have the strength to spare me a glance when I flew past, struggling to pretend I was struggling.

Those who grew up knowing my family name would always have the strength to glare. One boy tried to trip me when I overtook him. My reflexes were quick enough that I jumped out of the way, but immediately regretted it. I should have taken the trip to avoid moving so fast and drawing attention to myself. When I glanced his way, Commander Silken was watching, but I couldn't read his face.

I lost count of the laps, but we must have run miles when Commander Silken let out a piercing whistle allowing us to stop. I made myself drop to the ground with everyone else and let out a groan to match theirs. I pretended to wipe sweat off my forehead and was surprised to find it a little damp. I wasn't used to the warm weather.

Commander Silken gave us some time to recover, mainly for the benefit of the kids from the Squalor. A few of them crawled off the track and threw up the filling breakfasts their bodies weren't yet used too. One girl with a blue tinge in her black hair stood up with narrowed eyes after emptying her stomach. Daring us to think less of her. With a jolt I recognized her as the girl from the statue who'd smiled at me just the day before. I stared hard enough to draw her attention and received my second wink of the day. I looked away quickly, before she had a chance to read anything on my face.

A few feet away Oken climbed to his feet. My stomach swooped when he walked right to me and offered his hand. I let him help me up, pulling down more than I needed to, a trick my father trained me to use when he realized how much lighter I was than Bellovian people.

"I didn't know you could run like that. I never saw you out at the track at school or anything," Oken said.

As always when I brought up my family's wealth, I felt

shame. I forced myself to stand straight and meet his eyes. "We had an indoor path in our basement. I ran on there a lot."

"What are those like?" His eyes lit with curiosity. Not the dark resentment I usually got.

"It's like a rug almost but spins under the floor to match your speed." I attempted to show with my hands but felt ridiculous and tucked them behind my back.

"Sounds neat." Oken studied me a beat longer before giving me a small smile and jogging off toward Mayze. It took a few minutes for the shock from the whole encounter to wear off. Maybe he *had* been flirting with that wink during breakfast... but it was more likely he was buddying up to me because Commander Silken was watching me after recognizing my name.

As if summoned by my thoughts, Commander Silken walked by and gave me a nod. He wasn't disappointed and, better yet, didn't seem suspicious. I was doing fine. Pride I hadn't expected to feel at his approval bloomed in my chest.

CHAPTER 5

Commander Silken ordered us to line up again. "I want a sense of what I'm working with. Raise your right hands. Once they go down, keep them down." He eyed us and paced in front of the rows, glancing occasionally at his clipboard. "Keep your hand up if you ran regularly before coming here." Only a few people lowered their hands.

"Keep your hand up if you trained hand-to-hand combat regularly before coming here." No one lowered their hand. I caught myself looking at some of the kids from the Squalor now. The girl with blue-black hair met my eye with a raised eyebrow. I didn't let my face react.

"Keep your hand up if you grew up attending school." The kids from the Squalor dropped their hands. My stomach clenched with discomfort, my privileged upbringing hitting me full force. Not a day passed in which I hadn't dreaded attending school and complained about it afterward.

"Keep your hand up if you trained in a professional setting, meaning a training center or with a tutor." As a commander, my father counted. Most of us who still had hands up at this point were children whose parents were high-ranking commanders or administrators. Commander Silken made more marks on his clipboard.

"Keep your hand up if you have ever shot a gun." Hands fell all around me. Keeping mine raised, I stared straight ahead. Every head turned my direction. Hatred heated the air and pressed in tight.

We went over mechanics of guns in school, often loading and cleaning broken ones from the Front, but they couldn't afford the bullets needed to teach us all to shoot. Still, I was shocked my father was the only parent who had taken his children out to shoot with a family gun.

Knowing the crime rates in the Squalor and the daily murders there, I wouldn't doubt a few of those kids had practiced shooting too. I snuck a glance at the girl again, picturing stolen guns full of black-market bullets.

"Okay, children," Commander Silken's voice rang out when he finished making a note by my name. "Let's see how you handle yourselves at the shooting range. Follow me." He turned and led us off the track and onto the road toward the other end of base.

I jumped a little when I noticed the raven-haired girl matched my pace. Her steps were nearly silent. Her hair pasted on her forehead with sweat.

"One from the bottom, one from the top. I think I'd rather be invisible than hated, though," she said with a slight smirk.

I shrugged, keeping my face a perfect mask of indifference.

"How long do you think it'll be before he sends us out to get shot?" she continued, looking back at the other kids from the Squalor where they lagged behind. They weren't a talkative bunch.

"I doubt he'll send you."

She snorted. "Yeah? Why's that?"

"Your attitude marks you out as a fighter," I said, thinking of her defiant glares. "If you keep it up, he'll be looking at what you could be, since you haven't resigned yourself and limited your potential." We glanced back again, noting the stooped shoulders and weary steps of those following us.

She looked at me closer. "Alright, rich kid. You just know how this is all going to play out, don't you?"

"I have a pretty good idea." When she laughed, I gave her the briefest of smiles. I wasn't sure what it meant that she seemed to recognize me, or her smile back at the Squalor, but it was nice to talk to someone new. Someone who understood what it meant to be outcast. She held out her hand and I shook it, noting and then ignoring the dirt under her short nails.

"Rennie," she said. "Or Jaspers to this guy." She jerked a thumb toward the commander.

"Finley Larson, as you probably heard him announce."

"Of course. Your daddy set you up well, didn't he?" She smirked again; the look softened by the teasing glint in her eyes. They were not the common brown of the Bellovians, but a dark, navy blue.

"He's already bribed my way to the top," I said with an exaggerated shrug. "This is all just for show."

She laughed, but Dani heard as she came out of the toilets building. She scoffed and bumped into me roughly, sending me onto the concrete with her muscular mass. The line of kids paused to laugh and my face burned when I looked up into Oken's eyes. Instantly dropping my gaze, I climbed back to my feet. The left knee of my uniform was torn, the skin red and raw underneath.

Rennie was laughing too, but I couldn't blame her. "Damn, they really hate you!"

"You get used to it," I said.

"I don't know about that. Where I'm from she would have just gotten shoved through a window."

I smiled at that, enjoying the picture it painted despite myself. "Well, that's the Bellovian spirit, right?" Irony dripped heavy in my words before I caught myself. To my relief, Rennie's face didn't show any hint of offense at my criticism.

"Right. We're all about that Bellovian spirit in the Squalor." She mock punched my shoulder, harder than I expected given her slight frame.

We joined the cluster of bodies facing Commander Silken at the edge of the shooting range. Three tables were set up before a cleared field holding six targets at varying distances. From the first table to the last, the barrels of the guns got progressively longer: the first gun about the size of my hand and the last set up on the ground with a tripod and a scope. My father's gun was a middle-range gun the length of my forearm like the ones on the second table. Although it would shoot differently than the shortest and longest of the guns, my father told me not to overthink the differences. It was still basically the same idea. But Trish eyesight made me a good shot and I worried trying to use a scope for the first time would throw me off.

"If you're good with a gun it will go much further than hand-to-hand or how long you can run in circles," I muttered to Rennie. She looked surprised by the encouragement, but after a pause gave me a sly wink.

Commander Silken quickly ran through the slight

differences between the weapons and their names: pocket gun, short gun, the two mid guns, long gun, and finally scoped gun. Bellovian creativity at its finest. Next, he demonstrated loading and aiming each weapon with practiced movements. This varied little from gun to gun, but many of the faces around me looked bewildered by the end of the lesson.

I glanced at Oken. His eyebrows were drawn with concentration. In fact, him and Mayze wore the exact same expression. I almost laughed at this real sign of family resemblance.

Commander Silken called six names and they stepped forward nervously, Oken and Mayze among them. It took Oken a few shots, but he was the first to hit his target with a mid gun. Mayze still hadn't by the time her short gun was empty of bullets. Commander Silken was frowning when he waved the next group forward, then the next. Rennie and I went to the same table. I raised the short gun and sighted the target. I took half a breath in and zeroed in on the cardboard chest. I could do well here without giving away my abilities. I almost smiled as I squeezed the trigger. Six shots in a tight circle around the heart and one in the head. I was supposed to put two in the head, but I let one of my shots go wide, just in case. I breathed the rest of the way in and let it out through my nose.

Rennie landed all her shots. It chilled my insides to know she'd grown up with human targets, but I pushed the thought away when she set her gun down and smiled at me.

All eyes were on our table, the most successful by far.

"And here I thought this was where I'd outshine everyone," Rennie said.

"Sorry, but not that sorry." She laughed and we turned

from the table to take our spots in the line. I was glad we were now in the back row so I could avoid the glares for at least a moment.

In the next couple hours, we took a turn with each gun. Oken picked it up in little time and grew confident moving down the tables. Mayze did better with the long guns, especially when given a scope. Rennie and I were the most proficient shots, her nearly my equal with short range. A few of the other Squalor kids did a decent job, but they weren't nearly as proficient as Rennie. No one else particularly stood out by the time the last group was placing their guns back on the table.

We settled back into our lines and Commander Silken moved to stand in front of the group. He lifted his clipboard and read fifteen names off the list.

Those who stepped forward were all the Squalor kids except Rennie, a few others who looked exhausted, and a slightly overweight boy. I only recognized one kid from my school; a city administrator's son with a bad attitude. He was scowling.

"You all will be completing your training a little closer to the action," Commander Silken told them. "Prove yourselves well out there. Stay strong."

I was grateful to have made a friend in Rennie when she plopped down next to me in the mess hall. It was now clear the minimum week of training was no longer a guarantee. Fifteen of us already sent to the Front. The number sent flutters of panic to my stomach. I wished I could talk to my dad, ask him what this meant about the state of the war. For me and my chances. The pressure to stand out was nearly suffocating and it was not helping my situation. Dani and her friends from home whispered and shot me nasty looks from the next table. We were all still covered with mud from the obstacle course Commander Silken had sent us through before dinner, yet it did nothing to disguise the heat of Dani's glare.

Oken sat down with them, his back to me. Rody slapped his back and congratulated him loudly on being the best shot from home. I didn't even feel the sting of the words. When Mayze sat down across from me and blocked my view of her cousin's back, I wiped the surprise from my expression before the people at Oken's table turned with narrowed eyes. She pretended not to notice the glares drilling into her back. I knew from years of experience she could feel them.

"You did amazing today!" she said a little too brightly before tucking into her food.

"Thanks."

"Did your dad take you out to shoot? I've never heard of anyone else doing that."

"Yes. He didn't like going to war update meetings on Seventhday morning when he could avoid it. Said he got enough of them at work. We went out to shoot instead." When Mayze kept staring at me expectantly, I pushed on. Now that she was sitting here, I realized just how sad I'd been thinking I'd lost our slip of a friendship. "He grew up in Trent. With all that wildlife in the mountains, they need guns to survive and hunt. He misses it, so he took my brother and me out to shoot at squirrels and rabbits in the boulders outside the city. We did a lot of training out there too."

"Must have been nice to have that time with him," Mayze said. Her smile shook and I remembered the day she was pulled from class and informed her father was killed in action.

"It was." It didn't seem like enough words, but I had no idea how to comfort her. I'd yet to learn loss like that.

"You did well, too!" Mayze extended a hand across the table to Rennie, brushing off the moment. "Mayze Hale."

Rennie shook the hand. "Rennie Jaspers. Don't pretend you did that poorly. Those scopes are tricky; you'll have to tell me how you figured it out. I get the feeling princess over here was just born hitting the targets center. Absolutely no help."

"Princess?" I rounded on Rennie. Mayze clapped her hands over her mouth to stifle a giggle, her eyes shining over her fingers. I shook my head and fought the urge to share in their smiles.

"You all are having way too much fun over here," Oken said, suddenly behind Mayze. He had left his place at the other table and now slid into the seat next to his cousin, straddling the bench sideways and unafraid to meet the looks he received from his friends. My palms grew clammy.

"I think Jaspers just gave Larson a new name. Isn't that right, princess?" Mayze said. I rolled my eyes and busied my hands pulling the crust off my sandwich.

"Now, that's not fair. We've been calling her princess behind her back for years!" I couldn't really tell if Oken was joking when he said the words, but he smiled at me with nothing malicious in his expression.

"Alright, *pretty boy*," Mayze said. Oken narrowed his eyes at her, but the glare was unconvincing. I had definitely heard this nickname for Oken over the years. He lacked the harsh bulk most Bellovian men shared. His curls gave him too much of a boyish appearance to fit in with the scarred, crooked-nosed men around him. The nickname was given to my brother too, but Nico hardly let it bother him. Yet while being called pretty boy only questioned masculinity, princess was a harsh insult if it was not meant in jest. Bellovian people loathed monarchies. To them, the concept of royalty represented Floria, laziness, oppression, and all the hatred held toward their enemy.

"I can't believe he's already sending people to the Front." Mayze dropped her voice.

"Must be even worse than we thought out there," Rennie said. Oken and Mayze shot her a look, neither of them appreciating her lack of faith in the Bellovian army.

"My dad said the Florians have been holding back less since we killed their queen," I said.

"Makes sense," Oken said, looking away from Rennie with a frown. She continued eating like nothing was amiss.

Mayze fiddled with her fork. "I feel like I'll be next."

"I doubt it. Half the kids here still barely have any training, you'll be fine," I said.

"Oh, don't listen to her. She doesn't think I'll get sent away either." Oken laughed outright at Rennie's light tone and her eyes warmed as she experienced the magic of the sound.

"Who knew you were such an optimist?" Oken asked, smiling just for me.

I shrugged, grasping for a response while his smile drowned my thoughts.

There was a scrape of a bench as Dani stood behind Oken. She made a show of stretching, her muscles clearly visible under her tight uniform.

"All I know is Larson better watch her back. Knowing how to shoot a gun won't help the runt when it comes to hand-to-hand. Just wait. It'll be hilarious." She didn't bother to glance my way before she left the mess hall, the other kids from school laughing.

"Don't worry about her," Oken said quickly, eyes narrowed on Dani's back.

"I'm not." My answer wasn't so convincing. I was good at hand-to-hand, but it was also the hardest to hide my strength during. If Dani came at me, I couldn't misjudge. She would be the first to bring it to the commanders' attention if I slipped up. I didn't expect the chill of fear that came with the thought. I focused on keeping my features neutral.

I wouldn't slip up. There was too much at stake. A pang of longing for my mother's voice struck me and I stared at the table until I was fully Bellovian once more.

I woke to the bunk swinging violently beneath me. Something, no someone, grabbed my arm and yanked me out from under my blanket. I dropped to the floor hard, the air leaving my lungs in a choking gasp. Instant panic. In the haze I could only concentrate on clearing my face of emotions and not reacting with Trish speed. This order from my brain conflicted harshly with the instincts in my body and left me frozen. I struggled to get air back in.

Dani loomed over me, smug and sneering.

"What are you doing? Stop!" Mayze moved to climb from her bunk beneath my own. I still couldn't catch a breath.

"This doesn't concern you, Hale. Hold her back." Dani wasn't alone. More hands appeared over her shoulder. Mayze grunted, trying to fight them off. Dani's smile grew when her commands were heeded. She got in my face. "Daddy isn't here to help you now."

I finally got in a gasp of air, just in time to fight off the black at the edges of my vision and keep my face blank. It had always been my best defense against her. Dani's face twisted. I should be fighting. I should be trying to move. Instead, I watched her in fascination. I could read every thought in her head. Her expression was everything I'd ever feared from the Bellovians. Fear that always shifted into hatred and anger and violence.

One day it would be her and her people helpless to my will. One day. Only that thought kept me still.

Dani's first blow was straight to my nose. My head whipped back and hit the ground. Stars crowded my vision, but Dani didn't let me slump back. Her other fist was twisted into the fabric in the front of my shirt and she used it to keep me lifted in place.

Two more quick blows. They didn't hurt any more or less than the first one. Dani's fist was slicked with blood, her teeth bared. I could hear my pulse pounding in my ears, drowning the whispered cheering of the girls crowded behind Dani. I tasted blood. Mayze's shouts muffled behind someone's hand. Dani lifted me closer, spit flying as she spoke.

"You're going to back down, you hear me? Fail. Make us look good. You already look like a weak piece after this. Fade to the background with your little Squalor rat like you belong."

I think I kept my face blank. I couldn't even think of a response. Whatever look I gave Dani, the hand holding my shirt loosened and I caught myself on my elbows. I moved too fast, but her attention was on my face. Doubt filled her eyes. The hall went quiet. I heard drops of my blood on the concrete.

"She never even yelled," someone whispered. Fear and

adrenaline were coursing through my blood, but my perfectly made mask was doing as much as fighting back would. I couldn't let them see they had shaken me. How hard it was to breathe.

I smiled then, past the blood and the swelling of my face. Dani's eyes widened. With a strangled yell she brought her fist down. My head snapped back again with the force of her punch. I stayed down, curling instinctively when she kicked me in the stomach for good measure. I did what I could to keep my pained gasps quiet. Everything ached.

"Back down, Larson. Or you won't be getting up next time." I stared up at the ceiling and listened to the girls climb back into their beds.

"Finley?" Mayze's scrunched face hovered above me. Ignoring the desires of my body, I forced myself to move. I barely hid my wince as I pushed myself to my feet. I stumbled into the bedpost and smacked away the hand Mayze held out to steady me.

"I'm going to clean up," I said. My voice sounded muffled when it came out between my swollen lips and bitten tongue. How did I forget so much about my training that I'd bitten my tongue?

I wanted to curl up. I wanted to cry. I wanted my mom. Instead, I threw back my shoulders and walked out of the women's bunk. Rennie watched me pass. I couldn't read her expression; she didn't move from her bed. She was smart. I focused on my steps. If I could just make it to the privacy of the bathrooms, then I could give in.

When the doors of the bunk swung shut behind me, I leaned into the wall and let my eyes begin to blur, the pressure of tears heightening the throbbing pain of my nose. My hand left a smear of blood on the building as I walked. I could feel it hot and dripping down my chin. Humiliation flooded me. All those years of training. All those worries about giving myself away by proving so superior to the Bellovians. And I hadn't been able to move when faced with real fear. I just let her beat me. I choked on panic and let her draw blood. I'd been terrified.

At least they didn't know. My face was the only part of me that hadn't let me down. I pushed from the wall and kept walking toward the toilets. When my head got too light, I slumped up the steps to the nearest darkened doorway. I would just rest for a moment.

I was so focused on trying to calm my breathing, I didn't at first notice the voices drawing near. I pulled my legs in close and pressed into the shadows, ignoring the pain in my stomach where Dani had kicked me. I strained my ears and recognized Commander Silken's voice.

"... successfully."

"They're on their way back with her then?" The woman with him sounded skeptical.

"Yes. It is proving difficult as they near the Front, but they should cross within the next few days."

"But why even keep her alive?" the woman asked. She had a husky, rich quality to her voice, surprisingly pleasant even when her words raised the hair on my neck. "They'll have an easier time crossing without her."

"Command has decided she's more useful to us alive."

The woman snorted. "Useful? I can't imagine how."

"To start, she'll be a bargaining tool to keep them in line."

"Oh please. They're broken! There's no need."

"Every year they produce fewer crops. If we want to keep our alliance with Detono, we need to have something of value going in."

I furrowed my brow. Were they talking about...

"And you think the queen of Traesha is valuable?"

My breath caught. I covered my mouth, blood already crusting around my lips, though my nose still trickled blood. I suspected it was broken. It felt broken.

Commander Silken lowered his voice to a whisper even my ears struggled to catch. "Yes, she is valuable. You weren't there during the invasion. You didn't see the old queen. The instant we killed her and her guard, her people lost all their power. All their fight. If we use her daughter, maybe we can make them fight again, this time against the Florians."

"What can they do against anyone? Maybe the Trish were powerful once, but even then, they didn't have the spirit to fight. And like I said, they're broken now. We crushed them, just like we'll crush the Florians. Tell the Detonians that."

"Even so, it won't hurt to see if we can't use her to motivate her people. See if we can't use her death to threaten those who don't reach their quotas."

"Traesha is ours. We won. There are other threats we can make. I fail to see how this justifies the resources we're using—"

"Command agrees with me. We have the Trish, might as well use them. It's been decided. We'll bring her before them at the Conquering Celebration. Motivate the slaves to reach their quotas and, if they regain some strength, we'll force her to tell her people to take up arms."

"Like that will do any good. They aren't—"

At this point the doors of the building they entered shut behind them and cut off the woman's words. I sat frozen, hand over my mouth, warm blood pooling from my nose.

The queen was alive?

CHAPTER 6

I made it to the bathroom, cringing at the sound of the metal door clanging shut behind me. Stopping in front of the mirror, I stared into my blood-streaked face. My right eye was wide, the light-blue stark against the red backdrop. The left was swollen shut. Without giving myself a chance to think, I reached up and wrenched my broken nose back into place. Tears fell freely now. I took hitching gasps through the waves of pain. I looked down as the pain faded enough for the tears to stop, watching the blood drop and splatter into the porcelain sink.

The queen was alive. Alive and in the hands of the commanders. I even knew where she'd be. The knowledge stung. What could I possibly do with it? I'd heard of the ball the commanders held in Traesha annually to celebrate the successful invasion. My father went occasionally, more so for an excuse to see his mother on the way north. Since she died, he hadn't attended.

I let both my eyes close and sank down into a crouch, resting my forehead against the cool sink. What did this mean? What did this mean for me? Could I send word to my mother? Would it only hurt her like it was silently killing me? I lifted my head, looking into a face so puffy and discolored it was unrecognizable. The woman's words echoed; *they're broken.*

What could I do?

At least according to Silken there were no plans to kill the queen anytime soon. But no one knew to help her. None of the Trish were strong enough to do anything about this.

No one but me. I snorted at my reflection and watched myself wince.

But I was strong, wasn't I? My mother thought I would inherit the Trish gifts, that they would develop when I came of age. And I was trained. I might be the only potential ally the queen had who knew of her situation. Who knew she was still alive. And I was in league with the enemy. There was a chance I could use that to save her.

I stood and turned on the water. My blood spatters thinned and began spiraling down the drain. I cupped the water in my hands and began to wash my face. If I rose in the ranks, I could gain access to the queen. If I spent the rest of my time here working for an in, holding back less and impressing Commander Silken, maybe I would be promoted faster. Maybe I could get stationed somewhere with information about the Trish queen.

Maybe I could get an invitation to the Conquering Celebration.

Resolve tightened my chest before I was fully willing to give up on the plan my father sent me here with. My gut told me I would do what I could for the queen before my brain was ready to accept it. I would put myself at risk. I would stop holding back.

My stomach twisted and I swallowed, looking at my ruined face and replaying Dani's threats. I brought up another cupped handful of water to my face, hands shaking.

This week had to end with me on top. I needed to succeed in every mission. I needed stripes on my shoulder to give me access to the queen. I couldn't let them know I was Trish. I couldn't desert without them punishing my family for the betrayal. I had to get to the queen as a Bellovian. It was the only way to possibly help her and keep my family safe.

Above all, I had to keep my family safe.

"WHAT HAPPENED TO YOU?" Oken asked first thing the next morning, sitting down next to me at breakfast.

"Fell out of my bunk."

Mayze narrowed her eyes but didn't contradict me.

"Yeah, she's on the top bunk. Quite the drop," Rennie said. Her lips wobbled while she tried and failed to hold back a smile. "Damn, princess. She really did a number on you."

I did my best to roll my eyes with one still swollen shut.

"Who?" Oken asked.

"Don't worry about it," I said. Bellovians showed up every day covered in bruises from training and street fights. Did I really look so bad my face warranted this extra concern?

Whatever it looked like, I felt decent. I woke up this morning determined, my doubts diminished by sleep and replaced by the possibilities. I had a new purpose and no intention of letting Dani slow me down now that I needed to surpass everyone during training.

Silken's sharp whistle cut through the noise of the mess

hall, shifting attention away from me and my beaten face. I stood with the rest of the trainees to follow him out to the track, my hands clenching at my side from the sight of the commander's back. I needed to earn his trust to get to the queen but seeing him churned my stomach. Forcing the feeling down, I fell into line and ran with the rest of them, this time close on Oken's heels. I couldn't do too much better than yesterday, but I could show I was capable of improvement.

When Silken called for us to stop, I didn't drop with everyone else. I rested my arms on the top of my head and pretended to catch my breath.

"Gather around. You have a big test today." There were a few groans as people hauled themselves up from the ground. They cut off quickly when the commander shot a glare over his shoulder. Bellovian soldiers were not supposed to show so much weakness.

We were once again lined up before Silken. Off to our right on the paved road, a large group of soldiers going through more advanced training arrived and waited beside their cluster of cycles. They were joking and laughing and seemed to be making bets. I swallowed and turned my attention back to Silken when one pointed at me and then her eye, making her companions laugh.

No one was betting rations on me today.

"Your next test is simple. In fact, you need no explanation save for my telling you it will take place in the forest twenty minutes away from here. Those soldiers will take you to your starting points and provide you with the necessary equipment. They will also act as your team, so I suggest staying on their good side. Last point: you will be split into two groups and enter the forest from opposite ends. Two people, one from each side, will be after the same target. I recommend getting there first. That's all. Find your team."

Seeing us split from Silken, the soldiers formed groups of three and called us by name. My team groaned when I cut toward them, the woman who pointed to my eye the loudest among them. I kept my expression cool and lifted my chin. No words were necessary as they claimed two cycles and I got on behind the woman. We took off, the wind snatching any other words we may have shared.

It was a long twenty minutes on the back of a stranger's cycle. We traveled with the whole group for a while until we came to the point in the trees. Half the group separated to go higher on the hill. I heard my companion swear as we continued on lower ground. If the target was between the two groups, our team would be moving uphill. A distinct disadvantage.

More groups swerved to a stop at the base of the hill. Turning my head, I saw the soldiers begin unloading the backs of their cycles and handing devices to their leader for the test. My team was the last to stop at the furthest reach of the forest. One of the soldiers on the other bike whistled.

"Well, maybe you got the shit beat out of you, but for Commander Silken to put you in this section he must have faith in your abilities."

I couldn't tell if they were joking or not. I tipped my head back to take in the steep slope we would have to follow. "Here's hoping you lot can keep up."

The statement earned me a round of laughter. My driver was a little more open as she handed me a bulky pair of glasses. "Will these fit over all that swelling?" she asked, smirking.

A fresh round of laughter that I didn't mind. I even allowed a small, rueful smile as I took them from her. The glasses did hurt when resting on my nose, but I ignored it as best I could. A tiny speaker crackled on above my left ear. Words scrolled across the glasses' lenses and a monotone voice read them in my ear.

OBJECTIVE: BLOW UP ENEMY CARGO. CREATE A DIVERSION. LOSE NO TEAM MEMBERS.

Simple enough. I resisted the urge to remove the glasses and examine the technology as a compass arrow appeared in the corner of my vision, directing us to said enemy cargo. From the news my father brought home, I was familiar with the strange technological advancements Bellovians had achieved in recent years, yet the glasses were beyond my wildest imaginings. Where had the funds come from to produce them?

I gave my head a little shake, focusing on the task at hand as a gun was offered to me. The barrel was too bulky and the weight not quite right. I aimed at the ground to my right and fired a round, jumping when it exploded on the dry grass in a burst of yellow. I looked back to the trees. It would seem we were allowed to fire at each other. I enjoyed a moment of imagining Dani painted yellow. It felt right to picture her standing on the opposite side of the trees.

The last item handed to me appeared to be a fake grenade. "Sets off a sensor when you hit the target with it. Only get one, though," said the soldier who handed it to me.

I nodded. Message clear. There was no room to miss. I quickly noted my team was armed with the same guns as the ones I carried.

"I'm guessing there are people guarding the cargo we're supposed to blow," I said. "Be on guard and try to move quietly. We'll cut back and forth to accommodate the steep slope; it might add time, but we can't afford breathing too loud." I pointed to each soldier in turn. "You stay on our flank and watch our backs. You watch our left, you our right. Eyes sharp."

They nodded and exchanged grins, our confidence as a team growing as we formed a line and I led us into the trees.

The forest was quiet and peaceful. The trees reminded me of the silence that lingered in the rock formations surrounding Vichi. It made me miss my father, but thoughts of him and all his lessons while we hunted sharpened my instincts as we dove deeper into the forest. As I told my team, I walked us up a zigzagging path toward the target. We stayed quiet, each of us scanning our section for enemies. When their breathing grew heavy, I tried to mimic them, aware they watched me as close as the forest. Likely their observations were as much part of the test as whether or not I reached the target.

I refused to dwell on how much faster my opponent was likely moving. Hopefully, they were loud and clumsy traveling downhill and would alert those guarding the cargo. Hopefully, they had further to go so we weren't at such a disadvantage. I resolved to focus entirely on my team and getting us to the target. I would worry about the rest when the time came. Even if I lost, I would go by the book. Follow instructions. War wasn't a place for creativity, and because we were low-ranking soldiers, they would want to be sure we were obedient. My father told me this often enough. *"If you want to blend in with the Bellovians, you have to not think like us... get it? Don't think."* I allowed myself a small smile, remembering him laughing at his own joke.

I heard a boot skid on a rock ahead of us and held up a fist, halting my team. If we'd been traveling in a straight line, this person would be directly in our path. Luckily, we avoided them and I heard them continue down the slope, probably trying to intercept us. I waved my hand, signaling a slower, more cautious pace.

Finally, the arrow shifted so it was no longer above us, but a straight shot forward. My soldier watching our right got off a paint bullet and someone swore deeper in the trees. Our position compromised, I signaled for us to duck and move more quickly.

I spotted the glint of metal that was likely a cargo transport and the dark heads of the Bellovians guarding it. There were too many of them for my team to rush and we'd just lost our element of surprise. I thought quickly and noted a cluster of bushes at the base of a tree. My soldiers followed me there and knelt when I did.

I pointed up and patted my grenade, gesturing toward the cargo transport. Understanding cleared their faces and they followed my direction to take cover as I silently climbed the tree. I only had one shot and I wasn't close enough, but the forest was dense enough I jumped from one tree to the next without worrying I showed too much of my Trish abilities.

The cargo transport came fully into view. It was old and rusted. Broken down and probably only used for this test. Right as I readied to toss my grenade, I heard shouting higher on the hill. My opponent was here. No time to spare, I tossed my grenade.

Its rubber coat thumped against the side of the transport and an alarm blared in the forest. Yellow lights flashed, but I didn't stay to watch their reaction.

MISSION COMPLETE.

I returned to my team. Unsure if the completed mission meant we were out of pretend danger, I gestured for silence. I debated using a straight path down the hill but opted to avoid any twisted ankles and took us down with wide switchbacks again. My team followed as quietly as they could until the shouts from the target area faded enough that we let up on our caution and ran freely. My team even let out a few whoops as the trees grew sparse. Our cycles were near.

"That was the smoothest a trainee has led us through that!" One of them said, clapping me on my shoulder right where I'd hit the ground when Dani pulled me from bed. I swallowed a wince just as we reached the end of the trees.

All sense of victory died when we cleared the trees.

At first, I thought my sense of direction had failed. I didn't see our cycles. But when one of the soldiers swore, I followed their gaze to the cycle that had somehow fallen over in the bushes. I immediately dismissed the possibility of a strong wind and ventured closer.

The tires had been slashed and our other cycle was missing. I joined the chorus of swearing.

"It's going to take us ages to walk back," the woman soldier groaned. I pressed my lips and nodded.

There was no help for it. We righted the broken cycle and briefly debated leaving it behind. In the end we judged it wouldn't hurt the rims much if we didn't put weight on it. We began our trek, the cycle limping along as we pushed it.

We were probably halfway back when a transport truck came to get us. The driver was laughing when he stopped and helped load the cycle in the back. He and my team squeezed into the front of the cab, but I got in the truck bed with the cycle. When we pulled back up to the running track, Silken was waiting with his arms crossed. The rest of the trainees lounged in the grass, comfortable enough to establish they'd been waiting a long while. Oken's head came up at the sound of the truck doors, eyes blinking as he woke from a nap. That boy could sleep anywhere.

One look at Dani's smug expression and I knew exactly who was behind our mishap.

"Glad you could join us, Larson," Silken said. "Go sit while we discuss the results."

Frustration had been building since we found our cycle and his words had me swallowing a retort. Between my bruised face and missing cycle, Dani was succeeding before I even had a chance to try. I ignored Mayze's sympathetic glance and Rennie's questioning eyes and sat a short distance away. Silken and our teams went off the side, each taking a turn to speak with the commander. I listened to the concerns of the trainees around me with a hollow stomach. Of course, half were worried because they didn't reach their target first. A few anxiously picked at the paint drying on their uniforms, frowning as they did and wondering out loud how much they would be docked for getting shot. One boy burst out that he didn't even find his target. I was beginning to feel slightly better about my chances. Technically, returning the cycles undamaged may not be part of the test. The fact that I hit my target and kept my team safe had to mean something.

Finally, Silken returned. He glanced over his notes on his clipboard one last time. Huffing a sigh, he shook his head at all of us. Dread coiled in my stomach.

"Well, I won't be releasing any of you. Most of you tied for last. You either missed the target..." He paused to roll his eyes. "... lost one or more of your team members, failed to make time, or got yourself shot. Only three of you completed the mission adequately. Only one of you met expectations. This was a test to show leadership—we didn't think we'd have to look at anything else. You lot have a good deal of work ahead of you if you want to compete with Larson. One misplaced cycle isn't a testament to leadership; resorting to foul play, though..." He cut a hard look at Dani. She wilted. I bloomed. "Larson is the only true leader among you. Go eat, then come back here."

I tried not to look too smug, but my Bellovian blood got the better of me and my chin came up and my mouth quirked. A fist came flying toward me and I ducked to the side. Dani stumbled after her failed punch and Rennie burst into laughter as she came to my side to congratulate me. Silken shook his head again and walked away.

It was hard to feel too smug remembering Dani had already gotten the better of me and my face showed it.

On the way to mess, I could tell Rennie was itching to make a comment on Dani's failed punch and the stolen cycle. I spoke first. "You were one of the three who passed, weren't you?"

She shrugged. "I hit the target at least. What can I say? I'm good at sneaking around and causing trouble. Although, I guess telling my team to stay back with the cycles and wait for me might not have been the best idea."

I laughed at that. She proved her own abilities but missed the point of the test entirely. "Well, at least you blew up the truck."

"Eh, they didn't send me to the Front, that's about all I care about. Also, I think Silken's more pissed than he's letting on that Dani messed up one of their cycles. You should have seen his face when she pulled up without her team. She was telling Rody she sent her people ahead to blow up the cargo truck and just ran straight to sabotage her opponent getting home. You should have heard her bragging."

71

"Well, I think it's safe to say you did better than her at least."

"Like that was ever a concern." I couldn't help the laugh that escaped.

～

WE RETURNED TO THE FIELD. Several kids glanced anxiously toward the track and obstacle courses, but Silken had something else planned for us.

"We're finishing the day with hand-to-hand combat. Although, it looks like some of you already started practicing." The commander's eyes rested briefly on my face. I fought off a grimace.

He called out our names. Relief was a sweet rush when Silken paired me with Rennie. She smirked as we turned to each other and she called over her shoulder at Silken, "You should put rails on the sides of those taller bunks!"

There was a scattering of nervous laughter. For some reason, the jokes at my expense from Rennie didn't grate like they did from my classmates. I pushed her with an eye roll to disguise the laugh I nearly released.

"You won't be smiling by the end of this," I warned her.

"As long as I get a pretty bruise to match one of yours. I'm tired of you getting all the attention."

I discovered quickly that Rennie had great instincts and knew how to throw a punch but possessed little by way of form. I corrected her stance and when she looked more grateful than annoyed at the instruction, I started giving her more pointers. She was a fast learner, but when Silken caught me coaching her instead of sparring, he stopped us. He looked around for another person to partner me with. His eyes rested briefly on a grinning Dani and my heart stopped. The fear from last night returned before I could brace myself against it. But then Oken neatly dropped his partner with a punch, looking studiously bored. He caught the commander's eyes.

"Go work with Sars," Silken said. I fought the urge to sag with relief and hurried that way as Silken partnered Rennie with someone closer to her level.

"Nice work on that test," Oken said when I reached him. His smile was tight. He kept glancing toward Dani, thick brows furrowed.

My mouth was too dry to reply, so I just nodded. Now that the Dani-related fear and then relief had passed, I fully realized what was about to happen. I had no idea how to go about this. Sparing with Oken. My skin already tingled, pathetically anticipating his touch.

"Kicks!" Commander Silken shouted and my clenched stomach loosened. At least this way I could keep my distance. Oken stepped back, inviting me to strike first.

I positioned my feet, shifted my weight, and swung. I knew when my foot left the ground I was holding back too much. Kicks were always so hard to gage. Even knowing I swung too lightly, I was surprised by Oken's speed and strength. He snatched my foot out of the air with his left hand. It caught me off guard. My father was heavily right-hand dominant, something I'd never noticed until this moment. Oken easily lifted my leg and kicked the other one out from under me before I could orientate myself. I began to fall, hard, but he pulled up a bit on the leg in his hand to lessen the blow. I swore when I hit the dirt.

Rolling to my back, I couldn't stop the smile tugging at my lips from the challenge. Oken's tight expression cleared. A slow grin pulled up the corners of his mouth. His eyes crinkled. He was so pleased by my reaction that I let out a small laugh. Making this boy smile felt even better than winning the last challenge.

I braced my hands on either side of my head and pushed my body off the ground, landing back on my feet in a quick movement. I ignored how the rush of blood to my face made my bruises throb with pain.

"Lucky shot." The years of bantering with my father made it hard not to egg my opponent on.

"I'm a lucky person." We shifted back into our stances.

I went for another kick. He caught my foot again. Knowing now he didn't want me to fall hard, I kicked out with my other leg. The move caught him off guard and he pulled up, supporting my weight just like he did last time. He conveniently held me up as I twisted my body, my other foot clipping his shoulder. I landed on my right hand and spun on my palm to return to my feet. The kick was strong and Oken staggered to the side, but I hadn't hurt him.

He righted himself. "My turn."

I got ready to dodge. I couldn't keep my stoic mask in place. Both of us grinned like idiots.

After a time, Silken called for us to move on to ground work. Although the butterflies returned to my stomach, I found myself eager to test my strength against Oken's. He proved a good loser and graceful winner. Silken shot us a look every time Oken made me laugh by pretending to gag and choke too easily when I got an arm around his neck or writhing like crazy when I found control of the rolls from on top. The longer the training session lasted, the more energy he seemed to have. It was infectious.

He grew serious as we truly started testing each other. It was obvious he understood the mechanics behind his movements and flowed rapidly from one to the next, but he relied heavily on his Bellovian strength. I took advantage of my faster reflexes, and my speed kept us evenly matched. The competition built and I longed to let go of my restraint and fully test my abilities against him. I could tell he was holding back too, never even so much as brushing against my broken nose.

We were in a particularly heated roll, Oken sweating hard while we each looked for a hold on the other that would end the match. I was even panting a bit, the noon sun beating down on us in a way we never experienced back home. Oken suddenly maneuvered himself out from under me, early triumph in his eyes. He saw his mistake a split second after I did. My leg suddenly free, I swung it up with a grunt and caught his neck with it. He went down next to me, his weight flipping me on top of him. I grabbed hold of my ankle and caught him in the triangle of my leg. His face turned red as my hamstring pressed on his throat and he struggled hard for a moment, bridging and twisting beneath me. But I was unmovable. He gave up, tapping my lower back when he ran out of air. I crawled forward to let him breathe and his hand lingered, fingers trailing just longer than necessary and burning a path downward. My heart sputtered and I scrambled to my feet. I thought I heard Oken laugh as I busied my hands dusting myself off.

"Impressive, you two," Silken said. I looked up and was surprised to find we were the only pair left wrestling. The rest of the trainees watched us from where they had stopped to rest. Silken stood a few steps away, a gleam in his eyes. He looked like someone had given him a shiny new gun to play with. I may have redeemed myself from showing up covered in bruises, but my chest tightened at the look in his eyes. Doubt flooded me. I didn't want his attention so much after all. I straightened my back and pushed the thought away. This is what it took to succeed as a Bellovian. For now, I was a weapon to be used.

"Let's break for lunch here. Meet me back at the shooting range when you're finished," Silken said. I wouldn't be missing any shots today.

I turned to help Oken up. He accepted my hand. "Is there anything you can't do?" he asked, rubbing his throat.

"I'm terrible at the piano." I hadn't really meant for the words to be a joke, but Oken threw back his head and laughed. I was helpless against the smile on my face.

CHAPTER 7

For the rest of the week, my aim was precise, my blows perfectly placed, and, most shocking of all, my friendships solidified. It was hard to look around the mess table and see Rennie, Mayze, and Oken as enemies. I wanted to help the queen, but I couldn't hate them. Not like I used to. I had to be one of them if I was going to keep my family safe and learn more about her. It ate at me, feeling like I was constantly lying. Especially to Oken and Mayze—they were in clear support of the Bellovian cause. Both firmly believed winning the war was the way to save the many starving throughout the country.

Rennie was a little harder to read, but we'd caught each other's eyes while they spoke enough times for me to suspect she didn't agree. I longed to ask her thoughts. To ask what those in the Squalor believed about the war that was supposed to save them. I fought the need to confirm if rumors about a rebellion based in the Squalor were real. To know I wasn't alone in this country in my fight to take down the commanders. But there was too much at risk to ask her in a place like this.

So I did my part agreeing with the cousins, cheering for the Bellovian cause, and passing each test. All the while wondering if the day would come when I'd have to betray Oken and Mayze's trust. All the while knowing if they knew my secrets, they would turn me in as quickly as the next person. Expose me as Trish, sending me and my mother into slavery or possible death. But I couldn't give them up. Being with them felt foolishly safe. Dani faded to the background under Oken's stare and Mayze's sweetly vicious words. Our classmate's liking of them overshadowed their hatred of me and I was amazed to learn what it felt like to get through a meal without a glare cast my way.

Conversation was so easy. Rennie and Oken bounced jokes off one another until I thought I would cry from either laughing or thinking about my dad, his humor so aligned with Rennie's. We spent extra time every evening out in the field sparring or at the range practicing. I think Silken noticed. I felt like I was being watched constantly. I knew it could only help in my goal to find the queen for them to see me putting in the extra effort, but I hated the feeling. It seemed like any moment I would slip up and they would know my secrets. I convinced myself daily I'd shown too much, revealed my heritage and my plans. I checked my roots for silver morning and night, trying to find a time to dye them.

I kept my face blank, my stance loose and refused to talk myself into fear. If Rennie, Mayze, and Oken had yet to suspect, no one else should. The commanders around me only watched with cool, analytical gazes. Appraising, not suspicious. No hatred burning behind their eyes. They thought I was skilled and strong. That the Trish were weak and broken. I was fine.

I was fine.

I chanted this to myself every night, working to relax into sleep. I was fine. My family was fine. My ears practically perked in the direction of Dani's bunk down the aisle. I was fine.

On our seventh day at base, I caught the first hint of a sparkle at my roots and knew I was out of time. I'd need to slip into the toilets tonight to dye them. My thoughts were caught up in planning this when Silken took us to a classroom for the first time. By now there were only twenty of us left. The rest were all assigned to places along the Front, possibly already in the thick of war. We shuffled into the desks, all painfully aware that this was a break from the usual. The standard week of training was up. Most of us would be sent to the Front today. Only those showing true promise would remain for more advanced training.

The test was an exercise of memory. Silken read us a list, a series of numbers, or a set of directions, then waited a certain amount of time before telling us to copy his words on the paper in front of us. It was difficult, but when he finished I felt I had done a decent job. I worried about Rennie, though. She sat staring forward the entire time, hands clutched together under the desk and mouth pressed in a thin line.

Silken walked the room collecting our papers. He came to a stop in front of Rennie's blank sheet. She flattened her hands on the desk and looked up at him. Then she sucked in a breath and repeated all the lists, numbers, and directions. Her words perfectly matched those I had written down. The longer she spoke, the higher Silken's eyebrows climbed up his forehead.

"I can't write or read. But I'm not stupid," she finished.

Silken studied her closely for a long moment before he nodded and continued picking up papers. From my other side, Oken leaned forward and gave Rennie an impressed look. She winked back at him.

The commander sat down at the table in front of the room and read through our papers with a frown. As he separated them into stacks and shuffled between, he ignored us watching him. We fidgeted in our chairs. I kept looking outside to the trees in the distance and the other soldiers running drills. I'd never seen Oken so still, it unnerved me. Mayze looked like she might be sick. I started praying to my mother's gods, asking them to keep my friends away from the Front. Keep them with me just a bit longer. It occurred to me they might not care what happened to any of the Bellovians after what they'd done to Traesha, that I shouldn't care either, but I kept praying anyway.

Silken looked over his notes once more before nodding. My hands clenched as he stood. Mayze swallowed hard. Rennie's eyes narrowed on the paper in his hands. Finally, he stood up.

"Carns, Hale, Jaspers, Larson, Sars, Teal and Yike, please remain seated. The rest of you head down to mess."

Most of the other trainees pushed back their seats and left. My first thought was that we were being sent to the Front, but those leaving knew they had been the ones to fail before it sank in for me.

"Congratulations. You lot are the Bellovian army's newest team. Your mi—"

"Is one of us a commander?" Dani broke in, sitting forward in her desk. In her excitement she scooted the whole thing forward.

Silken's expression flattened. A thrill raced through me as he turned to her. "Don't make me regret placing you on this team, Carns. If you disrespect Commander Larson so thoroughly, she'll have every right to request you be replaced."

Victory. Pure and sweet and bitter. The Bellovian wanted to laugh in Dani's stunned face. The Trish sank deeper, buried under oncoming violence and obedience. I was dimly aware Oken was smiling at me, Rennie knocking on my desk in congratulations, Mayze relaxing with relief, two others I didn't know sitting in silence.

"You can't be serious!" Dani erupted.

"Keep questioning authority, Carns. See where that gets you in this war."

"*Sir*, I've proven myself a strong fighter. A good asset. I was the one who beat Larson the very first night! I—"

"Attacking a sleeping opponent. Very brave. I was especially impressed to hear you had four girls backing you. Too afraid to take her on your own?"

"Not afraid, sir. I'm a leader too!"

Commander Silken laughed and slapped his hands on Dani's desk, making her jump. He leaned in close. "No one respects you. I don't respect you. Don't even make me bring up how terribly you did on the mountain test. You have no idea how to work with others. You'll follow Larson. You'll learn from her calm and determination. Hopefully, you'll grow up. Reach some of the potential you have. Hot headedness is only encouraged at the Front. Don't make me regret not sending you there. Those who become commanders know when to strike back. Know when to keep their mouths shut. Know how to take a hit and keep fighting. I'll repeat what I said before: You have a lot to learn from Commander Larson."

Dani at last fell silent, blinking hard. The commander waited until he was sure she was finished. I looked at who was left. Rennie, Oken, Mayze. Teal was the girl I paced myself against during morning runs. She had gone to my school but hung around the other kids who clung to their hatred of me. Yike sat in the back corner of the room; his face impassive. He was a quiet, large boy; so strong even Oken shied away from him during hand-to-hand.

Silken walked back to his table. He crossed his arms and took the time to meet each of our gazes, lingering on mine. I focused on staying expressionless, unreadable. I was one step closer. Now was not the time to slip. I kept a firm hold on my panicking Trish ideals. This would help Traesha. Help the queen.

"We don't have the time for intensive training lately and we've found new soldiers learn just as well out in the field as they do on base. The Florians have gotten more aggressive over the last few months, so we need to send out competent teams once we form them and leave the heavy lifting to those with experience. You are all now in the position to move up the ranks quickly, so cooperate and don't let us down. Learn to trust and rely on each other, but especially on Commander Larson. She's one of the best we've seen. She'll be moving up quickly. If you want to as well, I suggest you make yourself invaluable to her." He shot a look at Dani. She'd never looked so small.

With little ceremony Silken pulled a new uniform out from behind the table and tossed it to me. It was the same basic idea as the black pants and shirt I already wore, but I had a feeling this one would actually fit. A red stripe patch was sewn onto the right shoulder. I ran my fingers over the stiff fuzz in wonder.

Silken continued, "Your mission is simple, more so just another test for us to make sure you have what it takes. It is, in fact, the same objective as the leadership test. Commander Larson will guide you to an enemy camp. Blow up their supply transport and return alive. The Florians think they are nearly past our defenses. We've let them work their way closer while at the same time separating them from their own base. Once you blow up their supplies, it'll cause the distraction we need to make a push and break their lines, allowing us to move forward for the first time in months."

Silken paused and pulled a pack from beneath the table. He took out a pair of glasses and held them up. These were sleeker than the ones we wore during the test, but I would bet they served a similar purpose. Those glasses alone could probably have fed a family in the Squalor for two years.

"These will guide you to the location we last marked the supply transport and help you see in the dark. They also have trackers, so we'll know your location and can guide you if the need arises." He pointed to the curve where the glasses sat behind the ear. "These also enable you to listen and talk to each other, picking up even whispers. Commander Larson, your earpiece has another small button here. Press it to communicate with me at base; your glasses will notify you when I am calling. And lastly..." He paused and put six more packs on the table. "... these are your packs. They hold everything you'll need for the mission. We want you to hike on foot to the Florian camp. It'll take all of tonight, most of tomorrow, and a few hours into the next night. If you're quick enough, that will leave you plenty of time to grab a couple of hours of sleep."

I nodded with the rest of the team, taking in the mission and the tight time frame we were to keep. The weight settled on my shoulders. I sat up straighter in my chair.

My plan to rise in ranks was going better than I ever

could have expected. It had taken my father two years to reach the title of commander. It would seem the war had changed and changed fast since he last tasted battle.

"Your ride is waiting outside. Grab a pack and hit the road. Stay strong."

My team cleared out, but I hung back, palms sweating. Everything had gone perfectly. Was I pressing my luck?

"Commander, may I have a word?" My voice shook a bit and I cleared my throat.

He nodded, expression warming from the one he'd held in front of the room. He seemed to grow younger. I suddenly saw him as he must have looked with my father. A young, scared soldier following the commander who was capable of drawing laughter even in the worst situation.

"I was wondering... If we complete our mission successfully, could I get an invite to the Conquering Celebration? I know commanders go..."

Silken's hands paused in gathering up his papers. My heart skipped a beat and I focused on keeping my thoughts hidden. He couldn't know how badly I wanted this.

"You want to go to Traesha? The celebration is in a week."

"It's just, my father's talked about the celebration a lot. I've always dreamed of being a commander and being able to go myself. See our greatest victory. I know the timing isn't great, but if I complete my mission to success, can I go?"

He considered me so long I clasped my hands together behind my back to keep them still. If he said yes, I would have access to the queen. I don't know what I could possibly do with that access, but just maybe my father would be there too. I could ask him for help. Ask him what I should do. It was a slim hope, he hadn't attended the celebration in years, but I found myself clinging to it.

"You want to go to Traesha... I'm not a good enough reference? You want to go rub elbows with the higher-ups already, don't you?" Commander Silken let out a laugh. I forced a smile. "I knew when I saw you the ambition was there. Your father was like that too. Saw a mission he wanted to lead? He knew exactly who to talk to. When he got tired of crawling in the mud, I swear he learned figures overnight and landed that comfortable job in City Center. I've always admired your father, and I think times are circling around. I want to be the mentor to you he was to me. I had my doubts when you let Carns get the better of you, but it clearly put you in the right headspace. You have what it takes to lead, Lars—Commander Larson. To tell you the truth, I am in the habit of bringing along my favorite of the volunteers each year. Give them the taste you want so badly. You complete this mission and give us the upper hand over the Florians, I'll consider bringing you along. Introduce you to whomever you want."

I flushed with a combination of relief and dread. I didn't want Silken for a mentor. I didn't want him remembering my father so fondly. I wanted to be good enough to stand out on my own. I wanted to hide in the background, so no one noticed anything was off about me. I wanted to go home and forget all this.

"I won't let you down, sir."

~

"I THINK I prefer princess over commander," Rennie broke the silence. We had been traveling for a while, sitting in the seats facing each other in the back of a team transport. Oken laughed.

"I might too," I said. As soon as the doors of the boxy transport had slammed shut behind us, my stomach dropped. I couldn't get it back up. I was in charge of a mission. Approaching the Front. The Florians. And now I must fight them to get to the queen. I'd have to act Bellovian. The knowledge made the gun at my side too heavy. The Florians had historically lived in peace with the Trish. I had no quarrel with them. I hated imagining what I would have to do in order to advance and avoid suspicion. Instead, I focused my thoughts on the Conquering Celebration. On seeing the queen and letting her know she had at least one ally among her enemies. Vague plans of retracing my parents' steps from when my father snuck my mother out of Traesha drifted in the back of my mind. But they would never come to pass. I couldn't leave the army, even if I found the queen. The punishment for desertion was clear. All of us had seen it. My family would die. It had been years since anyone risked desertion, but Hetta Busha's aunt was publicly executed because her husband was found with a full clip after an altercation at the Front. He hadn't shot at the Florians. His weakness ensured the death of him and his wife. No one was safe from the commanders in this war. There could be no fear. No mercy. No hesitation. I still remember how the crowd in City Center cheered when the woman's body slumped to the ground.

The most I could hope to do was send word to my parents. Maybe I would know someone working the event, someone my father knew who could carry a message back to him. Like Commander Gale. I couldn't remember if she attended but there was a chance I could send a message through her. Something coded might work.

I just needed to see the queen, make sure she was okay. I didn't know why the desire to even do just that hit me so strong. It could be my mother's stories spurring the desire. Magic could happen if the queen returned to the land. When her mother was killed during the invasion, someone must have taken the new queen, just a baby, out of Trae-sha. Since then, the imbalance hurt the land and weakened the people. I wanted to see the queen returned. I wanted to see if hope spread, if the land could flourish once more.

And I wanted to see her for myself. See if it woke anything in me too. A true test of how much my father's Bellovian blood corrupted my Trish. I could figure out the rest after that. Get a feel for how closely they watched her. Maybe rally a slave or two to help her, give them the inside knowledge they need to break her out. Plans kept forming, but I bit them off before they could develop fully. It was too risky to involve myself. My family came first.

Oken was working hard to get Yike talking, but after the third one-word response Oken pegged him as a man of few words and left him alone. Still, Yike looked happy enough to be included. He glanced in Mayze's direction repeatedly and I realized I wasn't the only person with a crush on one of the attractive cousins.

"Do you think we'll have to fight Florians on this mission?" Mayze asked. "Gifted ones?"

"C'mon, Maze. You know our parents said all those stories are made up. They never saw them attack with anything more than guns, just like us." Oken tugged on her braid, making her smile and swat his hand away.

Every Bellovian child grew up hearing rumors about how the evil Florians could breathe fire, control the metal of guns, heal bullet wounds without missing a step, and more.

Most shrugged these rumors off as simple folktales made up to make us feel better about the stalemate.

Most also shrugged off the stories of Trish abilities. Even after some Trish fought back with their lightning-fast speed, the Bellovians later pretended they'd imagined it in the heat of battle. Those who couldn't dismiss it laughed at the Trish for still being too weak to use their gifts. The commanders would say anything to keep the Bellovians confidently volunteering.

I knew better. The rumors were true. My mother was a full-blooded Trish and though she hid her gifts well, I'd seen her do incredible things. Once, when Nico was ten, he ran into my father's legs in the kitchen. My father had been carrying a knife and it fell from his grip at the impact. Before I could gasp, my mother, who had been standing next to me by the sink, was suddenly there. She plucked the knife out of the air before it could touch my brother and handed it back to my father.

I'd seen her jump from one spot to another in the blink of an eye like this several times. There was a word for this speed in Traesha, *nhasnen*, which would be most closely translated to skipping. True Trish speed was incredibly rare even before the attack. Most who possessed it were members of the *magsai* and killed alongside the former queen. Even with it being so uncommon, my mother watched me closely.

"True speed has been our family's gift as far back as our name carries," she told me a week before they called for volunteers. *"Your father's blood won't stop it. Be prepared, it comes with adulthood and often catches you by surprise. Your first skips will be terrifying until you learn to master them. But you will."*

She had been forcing confidence into her voice, though.

We were painfully aware a skip in front of the Bellovians could make me too large a threat. It could easily mean my imprisonment or death. The years my father put into training me would be for nothing if I suddenly developed this ability. It was the one aspect of my Trish heritage I hoped my father's blood would dilute.

I thought about the sword hanging above my parents' bed and how I fantasized about taking it to war. In these dreams I ran with Trish speed against my enemies, proving faster and more effective than any gun—even against those who could shoot flames or possessed equally terrifying powers. Those fantasies had been foolish, but at least I'd always been prepared to face the Florians and all their might. Looking at my team, I wished I could warn them without bringing up my mother and her knowledge of abilities as my source.

Oken caught my eye and smiled. I couldn't return it, my new reality for this war just beginning to dawn on me. I wondered if he had been in the square that day. If he cheered when Hetta's aunt died. Or any of the other family members meeting the same fate. Would he hesitate to kill me if I skipped in front of him or gave myself away?

But those thoughts felt forced and I couldn't hold them long. My stomach unclenched and my heart fluttered when his gaze didn't waver. Calm brown eyes trusting and crinkled, like he and I were in on a joke.

The world stilled when he stretched out his leg, boot tapping mine and staying there. The point of contact was everything. His red cheeks were fascinating. The quiet in my head brief and so sweet.

It was supposed to be me against everyone, making my way forward however I needed. I couldn't afford to lose myself in his smile. To remember how his hands felt on my skin. To wonder if his hair was as soft as it looked. If his—

Rennie called for my attention and I dragged my eyes away from our touching boots. Rennie had quickly made her way into my heart too. Mayze laughed at whatever Rennie said, but I couldn't focus on the words. My family would die if I left to save the queen; would my team be punished too?

My chest throbbed in the direction of Vichi, reminding me what was at stake there. The sacrifice wasn't worth considering.

Rennie said something even more ridiculous. I saw it when even Dani cracked a smile. I needed to focus. To succeed and get my team safely through the mission. Then I could think about the Conquering Celebration and the queen and why I even wanted to go.

The red stripe on my shoulder grew heavy. I was a commander now. I would use this armor to protect my family. I would use it to follow my original plan. If I gained access to Command Hall, I could still take them out from the inside, saving the queen and my family. Ending this war. That was where I would be most powerful. Now wasn't the time to get distracted.

CHAPTER 8

The road angled uphill and we swayed with the acceleration. I tightened my core to keep from sliding into Rennie. Bellovians did not believe in using the safety straps, only the occasional grabbing of the handholds on the walls next to our heads.

The truck moved swiftly over the bumps and dips that became more frequent the further into the hills we drove. The struggle of the engine and continuous ping of rocks hitting the undercarriage eventually made conversation difficult, so we fell quiet. I let the noise drown out my thoughts.

Oken tilted his head back and slept. Dani stared at the floor and bounced her knees. I'd yet to feel her glare but didn't dare hope for her cooperation once the sting of Silken's words faded. Mayze examined the end of her braid and I saw her hands tremble more than once. The other girl, Teal, was silent and tense, lips pressed thin and body still. I decided I liked her stoic energy, that it would do well in a difficult situation. I had a good team. Silken had picked the best and now it was on me to lead them. A good team was the key to success. I could taste it.

I closed my eyes to it all and sent up a prayer to the Trish goddess of peace. I was in no rush to get shot at or to shoot at anyone myself. I begged Finma, goddess of peace, to keep the way clear for us. For success to come easily. My mother would be proud; she insisted I needed to talk to the gods more. I had to admit it made me feel lighter, though I suspected it was the connection to her and not the gods that soothed me.

The truck finally jerked to a stop. Without even bothering to cut the engine, the driver got out and opened the back doors for us. The forest scene that greeted us was a daunting black wall against the night. I had only ever seen so many trees in my dreams. Wind rustled the leaves and a Trish melody flitted through my thoughts—

He sings the forest song
The trees whisper along

"Glasses on and powered up," the driver said. We jumped out of the truck and retrieved them from our bags. They nodded when we were all properly equipped. "Stay strong."

The wheels of the truck skidded over the dirt as they turned and drove back the way we came. I couldn't follow their cloud of dust long even with the moon shining and my glasses providing a red-tinted view of the nighttime world around us.

The screen in my glasses flickered and I heard a faint hiss in my ear as the earpiece turned on. A flashing red dot in the corner of my vision notified me of an incoming communication. I reached up and pressed the button at the base of the speaker on the glasses' frame.

"Commander Larson?" Silken's voice, so close in my ear, made me repress a shudder.

"Copy," I said. The team heard and turned to me expectantly.

"See the arrow?" A white arrow appeared at the bottom left of my sight. It was faint and flickered, but visible.

"Yes, sir."

"Follow it. Let me know if you have trouble. Your glasses are more advanced than your team's. Theirs are good for little more than tracking devices and night vision. Should something happen to you, pass your glasses on to your second in command." My eyes immediately went to Oken. My cheeks flushed red.

"Yes, sir."

"Good. Stay strong." The earpiece went dead and I took my finger off the button. The glasses were designed to pick up our voices to communicate more quickly with each other. I could hear my teammates' soft breathing in the speaker above my ear. I tried to ignore the annoyance bubbling and hoped I would get used to the sound so close and intimate.

"Fall in. Jaspers, take the rear." I trusted only Rennie's sharp eyes to guard my back.

I turned in the direction of the arrow pointing up the mountain, away from the gravel road. I tightened the straps of my pack and began the uphill hike through the trees, setting a pace I was fairly sure they could also maintain. My team followed. A timer appeared in the top left of my screen and a distance in miles in the right. I would use these to calculate if we were going fast enough, when we had time to rest, and to stay ahead of the troops following. It made my skin crawl knowing they were on our heels. I felt sandwiched between enemies: a Florian army holding the line on one side, Bellovian teams hoping to break through behind. It was hard to imagine us avoiding getting caught in the middle.

"Sharp eyes, team," I whispered, knowing Oken was the only one to catch any sleep on the way here. I almost wished I could lift my glasses, trusting my own senses more than the red night vision they created.

"Nothing is getting past me, princess," Oken responded in my ear. I was suddenly very aware of him walking directly behind me. Someone snorted with laughter, hearing the nickname in their earpiece and taking it for an insult. Likely Dani.

"Commander," I corrected him sharply. The word tasted bitter, but I needed respect now more than ever.

"Yes, Commander." Somehow the boy could sound equally amused and apologetic.

The sun was beginning to rise when I let my team break. Someone was panting and I suspected it was Rennie. We sat by a stream to refill our purifying bottles and eat the oat bars we found in our packs. Soon almost everyone dozed off.

Oken, alert but unworried, sat near me, leaning against a tree trunk. I took off my glasses so no one could hear me but him. He followed suit, tilting his head in question, his dark curls sweeping his forehead.

"I just wanted..." I stopped, feeling self-conscious. I pushed the embarrassment down with a deep breath and started over. "If anything happens to me, you are my second. Take my glasses, they show more than yours. I don't have to tell you the rest." Bellovian code was well known: complete the mission at all costs. They were to forget about me and push on, whether I was dead, captured, or too injured to continue. One life was a small cost when so many were excited to fill its place in battle.

Oken nodded, but I couldn't read the expression on his face. It was strange how he could do that. Before the last couple of weeks, I would have said Oken was an open book. Smiling and determined every day in school. He seemed so predictable. Since I'd really let myself start noticing him, I realized the smiles may be as much a cover as when I cleared my own face. When he let the smile die, I really didn't know what was happening behind his eyes.

The sun lit the forest, our red night vision fading to clear lenses. I woke the team, earning a couple of glares, but no words of complaint. The next leg of our hike was down-hill. While we were able to go at a faster pace, I cringed often as we crashed through the forest. Whenever someone stumbled, the domino effect often reached even me. I melted every time Oken's chest hit my back, his laughter brushing my ear. The third time it happened I rounded on the team, noticing Oken still stood too close while everyone else had righted themselves. He was grinning. I felt my lips wobble, but managed to smother a smile of my own.

"Walk further apart. Think about where you're putting your feet and how you're placing your weight. And try to stay *quiet*," I hissed. I heard a couple of grunts of acknowl-edgment and turned back to the path. The forest did get quieter behind me, but I knew in time they would forget once again and their steps would fall heavy like before.

I was grateful when the slope evened out and became leaves and soft dirt rather than twigs and rocks. After a couple of hours, I allowed another break and we ate sandwiches and bruised fruit. Everyone was red-faced, sweating and removing their new boots to examine blisters. I was glad I'd kept my old boots. They gave me no trouble. When I saw Mayze's face drain of color after removing her socks, I helped her pop some of the worst blisters and wrap her ankles and feet. Soon I was going from person to person. I noticed many of the blisters had been reopened, probably having formed during training. Teal's feet were by far the worst, and I wrapped them with extra care, thinking about how much pain she must have endured in the last week as she tried to keep up with me during morning runs.

Finished, I rinsed my hands in the stream nearby. I'd followed its path as best as I could while keeping with the arrow, but from this point on we would have to veer apart. Rennie joined me, removing her glasses to wipe the lenses studiously.

I copied the movement.

"You picked Sars?"

I winced. She must not have been sleeping when I made Oken my second. I lowered my glasses further and leaned closer to the water, letting its whispers drown my words. "He's more committed to the mission. To the commanders. It's safer for them."

Rennie considered my words. "More committed than you?"

We locked eyes. I let my face relax, showing more than usual. Just enough for Rennie's lips to quirk. My heart raced with the danger of letting my thoughts show. She nodded. "Your dad always said—"

"Larson! How long until we reach the target?" I jumped at Dani's barked question, forcibly turning myself from Rennie and clearing my face. How did she know my father? What was she going to say?

"Let's go two more hours," I said and waited while they groaned in unison. Some trained, stoic, Bellovian soldiers they were. "Then we'll get some sleep. We're about four hours of hiking from the target at our current pace." Their faces brightened as they realized the end was in sight. Rennie replaced her glasses and fell into place, ending the conversation and leaving me with far too many pressing questions.

Boots were pulled back on with winces and packs adjusted on sweaty backs. We left our camp. At this point, the trees around us felt never-ending and ancient. The tense silence and stillness of the leaves made my neck hairs stand. If I let myself think about it too hard, I got a strange sense that the trees were angry. The war was affecting more than just the people. I thought of the Trish hunting song I loved so much. There was no love in this forest, no deer, no universal songs. Only dead soldiers to mourn.

The trees swayed as if in response to my thoughts. My insides chilled. My team let out little sighs of relief from the first breeze we'd felt all day.

The two hours were slow-going. My thoughts spiraled as the forest burned orange and then dimmed with the sunset. When I signaled to make camp, my team sat heavily in the dirt. Night was falling quickly and bringing a biting cold with it.

"Rennie, you take first watch," I said. I hoped she would sit with me slightly apart from everyone and we could talk again, but the team huddled together against the chill of the night.

"Oh, push off," she muttered, propping her chin on a hand and glaring up at me. Nothing seemed to have changed, but her expression was more open and her smile more trusting. Something had been established between us, some connection I didn't understand.

"Just do it. Wake up the next person in half an hour."

I joined the team in pulling my thin sleeping bag from

the bottom of the pack and crawled in. Mayze lowered herself next to me and fell asleep almost immediately. I rolled and put my back to her, curling up on my left side like I always did to sleep. I barely kept myself from reacting when I realized it was Oken on my other side. He stared up at the canopy of leaves above us. His eyes dark in the moonlight, his skin soft and pale, hair a dancing black. He didn't look real. I clenched my hands into fists, fighting the urge to reach out and touch him.

Slowly he fell asleep, his body twitching occasionally as he relaxed, making me smile. I listened to his breathing even out, the hint of a snore on the edge of his breaths. My own body slipped into sleep.

I LEFT *the lavender warmth of home and ran to the center of Vichi. Dirt roads solidified into concrete. Someone had just plowed, and salt burned holes in the thin layer of packed snow. Dusty gray houses turned to clean windows set in steel walls. The buildings were taller, placed close together. I went straight to the heart of City Center, where Command Hall loomed, the longest and tallest building by far. Something tugged in my chest. I needed to go in. I set my hands on the main doors and they swung open at my touch.*

I heard a door click shut and turned toward my father's office. He'd just gone in. He'd be right there. I started toward him, but the pull in my chest begged me to go another way. He wasn't what I was searching for. I turned away, sadness and confusion flooding me. The confusion built until I wasn't sure which hall I was in. The panic of being lost hit me hard for the first time in my life and I spun in a circle, only to find four different identical halls branching out from where I stood. I'd never dreamed like this. Not even my dream shadow stood near to center me.

There was a cruel laugh and I couldn't tell which direction it came from. My heart was pounding and I spun once more to look, freezing when I noticed my hair had escaped its braid and fanned out around me, glowing silver and condemning. No one could see me now. It would expose me and my mother. The city officials and commanders walked these halls with guns at their hips. I needed to find my mother and dye my hair again.

I took off at a run down the hall in front of me, hoping it would lead me out of the building or upstairs back to my father's office. Maybe I could tap into Trish speed and run fast enough that no one would see me. Above all I prayed I wasn't running toward the laughter.

The pull in my chest tightened; this was the wrong way. My feet grew heavy. What I needed to find wasn't there. How was I supposed to find the basement? I needed to—

I jerked out of sleep. Teal was shaking my arm for my watch. I sat up and took deep breaths to calm my pounding heart. The forest was still. The trees crowding and solemn. I couldn't quite shake off my panic. That nightmare felt familiar, yet so different from the dreams I usually shared with my shadow.

Teal settled down to sleep, and I set my glasses on top of my head with no one awake to see how little use I had for them. I pulled them on only to check the timer. Slowly the minutes passed. When the time came, it was a relief to take my mind off the nightmare and wake Oken for his turn. He sat on his sleeping bag and backed up to lean against a tree. His posture was relaxed, but he wouldn't sleep.

After about ten minutes of shifting and trying to get comfortable, I knew it wouldn't happen. I dreaded returning to the nightmare, and it seemed no matter where I rolled a sharp rock was present.

"Can't sleep?" Oken whispered.

With a huff I sat back up. I scooted to sit next to him, pulling up my sleeping bag against the cold. As always, he seemed completely unaffected by the low temperature. I resisted the urge to move closer to his warmth.

"Nervous?" he asked once I stilled.

"I don't think so. I mean, maybe a little about getting shot at and all that. But the mission itself seems almost too straightforward. And they sent us out so quickly, that must mean they aren't worried about us much either. It's not like we're crossing the Front." I shrugged, looking up at the haunted forest around us. "Something feels off, though. I'm not sure what."

"I feel it, too." Oken laughed ruefully. "I was hoping you were in on it, whatever it was."

I shrugged.

"Oh well." He sighed. "This is war, right? My dad always said it was ninety percent mental games and we were just the players."

"What was the other ten percent?"

"Hiking."

I smiled at that. "Is he still enlisted?"

"No, he died a few years ago. His injuries from the war caught up with him. Mostly it was lung problems from some gas his unit got hit with."

His words surprised me. We usually knew when parents were killed. A commander came to class and a student returned with stooped shoulders. I supposed when a parent died away from the Front it didn't warrant a commander's visit. "I'm so sorry, Oken."

He cocked his head and I could feel the intensity of his

gaze behind his glasses. It was the wrong thing for a Bellovian to say. "I'm sure he fought strong" or something similar was the expression given to those in mourning. I tried to think of a way to save the moment. Something Bellovian, but the words that came to mind were too shallow. I couldn't force them.

I relaxed only when Oken's face cleared into a small smile. "Thanks, princess. He was in pain for a long time, so at least that's over. I just wish I could talk to him now. I'd whine about how some snob from City Center kicked my ass in training."

"Something tells me he wouldn't have much sympathy."

Oken coughed softly, holding back his laugh. "You've got that right." He paused and shifted, stretching out his long legs. I focused on that instead of the way he kept looking at me. His feet ended up inches from my own. I swallowed and bent my legs up, hugging them to my chest and resting my chin on the layer of sleeping bag over my knees. The night air suddenly wasn't so cold.

"You really aren't what I expected," he said.

"What did you expect?" I blushed when my question came out a soft whisper.

"For you not to understand. It's like you've had it hard too."

"I won't say my problems were nearly as bad as everyone else's." I thought about a lost home in Traesha I would never know. The hatred I grew up teaching myself to ignore. Yet, I'd never known hunger or death or feared the cold. "But I've still had problems."

"I'm sorry, Fin." Now he didn't sound like a Bellovian either. "I mean, I'm sorry I treated you like everyone else did. Only Mayze really talked to you in school. Even then I know it wasn't much. There was something about you, like you were detached. I still can't read your face most of the time. You just didn't seem to need anyone else, but it must have been lonely. If I'd known you were this pleasant, I would have made an effort sooner."

"Don't be sorry. I wasn't that lonely. I was... used to it."

Before arriving at base, I would have said I preferred it. My hatred of all Bellovians apart from my father and Nico had fueled my training and given me purpose. As a child, I never wanted to join the Bellovian children in their pretend war games and refused to go outside to build shelters and hurl snowballs when my home was so warm and safe. My mother stayed home most of the time, I could tell she felt safer hidden from the Bellovian streets too. She entertained me for hours on end with tales about Traesha. My father took me out to shoot and train regularly. Nico was my only and best friend. We even had a cat for a while that I talked to—mainly ridiculous stories about the boy sitting next to me now.

Had I been lonely? More like I was in the clouds, dreaming about what I could do with my Trish abilities or what Traesha had been like. What it would have been like to grow up there, far away from a war I would have to join to keep my family safe and the responsibility I felt to avenge my mother's home.

And if I was ever sad or lonely, there was a running path and training to take it out on. I didn't want to let Oken in on how often it came to that.

Oken and I fell silent, each of us lost in our thoughts. He had a soothing presence when quiet, something I hadn't expected from the loud-mouthed boy who regularly earned himself extra laps on the track after class.

Staring out into the dark trees, a melody came to my

mind. It was a song about a Florian igniter who fell in love with a Trish princess. He promised to burn down the world for her, but his rage and fire weren't what she wanted. She didn't accept his marriage offers and refused to watch him change for her. He used his flames to make large fires on the beach, and her people danced around them for hours. He used his flames to melt and blow glass into beautiful art. He worked in the forges and created the most elegant of *magsai* blades. He did everything he could to become like the peaceful Trish people around him, and she still refused him, marrying instead the Trish man tradition deemed appropriate for her. One winter night, the igniter finally left Traesha to return to Floria but wandered into the mountains to the south. He died from the cold there, having cast away his gift forever.

"I've never heard that one," Oken said. I stiffened. I hadn't meant to hum. I told myself it didn't mean anything. He couldn't make the connection to my mother's homeland. Bellovians didn't pay enough attention to art to know. "You have a pretty voice."

Oken gave me a sweet smile and turned his attention back to the woods. It was genuine. Not suspicious. My shoulders relaxed and his smile filled my thoughts, driving out the image of the Florian who could have burned the world, but turned Trish instead.

I MUST HAVE DRIFTED OFF, because the next thing I knew Oken was gently shaking my shoulder to wake me. I had no time to relish my dreamless sleep before realizing my head was resting in his lap. I hastily pushed myself away and began packing my bag, refusing to make eye contact with him. He went around camp waking up the others while I struggled to hide my embarrassment.

I focused myself on the mission and rolled up my sleeping bag. We had two and a half hours to reach the destination. By my estimations, it would take us two to get there at the pace we'd held so far. I had to account for an increase in Florian activity, though, and a need to move more carefully. The last leg would require extreme caution.

By the time our bags were packed I was ready to face everyone again, my face carefully void of expression even when Oken caught my eye. I saw a brief flicker of some emotion in his gaze right before I turned away. Regret? Disappointment?

I redirected my thoughts, clenching my jaw. This was exactly why I hoped he wouldn't volunteer.

"The Florians are close," I said, proud of the flat tone I managed. "If any of you forget to step quietly and carefully, I will make you climb up a tree and wait for us there. Watch your feet, but more importantly, watch for movement. It will take all of us being on our guard to get to our destination. Guns out, but fingers parallel to the barrel, no resting on the trigger. We don't need any misfires. This is what we've been working for, let's not screw it up."

I didn't wait for a response. I pulled down my glasses, let the red night vision set in, adjusted my grip on my gun, and began moving through the trees. Pride swelled when my feet made very little noise. I was getting better at this.

When my team followed, I could practically hear their concentration, but fortunately their feet were quieter than ever. Even at our cautious pace, the hike passed quickly. Despite the late hour and our quiet steps, I was surprised to meet with no resistance drawing closer to the Florian camp.

As I thought when Commander Silken described our simple objective, this was turning out to be too easy.

The hair on my arms rose and I could have sworn we were being watched, but even when I lifted my glasses, pretending to wipe sweat on my nose, I couldn't see anything. I listened hard but only heard my team breathing behind me and in my speaker. I even closed my eyes and discreetly sniffed the air, but I was downwind from my team and I could only smell them and the forest behind. I pressed us on, blaming lack of sleep and nerves for keeping me on edge.

We were only a hundred feet from the target now. Not daring to even whisper instructions, I lifted a fist and spread my fingers. The clock in the corner of my vision rapidly approached zero. My team fanned out behind me and we pressed forward in a wide V. I froze, halting my team, when Teal suddenly darted into the trees to my right, but she snuck around the Florian keeping watch with ease. We stayed crouched in the bushes and waited until Teal's hold on the man's neck had the Florian sliding to the ground. It left me slightly shaken that I hadn't seen the man myself. Teal nodded and waved a hand to single all clear. I unhooked the grenade from my belt and heard the gentle clicks of my team following suit. Our small bombs were not built to do much damage; we would have to throw all of them to explode the supply transport. This was a test of teamwork.

I saw a glint of metal in the moonlight and pushed down with my hand. We ducked low. Someone sucked in a breath and held it. There were canvas tents set up around the truck, four in total. I knew the occupants would be slaughtered by the troops behind us, but I hoped my own grenade would not cause them harm. I wasn't ready for that weight yet.

I signaled my team to get ready, and it crossed my mind that this transport looked exactly like the one we were taken to the mountains in, not like the supply transport I had been imagining. I looked around to make sure it was right, but it was the only vehicle nearby. The arrow on my glasses pointed right to it. I brought down my hand. We threw our grenades, turned, and ran.

I heard the explosives hit the metal of the truck and, a second later, a push of sound, and strong, warm wind hit my back. We crashed through the trees.

I pressed the button to connect with Silken. "Mission complete!"

There was yelling and the crackling of flames behind us. I waved my arm and turned my team in the direction of the new arrow that appeared to direct us. It must be taking us to the troops. I sprinted, ignoring the adrenaline coursing through my blood that urged me to go faster than the Bellovians around me. Instead, I paced myself with Teal once again. *Always focus.*

Suddenly the chaos shifted behind us. The roar of the fire cut off abruptly. A cold wind swept by, spreading too quickly from outside my clothes and into my bones. My movements grew stiff. My toes numbed and I stumbled. My team gasped around me. Rennie tripped and I doubled back to help her up. Her teeth chattered. Her eyes were wide when they met mine, lips turning blue. There was a moment of blinding confusion and then dread as I realized what was happening.

Florian gifts were at the Front.

Fear stole my breath. I forced myself to think and fell into the shadow of a tree, pulling Rennie with me and looking around the trunk to see who was approaching from behind. A twig snapped and I spun around, pressing into the bark, gun already aimed.

A girl our age stepped into view. She was stunning and severe, her smile more chilling than the sudden cold. Her colorless hair was in a tight bun that pulled up her equally pale eyebrows. I risked a quick look at my team and saw my shock mirrored on their faces. I'd never seen someone with hair like hers.

"What do we have here?" the girl's voice was a low purr, her accent a softened version of Bellovian Common Tongue. She smirked, red-painted lips a perfect curve. Her eyes landed on Oken, stepping in front of Mayze. I took half a breath in, my mind screaming as I began to tighten my grip on the trigger, the girl's forehead an easy target. Could I do it?

A hand snaked out from my left. I turned to see another girl. Stony, pale green eyes. With a fast jerk she'd snapped my wrist upward. The movement was so quick. I hadn't heard her approach. I felt the pain, though. The bones in my wrist, more fragile than I'd ever considered them to be, snapped. My hand went limp and the gun fell. For some reason, it felt more important than ever that I keep my face perfectly clear. Even as I choked on fear and agony. Even as shock blurred the world around the girl.

Rennie shouted. Yike roared to our left. But I couldn't fight back. Because this girl moved so fast. Because this girl had dark skin, an upturned nose, pale eyes.

This girl had silver hair.

She looked to the blonde Florian, and I followed her gaze, my eyes passing over Oken pulling Mayze away, but Mayze was caught in the Florian's gaze. The blonde's wicked smile twisted further as we watched. She brought her hands together in a clap. I heard the sharp sound and watched in amazement as a bright light flashed from between her palms. Soon the clap was all I heard; a ringing in my ears that wouldn't stop. The flash of light was all I could see. All my senses were robbed, yet the cold never left. The pain in my wrist never settled.

My last thought was a sharp sting of disappointment. I failed. I would never get to the celebration now. I wouldn't find the queen.

CHAPTER 9

S unlight beat down on my face. Squinting and lifting my uninjured arm to block it, I saw the light was coming in through the high barred window of the cell holding us. A quick count confirmed my team was still together. Unconscious and sprawled about like we'd been tossed inside with little care. My broken wrist appeared to be the only injury; an observation that made my cheeks grow warm. It was wrapped now in a makeshift brace, throbbing, but I could force the pain to the back of my mind like I did my nose and bruises on my face. I frowned toward Dani. She'd be the one to comment.

Yike was closest to me. I dodged the wild punch he threw when I shook him awake. His pale skin flushed and he apologized, but the blush faded to a murderous glare as he took in our surroundings. The cell was big enough to hold all seven of us rather comfortably. He paced the walls as I woke the others. The back one contained a window only Yike could see out of, not that he reported much of a view, just a lawn leading up to the forest. The wall opposite the window was made entirely of thick cage bars. There was another small room past them with a solid black door. A man in a navy Florian uniform stood at attention against the wall there. His stance never shifted, but I didn't like the way his eyes followed my movements. I lifted my chin and his eyes narrowed. My attention snagged on the ring of keys at his belt.

"So... what now?" Oken asked, voice lowered so the guard wouldn't hear.

"I guess we wait," I said.

And so we did. I tried to get my mind off the situation by planning how to help the queen, but the more I did, the more the cell pressed in. I already only had days to get to her. What could I do now?

Mayze nervously took her braid out and redid it. Yike followed her movements with his eyes and a thought suddenly struck me. My roots had been showing yesterday. Was it just yesterday? How long had we been stuck in here? How long would we be? I looked to Dani, engaged in a stare down with the guard. What would she do when she noticed? What would Oken or Yike or Teal do? Would they consider me among the enemies? They knew of the Trish as weak, but the stories of our gifts were enough for them to justify their attack, saying we were a true threat when Bellovi offered peace. Would they consider me one? A traitor and a spy? The possibilities spiraled as I imagined how long we could be stuck here. I fought down panic, knowing I should be more worried about our captors and the cage holding us.

Then real fear struck. What would the commanders do when we didn't return? Would they wait to clear out our bunks at base? Would they find the bottles of hair dye and feel the need to investigate, tracing them to my family and my mother, who looked even more Trish than I did?

How much danger had I put my family in?

I was really starting to work myself up when we heard keys in the door of the small room on the other side of our cage. The guard stepped aside as our captors entered. Without hesitation, Dani threw herself at the bars. The leading girl screamed and backed into the man behind her. He caught her easily, eyes narrowing. Even I couldn't stop a smirk as the rest of my team laughed.

The bars Dani held frosted over quickly and she let them go with a hiss, shaking out her hands. It was now the Florian girl's turn to smirk. I looked past her to the rest of the people coming into the room, remembering the girl from the forest with a jolt. My eyes craved the sight of another Trish.

The man steadying the first girl had shoulder-length auburn hair with a small braid down one side. I took in little else before my eyes skipped over him to the next two people to enter and my heart stopped.

There were two of them. A boy and girl with silver hair. Trish hair. I had never seen it grown out before. They were haunting and beautiful, moving with otherworldly grace in their light steps. I clenched my fists and stifled a cry of pain from the movement of my right hand. The agony was just what I needed to fight the urge to rush forward and tell them who I really was then and there. To tell them our queen was alive.

Yet I still waited for them to see me. To recognize me as one of their own. In that moment, I hated all my Bellovian blood that separated me from their grace and culture. These were my mother's people. Not me, with my bloodthirst and the satisfaction I craved from training. They looked angry, yes, but they didn't look consumed by the need to fight. That was me.

What were they doing here?

"They're just children," the Florian man said. He spoke in broken, accented Trish like my father's. I held my breath, waiting for one of the Trish to respond, speaking in the language I loved as elegantly as my mother did. They did not disappoint.

"Yes, Hinze. Probably around our age," the Trish boy said with a significant look.

"I doubt they know anything," the Trish girl said, her lip curled in disgust. The look jolted me. Maybe there was room for consuming hatred. The fire in her eyes reminded me of the feeling that churned in my stomach. Her hair was a lighter silver than the boy's and fell in a straight, heavy sheet to the middle of her back.

"What's going on?" Oken stepped up next to Dani, arms crossed.

I ripped my eyes away from the Trish couple, hoping it wasn't obvious I'd followed their conversation. I was sitting toward the back of the cell and no one was looking my way. I hardened my face, hiding the wonder and excitement I felt. I kept my arrogant, hateful Bellovian mask in place. If the commanders hadn't found my dye bottles, if we did get away, I needed to be the same girl I was when I left base. I couldn't tell them who I was or about the queen. My parents' lives depended on me.

"Which one of you is playing leader?" the Trish girl asked in Common Tongue. Her accent was the same one my mother worked so hard to get rid of over the years. But the sneer on her face was an expression I had never seen my mother wear.

I pushed myself off the wall and stepped forward, moving Teal out of my way.

"What's your name, girl?" she asked.

"Commander." I mirrored her glare.

The Florian boy, Hinze, came closer to the bars than the others dared to after Dani's move. It was unnerving to have her standing at my side now. She angled slightly toward me, body language a silent support of my movements.

"We just have a few questions to ask you," he said.

"I bet you do. I have some questions myself."

"I will answer yours if you answer mine." Hinze had an open face, kind eyes, and a seasoned way of speaking that didn't match his youth. He wouldn't last long in this war.

"Probably not."

"You won't speak with us." It wasn't a question. His eyes swept past me, disappointed but not surprised. Dani had a satisfied smile now. She knew as well as anyone I wouldn't break. "Any of you feel like saving us all a good deal of trouble and being forthcoming?" His question was met with glares as cold as Vichi.

"I'll answer some questions. Just let me out of this box," Yike said, flexing his muscles in a way I didn't think he was even aware of.

Hinze sighed. "I suppose it will have to be the hard way." He was the only one who seemed upset by the thought. "Who's first?"

"We'll take *Commander* first," the girl Trish said. The thought of making me break clearly appealed to her.

The short girl who had entered first stepped forward and raised her hands. The cold wind from the forest returned and hit everyone around me, pushing my team back from the bars. Hinze nodded to the guard, who opened the cage with a key from his ring. Hinze stepped inside and pulled me out, shutting the cell door behind me. The wind ceased, but the cold lingered.

"We'll return her in a bit," the Trish girl promised,

sickly sweet. She pulled out a pair of wrist bands and snapped them on my wrists, even over the cast. I didn't let the pain show from the extra pressure.

Oken stepped forward, eyes narrowed as he noticed the wrapping on my wrist. "It better be in one piece."

"Depends on how well she behaves." She jerked me forward by the bands. I caught my lip to keep from crying out. The pain was less surprising than the malicious intent. This wasn't what I expected from a Trish. Had the invasion changed them, or were my mother's stories too ideal?

I might have felt fear as I was led from my team, but it didn't process as Oken caught and held my gaze. Brown eyes molten with anger for me. His was the last face I saw before they led me from the room. I squared my shoulders.

They marched me down the hall. I resisted the temptation to fight them off, my mind instinctively running through the maneuvers that would break their holds and incapacitate those nearest to me. But I doubted I could take two Trish equal to me in speed and two gifted Florians. I didn't know his ability yet, but Hinze carried himself with a confidence born from power. He must hold a position of leadership, made obvious when the others fell into step behind him naturally and Florian soldiers we passed in the halls moved hastily out of his way, snapping to attention.

He took us to a room with nothing except chairs and a table with a clasp at its center. I was escorted to a chair and the chain connecting my wrist bands was placed in the clasp, securing my hands to the table. The two Florians took their seats on the other side of the table; the Trish boy and girl leaned against the wall behind them. They eyed me like a caged animal, ready to lash out. I eyed them like they weren't worth the effort of lashing out.

The Trish boy spoke first, clearly thinking I had no idea what they said. "You sure about this?"

Hinze sighed. "We need answers, Fisher. Even if the answer is she doesn't know anything." He paused and took a deep breath, switching Common Tongue of Bellovi and Floria. "What was your mission?"

I just looked at him. My left hand grew cold and stiff in the tight bands. My right hand, already stiff from the break, pulsed with warm pain.

"What's your name? There, we'll start with an easy one. What's the harm in answering that?"

There actually could be harm in that. Finley was the name of the very first royal family of Traesha, before the Hollis family came to power. This was something Bellovians would know if they'd ever bothered to learn the history of the land they had conquered, but I didn't have to worry about my name back home. The two Trish staring at me now would know its significance. My silence drew another sigh from Hinze. He stood abruptly.

"Ten minutes, Brea," he told the Florian girl who remained seated. She examined me closely. Frigid air rolled off her. Hinze and the two Trish people left the room.

"Just you and me, *Commander*," Brea sneered. She narrowed her eyes and the temperature dropped drastically, reminding me of the coldest day of winter back home. The air bit my lungs, making a full breath difficult and my skin pricked instantly with goosebumps. It stung to keep my eyes open. My broken wrist and nose ached so badly I couldn't hold back a grimace. The Florian girl sat completely unaffected, even though she wore nothing more than a light shirt and shorts. Our breath puffed into the air, clouding the space between us.

"Your name?" she prodded. I tried to clench my jaw, but my chattering teeth made it difficult.

My hands began to burn from the cold. I wondered if I was about to lose an ear or the tip of my nose, when suddenly the temperature changed again, rising as rapidly as it dropped. My hands and feet stung, like running them under hot water after walking home in the cold. I felt sweat bead too quickly on my forehead. The air no longer hurt to breathe but was heavy with heat. My tongue and throat dried and I longed for water. I started to pant. Right when the heat became unbearable, she dropped the temperature once again.

It felt like we sat in this cycle for ages. Eyebrows furrowed in concentration, she questioned me and searched for signs I would give in. When the ten minutes passed and Hinze found me still uncooperative, he left me with her for another ten. Each time we changed temperature I was sure she made it just a bit hotter or colder than it had been before. She was concentrating hard, the use of her ability requiring more effort the longer we sat. My body grew numb and my mind detached from the situation. My thoughts filled with the effort it took to draw air in and out in each extreme temperature.

Something tugged in my chest and suddenly I was lost in Command Hall yet again, walking the halls this time in no hurry. Concern that felt like someone else's flooded me. I knew I should be worried, but the escape to my nightmare was bliss. I wandered the building, searching idly. My thoughts slipping before they could form. Panic a distant roar.

I came to slowly, slumped in the chair, when they finally gave up. I slid off onto the floor when they released my numb hands. I couldn't hold back a cry of pain when my broken wrist hit the ground beneath me. It sounded weak and pathetic, but I couldn't force myself to care. Completely disoriented, I stared at my left wrist and the red line around it. Had I struggled? Or did it swell with the temperature changes? Either way, it was bleeding around the metal band. The pain was nothing compared to my other wrist, just a momentary distraction for my chaotic thoughts.

The Trish boy grabbed one of my arms and hauled me to my feet. "No one has gone this long," he hissed, a tinge of anger marring the beautiful flow of his Trish words.

"Well, Fisher, she should have talked," Brea said with a shrug, rising from her seat at the table. I could feel myself shaking, and for the first time in my life I was too weak to stand on my own. The world spun, my stomach churning with the sight. I leaned forward and lost whatever food had been in my stomach. Fisher struggled to keep his grip on my arm and jump out of the way at the same time.

Hinze and Fisher practically had to drag me back to the cell because I couldn't get my feet to step properly. The incompetence of my body was nothing I had ever felt before. It was more terrifying than those minutes alone with Brea. They dropped me behind the bars and shut me in with the Bellovians once again. I curled up, trying to warm myself and wishing for water to soothe my burning throat. I was shivering, drenched with sweat.

"She didn't talk. We'll see if any of you can say that much tomorrow." Hinze's words practically ensured none of my team would give him answers. He'd just made it a competition.

Food was brought, and I ate and drank what I could. But moments later I dragged myself to the corner when it threatened to come back up and did.

"What did they do to you?" I heard Oken ask. I was sitting curled against the bars, resting my cheek against the cool metal. I shook my head and groaned at the rush of dizziness the motion induced.

"Well, shit." I thought that might be Teal's voice.

"Try to get her to drink more water." Mayze there.

Soft brown eyes flooded my vision. Curls of hair I wished I could touch, but my hands ached too much. When he pulled me into his warmth to help me drink, sleep came almost instantly.

I was back in Vichi, outside on the snow-covered steps. I braced myself and reached to open the door. I was suddenly deep inside Command Hall's maze of hallways, hand still outstretched. I heard piano playing. Nico. I followed the sound, but when I drew close it became just a jarring striking of keys and not a soothing Trish melody. I opened the door that appeared and blocked my path. Inside was a white room. My old bed was in the center, my mother kneeling by the side, her back to me. I couldn't see myself around her but heard my child voice clearly. "What about the baby? The princess?"

"What about her?"

"Where is her resa magsai?*"*

A pause.

"I think it's time you went to your dreams, my child."

The image of my mother's back and my bed fell away, but my last question echoed through the shifting halls. I ran, searching for my mother now. She had to still be here. I needed her.

"Where is her resa magsai? *Where is her* resa magsai?*"*

I was crying. I heard a girl screaming and gunfire. The thud of a body thrown. There was no sound like motionless bones hitting the floor. I ducked, covering my head and cowering shamefully.

"Where is her resa magsai?*"*

A slip of paper fluttered to the ground at my feet. Nico's handwriting. Stisha colm.

"Where is her resa magsai?*" My child voice was getting louder.*

My chest ached so much I couldn't breathe. I thought I might be sick. The note shifted to ash in my trembling fingers.

"Where is her resa magsai?*"*

I woke up in the middle of the night, sweating and dry heaving. My chest still felt twisted, pulled toward Vichi. I missed my mother. My father's warm hugs. Nico's gentle comfort.

Oken, alert and ready, pushed a cup of water into my hands. I gulped it down, but it did little to bring relief. I hated to do it, but I moved away from his heat beside me. Everything burned.

"How can I help?" He sounded desperate. I leaned against the cool bars. A new guard stood expressionless outside the cell.

"I don't know." My voice was rough. My throat itched and I accepted the refilled glass of water Oken handed me.

"What was your dream?" he whispered.

I started, turning to look at Oken so fast my head swam. I swallowed hard. "Just a nightmare I have."

"You said something..." I froze. Had I been speaking Trish? "Something about a queen."

I couldn't read his expression. I couldn't think clearly. I started shivering again, the bars suddenly unbearable. Too cold and hard. "I... I heard something. Back at the training base. Commander Silken said the Trish queen was alive. That they had her." I wanted to regret saying the words, but it felt amazing to tell someone. Amazing to pretend Oken was on my side; that he would care about this knowledge as much as I did. I knew it was nonsense and dangerous, but I couldn't stop myself. "Commander Silken said they were going to reveal it at the Conquering Celebration in Traesha. He said if we succeeded in our mission, I could go."

"Why do you want to see the Trish queen, Finley?"

I shrugged. My teeth started to chatter. "I hoped my dad would be there." It was only half a lie.

"You'll see him again." I blinked at Oken. Without a thought, I crawled closer, resting my head on his shoulder and shivering into his warmth. He stiffened, but nothing had ever felt better.

That is, until he relaxed, his arms hesitantly coming up to wrap around me. That was bliss.

"Is your wrist okay?" He was still whispering. I barely focused on his words; my mind distracted by the sound of his heart beating.

"Broken."

He stiffened again. "Who?"

I shook my head, pressing my cheek closer. His arms tightened in response. "In the forest."

"Finley, you don't have to deal with all this on your own. Tell me who did it. Let me do something this time." I felt his head turn, toward Dani.

"Stop it. It won't help." My body completely melted into his chest. My eyelids grew heavy, but I was afraid of returning to Command Hall. I forced them open. "Oken?"

"Yes?"

"Why did you volunteer? You didn't have to." I couldn't have sounded less Bellovian.

Oken sighed and shuffled us back so he could lean against the wall. He lifted my forearm and moved my bandaged wrist gently so it rested on his shoulder. "We should keep this elevated to help the swelling," he said. I closed my eyes, thinking he wasn't going to answer the question. His arms secure around my waist, we sat in the silence for a few breaths.

Finally, he spoke. "I didn't have to volunteer. But... Mayze did. She won't ever admit it, but she was terrified. I needed to make sure she was okay."

I let my head tip back to smile up at him. It was as thrilling as asking him why he volunteered and telling him about the queen. He smiled back, expression turning teasing.

"What? Aren't you glad I did?"

I sighed and shook my head. "I still wish you hadn't."

His smile fell. I wanted to say something more, to bring the smile back, but I couldn't resist the darkness crowding my vision any longer. Sleep claimed me.

CHAPTER 10

The next morning, the Florian guards switched, slamming the door twice. My head was cushioned by one of Oken's arms where we lay side by side on the floor. I sat up with some regret. Only a hazy memory remained of how we got to that position. Rubbing my pounding forehead, I swallowed in an attempt to get rid of the itch tingling at the back of my throat.

Food was delivered. Bland but filling, my team grudgingly scarfed it down. Anyone who grew up in Vichi knew better than to turn down a meal. After eating I felt more aware, but still shivered violently and in the end failed to keep it down, making sure to throw up between the bars and keep it outside our cell. The guard's face curled in disgust and he called for someone to come clean it.

I was frustrated with my body; it had never failed me like this before. The weakness sank deeper and deeper into my limbs. My wrist was in constant pain. My throat felt like an itching, raw mess. I kept losing grip on half-formed thoughts and couldn't follow the conversations around me.

I shivered and tried to keep all this weakness from showing on my face.

Oken watched me warily but didn't offer his warmth. Curling up against him was no longer an option now that our team was awake. I already hated the uncertainty in their stares. A fever like this was a death sentence in Bellovi. Rennie took up pacing the cell, occasionally stopping to contemplate the barred wall as if she could figure out a way through. Dani did some exercises, taking too much space from the rest of us but at least her attention wasn't on me. Yike sat in a back corner, the glower made permanent on his face.

The outer door rattled with the sound of keys on the other side. Hinze and the Trish couple entered. My team jumped to their feet. I had to use the wall to join them, not nearly as aggressive a motion. A heat flash hit me and I broke out in a light sweat. Better than the shivering, but not by much. I barely smothered the cough that struck me.

"Anyone prepared to talk today?" Hinze asked. Arms were crossed in response. "Very well. Who's next then?"

For a beat no one moved, then I saw a look of determination cross Oken's face. I hastily pushed off the wall before he could volunteer himself.

"You're not touching them." I went to the door and held out my wrists, one scabbed over from the bands yesterday and the other swollen to my knuckles poking out from the wrapping. Hinze's eyes widened at the sight. How did a boy so softhearted expect to survive this war?

"Finley, don't be ridiculous." Oken tried to pull me back and take my place. The sweat on my arm made it easy to pull out of his grasp, although I stumbled into the bars.

Hinze turned to his companions. Fisher was staring at me. "Savha, her name..." he said in Trish.

"Just a coincidence," the girl answered, but she was looking at me closer now. "I say we take her. Why not? No way she'll last another day without talking."

"I don't know if she'll even last another day," Hinze muttered. I bit back a response and focused on keeping my face blank so they wouldn't know I understood. "What do you think, Fisher?"

Fisher ran a hand through his steely hair. "Let's take her. Don't give her to Brea, though. Just let her team worry about her for a bit. See if any of them are willing to talk when their leader doesn't come back for a while." His eyes went to Oken, who was red-faced and rigid by my side. His fingers twitched open and closed.

"You don't have to go," Rennie said, coming up behind me. "We'll take a turn. No need to prove anything." I gave her a small smile, knowing now I had little to fear and trying to communicate that she shouldn't worry. She frowned but said nothing else. The guard opened the cell door. Hinze grabbed my arm and led me out, touch firm but not to the point of hurting. I couldn't say the same for the guard who took my other arm.

"Stop!" Mayze yelled. I didn't look back to see if she was yelling at Hinze's back as they led me out or Oken, who I heard move forward as the cell door was closing.

The Florian guard's grip was tight enough to bruise as we walked down the halls once again. This time down a different path. We passed more soldiers. I couldn't distinguish them by rank or ability with them all wearing plain navy uniforms. I glimpsed a dining hall, a training room, and some offices. I stumbled every few steps, leaning into Hinze rather than the twitchy guard. My skin crawled when the blonde woman with the blinding light from the forest walked by. Hinze nodded at her. "Lilah."

"My prince." She dipped her head, her eyes lingering on Hinze before she continued.

"Prince?" I asked. I didn't recognize my voice and cleared my throat as best I could.

"Now, now. If you won't answer any of my questions, why would I answer yours?"

"Fair enough."

Fisher came up next to Hinze, drawing my attention away from the prince. "Why do you have a Trish name?" he asked in Common Tongue. I was surprised to note he didn't have a Trish accent.

"To remind me what weakness does to people," I said. The words burned, but my mother trained me well. No one was to know my heritage. I'd never thought to ask if that extended to any Florians or Trish I may come across. But she'd stressed the words. *No one.* I forced myself to raise my chin.

Fisher's face darkened and Savha hissed. Her silver hair fanned out as she moved forward and Fisher caught her arm. They moved so quickly. Unrestrained Trish speed. I longed to know what it must be like not to constantly check yourself. "There's no point, Savvy," he told her.

"Let's at least give her back to Brea." She spat the words. Fisher shook his head and pulled her away. They turned down the next corridor, shoulders tight. I was sad to see them go.

"That was cruel," Hinze said. "Your people have turned cruel."

I wanted to ask what he meant by "turned," but stopped myself. "We are strong."

He shrugged. "There are many kinds of strength. Compared to what the Trish have been through, your people's strength has never been tested."

His words didn't match his youth. A look of under-standing was imbedded in the metallic shine of his hazel eyes. They were beautiful eyes, rimmed with dark lashes and kindness. Filled even in their coloring with conflict. It surprised me when I didn't want to look away. My Bellovian upbringing had not taught me how to read people like him, but I resisted the part of myself comparing him to Nico. It made it hard to keep up my cool demeanor.

"If you want to examine what happened to their people, you'll find we did in fact surpass them in terms of strength."

The kindness drained from Hinze's face and he let go of my arm. I sagged into the grip of the Florian guard as a wracking cough erupted from my chest.

"Strength and brutality are two very different things." He addressed the guard holding me with both hands now. I could see him visibly work to ignore the painful sound of my cough. "Take her the rest of the way to solitary."

He directed me to be turned around so he could put me in wristbands, leaving them just a bit loose over my sore wrists.

"Sometimes being left to our own thoughts can be the worst form of punishment," Hinze said from behind me.

"Being alone with my thoughts is nothing new to me, *Prince*." I spat the title like any other Bellovian would.

Hinze shook his head and left me in the empty hall with the guard. He was breathing heavy, his grip tightening on my arms. When I looked up, the fear in his eyes made my mouth go dry. I debated calling the prince back but was caught in another coughing fit. I let it out full-force into the man's face. The guard's features twisted in disgust. He yanked me around and pushed me forward.

The tickle in my throat traveled upward and habit made

me turn my mouth into my shoulder when I sneezed loudly. The guard yelped and jerked me away from him, freeing one of his hands.

"No sudden moves!"

I froze. A series of clicks and the barrel of a short gun was shaking in my face. My father's training echoed. *"Always be steady with your gun. Fear makes mistakes. Your fear shows your capable of mistakes. You don't want your opponent ever thinking you aren't in control and deliberate."*

This man was not in control.

"It was just a sneeze," I said. I shifted my shoulders as if I could show him my cuffed hands. The movement only made his grip tighten on my arm.

"I don't want to hear it. I've been on the Front for too long to fall for any Bellovian games. Stay quiet and do as you're told. The prince trusted me to escort you, try anything and I won't hesitate to prove I'm worthy of his trust just like all those elites he travels with."

The Bellovian in me raged against his harsh tone, but I nodded. His grip on his gun was too tight, too ready. Too eager.

The tickle in my throat was unbearable. I barely had the strength to walk straight, let alone fight a sneeze or cough. The man kept looking up and down the hall, searching for help. He muttered something else about Bellovians and that I was weak. Assuring himself.

I jerked with a sneeze, unable to fight it any longer. With a shout he threw me against the wall. I barely turned my face in time to avoid hitting my nose full on, but instinct still made me twist and bring my head back.

The solid thud of the back of my skull connecting with his filled me with dread. The Florian guard swore so hard his voice cracked. He threw me hard to the ground. On my back, arms tied, I couldn't focus on keeping peace. Training took over and I swung a leg upward, kicking the gun from the guard's hand before he could fire it at me.

The gun was out of the way, but now his expression was murderous. Hand whipping back, he freed his knife from his belt. I planted my feet and kicked so I could roll over my shoulder and to my knees, intending to stand and run. But I rolled over my broken wrist and the pain was too sharp and sudden. I staggered, eyes watering, I found the wall with my shoulder and used it to get upright. I was so focused on catching my breath and blinking back tears, I lost sight of the guard for a few precious seconds.

His grunt of effort was the only warning. I went back to my knees right as he swung at the wall now above me. Wet heat down the side of my face was the first indication he'd gotten me with the knife. But the blood didn't block my vision and I was now fully standing, adrenaline dulling every pain. I tried to back away, bending back to avoid his next wild swing. He recovered as I straightened. It was then I saw the decision on his face. The certainty in his eyes as he caught control of his panic and remembered his own training. He adjusted his grip on the knife, took note of how little hallway was left for me to run before I hit the dead end.

He readied to make a killing blow.

My options were slim with my hands behind my back and no one likely to come to my aid. I was just the enemy. Another Bellovian with death in my heart and anger in my veins. They had six more of me in the cell. I wouldn't be missed and he knew it. His fear made him weak, his weakness made him angry. I understood all of this in the time it took him to fix his grip. In the time it took him to set his chin. I saw my own hatred in his eyes and knew I was about to die if I didn't fight back.

He lunged forward. I shifted my weight and swung, kicking how I practiced with my father all those years. Only, for the first time, I didn't hold back. It was Trish speed and Bellovian intent. I knew it was weaker than I was usually capable. I hoped it would be enough. *Please, Mags, let it be enough.*

My foot connected with the man's temple. He flew and hit the opposite wall, his head bouncing off the bricks with a sickening thud. I fell from the force of the blow, barely shifting in time to avoid falling on my broken wrist again. On my side, facing the guard, I coughed and gagged. Forced myself to stay conscious. I scooted back awkwardly from the blood that began to pool under my attacker's face. His eyes, now glossy in death, stared at me across the hall.

I was left to my own thoughts.

CHAPTER 11

My first kill. I couldn't look away. The color faded gradually from his face. The pool of blood crept closer to my boots. I bent my knees up to my chest and pressed as close to the opposite wall as I could with my hands bound behind my back. I took deep breaths. I would not cry over this man who had tried to kill me. I'd always known I'd have to kill. I would not cry. I rested my chin on my knees and stared back into his dead eyes. I would remember this moment and what war did to people. What it had made him. What it made me.

I didn't know how much time had passed before there was a shout down the hall. I thought about running, but I was caught in the dead stare of the man across from me.

Only when Savha came between us was I able to look away. "Fisher, get the gun." I followed her gaze to the weapon, then back to the confusion on her face. "What happened?"

"I sneezed," I answered, voice hollow.

Savha completely froze. The realization was slow to hit me, but when it did, my body went impossibly colder. She'd asked in Trish. I'd answered in Trish. Panic clipped my voice, "Please, you can't—"

She cut me off with a slashing motion of her hand as Fisher approached, gun in hand and eyebrows high. He'd heard too. The Florians were coming now, Hinze at the head of the group. Savha muttered something quickly in Fisher's ear, then went to meet Hinze. Fisher took up her position between me and the body. "He attacked you?" he asked in a low voice.

I nodded. It took effort to force out Common Tongue. All I wanted was the comfort of my mother's language. "He was scared and I kept sneezing and it made him jumpy and he pulled the gun and I... and I..."

Fisher nodded. He didn't look happy, but as Hinze approached with Savha, Fisher shifted slightly to stand between me and them.

"She isn't running. I don't even think she can stand. Let's just hear her out." Savha's soft tone caught me off guard. The unexpected kindness made my head swim and I blinked back tears. I would not cry.

"Get him out of here," she told the soldiers. The man's body was carried away. His head hung awkwardly, his dead eyes still seeking me out until they rounded the corner. "You go get Garris," she ordered the prince. Hinze hesitated, watching me close. I realized how open my face must be. For once it served me well, because his eyes softened and he left with a nod.

Savha turned and knelt in front of me. Fisher crouched behind her. She narrowed her eyes, but it wasn't a glare. She was looking for something in my face.

"Your name is Trish. You speak Trish," she said. "You're always watching us talk and you spoke it just now. How is that possible?"

I looked down the hall, swallowing. What should I say? What would my mother tell me to do? How much danger was the truth versus a lie?

I couldn't focus with the pool of blood so close.

Savha motioned for me to turn and removed my wristbands. I swayed with the movement. The adrenaline fading to dizziness and pain.

Footsteps approached again. "They can't know," I whispered, using Common Tongue just in case they heard.

Before either of them could respond, Hinze returned with another boy in tow. It seemed he had only just left.

"I'm Garris," the new boy said. "Can I see your hand, please?" He approached with careful steps and knelt to my level, his brown eyes gentle, their shape too round to be Bellovian.

There wasn't much more damage they could do to it at this point. I offered my hand to the boy and he took it gingerly. Tingling heat spread from his touch, pausing on my wrist. The relief was immediate and glorious. My eyes slid shut. Garris's power traveled up my arm, into my chest, taking away the need to cough. Warmth spread over my face, whisking away the bruises and mending the bump in my nose and the slice on my forehead. The shivering finally stopped and my tight, aching muscles loosened. I became alert and hungry. I opened my eyes and Garris smiled at me, but now that I felt stronger, I settled back into my natural blank expression.

Hinze looked unnerved. He addressed Savha in Trish. "Back to the cell?"

"Not yet. Fisher and I should take her outside. Give her a chance to calm down and tell us what happened. I think this was self-defense and it would be cruel to make her face her team like this." The fire I had come to expect from Savha entered her voice and I was grateful that for once it wasn't directed at me.

Hinze and Fisher exchanged a look before they shrugged at the same time. Savha clearly got her way often. She helped me to my feet, my wrist supporting my weight with no issue. Fully healed. She led me down the hall without another word. Fisher hurried to catch up. In moments, we were in the sunshine. I wasn't given very long to enjoy the feeling or take in the rest of the base before Savha led us into the shelter of the trees and turned to me.

"Explain. Now."

They both waited. Two Trish, silver hair shining, my age and living free in Floria. My imagination never prepared me for such a situation. My mother's warnings never accounted for the possibility. I could tell them everything, but would they believe it? I could tell them everything, but then they'd be the only people to know my family's secrets. They may be Trish, but I still couldn't give them my trust so easily. Could I?

What would put my family at the least amount of risk? They would call out the lie if I said Bellovians now taught Trish. Anyone at war with the Bellovians or who had seen what happened to Traesha knew they had no interest in Trish culture and would rather see it die than teach it. Savha crossed her arms, her face slowly closing off and distrust darkening her eyes.

I knew what to say. The decision made my stomach drop. I could accomplish everything I had set out to. It would take the truth, but that was already creeping forward each day I went without dying my hair. These were my people and I had a duty to them too. The pull in my stomach that always made me long for home shifted. The decision felt as right as when I chose to stand out and gain commandership.

I took a steadying breath. "My father was one of the Bellovians who attacked Traesha," I began. Their eyes widened when they heard my unaccented, perfect Trish. "He went into my mother's home and found her playing the piano. According to them, it was love right then and there. My father smuggled her back into Bellovi and they had me. I have to hide it, though. If they knew, they could kill me."

"They won't kill you, we have an alliance—" Fisher started.

"She's not talking about the Florians, Fish," Savha cut in, placing a hand on his arm.

"They can't know anything, in case we get back to the Bellovi. They would tell the commanders and put my family in danger."

They stared at me, the threat settling in. "So, you're Trish?" Fisher asked.

Savha answered before I could. "Half. She has the Bellovian hair. It's always been dominant. None of the kids that came after the invasion had silver hair, remember?"

Fisher nodded, and I was swept by sudden nausea. The Bellovians sexually assaulted the Trish? I thought Bellovi a safe place from such horrors. One of their biggest boasts was the equality between men and women, something they proudly informed us wasn't found in Floria. I suddenly understood it was more dangerous there for me than I had ever known.

"There's more that I need your help with," I said. "The queen is alive."

Savha scoffed. "She was killed in the invasion."

"No, her baby. The princess, now Queen Natasha. I overheard the commanders talking about how they found her. They're planning to reveal her at the Conquering Celebration. It's a ball they hold every year in—"

"I know what the Conquering Celebration is. I've worked it." My stomach swooped at Savha's words and the shuttered look in her eyes. She'd been enslaved.

"They want to use her to motivate the slaves." The word slave was hard to say in front of her. "To work harder in the fields... or make them fight against the Florians."

They considered my words and what going to war would mean for the peaceful people of Traesha. "We heard a rumor she was taken. I made Hinze bring us out here to check it out," Fisher finally admitted.

Savha frowned at him before turning back to me. "Why should we believe you?"

"Why would she tell us if she wasn't loyal to Traesha?" Fisher demanded.

"A trap?"

"Please," I cut in. "You have to go save her. I can help. My commander said he'd let me go to the celebration. I could figure out where they hold her and help you get to her."

"Like I said, we already planned to save her. We were close to answers when you blew up our transport," Fisher said. Savha elbowed his stomach, clearly feeling he'd said too much.

"What does your supply transport have to do with this?"

They shared a look. "Is that what you think you blew up in the forest?" Savha posed the question carefully.

"Yes? But really we were just making a distraction for those troops that attacked."

Savha and Fisher shared yet another look. I wanted to

cling to the mission I'd been given, but the looks on their faces told me I'd been lied to.

What had we done?

"We should head back in," Savha said. "We need to tell Hinze we've confirmed the rumor. There isn't much time to make a plan."

"You should come," Fisher put in. "You don't have to go back to the Bellovians. Especially not if you're afraid of them."

"I'm not afraid. I've lived with them my whole life. It'll be better to have me there on the inside, and this way they won't discover my secret and punish my family. I have to keep them safe. But you all could let us go, then I can get back sooner and make sure I get to the celebration. We only have four days." I could get back before they thought to clear out our cubbies and found my bottles of hair dye.

"Let you go just like that? All because you speak Trish? We have no way to know if you've even been telling the truth." Savha shook her head. "If you were truly loyal, you'd be doing everything you could to save the queen. We could easily fake your death or tell your team we're taking you somewhere else for questioning. If you go back to the Bellovians, who knows what else they'll make you do? Is it worth it?"

"I could rise high in their ranks. I trained to do just that. I'll be able to take them down from the inside. I'll be a better ally that way." I repeated the same words I had told myself over and over. I had to see my team to safety. I needed to look in Silken's eyes and know he didn't suspect. I was asking the two of them to give me trust and unwilling to return it, I knew that. But for the sake of my family, I had to do this on my own. I couldn't desert. It meant fighting for the Bellovians, but in the end it was the best option.

"So we let you go back to your team and when the celebration happens, you just let us in? You tell us where they're keeping her?"

"I'll do everything I can as long as I don't get caught."

"And when they tell you to shoot a slave that misbehaves or cut down more of our trees or monitor the fields or kill more Florians, you'll keep doing that as long as you don't get caught?"

We fell into silence. Only the birds chirping and breeze rustling in the sparse tree branches filled the air between us.

It was Fisher who broke the standstill. "I say we do what she wants. The Bellovians already know we want the queen; she'll be guarded no matter what. Returning Finley to them won't be giving away any of our secrets. And we have a bit of time, so if you change your mind, just say the word, Finley."

"You won't tell?"

"We'll have to tell Hinze. He won't put us at risk going to the celebration unless we give him good reason."

"And how will I help you? How will we stay in contact?"

"We have a way. If Hinze agrees, we'll pull you out again and explain."

The conversation was coming to an end and I was still unsatisfied. Something about returning to the cell and Dani's glare and Yike's flexing arms made my stomach turn. "What did we actually blow up?" I asked. Savha shook her head and turned away. I grabbed her arm and made her face me again. "What was it?"

"Another time," Fisher said, prying my hand off Savha arm.

"It might change her mind," Savha said slowly. "You won't want to go back to your team after you learn."

I shook my head. "I can't go with you. I won't put my family at risk. Not even for the queen."

"But think of Traesha! If you have any information, you—"

Fisher cut Savha off when, without warning, he pulled me in for a hug. I stiffened, but he was undeterred, reaching to pull Savha in close too. I was surprised by how easily she let him do it. "I'm glad we found you. A Trish is still a Trish, and we'll do what we can to help you."

"Don't make promises you can't keep, Fish," Savha said into the space between us, but her words were soft. I relaxed in their arms. This felt like being home, being surrounded by the smell of lavender and my mother's warmth. I was still shaken by my first kill. I hadn't realized how desperately I needed this form of comfort.

"We'll figure it out. But for now, let's just be happy we found another Trish. There are too few of us not to celebrate this." He gave one more squeeze and amazement washed over me. I knew he was trying to distract me, but it felt good to be hugged, to be accepted so easily. This was what my mother missed from her people.

The Florians were helping the Trish. They would find the queen. No matter how much it broke my heart to turn away and go back to the Bellovian cell, I needed to trust them to take care of it.

Fisher grabbed my arm right before we entered the room holding our cell. Everyone looked relieved to see me, then confused as they noticed my improved condition and unbound wrists. Maybe I should have asked the healer not to heal me completely. Savha and Fisher left me in the cell without another word. I reminded myself not to speak Trish as I turned to my team.

"Are you okay? What did they do to you?" Rennie asked. In the last couple days she had lost what little weight she'd gained during our time at base.

"I'm fine. I think they wanted to make you sweat is all. They didn't hurt me. They're too soft-hearted for this war."

Yike snorted with agreement. Teal let out an uncomfortable laugh.

"They *are* working with the Trish," Dani muttered, the only proof she needed for my claim.

Oken looked unconvinced and exhausted. How long had he stayed up last night checking on me? "You sure you're okay?" he asked.

"I'm fine. Really." Maybe I didn't look all that improved for them to still be so worried. Dead eyes flashed in my vision once more, now accompanied by the image of half-Trish children with black hair. I tried not to make it noticeable when I moved closer to Teal and Mayze, away from the men in the cell.

"Hale went to talk to the Florian," Dani said. She crossed her arms where she leaned against the bars.

Mayze shrunk under her glare, but her voice was steady when she replied. "It wasn't worth being tortured. I just told him our mission. By now the troops have attacked and nothing was lost by my talking."

I was oddly touched. "I guess you're right. I just worry that now they know, we've lost our value to them. I'm not sure what seven kids are worth to the commanders in terms of ransom or what use the Florians will have in keeping us."

Mayze worried her lip. Dani's face slipped into a deeper glare. Oken sighed and sat down, letting his head fall back against the wall across from me. He absently pulled on one of his curls and it sprung back into place when he let go. Watching him, a bit of the fear in my chest loosened. The dead eyes became a little harder to remember.

"I'm sick of this cell," Rennie muttered. She dropped down next to Oken. I surprised myself by feeling a flare of jealousy when she sat so close their shoulders touched. I pushed the feeling down. My emotions were a confused jumble best left ignored.

"Heard that," Dani said. I let myself marvel at how different she was away from the eyes of the commanders and the need to impress them. "War is turning out to be less exciting than I anticipated."

"Hope something happens soon. Or we get a chance to fight back," I said, the words immediate and hollow. I had a chance to fight back, right outside this cell. I could be leaving with Trish and gifted Florians today to look for the Trish queen. If only I didn't fear the Bellovians sitting around me so much. The first stirrings of regret hit, and I reminded myself I had time to decide. To think of a way to leave my team without it looking like I deserted. Except, no matter how much I thought about it, the bottles of hair dye were still at camp. I had no choice but to go back. No choice but to stick with my original plan.

Silence fell and the excitement of my return passed. I noticed Teal running her finger through the layer of dirt on the floor and inched closer to look at what she was doing. It was a picture of a mountain covered with pine trees she sketched out in detail with her nails. She'd patted down clouds overhead, the sun barely peeking through, its rays gentle strokes of her fingertips.

"That's amazing," I said.

Teal's cheeks went pink. "I drew a lot at home." She

shrugged. Drawing was considered a useless pastime in Bellovi. Right next to singing.

"What's your first name?" I asked.

She gave a surprised laugh, realizing I wouldn't know. "My name is Jenna."

I looked up and made eye contact with Yike.

"Bellot." A truly Bellovian name for the most Bellovian-looking person I knew.

"Nice to meet you," I said, cracking a smile. They returned it, no hate or resentment in their eyes. It was strange to sit in a room of Bellovians without a cold shoulder or glare cast my direction. Even Dani's face was open as she watched the exchange.

Jenna Teal began adding a flock of birds to her sky, fingers quick and sure. Mayze moved closer to me and watched Jenna work.

"You seem a lot better," she said. "You were really sick last night. And your face..."

"I was sick today, too. But then they brought in this guy named Garris. He's some kind of healer. He just grabbed my hands and I felt warm again and my cough went away. My wrist isn't even broken anymore." I flicked my hand a bit to demonstrate. Mayze's eyes widened, still amazed to hear the rumors of the Florian gifts confirmed.

"Why would they heal you?" Rennie asked, eyebrows drawing together.

"That Florian guy, the prince, he's the most softhearted of them all. I think he felt bad."

"He did seem upset when he talked with me," Mayze said.

"Wait, he's a prince?" Yike's face—I couldn't think of him as such a generic name as Bellot—darkened. "We should kill him. Send a message to the king and do something useful with ourselves while we're stuck here. Royalty never comes so close to the Front; we won't have another chance like this."

I hated the thought, but I nodded along with the rest of them. "When the opportunity arises." I doubted it would. "Just know that will probably be the last thing we ever do."

"You said yourself they don't have much need to keep us around," Mayze said. "They'll probably kill us anyway. Might as well get one step closer to winning this war."

"Remember when we got their queen?" Dani asked, voice wistful.

It was the most celebrated event in my memory. A year ago, word spread that an assassination attempt proved successful. A small group of Bellovians snuck into Floria and then their capital city, Helsa. They shot the queen where she stood at her husband's side while he gave a speech to their people. My father had scoffed and said the bullet missed the real target, the king, and made this war worse than it had been in ages. The number of people sent to the Front doubled to combat the wave of Florian attacks. All the while, Bellovian people barked out war songs and drank in the streets. Nico was gone every day playing at events where commanders gathered and patted themselves on the back. The assassins were killed after firing that single, poorly aimed bullet and made into statues I passed walking into City Center to go to school.

"They even gave us liquor with our rations in the Squalor to celebrate. I've never seen so many fights and shootings," Rennie said. She and I seemed to be the only ones who did not remember this time with fondness.

"It was great." Yike sighed. He was probably imagining the celebrations that would happen in our names when we killed the prince.

I wrapped my arms around my stomach, feeling cold again.

As the excitement of a new purpose faded, one by one my team fell asleep. Mayze's head ended up on my lap. I fought the urge to brush her hair from her face, knowing such tender actions were too Trish for this cell. I looked everywhere but where Rennie and Oken slept, her head on his shoulder, his cheek resting on top of it. I resolutely closed my eyes. When I opened them I was determined it would be morning and she would have moved away from him.

THE MAN I killed sat across from me in the cell. His eyes were glassy, face stuck in an expression of fear. He just sat there, staring at me. It seemed to last for hours, until suddenly, with Trish speed I had only seen from my mother, he was next to me, grabbing my arm again—

I screamed and jerked awake as I ripped my arm from his cold dead hands. But instead of the Florian guard, it was Oken beside me, his face frozen in shock from my scream and hand still in midair.

"Sorry. I'm sorry. It was a nightmare," I gasped, my heart still pounding in my chest. Oken backed away, tucking his hand behind him.

"No, *I'm* sorry. Just trying to wake you up," he said.

My face burning, I realized everyone else was awake, but it wasn't my scream that woke them.

"They're shooting out there," Rennie said, the whites of her eyes stark in the dim morning light. There was a flash of white light outside accompanied by a boom.

"Grenades," Yike said. He strained to see out the

143

window. The next flash was yellow, the pitch of the explosion familiar. Just like the grenades we threw. "Bellovian grenades."

We stood. Excitement mounted around me, but I felt only a hollow dread and some of the terror left from my dream. A cold sweat down my back. The door outside our cell opened. Savha came in, her light silver hair practically glowing.

"There were tracking devices in our equipment," I said to no one in particular. Understanding crossed Savha's face. I turned from the window and faced her. "What did we blow up?" I asked again as a scream sounded outside.

She barely hesitated this time. "Bellovian commanders we captured for questioning about the queen." She answered in heavily accented Common Tongue, but only Rennie was paying attention to us. Her sharp eyes missed very little. She raised an eyebrow, but I only spared her a glance, my mind whirling.

The commanders' plan became suddenly clear. An explosion boomed closer to our cell and we backed up against the barred wall. They sent us to kill our own captured commanders—commanders with information about the queen that would help the Florians find her. That would confirm she was alive. They had us each throw a bomb. A line of executioners. I rubbed my temples. Commander Silken probably planned for us to get taken. We had no information, but we did hold tracking devices that led straight to this base and the powerful Florians and Trish people within.

The guard yesterday wasn't my first kill.

"Only a few volunteers are staying to slow them down," Savha switched to Trish, standing directly behind me and pitching her voice so low I was sure I was the only one who could hear over the sounds of war. I didn't look to see if Rennie was still watching. "Hinze evacuated the rest after the girl talked. It was all too strange. We're leaving the Bellovians here to be found. This is your last chance. Come with us. Stop helping the Bellovians slaughter themselves, the Florians, and our people. Help us find the queen."

My heart dragged with a longing so deep I couldn't draw in air. My former resolve to do what I could to help the queen nagged, encompassing my thoughts and tempting me so much I almost nodded. I could still feel the force of my kick. The hard metal of a grenade in my hands. They would ask me to do so much worse.

Yet the bottles of dye remained at base. My mother was safe. My father within reach as a fellow commander. If I left now, my team would tell Commander Silken. I would be a traitor. A deserter. I pictured my parents dying in the square. Bodies falling limp.

If I stayed, we might go back to base. I could dye my hair and continue hiding what I was. Lead more missions. Kill more Florians. My family would be safe.

"Come with us," Savha whispered behind me.

I pretended not to understand. I kept my attention on my team, on Oken, Mayze, and Rennie. I couldn't stand the thought of them turning on me. Turning my family in. The door slammed when Savha left.

Keeping the disappointment from my face, I opened my mouth to speak, hoping I could do so with a steady voice. I was saved from trying when a Bellovian grenade hit the bars of our window with a *tink* that was misleadingly harmless compared to the explosion that followed just outside.

With ringing ears and dust-covered bodies, we rushed forward to climb out of the hole left in the wall. Dani paused when we were on the grass, smiling at me for the first time through the dust that drifted around her face.

"Larson, we're free!" She laughed and the sound was surprisingly high and open. The ache in my chest slightly eased. I could do this. I could stay with them. If I could gain a smile from Dani Carns, I could earn the commanders' trust and access I needed. My plan was solid. It didn't matter what I had to give up. Dead eyes might haunt me, but I could save so many from the same fate if I did this right. Then Hinze's team would save the queen. It would all work out for the best.

We ran toward the Bellovian soldiers emerging from the trees. Dani let out a Bellovian war whoop and we all answered it. I couldn't resist glancing behind me. Across the field, two silver heads were climbing into the back of a transport. My heart squeezed. The prince stood with his hand on one of the doors watching the abandoned building, the one-sided fight. Looking at me.

I tripped on something heavy in my path. Something that hadn't been there seconds before. On my stomach, I looked back to my feet. Dani Carns, hair clearly black and braided in the light of the dawn, lay dead on the ground. A Bellovian bullet hole in her skull and the smile she gave me frozen on her face.

CHAPTER 12

I couldn't even scream. I scrambled away. Memories hit hard, a childhood of knowing Dani and suddenly she wasn't there behind her dark eyes. She'd been the first person to hit me. The first shock of pain that fueled my true hatred of Bellovians and what they stood for. The first inspiration to learn to fight back. All my life I'd lived in fear of her. I'd tensed at the sight of her. Now the threat was gone. Her life stripped. My heart pounded. Bile rose in the back of my throat. I could hear shouting and bullets still being fired, now aimed at the truck where Hinze stood watching me, waiting. The dead Bellovian girl meant nothing to the rest of the world. They killed her. They killed her.

I realized then I never could have. I didn't truly hate her. I didn't belong here. This was wrong. So wrong.

Oken shuffled back to help me up, his face white and eyes fixed on our fallen team member. They'd been friends. He'd trained with her. But I could see he didn't get it. He didn't understand the Bellovians had done this, done all of this. He didn't feel the disgust. The anger. There's no way they could have mistaken us for Florians. They didn't care where their bullets went. Who we threw grenades at. Who was sent to the Front. How young or hungry their soldiers were.

I couldn't stand among them. I couldn't be the one sending Bellovians to their death. Because the hate died with the seventeen-year-old girl at my feet who had never learned any better. She would never have a chance.

I took Oken's hand, keeping my grip on it even when I was standing. I stared at Dani, dead at our feet. I didn't realize my cheeks were wet until Oken brushed the tears away with the back of his hand. He put his dampened knuckles under my chin, lifting it.

"We have to keep going, princess."

I shook my head. More tears fell. I was going to get my family killed. I took a deep breath and reached to cup Oken's warm cheek. I brushed his cheekbone with my thumb. His eyes went impossibly soft. A Bellovian shouldn't be capable of that expression. But of course they were. Even Dani could smile at me.

I wanted him to look at me like that forever. I ached for him to keep looking at me.

But he was one of them. Loyal to the ones who made us blow up our commanders. They executed innocent family members without blinking. All that mattered was victory in war.

They had destroyed Traesha. Broken its people. But broken people could be fixed, as long as they were breathing.

The commanders had to be stopped. Dani's dead eyes would haunt me. I couldn't fight beside her careless killers any longer.

"Until I see you next," I whispered in Trish.

Shock hardened Oken's beautiful eyes. He frowned, stepping back. It hurt more than I could have prepared myself for. I dropped my hand and forced my eyes away. I turned and ran, jumping over Dani's body. The dirt puffed up from the bullets struck the ground at my feet. Hinze was still next to the truck, so foolish and hopeful. They were all waving, hurrying me on. But it was too far, there were too many bullets, all now trained on me. I put on one last, desperate burst of speed, wanting nothing more than to be at the transport and away from the Bellovians in that second.

And suddenly I was. Hinze blinked, as shocked by my show of true Trish speed as I was. He quickly recovered and practically threw me inside the transport. He slammed the doors shut from the outside.

"We can't leave him!" My voice came out shrill, but no one else reacted. Not even when Hinze jumped into the transport *through* the closed doors.

He saw my stunned expression and grinned. "You're not the only one with a useful gift."

The tires spun briefly in the gravel when the engine revved, then caught. We took off at full speed, driving in a straight line despite the forest I knew was in our path. Hinze stood between the rows, feet spread and hands braced on the ceiling. A tree swept through the truck. Then another and another. Looking at my feet, I saw the tops of rocks and bushes passing through the floor. We moved through them all effortlessly. I began to grasp Hinze's incredible ability.

We drove literally through the forest for about ten minutes at top speed before the truck found a road and the driver called back that we were in the clear. Hinze fell into a seat, breathing hard and trembling. His forehead was slicked with sweat.

"Well, wasn't *that* exciting," Fisher said, breaking the silence. We let out shaky laughs. Mine turned quickly into a sob that shocked everyone, myself included. Savha threw an arm over my shoulder.

"Dani... They shot her. I couldn't stay but... my family. They'll kill them. They saw... I skipped." I sounded hysterical even to my own ears. "My mom and the hair dye. I deserted. They'll kill her. They killed Dani. They—"

Hinze took my face in his hands, kneeling in the aisle between the seats. His sudden touch startled me enough to momentarily shut me up. His hands were warm and his skin impossibly soft.

"I will do everything in my power to ensure they're warned. We're in contact with the rebellion in Vichi. They might be able to help. Just try to calm down. Breathe, okay?" I nodded in his hands and he let me go. I drew a shuddering breath.

Hinze moved toward the front of the truck. In another situation I might have laughed to see him simply stick his head through the wall to talk to the driver. He pulled back a second later.

"What's your family name?"

"Larson. My dad's Teo Larson, he works at Command Hall." Hinze nodded and his head disappeared again.

"Londe's up there," Savha said, as if that should mean something to me.

Fisher leaned around her and patted my knee. "If there's anything that can be done, he and Hinze will do it."

"There's really a rebellion?" I asked.

Their nods were pitying, but I didn't care. If there was a rebellion, there might be hope for my family. If they were warned, my father could get my mother out of Vichi. He knew the boulders surrounding the city and the land better than anyone. After a few minutes of standing halfway through the wall, Hinze helped the girl who had been riding passenger into the back so he could take her seat. She sat down next to the Florian girl who tortured me, Brea, and buckled herself in.

"What's the news, Mesa?" Savha asked her in Trish. Mesa answered in Common Tongue and I got the sense that mixed conversations like this were normal in this group.

"Londe's trying to get a hold of our contact in the rebellion."

"Who is in the rebellion? How are you contacting them?" My voice cracked.

Mesa pursed her lips like she didn't want to answer.

"How are things at the base?" Lilah asked before anyone could tell me.

"We lost it but are holding the line just past it. The fact that they're now so close to Honna is our biggest concern," Mesa said.

"Is the king going to push back?" Brea asked. My brain was stuck on the existence of a rebellion. People in Vichi who could help my family. It seemed too much to hope for.

"I think so. We'll probably get sent back in once rein-forcements come. Shouldn't take too long. The king is getting impatient and Hinze thinks he's going to send in the elites."

"Imagine it finally being over," Brea said.

I could hear the tones of Hinze's voice up front, speaking quickly. I blocked out the conversation and started to pray. I begged Tash, the god of love, to watch over my family. I couldn't say if I was praying so much now because I believed or because I knew it would please my mother and she'd be glad I at least tried. The road grew less rocky and I tried to relax against the seat. About an hour later, a metal gate passed through us and the truck jerked to a stop. I slid roughly into Savha.

"That wouldn't happen if you'd put on your straps," she muttered. I gave her a small smile and scooted away.

The doors in the back of the truck were thrown open by the driver, Hinze at his side. I climbed out first and went straight for the prince. Hinze held out his hands to slow me. "We got word to our contact in Vichi. They're trying to get the message to the Larson household. There isn't much more I can do now, but I told them to return word if they can. Without abilities it's more difficult to get messages out of Bellovi than in, but we're doing our best."

I fought the urge to hug him. "Thank you, Hinze."

He waved the thanks away. "Of course. Let's just call it even for me giving the order to have you tortured." He said the words lightly, but I saw the deep need for forgiveness in his features.

"Deal."

We were parked in front of a large mansion. The size of the highest ranking commanders' homes in City Center, but completely different from any building I'd seen before. The walls were made of stacked, rich brown logs and the windows gleamed with the reflection of the surrounding forest. Plants grew along the base and a cobblestone path led to the front door. It sat on the crest of a hill. Down the drive, past a large iron gate, at the bottom of the hill's slope, was a small bustling town.

"Honna," Hinze told me, following my gaze. He swept an arm toward the mansion. "And this is the royal home here. We'll rest up and figure out what's next. We only have three days to plan, so whenever you're up for it, we need all the information you have on the queen."

I nodded and Hinze led us inside. A flustered house-keeper met him at the door.

"Your Highness! We weren't expecting you." He sounded more inconvenienced than apologetic.

Hinze's lips pressed together as he fought a smile. "We suddenly found ourselves without a base to stay in. Don't worry yourself, Lanis. I'm sure the house is in excellent condition."

"Still, if you had sent word I would have prepared better!"

Hinze laughed and I agreed the housekeeper sounded ridiculous. I had never been in a cleaner room. The flag-stone floors of rich dark colors sparkled like a clear river bottom, reflecting the light from the grand chandelier in the ceiling. Its many crystals dripped toward the floor, casting the room in warmth with little effort. Two stair-cases crept up either side of the foyer, a hall beneath them and two more branching on both sides of the room.

"I think we'll manage. Just need a nice bath, a warm meal, and a bed to sleep in."

"Oh, fine. Just take your shoes off." Lanis turned and began barking orders that echoed over the stone floors. I decided his amplified voice must hint at an ability.

We turned to the wall to do as we were told. My stomach dropped when I noticed Dani's blood smeared and splattered across my boots and pants. I bent and began undoing the laces, taking care not to touch the stains and ignoring how my fingers shook.

"Miss? I'll take you to your room now if you are ready," a voice said behind me. I turned to a boy probably a year younger than me. His smile spoke of forced politeness and only faltered briefly when he looked down and saw the bloody mess of my boots. I followed him up the set of stairs to the right.

The top of the staircases twisted inward into another short set of stairs with a wide base that narrowed at the top. A pair of mahogany doors opened to what I assumed were the royal chambers. Hinze was walking in that direction, his steps slow and deliberate.

Hinze's team was going to the rooms to the left of the landing, but the boy led me down the hall to the right. I glanced over my shoulder and watched Savha and Fisher go in the same doorway. I swallowed my surprise. With all their casual touches I should have guessed they were a couple.

The hallway we walked down twisted and turned enough to leave me wondering what could possibly be kept behind all the doors. The carpet turned to scuffed wooden floors and the paintings on the walls dulled with a layer of dust.

"Here we are. The room should be fully stocked. Someone will bring you a change of clothes shortly. We'll be around if you find yourself in need of anything." The boy turned on his heels and hurried further down the hall. Right before rounding the corner, he glanced back, for the first time revealing the fear in his eyes.

I sighed and pushed open the door. The room was elegant in its simplicity. A cream rug so thick my feet sunk into it covered most of the floor. The bed sat to the right; the white sheets tucked without a single wrinkle. An open door led to the bathroom. I immediately went that direction, pulling off my commander uniform and throwing it into the corner, where I hoped to never see it again. Once the tub was filled with the hottest water I could stand, I sank into it and began to scrub my body red and raw, double and triple-checking for blood.

The clothes they brought me consisted of a black knitted cardigan and a gray dress that flowed out around my knees. I had never worn anything like it. In Bellovi, the only dress I owned was a formal, shapeless, heavy, black thing for events like the life celebration of the last lead commander. This dress was made of the softest fabric I ever felt. Delicate, loose, yet restricting at the same time as I feared tearing it. It made me feel three years younger. I pulled at it helplessly a few times, looking for more length, before putting on the short socks. They were slightly too big and bunched at the ankle but they made me feel less bare. I stared down at my legs. They had never been so exposed before. How would I stay warm? No, that wasn't a problem here. The weather was cool, but nothing compared to the frigid air of Vichi.

Taking a breath to brace myself, I went to the mirror next. It was almost a shock to recognize the girl there. Since I'd last seen myself, I had killed by grenade and hand-to-hand. I had been tortured and held in sleep by a Bellovian boy. I had exposed my heritage and deserted. But it was still me, just in a dress. I didn't know how to feel. I began mechanically working through the wet tangles of my hair. The silver at my roots was clearly visible, but only because I was looking for it. I hoped. Likely others would brush it off as a trick of the light. It wouldn't be long before it became truly noticeable. I pushed down my part to look closer and noticed the silver seemed different from Savha's light shade and Fisher's steal. What would my natural color be? Savha's words still rang in my head. *Bellovian hair is dominant. All of the kids that came after the invasion had black hair, remember?* The words were still chilling. I twisted a wet strand around my finger. My mother always said her family's blood ran thick and strong. She claimed there was more Trish in me than I knew, confident in the blood passed down mother to mother along with our name.

I thought about my excitement during training, how even now I missed the burn in my muscle and the thrill of winning a match. I never agreed with her. The Bellovian in me craved violence and a challenge. Yet my hair confirmed her suspicions. Not to mention my newly discovered ability to skip. Her blood *did* run strong.

I let myself fall into the memory of that moment. The horror of seeing Dani's body, the dread when I turned to say goodbye to Oken, unable to deny that last look at him even as I doomed my family to his people. The feel of his warm cheek under my hand. I closed my fist, a useless attempt to trap the sensation in my palm.

Then, the need to move quickly. Even in the devastation of that moment I felt a thrill, a release, as I refused to hold back and ran. My feet flew faster than I could comprehend. Hinze, who I had been looking at, had seemed to grow in the blink of an eye when I had drawn close. He'd looked so shocked, I smiled at my reflection now, remembering.

I wanted to do it again.

CHAPTER 13

Eager to begin the search for the queen, I hurried back through the halls to find the Florians and make a plan. At the stair landing I heard voices and rounded the corner to a sitting room with a fire burning in a pit at its center and couches surrounding it. I took in everyone there, forcing myself to remember their names and abilities. Savha was easy. Then Brea, who tortured me with her gift of controlling the temperature around her. Lilah, who rid people of their senses with a clap of her hands. Garris the healer. Then it got trickier. There was the driver, Londe, blond like Lilah, with strange, light-gray eyes that looked nearly Trish. He helped Hinze send the message to Vichi, but I had no idea how. There was the girl with short hair named Mesa. She hadn't revealed an ability thus far. I made a mental note to figure out her role.

Tension filled the room with my entrance, instantly crawling under my skin. Likely it would be a long time before I was accepted in this group, even if Savha, Fisher, and Hinze welcomed my presence. Conversation stopped. I squared my shoulders and lifted my chin under their scrutiny. Footsteps on the stairs announced Fisher's arrival. "Hinze's sleeping. He overdid it getting us here."

"Why don't we go get supplies in town while he sleeps? I can't just sit around right now," Savha said, jumping to her feet.

"Me neither," I said. My body was alight with an anxious energy. The thought of sitting around in this tension was agony.

"Good idea." Fisher turned me to the stairs. Savha hurried to follow. I could practically hear the room of Florians behind us relax. We descended the steps and Savha took up Fisher's hand. When we got to the door, it was a relief to find my boots cleaned. Yet my heart dropped. No more traces of Dani Carns.

Outside the sun beat down on us. I felt so much closer to it here than I ever did in Vichi. I could smell dirt, not mud, and the flowers blooming in the expansive gardens to the left of us. The colors were breathtaking, but I had little time to admire them before Savha and Fisher reached the gate and waited for me. My heart raced at the ease of their speed and the thrill of keeping up. Rather than bothering with the heavy lock, they scaled it. Their light bodies agile. Their motions effortless. I followed them, running the last few steps to the gate and jumping high enough to grab the top rung and swing my legs over. I dropped to the other side, barely making a sound on the cobblestone road. My movements were so fast, not anything like how I moved in Vichi. Even this simple release of energy and restraint had me smiling at their backs.

Savha and Fisher chatted as we walked into town and among the shops lining the square. Every building sported potted flowers and wooden walls from the forest surrounding us. The colors were vibrant against a clear blue sky. The people here talked with simple familiarity and unhurried warmth. Nothing like the head-ducking and weary rush of getting out of Vichi's cold streets.

My companions were constantly touching. Even without looking, they always knew where the other was. It reminded me painfully of my parents. It made me think of Oken. Fisher smiled while Savha haggled tirelessly with shopkeepers in her accented Common Tongue. His proud expression reminded me of the times I'd caught Oken smiling at me while I surpassed all the other trainees at base. Laughing in the face of the Bellovian anger I caused. I pushed the image of his floppy black hair and golden eyes from my mind. By now he'd likely told the commanders of my Trish farewell. The memory of the betrayal in his eyes stung. I closed my fist again, remembering the feel of his skin.

We were between shops when Savha turned to me, a bag of dried fruit hanging from one arm, and she looped the other through mine.

"How did you do it?" she asked.

"I was just focusing on running fast... it just clicked." I'd known immediately what she was talking about. My ability to skip was at the forefront of both our minds. So much easier to focus on than everything else that had occurred recently.

She frowned a bit. "None of the half-Bellovians in Traesha could skip."

"Well, they're all just now coming of age, Savha," Fisher said. "It's been a year since you got away. Now that they're getting old enough, like Finley, maybe some can."

"I guess. But none of the half Florians could skip either from what I heard. The abilities cancelled each other out."

159

Fisher considered that. "Maybe it just couples well with Bellovian blood."

"My mother always suspected I would be able to skip. She said her family's blood ran strong." I shrugged. Curiosity lit Fisher's eyes, but he held in any questions.

"You do look Trish. Besides the hair. The Bellovians never suspected?"

"They had too many other things they disliked about me. And my skin was paler in the cold. I didn't get much sun. It was so cold, even inside, that I wasn't often without a hat or a scarf. And I always made an effort to hang back and try not to draw attention."

Fisher nodded, content with the answer without my having to explain my family's privilege and the hatred it garnered when people saw my clothing. How they didn't look past that. "What was skipping like?" he asked.

"It was..." I couldn't think of the words.

"Amazing," Savha said, seeing the look on my face and sounding dreamy. I couldn't deny it. I had never felt anything like it. "Maybe..." Savha paused, looking almost embarrassed. "Maybe you could try to teach me? I probably can't skip, but other things. You know how to fight, right?"

"Of course." I paused in my steps, Savha and Fisher halting next to me. Even my mother knew how to fight. "You don't?"

"I was raised a slave in Traesha, what do you think?"

I was staggered. I'd never met someone who couldn't defend themselves. "But you broke my wrist!"

"That was just instinct. I want to learn how to control it."

"Why haven't the Florians taught you?"

"I mean, there were lessons at the palace," Fisher said, rubbing the back of his neck. "That's where I was raised.

My parents were ambassadors there when the invasion happened and involved with the Trish refugees, but none of us had much interest in learning to fight. It's important to hold on to the culture when we don't have the land, you know? Those who trained at the palace were those with abilities, the elites. Mostly from powerful families. And Hinze and I have always been best friends. I knew he'd come to the war one day, being the most protected of his siblings, but training with him mainly focused on learning to shoot. Since I was always with him, a fight would involve him grabbing my arm and protecting us both while we shot," Fisher finished with a shrug.

"But..." It felt like hearing that they all simply gave up. But that was the Bellovian in me judging. Most Trish didn't feel my need to strike back. It wasn't a natural feeling for them. My insides chilled with the reminder. "So the army at the Front *is* all gifted?"

"Not exactly. There are some teams of elites like Hinze's, but for the most part the border is protected by criminals or volunteers who had trouble finding work elsewhere. The elites keep things calm enough to protect the ungifted from too much danger, but the king has held off on using their full force. Before the queen was killed, his attention was on Detono and making sure they felt too threatened to try anything."

I opened my mouth to ask what the small island east of Floria had to do with anything, but Savha broke in first. "So, will you teach us? The basics at least?"

I nodded slowly. What even were the basics? I could barely remember my first lessons. Satisfied with my nod, Savha steered us toward the next shop. As we walked, Fisher moved on to lighter topics of conversation. He told me about his travels here with his parents. Apparently, it snowed in this area but only in the dead of winter. People came to do activities like snow hiking with wide, circular shoes. It made me laugh to think about people being out in the snow for fun and not necessity.

"Oh Fish, look at this one! I think your mother would love it!"

"We aren't shopping for pleasure, Savvy. I thought you needed a bag to carry when we leave..." Fisher was drawn away at Savha's call. I smiled at his half-hearted protests.

I came across a rack of hats with a soft leathery feel. I picked up a maroon one, my mother's favorite color. I thought about my silver roots growing in and Savha's words once again. I put on the hat, pulling down on the slim brim, and frowned at myself in the small mirror to the side of the rack. Even away from Bellovian eyes, I wasn't ready to show my true colors. I took the hat off and decided to buy it when I remembered I had no money. How ironic I had to leave Bellovi to become poor. With a twinge of disappointment, I moved to return it to the rack.

"Here," Fisher said, suddenly at my side. "It's on me."

Before I could protest he plucked the hat from my hand and went to Savha, who he would never deprive of an opportunity to haggle.

WALKING streets lined with flowers and tufts of grass in a dress and my new hat, speaking Trish openly in public for the first time, I had never felt less Bellovian. My steps were light and I came to enjoy the brush of fabric around my knees and the touch of wind on my legs. I was entirely caught in the conversation with Savha and Fisher. They kept the topics light and I heard stories of the Florian palace and the Trish living there and in the capital city of Helsa. An entire community had escaped the Bellovian invasion, more than I could ever have hoped. Still too few, but it was better than none. There was still hope and life after the Bellovians.

My enjoyment didn't last. It wasn't until Fisher and Savha went into a small butcher's and I told them I would wait outside, the smell of blood too fresh, that I noticed the looks I was getting. When the minutes ticked by and the people passing saw me alone, not with their prince's Trish friends, things took a turn for the worst. I became a Bellovian standing in the middle of a town just inside the Front. A Florian bumped me roughly as he passed. He mumbled something that sounded like "rebel scum."

I caught my balance and kept the confusion from my face, but just barely. If they knew I was rebelling, why would that make me the enemy? I watched him go, fighting the urge to demand an answer. But when I looked away, it was into glaring faces. I was used to such looks, so I suppose that's why I hadn't thought much about the glares until then. I swallowed, suddenly very conscious of my black-as-night hair. A group of young boys ran up. The leader spit on my boots, freshly cleaned of Dani's blood. Their voices cracked and echoed, they laughed and jeered as they were welcomed back into the defensive crowd gathering. The adults around chuckled at their antics. I felt my face heat. I raised my chin and met their eyes. The stoniness of my gaze made their laughs falter.

"What are you doing here?" an older man yelled in a shaking voice.

"I'm just shopping. I'm here with—"

"You aren't wanted here!"

"Your kind only bring death!"

I kept my face unreadable. At that moment it didn't matter to me that my hair was dyed black and I was only half Bellovian. I felt insulted. I felt proud. I felt like I did every day walking the streets of City Center and at school with people hurling insults my way. They didn't know me. Their hatred wasn't grounded.

Another man checked me with his shoulder, the force pushing me into the middle of the street. He turned, pointing a finger at me. "They say the prince befriended a Bellovian who killed one of our soldiers!"

"Shame such a pretty face should be wasted on a blood-thirsty creature," another man spat. Those words sank quick and hard, making me swallow and step away. Insults in Bellovi were only about my stature and weakness. Not my appearance. I felt like the space around me wasn't right. I didn't know how to fit. The eyes on me were different. I fought the urge to duck my head or turn to look for Savha and Fisher.

A woman laughed at the man's words, encouraging him. He lifted a hand and I ducked out of his reach. This put me further away from the butcher shop and deeper into the crowd. They swarmed around me. My feet slid into stance. No one here would protest or defend me.

This was everything I feared happening in Bellovi if they'd found out I was Trish. My worst nightmare.

"Get out!" I ducked out of the way of the red fruit thrown at my head.

"Your people killed my son!"

"You burned our trees, our land! Murdered our queen! How dare you try to sneak through our town!"

"I'll show you the way out." The latest speaker made to grab me again. I struck out with a fist and hit his soft stomach. He doubled up instantly.

"Don't touch me," I hissed. The blow was met with calls of displeasure, fearful cries. The faces surrounding me shifted again as I became a threat. The same face of the guard before I was forced to defend myself. Where were Fisher and Savha? A town officer approached, elbowing his way through the crowd accusing me of murder and espionage. He made a grab at me. I dodged him easily.

"If you cooperate this will go much easier," he said through gritted teeth, hatred dark in his eyes. With him there to protect them, people were laughing, hurling insults, spitting. A glob hit my cheek, warm and slimy. I saw the top of Fisher's silver head. He and Savha were pushing their way toward me.

The officer grabbed my arm and yanked me into him while I was distracted. I pushed his elbow upward with my other hand and ducked under with a twist. He lost his grip and I spun away, losing him in the crowd easily.

I craned my neck to look for my Trish friends. Another officer came up behind me and grabbed the arm I had just freed, shouting to his partner. I ground my teeth in frustration. I spun to face him and his grip held firm, too warm on my skin. He was big enough for his hand to completely encircle my bicep. I dropped and his body bent with the weight of me, unprepared. I kicked out at his knee and sent him to the ground. He landed heavily, but kept his grip on my arm, now nearly burning. I rolled over his hand and the grip finally broke under my weight, but not before another flash of heat. And then pain.

It was only then I realized I was fighting a gifted Florian. Fire burned in his eyes.

I rolled back over my shoulder, using my hands to push to my feet. My bicep flared with pain and the breeze bit at the wound. A quick glance down showed blistered flesh, my cardigan sleeve staying up by mere threads. The gifted officer was trying to stand, his knee giving him trouble now. I should have kicked him harder.

The crowd backed away at the sight of the flames engulfing his hands. An excited hush fell. His partner approached from the side, gun drawn. My eyes stung and my bicep ached with a pain entirely different from the throb of a snapped bone or bruised skin. It was overpowering. I wanted to fight, but there were too many people. Fire was too dangerous a weapon. Too effective. I might have pride, but faced with his burning hands, it crumbled. I turned and pushed my way through the crowd, throwing elbows and fists whenever necessary. I burst out of the clustered bodies. Some followed but I knew they wouldn't be fast enough. Not by a long shot.

I tried to access my Trish speed again, but it was beyond my grasp. I sprinted back through the shops and back uphill. Climbing the gate was more difficult this time, but I ignored the searing pain of my burn and clambered over, dropping to the ground on the other side with a gasp. I tried to calm my breathing when I reached the door of the mansion. Wiping the spit off my cheek, I opened it, stepped inside, and knelt to take off my boots.

"You're back!" I glanced up and saw Hinze looking up from a letter in his hands, halfway down the stairs. He wore a white shirt and an unbuttoned red sweater. The tension he'd carried in his shoulders at the base was gone.

"You're probably hungry, unless you ate in town..." He trailed off when whatever expression he'd caught on my face registered. I quickly cleared it and stood, keeping my body angled so he didn't see my arm.

"I think I'll just go lay down in my room for a bit," I said. I sounded a bit breathless, but my voice didn't shake.

He folded his letter, stashing it in his pocket. "Finley, what happened? Where are Savvy and Fisher?"

I couldn't stand the kind look in his eyes. I ducked my head and moved for the other set of stairs, keeping my arm angled out of his sight. "I just got tired. It's been a long day."

He didn't move to follow me and for that I was grateful. I hurried up the stairs and ran on silent feet to my room.

CHAPTER 14

Taking off the cardigan was difficult. I winced every time it brushed the burn on my right arm. I felt light-headed but couldn't hold in my gasps. My left hand shook as I used cold water from the sink to clean the wound. I was bringing up another cupped handful when there were two quick knocks on my door and it was pushed open.

I wasn't even surprised when Hinze strode in, just embarrassed to be caught bending so awkwardly over the sink. His frown deepened when he saw the handprint of blisters that marred my skin. He didn't say anything for a long moment and I couldn't place the expression on his face. I straightened, water trickling down my arm.

"Send Garris to my chambers," he finally bit out. The boy who led him to my room took off down the hallway. "If you wouldn't mind," Hinze said to me next, holding out a hand. He seemed to be working to control his voice.

I didn't want to go at first. I wanted to be alone. To hide in my room like I had so many times when people became too much to bear. But the pain in my arm and promise of Garris's healing touch propelled me forward.

When I took his hand, Hinze gripped my fingers and a sensation of weightlessness came over me. He led me from my room without another word. We went down the hall and up the stairs with the mahogany doors. The bounce of my steps made my arm throb. I held it out awkwardly from my body, trying not to wince from the exposure to the air but unable to stand it touching the side of my ribs.

There were three doorways at the top of the stairs and Hinze went to the one on the left. I took in the beauty of the carvings on the door. A forest and mountain that reminded me of Jenna's drawing on the floor of our prison cell.

I yanked back with a startled yell when Hinze went right up to the door without reaching for the gold handle. He didn't pause but pulled me through, seeming too lost in his thoughts to notice my reaction or my embarrassment that quickly followed.

I found myself in the largest bedroom I'd ever seen. A fire crackled in the hearth and a canopied bed took up the back wall. There was a small set of stairs up to a high-ceilinged loft to our left. The wall below the stairs was made up of shelves of books. The sight was as unfamiliar to me as the garden outside. I'd never seen a library before, only heard my mother's descriptions of the ones she knew in Traesha.

Hinze went to the stocked bar on the wall opposite of the stairs. He was pouring us glasses of deep red wine when a knock sounded at the door.

"It's open," he called. Garris walked in and quickly noted the burn on my arm, his eyes accustomed to looking for what needed fixing.

"May I?" I nodded and held out my arm to him, unable

to hold back a wince at the movement. Garris placed his hand over the burned skin. The feeling of spreading water rippled across the burn. When he let go my skin looked rough, scarred with thin lines, bumps and divots, and a shiny redness. All forming the shape of a man's hand. But it no longer hurt.

"I'm sorry. Some healers are strong enough to heal the scars," he said, frowning down at his work and twisting my arm gently to examine the mark that now circled my bicep.

"Thank you, Garris. A few scars don't bother me."

He smiled a bit, hearing the sincerity in my voice. "Be careful, okay? Those igniters generally have personalities to match their flames."

"I will."

He glanced at Hinze's turned back and left the room when nothing else was needed of him.

Hinze finished his task and came toward me with the two drinks.

"Let's go up there," he said, pointing to the loft with his chin. I went up the stairs and paused at the top. The room stretched back further than I imagined. Most of the space was taken up by a long table littered with papers, open books, and a large map. In the back of the room were two cushioned seats; the lamp standing in between them cast a soft yellow glow over the table.

I took the glass Hinze offered and walked to the map. My braid slipped over my shoulder as I leaned forward to look at it. It was different from those I studied at school. Floria was large and prominent, Bellovi tucked into the bottom corner. At school, Bellovi was always center, Floria condensed to seem less threatening. I shook my head at further evidence of the lies we'd been taught to keep us motivated to fight. Traesha sat north of Bellovi, surrounded by mountains and a vast forest. The trees funneled down-ward, curving so the lowest reaches separated Floria and Bellovi. This section was labeled "Front."

The ocean surrounded our three countries. I'd never seen the water drawn on a map, the Bellovians were only concerned with our immediate enemies. The ice and glac-iers extending past Bellovi were of little interest. On this map, the ocean was spotted with islands, the largest being to the east of Floria. The word Detono marked its name in the center. I frowned, remembering how Savha mentioned it. I could swear my father or mother had talked about the country, but not in a way that made it memorable. From my parents, I knew the world was bigger than what Bellovians taught, yet it was still strange to see it remade and drawn out. It was so much bigger than I could fathom, so unex-plored past the edges of even this map. Feeling small, I turned to Hinze. The words the Florians shouted in the square still rang in my ears.

"Why did they call me rebel scum? If they knew I was rebelling from the Bellovians, I don't understand why they were so hateful."

Hinze pulled out a seat for me and I hesitated briefly over the strange manners before I sat. I drank from the glass, and the tart liquid tingled in my jaw and warmed my stomach. Hinze was more at ease now with a drink in his hand and my arm healed.

"They weren't accusing you of deserting from the Bello-vians," he said, the pattern of his words and low timbre of his voice filling the space around us. I sat back in the chair and sipped absently, losing myself to the sound. I was beginning to note the different accents between Florian Common Tongue and Bellovian. His words were softer, the vowels held just a beat longer. The hard emphasis Bellovian people put on letters like "k" and "r" was softened. Hinze's voice was nearly musical. "How much do you know of Bellovi's history?"

"Not much, I guess. My mother had never heard of the country before the rebellion and my father only learned the truth about the outside world from her."

Hinze nodded. "She wouldn't have heard of Bellovi from us. It was the shameful secret we kept from the Trish, wanting them to think we valued peace in the same way they did. The questions they asked were always about our culture and art, so war was an easy subject to avoid."

I raised an eyebrow and Hinze's lips twisted into a rueful smile. "Bellovi used to fall under our reign. Floria has always been a people connected by our abilities. Each bloodline passes on gifts of a similar vein, like Brea's family all have some level of control over the environment around them. Back then, gifts were more static and predictable. The powerful families oversaw different sections of Floria and answered to the king. The Bellovi family's gift was incredible strength, and there were quite a few of them." I swallowed. The Bellovians still boasted about their strength. I always thought it was more propaganda to give the people hope in the war. Was it more than that?

Hinze continued, "Florent Bellovi decided his people were strong enough to stand on their own. He was tired of following the rule of a distant king. Many of our prisoners and criminals were sent to work in the coal mines, the strength of the Bellovian guards was enough to keep them compliant. Florent felt my great-great-grandfather owed him more land than the coal mines and tundra he occupied. He led a bloody rebellion that went on for years, until the king decided to give him the land the Bellovi family held, but no more. The cold corner of Floria wasn't worth the effort it would take to stomp out the rebellion entirely and criminals could simply be sent to fight them off. So the Front was established, the train track that carried coal into our country was severed and we found other ways to power our land, mostly relying on abilities."

I sighed. "But the fight became everything to Bellovi. It's all they have."

Hinze nodded. "My family should have known cutting them out like that would motivate them more than anything to gain more land. I think my grandfathers and even father basically forgot about the Bellovi, just kept holding the line with the same kind of weapons the Bellovians were using, buying them from Detono even as tensions rose between us and the island. So my family focused on keeping things peaceful with Detono. That is, until Bellovi overthrew Traesha. That was a great shock, but it took us a long time to even realize what had happened. It wasn't until those who escaped reached us that we knew. So many had died of a population already so small. Only about a hundred made it here." My throat dried hearing this. Traesha was small. Almost entirely made up of one single city, the people avoided population growth in fear of having to cut more into the forest surrounding them. My mother told me of the birth control methods they used and how serious an undertaking it was to have a child. Unlike Bellovi, where family sizes were huge and many saw it as a duty to raise new soldiers after they themselves retired from action.

"My grandfather thought Traesha was a lost cause and extended the patrol along the forest border, but did little else. He was already at the end of his reign and left it for my father to deal with. My father saw the Bellovians may be more a threat with Traesha's resources to back them, but that was the year Detono went on strike in response to a raised tax at our ports." Hinze took a long drink from his glass, finishing it. He stared out the window across from us at the now setting sun. My stomach was in knots, hands curled into fists. Traesha hadn't received aid because of a financial issue?

"It wasn't until my mother was murdered in front of us all that my father saw the Bellovians as a serious threat. The team was taken out, but our people rioted and demanded the Bellovian rebellion crushed once and for all. My mother was very loved." Hinze paused to take a breath, looking at his glass like he wished it wasn't empty and reaching up to fiddle with the small braid in his hair. "My father sent me to keep track of the lines and tell him when it was time for a push. Since I am the third born, he had little use for me at court. Not to mention how convenient my gift has proved to be out here."

I set down my own empty glass. "But you're doing more than watching the lines."

"Yes." Hinze smiled. He liked that I knew that. "We, ah, learned that the Trish queen had been discovered and captured."

"How?"

"The same way we tried to get information out of you. A commander had fallen behind the rest. It's not the first time they've sent spies across the Front. We used to let people cross, many were just trying to get away from the commanders. But that's how the team got through to kill my mother. We can't trust the Bellovians anymore."

"That's why they attacked me today."

We fell silent as I looked to the map with fresh eyes. My stomach grumbled. Hinze heard and went to the wall, pulling a string. When the door to his chambers opened, he called down for food and more wine.

"My, do you have it easy," I said. "They hated me for my family's wealth in Vichi. I can't even imagine how they'd feel about this." I waved a hand at the string.

"As much as they disliked you, my royal title would probably top that alone."

"Well, they did call me princess," I said. An unexpected stab of pain came at those words. I wondered what had happened to my team. I stared at Bellovi on the map as if it would tell me. It surprised me how much I missed them, a pull in my chest making it difficult to concentrate on the prince sitting next to me.

"We're going to find her. The queen," Hinze said. "We'll complete the triangle and form a stronger alliance than before."

I was startled to hear the Florian boy mention the triangle. It took me back to bedtime stories with my mother.

There is a triangle that blesses our land and keeps our magic strong, my mother would whisper to me, tucking me in. She was the only person who ever described abilities as magic, but only when she spoke about the Traesha. She would point a finger in the air while she talked about the triangle. *The people tend the land and the gifted make up the* magsai. *They protect the kingdom. Mags blesses them with the strength to do so, using the bond between* resa *and the queen to solidify their power.* My eyes would follow her finger upward diagonally, imagining the line she outlined from the bottom right of the triangle to the top. *The queen and her family handle disputes and create alliances with Floria and the islands. They live their lives as an example of peace and Finma blesses them.* Her finger went downward to the final point. Even when I was young,

I was saddened when my mother still spoke of Traesha in the present tense. *The land, blessed and cared for by Tash, god of love, supports us all. It whispers the secrets of the world and feeds us every year. We must always thank the land and to do so, we give love freely. Tash only asks for open hearts and* fisha grens *in exchange for her blessings. Together the gods watch over us and balance the triangle that keeps us strong.* She retraced the triangle in the air and kissed my forehead, showing me how easy it was for her to give *fisha grens*. Gentle loving.

Hinze continued talking, pulling me from my memories. "Maybe we could even reform the *magsai*."

I frowned. "I don't know... they have always been led by the *resa magsai*. We'd need them too."

"The *resa magsai*? I've heard the title, but I didn't know they were so significant."

I frowned; what if the knowledge was held in secret by the Trish? How else would he know about the triangle and not this figure? But at Hinze's open expression, I gave in and did my best to explain, the wine loosening my tongue. "There were always *magsai* being recruited. They were trained from children until adulthood. Those who developed Trish speed joined the guard, others became ambassadors or advisors—"

"Like Fisher's parents."

"Exactly. But every queen had a *resa magsai*, a person born on the same day they were. Some say the same minute. They were bonded by the gods and through that bond the queen and *magsai*, all the *magsai*, formed their power."

Hinze's eyebrows drew together. "Bonded?"

"Yes. That's what my mother always said at least. Her mother was a *magsai*, but I never really understood what she meant by bond. If we can find the queen and the *resa magsai*, someone who'd be exactly the queen's age, and save them too, then maybe we could hope to reform the *magsai*."

"How old is the queen?"

"A year or two older than me, I think. She was born shortly before the invasion, that's all I know."

"So, if we could find them, they would be even more helpful in leading us to the queen and helping the people?"

"Yes, but we have no way to do that. They could be dead."

Hinze shrugged. "Bellovians didn't kill many children. I don't think we should discount the idea. Maybe they'll even come to us during the celebration, or to the queen while we're there."

"Maybe." The idea didn't seem likely, but it didn't matter. The queen had me now, committed fully to helping her. I had to believe I could do this and putting my family in danger would pay off. This was my mission now and I wouldn't fail again.

CHAPTER 15

I'd been here enough times to know I was dreaming. Command Hall was a gleaming maze. I forced down the panic and began my search. The pull in my chest tugged and I followed it at down the halls, frustratingly unable to skip in my dreamscape. I heard a laugh. Contagious and effortless. I would know the sound anywhere. I put on a burst of speed toward it, ignoring when the pull tugged the opposite way. I reached the door the laugh came from and threw it open, expecting to see Oken's smiling eyes on the other side.

I stumbled back. Dani was dead on the ground. Her deep brown eyes accusing and glossy. The smile, the only one she'd even given me, slowly began to turn to a familiar nasty frown. She spoke, eyes still lifeless. "You deserved every hurt. You did this to me. You failed our team. You failed your family. You did this!"

My stomach roiled and I ran for the next room. It was wrong wrong wrong. I needed to go another way. But I wanted to find Oken. I knew he was here. The light and butterflies he induced just out of reach. I could taste it on the tip of my tongue. I couldn't stop my hand from trying the door.

Inside, the man I killed lay in a puddle of his own blood. His eyes held fear of me. Justified fear.

The panic was at full force now. I backed away, but when I started to turn, he shifted, a rotting hand reaching out for me. I sprinted to the next door, so relieved to see Hinze smiling on the other side. I walked forward and took the hand he offered. His hazel eyes darkened when our fingers met and the hunger there had me trying to pull away. He tightened his grip. I threw my body into trying to free myself, feet slipping from under me. I heard a girl scream. The crack of gunfire echoed down the halls. Someone was sobbing. My chest ached.

The pressure of Hinze's hand disappeared. He used his ability with a smirk. I free fell into the dark. A scream built in my chest, about to erupt. I glimpsed the basement and a small, hunched figure. A pulse in my chest, outside my own wildly beating heart. I reached but fell past into the darkness.

Knocking on my door brought me abruptly from my dream. I went still, trying to calm my breathing. When the knock repeated, I untwisted myself from the blanket and went to answer.

"Clothes for you, miss," a young, red-haired girl said when I opened the door. She thrust a bundle into my arms. "And breakfast is served in the main dining room." We spent a moment staring at each other. I'd never seen someone with red hair. She'd probably never seen a Bellovian. Remembering ourselves at the same time, she stepped away and I shut the door. I leaned against it, trying to shake the dream. The memory of Hinze's smirk chilled me. Last night we'd parted on good terms, with him walking me to my room and offering to find me a better one near the rest of his people. I wanted to stay here and he'd taken my answer with a smile and walked me through the door without thought, bidding me goodnight with only his upper body sticking through. I almost laughed at the time, but with the dream clinging his ease of access made the hair on my arms rise.

Today the clothes included thin leggings and a simple shirt. Better to move in than another short dress. I readied for the day and hurried to the main floor. I wanted to move forward. Past the dream and constant worry for my family. It was time to make a plan and I was determined to use all the resources a prince of Floria could offer. I followed the sound of voices down a hallway lined with portraits of past Florian royalty to the dining room where I was immediately assailed by the smell of bacon. The table in the center of the room was a huge slab of wood that could easily fit twenty people but now only held Garris, Brea, Lilah, Fisher, and Savha.

"Where's Hinze?" I asked. They turned to me with varying degrees of welcome. Brea and Lilah's faces were closed off and on the verge of glares. Practically smiles compared to Bellovian stares. Fisher was grinning, Savha yawning as if my presence was already a constant not worth remarking on. Garris's eyes dipped to the scar on my arm, guilt etching his face in a way I found mildly irritating. Scars were nothing to note in Vichi.

"He'll be down in a minute, I'm sure. He and Londe were communicating with the king this morning," Fisher said.

"How?"

"Good morning to you too, Finley," Savha said. "Londe's ability makes it possible. Just like how he's been killing himself trying to get a hold of your family."

"Oh." Food was set up buffet-style against the closest wall. I loaded a plate without paying much attention to anything besides the vast quantity. How many would this feed in the Squalor? "I was hoping we could start planning our next steps."

"We will. Just relax. These things take time and delicacy and the king's approval, which I'm sure Hinze is asking for now."

My heart sank as I sat down across from Savha. "What if the king says no?"

"He won't," Fisher was quick to assure me.

Savha just winked and I relaxed slightly. Nothing was going to stop me from making my desertion worth it. I was going to that celebration no matter what.

With this lull in the conversation, I began to eat. I had never had anything like the food on my plate. So rich I felt full far too quickly, yet I couldn't stop sampling. Fruit in such bright colors they seemed painted. Bacon so thick I wasn't sure it even counted as bacon. Fluffed breads covered in sugar that were far too sweet for me. It wasn't until I took a pause to breathe that I noticed the whole table staring at me. "I'm sorry, what?"

"We were just asking what happened yesterday and if you're okay. That was quite the angry mob," Savha said. Her words were teasing, but I felt the eyes of the Florians around me and wondered just how closely their feelings for me mirrored those of the people in town. Lilah drummed her long nails on her coffee mug.

"Oh, I'm fine. They just saw I was Bellovian and got angry. I probably should have expected it." I shrugged.

"What's that supposed to mean?" Brea asked.

"Well, we are at war. I don't expect anyone here to be falling over themselves to befriend me." It wasn't as if they were.

"*We* are at war? You side with the Bellovians still?" Lilah asked. Nothing I said was coming out right. Even Garris looked wary now.

"No, I meant our countries. I look like a Bellovian."

"Not really. Just your hair." Lilah was on the lookout for any opportunity to contradict me.

"Well, my mom isn't Bellovian."

"She's really Trish?" Mesa asked as she entered the dining room. She looked skeptical but had a layer of curiosity beneath it rather than the disbelief Lilah and Brea exhibited. I still didn't know Mesa's ability. She had shoulder-length brown hair and sure movements. A bodily awareness I saw throughout Bellovi and now knew to associate with training.

"She's Trish," Fisher affirmed. "Finley's going to help us find our queen."

"How would you help?" Mesa asked, sitting down next to Savha with a plate full of fluffy pancakes drowned in so much syrup I fought a cringe.

Hinze and Londe finally came in. The prince took the seat next to me and snatched a piece of bacon off my plate. I ignored the eyebrow Savha raised in my direction and the memories of my nightmare his presence stirred.

"I can find her," I told Mesa. "I've trained my whole life for missions like this."

She raised an eyebrow. "Missions to strike against us, you mean. Not your own people."

"This isn't a strike against the Trish," I said. The words felt surprisingly right after being forced to identify as Bellovian my entire life.

Hinze waited a beat to see if Mesa had a response. "A few announcements." With those three words he claimed the attention of the table. "First, my sister's travels will be bringing her to Honna this afternoon." Lanis entered the room when Hinze said this. His face drained of color, nearly matching his flour-covered apron.

"No!" The horror contained in this singular word had Hinze fighting a smile.

"Don't worry too—" he began, but Lanis had already fled the room. Hinze grimaced when his voice boomed through the halls, yelling at the maids and threatening the entire staff should he spot one hair out of place.

"As I was saying, my sister will be here this afternoon. This being the case, we'll have to leave tomorrow morning." A shot of adrenaline thrilled my body at his words.

"Leave so soon?" Lilah asked. "We don't even have a plan."

"We will once Finley helps us make one."

"And the king is fine with this mission?" Mesa asked.

Hinze ignored the question and turned to me, the whole table following his lead. Some with scowls. Some with smiles. Even Londe's strangely intense gaze was open. "Where do we start, Finley?"

I straightened and lifted my chin as I pushed away my plate. "I'll need paper. Savha, can you help me make a map?"

THE PLAN WAS NEARLY FINALIZED by the time the second maid ran through the dining room on the verge of tears. Hinze sank lower in his seat. "I feel as though I should compensate them for emotional damages."

"Is your sister so particular?" I asked.

"She's…" Hinze couldn't think of a word. He sighed and shrugged. "Yes, actually, she is."

"We should probably give them some room," Londe

said. His voice was softer than I first expected, a pleasing cadence to his words.

"Brilliant idea." Hinze jumped to his feet.

"Let's show Finley the gardens!" Fisher said.

"Fisher and his flowers." Savha shook her head at him.

Fisher grinned, leaning close and nuzzling her shoulder. "Anyone looking at you would know how much I love beautiful things."

Savha's face went bright red. Fisher looked supremely proud of himself. He tilted his head to kiss her cheek and she halfheartedly pushed him away with a laugh.

Once standing, I fully realized just how long we'd been sitting around the table. I now had three pages of writing and drawings and a plan I felt confident in. Through Savha's memories and communications with Fisher's parents using Londe's mysterious ability, I had sketches of the Trish castle. It consisted of three towers connected by arched hallways. The celebration would be held in the east tower. The first floor was a ballroom and above this the kitchen where Savha collected platters of food to distribute below. Florian abilities made planning almost too simple and easy. Mesa, with her dark brown hair, and I would sneak into the celebration as guests. Londe was certain he could get us invitations through the rebellion, an organization that grew larger and more powerful in my head the more I learned about it. Savha and Fisher would don the outfits the slaves wore while working. Hinze would be in position in the kitchen above, finding a spot in the chaos to hide with Lilah, Garris, and Londe until we could signal them it was time. Mesa and I would make our way to the head of the room and create a distraction to draw the attention of the crowd so Lilah could use her ability to incapacitate the commanders, leaving us free to search for the queen.

"But I can't hold them that long, there's too many," Lilah had protested then.

"The queen should be close by. They want to show her to the room, flaunt the accomplishment and power," I told her. She still looked skeptical, at which point Londe broke in.

"We might be able to have members of the rebellion look for her. They have some members that are higher up in the ranks. I could signal them to send people with them to the ballroom and they could look for her."

I didn't love having to trust so many people I didn't know, but in the end I agreed to hold off further planning until Londe was able to contact the rebels.

"But would they really want to help the Trish? Aren't they just against the commanders?"

"They'll want to help the Trish," Londe assured me with a smile that promised more than his words. I was getting the feeling he knew more than he was letting on and couldn't imagine what it was or why he was keeping quiet.

This much of the plan set, we left the manor for the gardens out back. The view was stunning. Like nothing that could ever exist in frozen Bellovi. My experience of plant life went as far as my dreams, which I didn't count, and the forest I walked through on my single mission. Here every color imaginable bloomed in patterns along a narrow gravel path. Fisher took Savha's hand and led her through the rows of flowers, occasionally picking one and trying to hand it to her. She laughed and waved them away.

Garris, Mesa, Londe, Brea, and Lilah turned for the wall of

large, trimmed hedges. Garris's attention was captured by some bushes near the entrance and he knelt to examine them closer. Mesa darted into an opening with a laugh. Londe smiled and followed quickly. Lilah and Brea were too enrapt in their conversation to take part and walked inside at their own pace.

"That's the maze," Hinze said, still at my side. "I would offer to race you, but I always seem to win."

I snorted, imagining him walking straight through the bushes while I ran uselessly down the twists and turns. "I'm sure that does take all the fun out of it for you."

"Indeed." He began walking down the path between the flowers and maze toward the lawn. "Although, if I remember correctly, you *are* quite fast." He tried to bring up my Trish ability nonchalantly, but when he looked at me out of the corner of his eye, he betrayed the curiosity he felt.

"My mom thought I might have the ability to skip. She does and said her family has always been gifted with it. That was my first time."

"You skip?" he asked, laughing.

"No, I'm running when I do it. That's just the best way to translate it. Skip from one place to next."

"What's the Trish word?"

"*Nhasnen.*"

"*Nhasnen,*" Hinze tried the word, but it sounded nasally and awkward on his tongue. "Is it not very common? I've heard of it, but never seen anyone do it."

"My mom always made it sound rare, but I don't really know. Definitely all the *magsai* guards and the royal family could do it." My chest throbbed talking about my mother and my thoughts turned to Vichi. Homesickness washed over me and I forced down the longing to return. The pull in my chest twinged in response, resisting my efforts.

Hinze nodded. Those were the people first killed in the

invasion, so it made sense he'd never met someone who could skip. We walked in silence for a bit before he picked a spot in the grass and sat down, legs sprawled out in front of him. I crossed my ankles and sat next to him, enjoying the breeze that carried the scent of flowers. I tried to distinguish each scent, but they swirled together too well. After his eager assistance with the plan and a morning side by side, my wariness of Hinze had eased. I could brush off my nightmare surrounded by colors and sunshine.

Hinze leaned back on his hands and tipped his face to the sun. The breeze picked up and shifted through his brown hair, the small braid on the right side still in place. In Bellovi, most men kept their hair cut short or opted for the same braid I currently wore. I found I liked the look of Hinze's longer hair and the small braid he kept in it. He was as far from Bellovian as a person could get.

I stopped myself when I noticed the thought rang hollow in my own head. When had the faces of my team replaced the image of commanders when I thought of Bellovians? When did sympathy for those starving in the Squalor and being shot by friendly fire replace my feelings of hatred?

I shook away the thought as Savha and Fisher made their way over to us. The Bellovians in charge were why I was here. I needed to hold onto the burning hatred as long as it took to take them out. Fisher tossed his bouquet of flowers into the air over my head and I laughed, watching their beautiful colors rain down around me.

"I can't believe we're actually doing this," Savha said. She and Fisher gracefully lowered themselves into the grass. Did I look so weightless when I moved? Or did my body still mimic the Bellovians after so many years?

"It's about time we had a real lead," Hinze said. "And

the rebel we're in contact with has been eager to make this happen."

"How exactly does Londe's gift work?"

"He'll have to show you before we get to the celebration. There's a way to invite him in. He can't read minds but speaks into them." Hinze gestured to where Londe and Mesa had just exited the maze, out of breath and smiling. Londe was a painting of light colors. I was still getting used to seeing blond hair. His eyes were unfocused in a dazed look, like he wasn't entirely present in the moment. Mesa tapped his arm and his attention returned to where she stood nearly a head shorter than him.

"It's happening! We're going to free Traesha!" Savha threw her arms around me so tight we fell into the grass and crushed Fisher's flowers. I laughed at her sudden show of affection, feeling lighter than I did from Hinze's touch.

"We're going to find the queen," she whispered these last words in my ear, making the hairs on the back of my neck tingle.

I swallowed down the thrill of excitement, flaring with shame when the Bellovian in me came to attention. Eager for the challenge and possible fight.

CHAPTER 16

Before long, the rest of the Florians joined us. For the first time I appreciated Brea's powers. The noon sun grew warm, but our circle in the grass was pleasantly cool. After sitting around the table and strategizing as we had, the Florians looked at me differently. Something akin to respect had blossomed the more of the commanders' secret I'd shared and the more passion they saw I held for the Trish people. The hard looks were gone. It made me feel entirely more confident in the mission to know we were that much closer to trust and willing to work together.

Savha jumped to her feet. "Finley, will you teach me how to fight now?"

The way she phrased it made me laugh, thinking about the years it had taken me to learn. But I shrugged and stood. The Florians and Fisher did nothing to disguise their interest as Savha and I walked a short distance away.

I still wasn't sure where to even begin. "Let's see what you can do."

"What I can do?"

"Yes. Just try to land a hit." I sank into my stance and waited. Savha stood straight, rigid and frowning. When she lunged at me all it took was a step to the side on my part for her to lose her balance and stumble. I stood up and couldn't stop a frown of my own. This suddenly became a daunting task. Hinze let out a laugh.

"Oh, I'd like to see *you* do better," Savha bit out, cheeks red.

"Please. Hinze doesn't need to know how to fight." Lilah laughed. Savha turned to include the girl in her fierce glare.

"I'm game to try." When Hinze got up, except for Garris, the rest of his team was quick to follow. Lilah quicker than the rest, despite her words. They all seemed so much younger in that instant, wanting to fit in with their prince and leader.

I felt unprepared when they all turned to face me expectantly. "I suppose we should start with stances."

It quickly became evident Fisher, Hinze, and Londe had minimal training. At least they could get into a stance without my instruction. Their punches were hesitant but movements practiced. Garris edged them on from where he relaxed in the grass, offering to heal any bruises they left on each other. When Hinze suggested he join, Garris saw little point. He claimed his place would always be behind the battle lines.

Only Mesa had confidence backing her movements. "It's been decades since someone was born with an ability in my village, but being so close to the Detonian coast, we all had to learn to defend ourselves," she explained when she caught my approving look. My liking for the girl heightened. "Good luck with them, though."

"Well, it'll be easier now that I know I have help." I pushed her toward the boys with a grin. She sighed and took the hint, leading them in an exercise while I tried to catch the others up.

"Why have none of you trained?" I asked. My real question—why hadn't I seen any women soldiers at base? Why was Mesa the only girl here who knew anything about fighting?

Lilah rolled her eyes and snapped her fingers. I can only assume not a lot of time passed before she snapped again and I returned to my senses. I glared at her. "I *am* trained," she said. "Highly."

"Do you want me to demonstrate my abilities on you again?" Brea asked sweetly.

"Fine. You aren't useless in a fight. But don't you—"

Lilah cut me off. "Just show us the basics, Bellovian. We're only doing this to make the prince happy."

Sahva's shoulders fell. She didn't have powers or training and now, not even motivated partners to learn with. So I went through the very, very basics. I repositioned Brea and Lilah's fists three times. Made them go in and out of their stances repeatedly. Within five minutes they were sufficiently bored and quit. Savha and I watched them march back toward the house.

I turned to smile at her. "Okay, let's actually get to work."

Savha's answering smile was brilliant. She was a fast learner with perfect muscle memory. Working one-on-one, we soon caught up and surpassed the boys. I found myself grinning as we moved into more complicated movements. I called over Fisher, thrilled to practice with people who could keep up with me. I couldn't fully test myself against them, but it was freeing not to hide my speed. Both were gracious when I bested them time after time and then

191

explained what they did wrong, walking them back through the fight slowly.

"How do you remember every hit?" Hinze asked.

I shrugged. "This was my life."

His eyes dimmed. "That's sad."

I raised an eyebrow at him. "Besides my family, fighting was the only thing I loved in Bellovi."

Fisher looked uncomfortable. Savha pitying. My words were so far from Trish ideals, the looks on their faces made me ashamed I said them. Ashamed they were so true.

"And that's why you'll do better in this war than any of them," Mesa said. The shame closing my throat loosened at the understanding in her eyes.

"You wanted to fight in the war?" Londe asked.

"Not necessarily. I don't want to have to kill people, but it was the reality I lived in."

"But I thought you were enlisted on a volunteer basis." Londe might be the only one in regular contact with the Bellovians, but that hadn't put him any closer to understanding life in Vichi. By now Hinze was reclining in the grass again. I sat across from him and Savha, and Fisher dropped to the ground. Londe did so cautiously, watching me close.

I sighed. "I have an older brother. He's Bellovian, from my father's first marriage. But he... my parents could tell he didn't have war in his nature even when he was young. My father made him learn to shoot, but he missed every target. Finally, my father had to accept Nico could shoot and knew how to aim, otherwise he would have at least hit something by accident. Trying to teach him to fight was another matter entirely. Nico refused. He never landed a blow. When my mother taught him to play the piano he poured his entire being into learning, knowing it was the only skill my parents could give him to keep him from having to volunteer. If you don't show you excel at something early in our schools, you're placed in classes that focus only on warfare and it's expected that you'll volunteer and be happy about it. Unless you have another career option, it's suspicious and unpatriotic not to make use of that education and volunteer yourself. Nico got away with making another path, but if I hadn't volunteered it would have drawn too much attention to my family and possibly our Trish secrets. So, I volunteered and planned to use the position to try and take down the commanders from within."

I pulled up a few blades of grass. Talking about Nico made my throat tight. I missed him so much. There was so much I wanted to tell him. About training. About the queen. About finding Savha and Fisher. About Oken. He'd suffered listening to me gush about Oken for years. When Nico gave me that look, the one with his nearly black eyes crinkled at the corners, his smile knowing, I felt like I could do anything. There was no better feeling in the world than when Nico was proud of me. Even for little things, like getting up the courage to talk to a boy. I wished he was here to see me plotting the queen's rescue.

"That's amazing. That you would volunteer for your family." I couldn't meet the warmth in Hinze's gaze. Because in the end, I hadn't kept them safe at all. At least Nico had his alias. They'd probably be searching the city for Nico Larson, but as long as he wasn't with my parents, Hapton Travs could stay hidden.

"Let's keep practicing," I said, standing to move past the moment. My chest was heavy and I was anxious to lighten it. Training was always the best way to do so.

Sometime passed and I showed the group a hold on Hinze similar to the wrist grab my father used to catch me

193

in. I had pushed his arm high behind his back, forcing him to bend at the waist, when I heard a shout behind us. I let go of Hinze and turned in time to see a jet of flames spitting toward me. I hit the ground and they over me, heart racing and bicep twinging in remembered pain. The flames passed harmlessly through Hinze where he stood.

"Stop! Stand down!" I'd never heard Hinze speak with such authority.

"What are you doing, Hinze? Are you insane? Letting some Bellovian put her hands on you?" A girl who could only be Hinze's sister, Princess Chelsa, demanded. She and the men flanking her looked furious. Her guards had drawn their guns, all pointed at me. The barrels followed my movements while I got to my feet.

"Don't move!" one of the men shouted. His hands burst into flame. I should have been afraid, but annoyance flashed through me. Especially when Hinze grabbed my arm and I was protected by his ability. The invincible feeling was a rush. The man's flames, now useless against me, sputtered and went out. He looked to Princess Chelsa for direction.

"Chels, calm down. She's half Trish. She came with us when our base was taken."

"Oh, how convenient for her. I suppose this is the same Bellovian prisoner that killed one of your guards? I heard the rumor, but I didn't think even you would allow such a thing without retribution."

"She was defending herself and she deserves to be here. She's half Trish!" Savha repeated. She stepped in front of me, forcing the men to lower their guns.

"So she says. Where's your proof?" asked one of the men. I started when I heard his accent. Savha did too. He was older so until he drew my attention, I hadn't noticed his gray hair wasn't just gray but streaked with shining silver. He had pale yellow eyes that could only belong to a Trish person. On his belt was a sheathed sword. A sword just like the one hanging over my parent's bed.

I went still. He was a *magsai*.

"She speaks Trish," Fisher said.

"Anyone can learn a language." The *magsai* gestured to the Florians around us following the conversation with ease.

"My mother *is* Trish." I pulled out of Hinze's grasp and stepped around Savha. I didn't need anyone protecting me.

"What's her name?" I hesitated. My mother's lessons of secrecy were so ingrained I couldn't get the words out even to one of Traesha's protectors. When I stayed silent too long the *magsai* snorted. "Put her in bands."

"Stop! Chelsa, just hear me out," Hinze said.

Chelsa flicked her hand at a guard and he approached with a smile. My heartbeat quickened. I shifted into my stance.

"What? You think you can fight me?" he asked. The guards laughed.

I looked him up and down quickly. I let my face show just how unimpressed I was. "I think I could fight *him*." I switched into Trish and pointed at the *magsai*. My words were met with another round of laughter.

Hinze saw my fists clench and tried to step between us. "We don't have time for this. We only have three days until the—"

"Oh, she's clearly Bellovian." The *magsai* cut Hinze off and sneered at me.

Chelsa stepped forward. "Lilah, blind her. Put her in the bands." I hadn't seen Lilah and Brea return. When I glanced their way, Lilah shrugged and lifted her hands to clap.

Before I could remember to look away, the world went white.

I CAME BACK to awareness just as the door was shutting me in. I jumped up to try and catch it, but accidentally tapped into my Trish speed and slammed into the door, closing it even faster. I swore and rubbed the shoulder that took the blow. Turning, I saw I was in the wine cellar. The cot they left me on lay in the middle of the narrow room. I hurried to the sole window and pulled myself up to see outside. My view was level with the ground of the garden, a large bush of roses blocking my sight.

I swore again and sank down onto the cot, dropping my face into my hands. I replayed my mother's words in my head. Words that effectively landed me in this situation. *Tell no one our name, Finley. It carries too much history. You must use your father's until the time is right. You will have no doubt when that time arrives.* She offered no further guidance on the issue. She would have trusted a *magsai*, though... wouldn't she? All I could see was the severity in her eyes as she told me those words. Every time she reminded me. That I even questioned if I could tell him meant I had too much doubt to risk it. But I hated that I landed here without even knowing the reason I had to keep it secret. I thought of all the whispered conversations between my parents, or the ones I could swear were happening, but my mother always heard me approaching and cut them off. I was missing something. Something huge. For the first time a rush of anger toward my parents swept in. It felt wrong after putting them in so much danger, but my jaw clenched regardless. I hated being in the dark.

The room seemed to dim as helplessness grew. If my mother was dead, all the questions I had about the queen and *magsai* could only be answered by the man who locked me up. I wished desperately for better control of my Trish gifts. I could have proven my heritage easily with one skip. But the only person who could help me learn control wouldn't listen. I touched my hat, thinking about the roots growing more visible by the day.

I groaned and flopped back on the cot, thoughts returning to my mother and my home in Vichi. My heart gave a painful squeeze. Then another, surprising me with the intensity of the pull I felt toward the city I had grown up in. A deep sense of loss overcame me. I pressed a hand to my chest and curled forward, my sight blurring with tears. I wanted to save the queen in Traesha, but my body ached to return to Vichi. With the desperation of my reoccurring dream, I needed to go home.

A thump behind me made me gasp and jump to my feet. Hinze was standing under the window, a wry smile on his face.

"Thanks for not screaming. I didn't think that through. I didn't mean to scare you."

It took me a beat to find my voice. "What's happening?"

"Chelsa thinks I went off to the maze to pout." He rolled his eyes. "I am so sorry about her. She's convinced the commanders did everything they could to pass you off as Trish so you could get into the palace and assassinate my father. She's being absolutely ridiculous."

"I mean, that's not so ridiculous. It would have been a solid plan. I never even expected you guys to believe me in the first place."

"But I saw you skip. Only a Trish can do that." He pitched his voice higher. "*You sure you didn't just imagine it,*

Hinze? She could just be a good runner. You've never seen someone with Trish speed, so how would you know? Sam, you should probably show him what it looks like. Gah!" He dramatically threw himself onto the cot.

"I'm *so* sorry to see how much you're suffering over this," I said, gesturing to my makeshift cell.

He grinned, charmingly sheepish. "Sorry. Anyway, what I really wanted to tell you is my father gave the okay to go to Traesha. I think Chelsa told him I needed the distraction to forget about you."

"So, you're still going?"

"*We're* still going. And now the *magsai*, Sam, wants to come too, so we'll have all the layout of the palace." With his Florian accent, Hinze put too much emphasis on the "g" in *magsai*. I was still thrilled to hear this.

"That's great." I would have the two days of travel to convince the *magsai* to help me with my abilities. Get him to trust me. Answer my questions.

"It's all coming together. We leave tomorrow, early. I'll come down and sneak you into the transport before everyone else. I already asked Sam to drive, so he won't see you back there. Be ready in the morning. Don't scream." He winked and we heard Chelsa's voice calling for him outside.

"Try not to get too bored," he said. He went to the window and pulled himself out through the glass, pausing just long enough to shoot me an excited grin before he ran off to meet his sister.

I sank back onto the cot, head light with relief. It was still happening. We were going to Traesha.

CHAPTER 17

"I'm beginning to really appreciate this gift of yours," I whispered as Hinze pulled me through the wine cellar wall into the garden. The flowers sparkled with heavy drops of dew. Hinze tightened his grip on my hand.

"It has its uses." We rounded the mansion and jumped into the back of the transport, not bothering with the doors. "Shouldn't be long. Everyone was heading to breakfast. Stay quiet until we're well out of town, we don't want Sam hearing you until it's too late to turn back."

Hinze turned, about to leave. I reached for his arm and my hand passed through, giving me the strange sensation he wasn't actually there at all. He noticed my movement and turned expectantly.

"Why do you trust me?" I asked. "Besides seeing me run. Chelsa was right: being from Bellovi, I could still be dangerous even if I am Trish."

Hinze shrugged. "You conceal your thoughts well, but not when we talk about Traesha or the lost queen. Saving her means as much to you as it does Savha, Fisher, and Sam. I wouldn't take that away from anyone."

After he left, I couldn't stand still. I was going to Traesha. I was really going to Traesha. Thank the gods. I thought of all my mom's faraway looks and stories and pain. There was a chance I could go get it back for her. I noticed I was wringing my hands and shook them out. We had so little time. Today was Firstday. By tonight we should reach the forest of Traesha, leaving us only until the night of Thirday to travel through the forest and get ourselves into position. In that time I had to get Sam's trust and work out any issues in the plan. I had to make sure Mesa and I were properly disguised. I had to avoid being distracted by the sights of Traesha and ready to meet the queen.

A week ago I hadn't even been made commander. If I could go from there to here in so little time, in three days I could be finished with this mission successfully and be the queen's ally. At least, I told myself this was the case.

Voices approached. I rushed to the corner to be out of sight when they opened the doors. In my excitement, I skipped and nearly slammed loudly into the wall. I let out a sigh of relief when I stopped in time. The small show of control felt like a good omen.

Everyone climbed in and took their seats, pointedly not looking in my direction. Hinze was last and pulled the doors together to hide me more when his sister approached to say goodbye.

"Remember, you are not to trust any of the Bellovians. I don't care if they speak Trish or Detonian or what. Make sure no one can even touch you." She pitched her voice lower so only Hinze, and I, could hear. "I wouldn't even trust the Trish people you meet up there. We need their alliance, but that doesn't mean they'll understand they need it too. Who knows how much the Bellovians have changed them? Get the queen on our side first and foremost. Bring her back to Helsa so Father can convince her to maintain the alliance. He has a plan. Don't mess this up, Hinze."

"Much love, Chelsa," Hinze replied. "Take care of yourself." He slammed the doors and pounded on them twice to let Sam know to leave.

Lilah sat closest to me. "How was your time in solitary?" she asked in a whisper. I was surprised by the teasing gleam in her eyes. Maybe even a hint of guilt for landing me there.

"Better than my time with Brea." Lilah laughed, a sound pleasantly low and full. Hinze smiled at us and buckled himself into the seat across from me.

We drove for hours, flying down the road at a speed that had the engine whining. We stopped briefly to relieve ourselves, Hinze leading me out the side of the transport so Sam wouldn't see. We nearly left Brea when Sam started the transport back up in a hurry. Her shouts from the trees barely stopped Mesa from shutting the doors on her. I appreciated his urgency.

When Londe sent Hinze word that we were stopping again, he turned to me with an encouraging smile. "I think we're far enough away now. Sam won't make us turn back to take you to Chelsa."

"You better be right," I said. "We don't have time for that kind of drama."

"Don't worry, dear." The endearment made me blush. It sounded strange coming from his young face. Impossible not to notice. I looked down to ignore the looks I got when the others heard it, something squirming tight in my stomach.

Londe opened the back doors for us to a wall of trees like those at the Front. No, not like the Front. I realized with a jolt they were familiar because they were just like the trees in my dreams. I frowned up at them and reminded myself I was awake. My mind floated, displaced.

"What's this?" Sam asked, catching sight of me and pulling my attention away from the forest of my subconscious.

Hinze grabbed my arm, making me weightless and untouchable. "She's coming. Go back and tell Chelsa if you want, we'll be continuing on to Traesha."

Sam turned to Londe. "Inform the king at once!"

Londe crossed his arms. "Not happening. I've been coordinating with the Bellovian rebels for hours. The plan is already in motion. Nothing is compromising it."

"*She's* going to compromise it! I can't risk the queen—"

"You wouldn't even know she was alive if not for me!" I broke in.

Sam turned to me, yellow eyes burning with anger. "And how did you know? From the commanders in the army you fought for? The very commanders who murdered the queen's grandfather and captured her?"

"And what would you know of it? Shouldn't you have been there to protect her? I thought you were a *magsai*."

Sam's knuckles turned white where he gripped the hilt of his sword. I itched to step out of Hinze's grip and test myself. I pushed down the Bellovian desire.

Fisher stepped forward. "We trust Finley. She has every right to be here."

"This is ridiculous!" Sam went to get back in the transport, but Hinze touched its side and Sam's hand passed right through.

"I will leave you here to run after us or to my father.

Finley is coming. This is not a negotiation." When Hinze spoke like a prince it was a powerful thing.

The anger was still there, but I could see Sam relenting. Hinze started to remove his hand from the transport.

"Wait!" I stepped forward. "You'll also teach me everything you can until we get to Traesha. I want to learn to control my speed. And use a sword."

"You will not touch this blade."

"Fine. But teach me to control my skips or you won't be coming. I want to really help. Your queen is worth this request."

Sam glowered from me to Hinze. The prince kept his hand firmly on the transport and met Sam's glare. Finally, the *magsai* blew out a breath.

"Fine. When we stop for the night I will give you a lesson. It'll be easier for you once we reach Traesha. And do not pretend to know anything about my queen."

Hinze smiled and removed his hand from the transport. Sam wrenched open the door, got in and slammed it behind him, so quickly I could feel the effort it took my eyes to follow the movement. Hinze jumped next to me, he hadn't seen Sam move at all. Soon we were back on the road and one step closer.

We stopped next at the end of the road. The valley to Traesha. Stepping out of the transport, we were greeted by a surreal view. On the other side of the road Florian trees grew close together, a wall protecting the entrance to the valley. Mountains rose on either side, their height giving me a sense of vertigo as I tilted my head to take them in. Kissing the trees like smoke, clouds drifted high above. I could easily imagine climbing the mountain to their height. I never knew it was possible to touch the sky. The thought filled me with hope, making my throat tight. I was so far from the oppressing flat cold of Vichi. No wonder my mother passed the years there with her eyes full of distant dreams.

Our packs were unloaded in silence, all of us pausing every few moments to look at the breathtaking view. We left the transport behind and walked into the hush of the forest. For a time, it was only the sound of twigs snapping and our breathing. Birds called. A trickling clear stream. These trees were far more welcoming than the ones along the Front. Like I used to in my dreams, I relaxed under their presence.

I found myself walking next to Londe. His face was unfocused in a way that suggested he was communicating with someone far away. When he tripped on a rock and returned his attention, he caught me staring.

"How does it work?" I asked.

"Picture in your mind's eye that we are talking. With closed lips—that usually keeps people from speaking their half of the conversation out loud. But still, imagine we are speaking or you might let more thoughts come across than you intend. The visual you create is the invitation I need to communicate."

"Now?"

"Why not?"

I gave him a skeptical look, then flexed my imagination, doing what he said.

"See? It isn't hard." Londe's voice sounded clearly in my mind. I stumbled and lost the image. I watched Londe's eyes refocused on me, amused now. I tried again.

"Is it hard for you?" I asked.

"Only at far distances. It's been nice as we approach the rebels. I can finally talk with him without straining myself."

"Who is him?"

204

"I communicate mostly with one rebel. The others are wary of letting me in their heads, and my presence must be welcome or people can dispel me easily like you did just then. If I force my presence, it can be a painful experience."

The thought made me shudder. *"How long have you been in contact with the rebels?"*

"Two years. I've been Hinze's messenger since we were twelve, though. My family often works alongside important people, passing messages along. When we started finding the notes carried by the rebels to the Front, we sent messages back and established communication."

"Notes?"

"Yes. It isn't often, but sometimes messages are found with the bodies along the Front describing the resistance forming in Vichi. Usually with people from the Squalor. Most of the rebels come from there."

My steps faltered. I thought about the kids who could barely run a mile that first day at base. Maybe I was just imagining it now, but some of them walked away with steely looks in their eyes when Silken discontinued their training. I wondered what they carried with them when they met their fates at the Front. I thought of Rennie's determined glares, her shock at making it so far in training. I felt the hatred I'd clung to for all Bellovians slip once again.

"That's amazing."

"They are." I severed the mental image I held to look at Londe now. The fondness of his smile was genuine. I returned it, glad to find someone else who valued the people of Bellovi who deserved it.

～

WE HOPED to reach the trees of Traesha before nightfall and set our pace accordingly. The setting sun illuminated the leaves with an orange glow. I felt a strange sensation in my gut. The smell rolling off the trees was intoxicating, sharp and familiar. They had almost doubled in size from the trees we saw when we first entered the forest. I realized the deep red brown of the bark was not due to the sunset. These were different trees entirely. The grass changed from sparse and gravelly to thick and green despite growing in the shadows. Magic. The breeze was as gentle as a welcoming smile. My heart thrilled. I was in Traesha.

The leaves rustled above us, sounding like incoherent whispering. Fisher froze in his stride when he heard it. Savha smiled at him and took his hand to urge him on. "The trees are always whispering nonsense," she said in a low voice. I could tell from her smile how important it was to her that Fisher was finally in Traesha. Her memories of this place consisted of slavery, death, and a narrow escape, yet even so she stared up at the trees with the fondness of a loved one.

The humid air carried the smell of home. My mind swam with memories of my mother, the warmth of lavender clinging to her shirt every time she held me close and sang, *He sings the forest song, the trees whisper along.* As soon as I thought the words, the whispers shifted. Their volume rose and the birds in their branches whistled the melody as if they'd plucked it from my mind. I stumbled in surprise.

A memory surfaced that I hadn't thought about in years: *"There is nothing in this world like the forest protecting Traesha, Finley,"* my mother whispered, leaning in close. *"The gods made it for us with loving care,* fisha grens. *I dream of its music. Some say the trees can read the stars. Some say they read our hearts and understand our futures. Some say the dead we bury among their roots speak through them. Others still believe they whisper the words of Tash. Wherever the predictions come from, the trees speak directly to few people, fewer even than those with true speed. But we all listen."*

I wanted to be alone, to bask in the presence of the ancient trees uninterrupted. I wanted to ask them every question I'd ever had. Why did I feel the need to return to Vichi even more now that I was finally here? Why was the Florian forest so familiar? Where did my haunting, reoccurring Command Hall dream come from? Why couldn't I share my name? What was my mother hiding? I closed my eyes and listened.

Go and see, singer. Go and see. I froze. The trees formed clear words. The hissing tones of the Trish language made more sense than ever when the leaves whispered softly.

I hurried to catch up when Hinze glanced back at me, the only one to notice I stopped. I found a place next to Fisher and Savha where they walked hand in hand.

The queen. The queen. The trees hissed.

We're going to get her, I told them back in my mind. I looked around, but no one else seemed to understand the trees' words. The branches shook with an urgency. *She's at the celebration,* I found myself assuring them. *We're going to get her.*

The trees weren't satisfied with my answer. The song they picked out of my thoughts continued at a faster tempo until the birds whistling it suddenly took off with a ruffle of feathers. I caught Sam looking at me but couldn't read his expression.

"They don't feel it," Fisher marveled. We lagged behind the group. "Traesha only calls to its people. It's a magic we were gifted when they were gifted with abilities. The land, the people, and the royal family... My parents tried to explain it to me, but I didn't get it until now. It feels like... like..." He searched for the word.

"Belonging." Savha sighed and leaned in closer to him. Fisher smiled, nodded, and pressed a kiss to her temple. I couldn't have agreed more.

The forest woke my senses. I hadn't even known they'd been deadened. I could hear and breathe and move easier. The land released some reserve of strength suppressed during my cold life of hiding. If I started to run, I had little doubt it would be the fastest I had ever gone. The land was magic. It was the power and warmth of my mother's arms. *I* was magic and power and the heat of energy.

We set up camp. I went straight to Sam when the others were settled. "I'm ready for my lesson."

Sam sighed and beckoned for me to follow him deeper into the forest. "You feel it then? How the land calls upon our gifts?" he said once we were a distance away.

I nodded, wondering when he decided to believe I was Trish. "Yes, but I still need control. The power here won't help me when I'm in Vichi." The leaves above shuddered.

"You plan to return to Vichi?" He was instantly suspicious.

"I..." I frowned. Why had I said that? Of course I didn't plan to go to Vichi. I made myself stop rubbing my chest. "No... I really don't. I misspoke. I meant Floria, I guess. The queen will have to go there to speak with the king."

"And why would she take you?"

"Because I'm gifted!" I cringed at the words, it sounded like I was bragging and whining at the same time. "She must need new *magsai*."

Sam lifted an eyebrow. "You really think you'd qualify?"

"Why do you think I want you to teach me?"

He laughed a bit. We walked in silence while I struggled to swallow my anger. But I did swallow it. I still had so many questions and needed him happy with me enough to answer them.

"What about the *resa magsai*?" I cringed when the question brought back memories of my nightmare.

"What do you mean?"

"Do you think they're alive?"

Sam frowned. "They could be. For as liberally as the Bellovians slaughtered us, they did not kill many children during the initial invasion."

"So, shouldn't we look for them? Ask around for someone the queen's age?"

"No." Sam pushed forward and I had to hurry to keep up. It was strange being slower than someone.

"Why not?" I put on a burst of speed and stopped in front of Sam, hands planted on my hips. The stance reminded me of my mother during her stubborn moments and I felt a pang of homesickness. I pushed the feeling away. "Isn't the bond between the *resa* and queen a source of the people's power?"

"It is."

"So why wouldn't we look for the *resa magsai*?" The struggle to keep my frustration from my tone was getting the better of me.

Sam took a moment to answer, studying me. He was only a bit taller than me and I straightened my back under his gaze. "Because the bond will lead the *resa magsai* to the queen. We won't have to look for them. They'll find her."

"Why haven't they yet?"

"The queen is just coming into her Trish abilities. Therefore, so is the *resa magsai*. The bond exists before their abilities set in, yes, but it will be strong enough to bring the two together once they fully develop."

I considered this. It did make sense. "Then once the *resa magsai* finds the queen, the people will be stronger?"

Sam sighed. "I don't know. The triangle has never been broken before, so while I can say I've felt weaker since the invasion, I can't say returning all the pieces will magically make us strong again. It may return us to our former strength, but even then, few had true Trish speed. I can't say it will be enough."

"What *will* be enough?"

Sam kept walking. My stomach fell as I scrambled to keep up. "Do you think we can save Traesha?" More silence. "Sam, what will be enough?" I ran and stopped in front of him again. He glared down at me.

"It will be enough for me to save my queen. To stand by her side. To do whatever she determines needs to be done with whatever power we can give her." He stepped around me.

"That's not an answer."

"It's the only answer I can give."

I huffed and followed him until he stopped at a small clearing. He started right in with his lesson. "Our gifts, like our speed before skipping develops, are natural. Born of instincts. But every instinct can be honed with practice. You need to place deliberate thought into skipping, yet let it happen without instruction."

"Well, that's very helpful." I couldn't keep the sarcasm from my tone.

Try, singer. Try.

I craned my neck to look up at the trees again. Sam caught the movement and shock widened his eyes. "You understand them?"

Ignoring him, I turned away and looked through the trees. "Won't I hit something if I try to skip here?"

Have no fear, singer. Have no fear.

"No. Your reflexes will quicken along with everything else." It was hard to listen to them both at the same time.

I started off at a jog, Sam at my side. He was more patient now as he coached me, looking up at the trees every few steps and watching me close between glances.

"Stop concentrating so hard. Remember how it felt to skip before. Lose yourself in the memory of that moment. How did your body move? How did you breathe? What emotions spurred you?"

I let my mind relax. The trees surrounded me. A deer jumped and ran to our right and I raced it. I made myself remember the rush of my few skips. The lingering warmth of Oken's skin in my palm that first time. The adrenaline. The shock of seeing Dani's life cut down.

I thought about the queen. I was doing this for her. To save this land I already loved so much it pained me. I didn't even notice at first when Sam stopped talking, the forest a blur around me. I whooped and let out a laugh. Sam was looking at me funny when I glanced at him, but I couldn't care less faced with the freedom and rush of skipping.

THAT NIGHT I couldn't sleep. Traesha's energy crackled under my skin. Skipping hadn't eased it at all. In fact, I was even more restless and alert after the last hour I spent working with Sam. I was nearly overwhelmed by my new senses. I could smell everything, hear everything, feel everything. The taste of the forest's power tingled on my lips. Savha and Fisher tossed and turned across the camp from me and I knew they felt it too.

Even so, there was a pressing need distracting me, taking my thoughts far away. I worried for my parents. My mother hiding in our small home. The long hours my father passed at Command Hall. The pull in my chest toward Vichi had become a physical ache. When sleep did come, my nightmare plagued me so entirely I woke abruptly ten steps away from my bedroll. My body had been walking in Vichi's direction, completely outside of my control.

I felt the first thrill of fear for the power this place held.

CHAPTER 18

In the morning we sat in a close circle and ate from the cheeses and bread we carried with us. Even with few hours of sleep, my body felt oversaturated with energy. My knees bounced as I explained my plan to Sam.

"It's relatively simple. This celebration has never been attacked and as far as they're aware, no Florians know they have the queen or that she's here." I explained each of our positions, briefly debated with Savha if Sam should pose with her and Fisher as a slave. We ruled it out, deciding his speed could be used elsewhere, especially if it freed up Hinze to use his powers.

"So I bring Lilah to the front of the room, she captures them, and what?" Sam asked.

"Not the entire room. The rebels have assured us they are in a position to make a signal so the Trish know to look away and avoid Lilah's power. Then, with their help, we tie up the commanders. By the time Lilah's hold gives out, we'll outnumber the untied Bellovians and have the queen's voice to rally the people."

Sam's expression narrowed. "I don't like it. No Bellovians should have access to our plan. How do we know these rebels are trustworthy?"

Now Londe's expression matched Sam's. "They are. I know my contact far better than I know you. He'll be giving the signal."

"We're leaving too much up to chance. Too much relies on people who have already been used far too much these last eighteen years. It's too rushed."

My chest squeezed at the thought of stopping. I needed this mission. I needed to get to the queen. There were risks, but looking at Hinze, I knew we were both willing to take them. Silken could be there, or one of my father's coworkers, but I could go unnoticed and, with Hinze, untouchable. "Of course our plan is rushed. The celebration is tomorrow night! It's the only time we will know exactly where the queen is. With the Florians' abilities and the rebellion's inside knowledge, it will work."

"You mean it has to work."

I tipped my chin up and met Sam's strange yellow eyes.

"Alright, one more time," Garris broke in. Even though his role was healer on standby, he still seemed the most determined to get the plan straight in his head, especially with the changes from Sam's presence.

I explained once more, slowly and making eye contact with each member of the plan as I went. I was slipping into lessons learned during strategy and leadership classes in school and didn't know how to feel about that. "Tomorrow night, we'll be sneaking into the celebration. Fisher and Savvy will be posed as slaves. Savvy has filled Fisher in about everything he should expect and how he should act. Once the signal is sounded, Sam and Lilah will go in from the back entrance and skip to the stage right when Mesa and I draw the crowd's attention. Hinze,

Garris, Brea, and Londe will be above the ballroom in the kitchens."

"It's a huge space," Sam cut in. "With many pantries to hide in. The bread room will put you along the back wall. There are stairs close by too, in case you get separated."

I nodded. "That would be a good place for you to coordinate and drop in if needed. But your primary purpose will be warning the Trish working in the kitchens. Try to get them out or ready to help right before the signal. Just don't tip the commanders off."

I went over a few minor details, but there wasn't much more we could plan in the time we had. We packed up and finished hiking the valley in silence. The trees kept whispering about the queen, our anticipation evidently contagious. I expected to find Bellovian guards patrolling, but we saw no one. The trees stirred when I wondered about it. The forest darkened briefly.

Unwelcome. Unwelcome. A branch whipped out above me, apart from the wind or any other natural plant activity. I didn't fight a smug smile. The land wasn't dead. It was still fighting, and it welcomed me. Never had I felt more secure in my Trish heritage.

I was sad to leave the cover of the trees when we reached the edge of the forest. We entered one of the sprawling farms that fed the people of Bellovi. The ones who could afford it, that is. The field was stiff with rows of corn stalks. Most of them were even taller than Londe. Many tinged with brown. They rustled together with a dry sound so different to the lively trees we'd just left. We crept down one of the rows, listening hard for slaves and Bellovian guards. It was easy to avoid them with four Trish on alert.

I walked at the end of the line. Sam gestured for us to

move over a row again when he heard something. Everyone linked up, holding hands so Hinze could help us slip through the wall of corn silently. I hesitated. Savha narrowed her eyes at me when I didn't take her hand. She had to stretch her arms out when Fisher didn't realize we'd stopped and jumped through without us. I was listening close to what Sam had heard to make him turn.

"Please!" a girl's voice. Savha's head snapped in her direction, but Fisher pulled at her arm and with a fearful look she went through the wall of corn without me.

"Finley, don't," she whispered from the other side.

A crack sounded. I couldn't stand still any longer. The girl ahead cried out and I started down the rows.

"Finley, no!" Fisher hissed from the other side of the rows. I caught his eye through the stalks and squared my shoulders before I skipped forward, away from them. When I reached the voices, I crashed through the brittle stalks.

The Bellovian swore, spinning away from the Trish girl on the ground. She was covered in dirt, her silver hair in a ragged braid down her back, lip bleeding. Her lavender eyes widened in terror.

"What are you doing here?" The Bellovian reached for her gun, but my black braid made her hesitate.

"You're needed..." I couldn't think of a lie. I was completely out of my element.

She reached for her earpiece and I skipped forward. But after only one lesson, I still lacked control. We collided and fell in a tangle of limbs, the Trish girl scrambling away with a scream. I winced at the sound, sure it would draw more attention.

"Go!" I hissed at her in Trish. Confusion masked the girl's face but understanding cleared the Bellovian's. She roared and I was still so thrown off by my wild skip and the girl's scream that the Bellovian succeeded in freeing her arm. I whipped my head to the side in time to avoid her first blow. I gritted my teeth and got my feet under me, bucking the woman's bulk over my head and twisting violently to end up on top. We rolled a few times, my movements more uncertain than ever as I feared slipping into Trish speed and losing my rhythm. The Trish girl took off running, the patter of her feet flooding me with relief.

The woman managed to hook her arm around my throat. I gagged and snapped my head to the side. Pain exploded in my ear as I hit her jaw, and her grip slipped enough for me to get her arm over my head. With a grunt, I threw an elbow into her solid stomach. She wheezed, but continued to fight. I spun and hit the same spot with my fist, this time putting enough speed behind the blow that she doubled up, gasping for air. I drew my head back and rammed her with a headbutt hard enough to knock her unconscious. When I was sure she wouldn't be waking up for a good while, I rolled away, breathing heavily. From my place on the ground next to her, I plucked her earpiece out.

I tucked it into the ear that wasn't hot and throbbing and listened closely, exhaling only when I was certain the thing was off. I rolled over my shoulder and onto my feet. With two stomps the earpiece was left shattered in the dirt. I looked up to see the slave girl had returned, trembling as she reached for the sack of corn she'd dropped. At her side stood a Trish boy with matching lavender eyes. He looked about nineteen. Angry and alert. The right age to be the *resa magsai*. The chances were slim, but still I wondered, heart racing.

"Who are you?" He kept his voice hushed, Trish words a breathed whisper.

"We're here to..." I faltered, unsure what to tell them.

How much hope I should give. His eyes narrowed in distrust. The tattered black clothes he wore hung from his shoulders as if too tired to hold form any longer, yet his back was straight as he took me in. Then his eyes dropped to the limp Bellovian at my feet.

"Whatever you're trying, it won't work. You'll only make things harder for us. Leave now, before they know you're here."

"We're here to help. We *can* help."

The boy's eyes widened. I followed his gaze to see Savha, Hinze, and Sam come through the corn. Sam looked furious. Shock paled Savha's features.

"Trace?"

"What in Mags's name are you doing back here? Didn't you ruin enough trying to escape in the first place?" The boy lifted a hand and I fought a cringe seeing the mangled stumps that had been the last two fingers on his right hand. "One for helping you. One for helping your father. They made me dig his grave right after they cut them off."

Sahva's face crumpled. "Trace..."

Hinze's grip on her arm kept her from moving forward. "We're here to help now. You can aid us by spreading the word. We have a plan to free the slaves at the celebration and subdue the commanders."

Trace laughed. The girl still next to him kept glancing from him to us so fast I imagined she must be making herself dizzy.

"What? With the last *magsai*, a few Trish and an impulsive Bellovian? Where's your army, Florian? Where are your weapons? Where is the king's might if you're finally acting on our alliance?"

"There are more of us."

"Hidden here with you? If they can hide so easily, it will

not be enough. They won't blink before they kill you all. If you truly wanted to help us, you would have picked any other time to come. A time when the most powerful and cruel commanders weren't gathered. If you cared about us slaves, you wouldn't be making a spectacle of this mission."

"We're looking for the queen," I said. My hope that he might be *resa magsai* drew the words from me and earned me a sharp enough look that my hope grew.

The girl gasped. "The queen?" The wonder lighting her features died when the boy glared at her.

"The queen is dead." His voice was too flat.

"No, she's not," I said. "She's been captured by the commanders. They're bringing her to the celebration."

A hint of a smile lifted the girl's lips. She clasped her hands in front of her, fingers blackened with dirt and her nails short and broken.

The boy wasn't convinced. "If this is true, I fail to see how it benefits us. She has spent her life hiding from her duty while we all suffer here. The land is dying. Our people are dying. And she hid like a coward. What will finding her change?"

Sam rushed forward and I lunged, grabbing his arm to stop him. I'm not sure why I did. The boy's words filled my own ears with a dull ringing. I clenched my jaw.

"The queen is a child. Her Trish abilities only now forming—"

"We're all just children." The boy turned away.

"Trace, listen!" Savha stepped forward.

He stopped her with a glare. "We're all just children and now Wilsa and I are behind on our quotas. Excuse me, but I'm in no hurry to lose another finger."

"Please! At least spread the word! Let the Trish working the ball know to look for us," Savha tried.

He laughed and reached to pick up his sack. The girl adjusted her own on her shoulder, eyes downcast. "Kill and hide the Bellovian unless you want Wilsa punished. You owe us that much for what you're going to bring down on us with your foolish plan. Until we see you next," he said, his words bitter.

Savha had frustrated tears in her eyes as she clutched Hinze's hand. I looked down at the Bellovian lying in the dirt at my feet.

"Clean up your mess," Sam spat at me, ripping his arm out of my grip. All progress we'd made in the forest gone. I was an impulsive and cruel Bellovian once more. My hands shook as I knelt at the Bellovian's head, her long black braid the same as my own. Only Hinze stayed to see what I would do. He came forward and knelt across from me.

"I hit her so hard. She won't wake up anytime soon. Maybe it would be okay if we left her," I whispered.

Hinze looked down at the woman, then up at me. He kept those metallic, glimmering hazel eyes trained on my face as he laid a hand on the woman's body. With his ability he sank her into the ground, all the way up to his shoulder. My chest tightened, choking me as I imagined the woman's death when he let go and climbed to his feet.

"This mission cannot fail," he said in his accented Trish.

I took the hand he offered. I glanced back before we crossed the wall of stalks to rejoin the team. The only thing marking where the woman had been was the broken earpiece in the dirt. I shivered and Hinze's hand tightened around my own. He was shaking too.

～

WE REACHED a small neighborhood just outside Shalta, the main city of Traesha. We were slightly elevated and Shalta was close enough that I could see the stark white of the three castle towers in the distance. The ocean stretched out beyond. Savha came up next to me and took in the sight, squeezing my hand.

Hinze took the lead and snuck us through the streets, pausing every once in a while to walk through a wall or fence and check the coast was clear. It made my stomach drop to see him use his powers now, after watching the Bellovian sunk so easily into the ground.

The homes seemed deserted. Fisher commented as much to Savha. With a flat voice she explained, "Most of the slaves and Bellovians are already in Shalta preparing for the celebration. Or they're still out in the fields."

We found a house big enough for us on the edge of town with a good view of the city. Mesa worked the lock and we stepped inside. The wall held the Bellovi flag depicting two crossed hammers. Red against black. Those were the favored weapons of the Bellovian people before the time of guns. Now that I knew Bellovian strength was a Florian ability, the weapon choice made more sense than ever. The furniture was sparse, the flag the only decoration. The family living here would be in Shalta until the celebrations were over, so we set up camp for the night and raided the cabinets for food.

Mesa and I ended up sharing one of the rooms upstairs. She was quiet as we each claimed one of the narrow beds. She was quiet all the time, really. She wasn't as close to Hinze as Londe, Garris, and Fisher. She always stood in the shadow of Lilah and Brea's friendship, their abilities, and their boisterous confidence. I liked Mesa more because of this, recognizing someone else who lived on the outskirts.

"You said you were from a town on the coast? That you had to learn to fight off the Detonians?" I asked. I had bathed down the hall and was drying my hair with a scratchy brown towel I found. In the dim lighting of the room I didn't worry about my roots, but tomorrow I would cover them, just in case. Luckily, we had found extra black makeup that Bellovians used. I would color in my roots and use it to darken Mesa's hair, blending us in better.

"Yes, partly. Detonians rarely come to my town. Only when they send an ambassador and need to dock there, but even so they usually go to Ross Port, further to the south. Detono has control of the waters and an uneasy peace with Floria, so many of us sail there and spy on them for a living. We earn most of our income that way, but without abilities we learned to defend ourselves when we go over. They don't have abilities on the island either, so we're usually fine with just our skills at fighting and shooting. We've developed our fighting technique for generations and start training when we're kids, even the girls. We make better spies. Less suspicious." Pride lifted her chin and I saw in her eyes years of pushing to prove herself against the men around her.

"But most Florians don't bother to learn to fight at all, right? Even those without abilities?"

"Right. And unless they go to the Front, they don't bother learning to handle a gun either."

I shook my head, unable to imagine such a world. Fights broke out regularly in Vichi, at school, in the streets, during training sessions. Bruises, scars, wrapped fists, and broken noses were so common I rarely noticed them. Everyone pushed their bodies to the max and enjoyed it. I loved the feel of a solid punch or the whoosh of air when I flipped out of a hold to make a kick more than I probably should. Much more than any Trish person would.

"But how do they defend themselves?"

"If you have an ability, you use it. If you don't, you thank the elites for protecting you."

"Don't they feel helpless?"

Mesa's short hair fell over her shoulder as she tilted her head. "The first time I went to Helsa it was with my father to trade secrets. There is a clear distinction between the gifted and those who aren't, but for the most part I think people are fine with the circumstances. Since Bellovi fractioned off, those with abilities pride themselves on being fair and honest, like they want to prove the Bellovians overreacted. They try not to let us without gifts feel too inferior. And without gifts, most Florians have worked to hone different talents. The art and music in the city are incredible and the gifted get none of the credit. It's understood they spend most of their time practicing their abilities and keeping us safe. Some take advantage of the power, sure. I can't look at your arm and think everything in Floria is just fine." We both glanced to the scar in the shape of the igniter's hand wrapped around my bicep.

"People are too poor to care about art in Bellovi," I said.

"I hope when the war is over they won't be too proud to accept the benefits of living under Florian rule then."

"You don't believe they have a chance of winning?"

"I've seen terrifying gifts since Hinze befriended me. The elites train at the palace often. There's nothing in this world like them. If the Florians wanted, they could burn Bellovi to the ground. I can't imagine how a people could fight that kind of power." Mesa looked out the window and I followed her gaze. The rows of corn were mesmerizing. The forest beyond stood tall. The energy I felt among the

KELLY COLE

trees was still here but muted in this Bellovian occupied home.

Everything I'd learned since leaving Bellovi wasn't adding up. Hinze had made the war sound so simple, but I couldn't imagine it was as easy as establishing a border for the old Florian kings. Not when the Bellovians' strength was so formidable. Maybe destroying the railroad and cutting off resources should have been enough to end things, but the Bellovians have always found a way to keep the fight going. They killed a Florian queen with only the barest shift at the Front as a consequence. It didn't make sense when the Florians had the power to stamp them out this whole time. I suspected there was something else the Bellovians had. Something that made their strength more of a threat.

"Are you nervous for tomorrow?" I asked.

Mesa laughed a little. "I've been training my whole life for exactly this sort of mission. I'm just nervous you'll mess us up."

I smiled back at her ruefully. "I've trained my whole life to act like a Bellovian. You might find they're a little harder to blend in with than the Detonians."

"I guess we'll just have to wait and see who the better asset is." Mesa stood and began readying for bed, which really just involved her removing the knives she had hidden on her person. When the sixth one hit the nightstand, I smiled at the rush of competition.

"I guess so."

～

"Are we ready?" Hinze asked. His eyebrows knotted over his conflicted eyes as he looked down at me.

We were hiding in an alley between two brightly painted buildings in the middle of Shalta. I had tried to take in the city as much as possible when we hurried through the streets, but running with Hinze through buildings hadn't provided much of a view. Although I now knew most of the businesses and homes this close to the castle were taken over by Bellovians or left abandoned. With horrible clarity, I took in every Bellovian flag and realized just how many of the Trish were killed during the invasion. The fury I held between my shoulder blades hadn't eased all morning and a cold dread coiled tight in my stomach. How did a country come back from something like this?

Like Mesa and I, Hinze was dressed entirely in black. He stood ready to slip through the walls and be where he was needed. He'd already gotten Brea, Lilah, Sam, and Garris into their respective positions. At Sam's directions, he'd slipped them into the walls, straight into supply closets and empty rooms. Londe was similarly dressed next to him, his eyes unfocused while he communicated with the rest of our crew and the rebels stationed inside. He looked exhausted. I hadn't seen his eyes focus once today. He and Hinze remained hand in hand so Londe could keep up contact all morning while Hinze guided him around without letting him run into anything. Hinze was starting to look strained, too. This worried me. They both still had so much to do today. We all did.

"Ready as we'll ever be." Mesa finished checking the straps around the knife at her calf and stood, letting her shapeless black dress fall back into place and brushing off her hands.

"Just create a big enough distraction to get everyone's attention up front," Hinze said. "Lilah will handle the rest.

But her power doesn't work unless people are looking at her."

"We know," Mesa said. She and I shared a look.

Hinze wasn't assured. "But wait for the signal. If you do something before Lilah's in position—"

We shared the look again. "I came up with this plan. We got it," I said.

"Well, I'm not sure what the signal is yet. The rebel in charge of setting it off hasn't responded. Londe says he's probably just around the commanders and needs to focus, but he said it will be obvious to the Trish. So just make sure you're sure before you act. Lilah has to be ready..."

We were both glaring at Hinze now. I could see he wanted to elaborate even further but went quiet seeing our faces.

Not for long. "Make sure—" he started.

"Hinze. They know." Londe came out of his daze for the first time today long enough to say those words.

Hinze blew out a breath and handed us the forged invitations he'd gotten from behind a loose brick in the wall where the rebel left it. When he handed me mine, he held on for longer than necessary, his eyes lingering on my face. I felt an itch of irritation in response to the worry in his hazel eyes. He wasn't nearly as anxious about letting Mesa go in. Did he think I couldn't handle this?

I turned from Hinze and checked Mesa's appearance one last time, making sure I hadn't missed something obvious. Her short hair was pulled back and tied at the nape of her neck. It wasn't a braid, but I doubted she would draw much attention. I had darkened her hair and my roots and rimmed our eyes with intense black. This was the only makeup Bellovian people wore. It gave us a fierce look and ferocity was always in style in Bellovi.

"Worry about yourself," I said when I realized Hinze was *still* staring. "Mesa and I know what we're doing."

Hinze forced a smile.

Londe's attention focused on me. "Stay strong." The Bellovian phrase sounded only slightly ironic. "Be good," he said to Mesa with a wink, making her grin. Then to Hinze, "Everyone is in position. We need to move."

Hinze caught my eye again. I lifted my chin and narrowed my eyes enough to show just how little I appreciated his concern. Worry was too close to doubt. He shook his head at me, a strained smile playing on his lips, and they slipped into the building on our right.

Excitement fluttered in my stomach. I pulled at my dress, hating it. I'd worn similar outfits to commander events with my father. Many women preferred formal clothing with pants and a nice jacket, but such outfits were more expensive. It wasn't surprising that these dresses were all we could find in the houses we searched. Mesa and I stepped out of the alley and into the line of partygoers. The castle rose up in front of us, tall and elegant. I craned my neck to get a better view of the three white towers. The coned roofs so high above were a dark gold swallowing the light of the moon. On the tip of the middle one, the tallest by far, the Bellovian flag flapped in the breeze coming off the ocean. The two other towers flanked the middle, just set a bit further back. The balconies, glassless windows, and doors were all bordered with the same thick, dark gold. By now I could see shimmering veins of it even running through the white stones of the tower wall like the gray that swirled and streaked through marble.

Three towers of the castle. Three gods: one for love, one for peace, one for strength. Three was a powerful number here. I resisted the urge to trace a triangle in the air and I found myself praying as we neared. *Please, bless our efforts and restore the Trish power tonight. Help us free the queen. I'll complete the triangle; you provide the magic.* I couldn't have said which of the gods I was bargaining with.

The towers were connected at the base by arched open halls. I could see Bellovians walking from the middle tower to the one on the right. My skin crawled watching them strut through our sacred castle, but I kept my blank expression intact.

The low-ranking commander checking invitations at the door barely glanced at ours. As I expected, their guards were down. Nothing had ever gone amiss for them at this celebration. Stepping inside, I caught sight of a slave with a silver braid down her back and for the first time understood what defeat looked like. I sent up another quick prayer, this one to Mags. Our actions tonight needed to be enough motivation for them to fight back. It would take all of us to reclaim Traesha. Each of us needed strength.

Inside, the floor was white tile flecked with yet more gold. The walls were a calming shade of light green bearing paintings so intricate I could lose myself in them. I thought of Jenna and her love of art. Thinking of her reminded me of my Bellovian team, thoughts touching on Oken as they always seemed to. I pushed the memories and worry away. I barely had time to glance up the spiraling staircase wrapping the inside of the first tower before the crowd pushed us down the hall to the ballroom.

The room's grand entrance was an archway resembling two maroon trees joined together by their leaves at the top. Some of the taller Bellovians needed to duck to avoid the golden and green leaves. I saw Savha scurry past in her slave uniform. Tonight couldn't be easy for her. I also thought I saw Dani, but when I looked back the girl had turned her head and I remembered with a painful clench in my chest that Dani was dead. I kept my face blank. Now was not the time to give into emotions. I hadn't realized how easy it had been to hold that memory at bay when surrounded by Trish and Florians. Now, with all the heads of black hair around me, I could only see their soldiers running out of the trees, guns firing without care.

The ballroom itself was like walking into a gold accented forest. The pillars throughout were carved and painted to look like trees, opening at the top to resemble branches. The ceiling was textured to look like a canopy of leaves. The walls were painted with beautiful detail to resemble forest scenes: prancing deer, swooping owls, trickling streams. I focused on that beauty rather than the emotions gathering tighter and tighter in my chest.

My mother had described a Trish ball to me once. She attended when she was my age now, just deemed old enough to be a woman at seventeen. It had been the same week of her first skip and she always smiled at the memories of that time. The very first dance was with some handsome young man. She said they stayed together the whole night. She grabbed my hands and showed me how they danced: twirling me, lifting me in the air, and dipping me close to the ground. A distant, glowing happiness in her eyes the entire time.

I took in the ballroom. How many hours had she spent in this room lost in her own memories? Was the handsome young man she danced with among the slaves lined up against the wall holding a platter of food and drink? Or was he dead like so many others?

The crowd of tall Bellovians shifted enough for me to see a slightly raised platform with another arch of trees over it against the far wall. It was designed for a band to play on, the arches lined in a way that allowed music to carry. Someone started playing the piano there. I jolted to a stop, Mesa crashing into my back. I knew the song, an old Bellovian war ballad.

And only Nico's hands could play so perfectly.

CHAPTER 19

How could I not have imagined him being here? Never even considered the possibility? He'd never worked the celebration before, but there he was. Eyes dimmed and lips pressed tight, he played flawlessly. He couldn't risk his favorite Trish melodies here. Not with so many of us in the crowd.

I felt detached as I straightened, stepping away from Mesa so she could right herself. I was vaguely aware of her glare, but couldn't take my eyes from the front of the room. Nico had dark circles under his eyes. His shoulders were drooped, not pulled straight back in the posture my mother forced him to keep while at a piano bench. He'd lost weight. A lot of weight. I knew my brother well enough to read the depths of his dark eyes from here.

Grief.

"Oh no." My voice was thin. Mesa followed my gaze to the piano. She grabbed my arm and pulled me off to the side roughly enough to finally pull my attention off my brother. A slave approached with drinks. It wasn't until he spoke that I realized it was Fisher.

"What is it?" he asked, holding out the platter and blocking me from the view of the room.

Mesa grabbed each of us a drink and replied out of the corner of her mouth, keeping her eyes on the crowd of Bellovians talking loudly. No one danced. "Yes, care to explain?" she asked.

I swallowed. "It's my brother. Playing the piano. He doesn't... He looks... I think my parents..."

Fisher was nodding before I had to finish. "I'll contact Londe. Hinze will come get you out."

I shook my head and took a deep breath, refusing to mourn before I knew anything for certain. I had to talk to Nico. I took a sip of my drink, the alcohol burning my throat. I let the slight pain center me and cleared the expression from my face.

"No, I'm fine. Let's go."

Mesa narrowed her eyes at me, thinking quickly. Weighing the risk of a breakdown. I met her gaze, concentrating on keeping my mask in place. After a beat, her frown cleared and she nodded. "Keep it together."

I pulled my shoulders back and turned to rejoin the crowd, only to whirl back around.

"Oh, what *now*?" Mesa barely concealed her frustration. Even as I internally panicked, I recognized that fear fueled her narrowed eyes.

I curled my fingers into my chest, using the Bellovian gesture that meant quietly follow without thinking. Mesa got the message and we ducked through the bodies and away from Fisher. I lowered my voice and kept my face angled away from the other side of the room.

"My old commander is here. I don't think he saw me."

"Your... you didn't think to warn us you'd actually know these people?" Mesa was sufficiently angry now. She crossed her arms and looked over my shoulder, searching for anyone watching too close.

I *had* thought about Silken being here. I debated with myself for hours about whether or not I should warn the team. I didn't, though. I was too worried they wouldn't let me come along. And I had to save the queen. This was all that mattered.

Yet my eyes kept going to the devastation on Nico's face. It was all I could do to keep my face clear. I should be looking for Silken or anyone else who may recognize me. I should be looking for our means of causing a distraction.

"Finley! Focus!" I pulled my gaze from the piano. Mesa leaned in close, the fury in her voice tangible. "Did you know he would be here?"

"No, I never imagined Nico—"

"Not your brother, you idiot! Your commander! Did you set us up?"

"No! Well, I knew he was planning to attend. He's the one I heard talking about the queen. I thought there would be too many people... that he wouldn't see me—"

Mesa smiled, but there was no kindness in it. It was a hundred times more terrifying than her glare. "If this mission fails, if anyone so much as cuts themselves, that's on you. And I swear, I will kill you myself." She turned for the front of the room but paused and pointed a finger at my face. "For the record, I'm by far the better asset."

Her threat hung in the air between us, but I felt no fear of her. Not in Traesha, with its power humming in my blood. Not surrounded by Bellovians, their muscles and confidence reminding me of my training. I had bigger concerns than an angry Florian. Silence fell over the room. We turned to see Silken take the stage. Nico sat off to the side, hands resting in his lap, expression empty.

"Welcome, my fellow commanders!" I shifted a bit, ducking out of Silken's sight from the stage. My stomach was in knots. My palms slicked with sweat. It was time. He was going to announce the queen's presence. "This is our eighteenth year celebrating the conquering of this land. While there is cause to celebrate still, I fear Traesha and its people are no longer the prize they once were."

Londe brushed my consciousness. *The rebels say this speech was unplanned. Get into position. Be on your guard.* I returned my focus in time to see Mesa's face go blank while she received the same message. When our eyes met, indecision showed in hers. I nodded, determined and trying to be reassuring. Her look faltered and she gave me a slow nod back. She wasn't going to tell Londe I'd nearly been recognized. Not yet. We began making our way to the front of the room. I kept my face tilted away from the stage.

"We've made much progress in the last year. We've killed a worthless Florian queen..." Silken paused for the cheering. I clenched my fists, hoping Hinze couldn't hear wherever he was. "And we've made some powerful allies."

Mesa's eyes widened. By now we were nearly in position, standing behind the broad shoulders of a couple watching the stage. I saw Mesa's eyes unfocus again, talking to Londe. Was she giving me up? I swallowed my nerves.

"And tonight, we celebrate it all! Including a special reveal I hope you'll enjoy."

I peeked around the Bellovian woman I stood behind. Just in time to see Silken's smile and for his eyes to catch mine. My stomach dropped and it took everything in me not to let my face react. Because he didn't look surprised. Because he looked away after, as though my presence was of little consequence. His dismissal was so much worse than any alarm he could have raised. My hands began to shake and my mind whirled. But I forced in a breath. Whatever he thought of my presence here, he didn't know about the gifted Florians I had brought. How the queen would rally our people against him. He didn't know his people didn't stand a chance. He'd realize soon enough they were outnumbered.

Finley... I don't like what Mesa's telling me.

I let my eyes slide shut and took another breath before responding. All that mattered was getting the queen. Ending Bellovian rule. I let that focus center me as I joined Londe in communicating. *My commander saw me, but there's little he can do to interrupt the plan. He'll fall under Lilah's power like everyone else.*

We have a lot of people here risking their lives. You sure you don't want to fall back?

This is too important. There's a reason we're here risking our lives.

A pause that had my hands sweating. *Alright. We trust you. The signal will sound soon. Take out your commander quickly so he doesn't ruin anything.*

I almost smiled as I came back fully into my mind. This plan would work. It had to work. Mesa's expression was so hard she truly could have passed for a Bellovian. I met her gaze and let her see how determined I was. The plan was set. Hinze was invincible. Sam was a *magsai*. Lilah could render them all blind and useless. I stood up straighter and focused on the conclusion of Silken's speech.

"The reveal will take place in a few moments. I just have to make sure everything is in place."

Mesa and I shared yet another look and Silken stepped off the stage through a side door. It was time. Mesa's fingers curled and straightened with nerves. The celebration resumed around us, conversations loud and growing sloppy the more trays of drinks made their rounds. A man bumped into Mesa and didn't even glance down to apologize.

"No one is paying attention to us," she said.

"We're too small."

"What?"

I sighed and gestured to a group of commanders a few paces away. Nico had started up the music again. Three men were talking to the woman. She stood as tall as any of them. Her dress was sleeveless, showing off the cords of muscles twisting her arms. She had a square chin and a thick layer of black liner around her eyes. Her braid was pulled so tight it lifted her eyebrows. Strapped to her back, the closest decoration the Bellovians had to jewelry, was a *magsai* sword. A trophy claiming she was part of the invasion. A man approached the cluster, two drinks in his hands and looking for an in.

"I told you we would go unnoticed. That's who they're interested in. Imagine the strength of their children."

Mesa frowned. "Our distraction will have to be big."

We went quiet again. Londe said the signal would be soon, but each second dragged. I caught sight of Savha and Fisher making their way among the slaves, whispering words in Trish that earned them looks of distrust or timid hope. I asked Mags to make them listen. Three minutes passed. Mesa could hardly stand still and had finished her drink. She was looking for somewhere to put the empty glass when the song ended.

Nico moved smoothly into the next piece. The mood in the room shifted. He played louder, more boldly. His features were still unreadable, but his back straightened and he regarded the edges of the crowd. His fingers struck out the quick, lively cords of the Trish national anthem. With a wash of shock, I understood his role tonight.

"That's the signal!" I barely refrained from shouting the words. Mesa didn't question me or hesitate. We moved forward as one to the largest commander at the front of the room. I almost backed down when I saw five stripes on his shoulder, but Mesa never slowed. She smashed an elbow down on the commander's forearm, sending this drink crashing to the floor. He roared and lunged at her, but she ducked under his arm and behind him, jabbing her small fist into his side. His face didn't even register the blow. Before he could spin to face her again, I jumped forward and threw a punch at his jaw. My hand snapped forward with blinding speed and my breath momentarily caught when he dropped. He moaned from the ground and I staggered in relief. Not dead.

Mesa and I succeeded. When Lilah and Sam appeared on stage the Bellovians were already looking in her direction. Lilah jumped off the *magsai's* back. I closed my eyes. There was shouting, but Lilah's clap quickly silenced them. When I looked, her face drained of color from the effort of holding the entire room.

It was surreal watching my plan slip from one step to the next. The slaves rushed forward. Savha and Fisher had spread the word to close their eyes when the signal sounded. At the sound of their national anthem, they had done so. Hinze was yelling from the far wall, using his gift to render the whole thing permeable. Slaves who chose to stand their ground began tying up the commanders with anything they could find while the others ran for safety out of the large exit Hinze created. I could see him straining as much as Lilah. Their powers wouldn't hold for longer. It had to be enough.

I whipped around, looking to the front of the room again for Nico. My breath caught. Silken had returned through the stage door, his gun aimed at Lilah. I saw Sam shift, but the commander already pulled the trigger. Sam only succeeded in ruining the commander's aim when he grabbed Silken's arm. The bullet hit Lilah in the stomach when she turned, not her heart.

If it had felt surreal thinking my plan was succeeding, that was nothing compared to watching it fail.

Mesa cried out and began shoving her way through the crowd, but the commanders were stumbling, their eyes blinking slowly as Lilah struggled to hold them. Only about a third had been tied when she collapsed to the floor on the stage. Chaos erupted. Some began fighting with the Trish slaves. Even more silver heads were running to the exit now while Hinze held it open for them. I could see how badly he wanted to move. Garris and Londe ran to the stage through the side door. I heard gunfire behind me and Hinze ran toward the sound without a thought. I took a few steps in that direction, but another shout from Mesa turned my attention back to the stage. Slaves crashed into the solid wall with desperate cries.

"No!" My protest was lost in the escalating noise of the crowd as commanders broke free of their bindings. My vision focused in on Nico, making his way toward Lilah. He would give himself up trying to help her. I ran in his direction. Silken broke out of Sam's hold, throwing the *magsai* against the wall. I cringed at the volume of the thud. Nico's steps faltered, unsure who to go to, but Garris reached Lilah. Sam pushed onto his elbows, shaking his head to clear it and wincing. I remembered him saying he was weaker without the queen. Watching the Trish run and pushing through the chaos myself, my desperation to find her spiked. Where was she? Should I find her to help the slaves fight back or stand and fight?

A commander took the choice from me. They recognized me from the start of the attack and took advantage of my hesitation. Their practiced fist struck out while I looked toward the stage and hit so hard I fell to one knee. I quickly recovered and kicked out, but by then I'd attracted attention from too many. I fought the crowd, ducking and skipping with little control. At one point a man ran at me, lifting me off the ground with his shoulder. I didn't even feel fear as I was afforded a glimpse of the stage. Garris was pulling Lilah to her feet. Relief flooded me right as a fist connected with my nose.

A crunch. Blood. A rush of shocking pain. This was what it took for me to realize my training did not prepare me for the realities of war. But it was happening all around me. Frustration welled as I finally got a grip and was able to flip out of the man's hold. Another kick and a few punches and I momentarily cleared the area surrounding me. I sucked in a breath and turned toward the stage to help my brother and friends.

Only to come face to face with Oken.

I halted, confusion welling at the sight of him. The emotions induced so at odds with everything I had felt thus far today. My head spun looking into his golden eyes. Taking in his curls and the strange lack of a smile on his face. I opened my mouth but couldn't form words.

"Sars, detain her!" I had made it close enough to the stage to hear Silken's barked command. Oken winced as he efficiently got in my space and slipped behind me, holding my biceps firmly. Some other Bellovian stepped forward and tied my hands together.

I hadn't even tried to fight Oken. A flush of embarrassment and shame hit so hard I almost hung my head. It took everything to keep my chin raised. In doing so, my eyes found Nico again. His face paled at the sight of me. He jerked into motion toward me, but I shook my head quickly once. Thank the gods he stopped and wrestled his features back into careful blankness.

My thoughts whirled. Worlds collided. Who did I help? My brother? My mother's people? The Florians who got me here? Was I willing to hurt the boy holding my arms and trying to whisper reassurances in my ear?

"Did you tell him?" I asked.

"Tell who what?"

"Silken. Did you tell him I was interested in the Trish queen?"

Silence behind me. Then, "No, not really. I told them about how they tortured you. How you got sick and were having weird dreams..."

Something in my chest cracked. "You told him."

"I'm confused. What does this have to do with the queen? But that doesn't matter." It did. It was all that mattered. The pull in my chest tugged toward Vichi. I'd risked everything leaving. Everything by coming here. "Don't act so betrayed, Finley. You're the one that left us. Dani was shot and you... You deserted and—"

Gunfire sounded close behind Oken's back. He yanked me into his chest and ducked, forcing me down and angling us away from the sound. The movement sent the blood to my face, bringing a dizzying rush of pain. I ground my jaw in frustration. I should be used to this by now. When I could, I craned my neck to look, already picturing Nico's dead body on the stage.

But it wasn't Nico on the ground. Lilah shrieked. Garris lay at her feet, unmoving. I couldn't look away and barely felt it as I sagged into Oken. The volume of Lilah's cry must have drawn everyone's attention and the crowd fell silent again, back under her power. I don't know if she even realized as she stared at Garris's body.

Oken supported me. Mesa was right. This was my fault. An acid taste filled my mouth. This plan was rushed and stupid. I'd felt so powerful with the Florians on my side and yet...

Oken's grip on my arm never slackened. "Finley?" his voice cracked. He shook me gently.

I tore my eyes away from Garris's limp form. His unblinking stare. Oken had been watching me the entire time, not even looking up at Lilah's scream. Her hold had missed him. Worse still, Silken had been watching us closely, also in full control of his senses.

His face grim, Silken spoke over the silent crowd, "Larson, you fight and the members of your team present will face the consequences." A significant look at Oken. "Sars, to me."

Oken sucked in a breath. I knew he would follow orders. My vision was blurring. Tears? Panic? My chest was too tight to pull in a breath. I looked back to Garris. Oken turned toward Silken, dragging me onto the stage and out the door. We left the sound of Lilah's crying and the eerily still room.

"Oken, please, let me go," I whispered. Silken was walking fast, far enough ahead not to hear.

"I'm sorry, Finley. You know what they'll do to my family."

I fought tears of frustration. "Please, Oken, I..."

His steps slowed just enough to give me a moment of hope. His lips close to my hair. "You what?"

Could I persuade him? Use whatever was blooming

between us? His telling Silken about my dream was likely what tipped the commander off to this attack, that and my request to come in the first place. But while his hold was firm, it wasn't painful. His warmth at my back nonthreatening. "I have to save the queen."

"She isn't here."

I stumbled. "No. You're lying."

"I wouldn't lie to you. Finley, you're one of top trainees to leave basic. I'm sure you could just talk to Commander Silken, he seems genuinely sympathetic about what happened with Dani. He could help figure something out—"

"Hurry up, Sars!" Oken jumped and hurried forward. He still believed in the commanders. In the broken and oppressive system. And I couldn't fight him. I couldn't leave him behind to be punished because I skipped and broke out of his hold. I would have to deal with Silken and face the consequences for desertion. Oken pulled me up a set of stairs and through the door Silken held open.

"Tie her here." Silken pointed at a chair set up in the middle of the room. Ropes were already waiting, coiled on the ground. Oken guided me to sit down and Silken watched him set to work binding my feet to the chair legs and then moving to the back to tie my bound wrists to the chair behind me. I watched the commander the entire time, keeping my face blank. I raised my chin and centered my thoughts on what was happening here and now. Away from the ballroom. I was no use to anyone if I didn't get it together and think. Oken couldn't be punished if I got away after his part. After he was gone, and I could stop thinking about how near he was. *Always focus.*

Oken's hands were quick and steady. His fingers kept brushing my bare forearms. I must be sick to still shiver at his touch. Cool metal pressed into my hand. I closed my fists without a thought. The edge of a blade cut into my right palm, the smooth handle hidden in my left. Only the years of training kept my face from giving anything away. Oken stepped away and the commander approached. I was acutely aware of the blood pooling between my fingers, hot and fast.

"Wait outside."

"Yes, sir." Oken left the room without looking at me. I watched his back until the door shut between us. Once he was safely away, I was able to pull in a breath.

"I knew having him here would get to you," Silken said. When I spat at his feet, Silken only shook his head. He stepped closer, right into the glob. "Larson, I'm trying to help. I know it was a shock seeing your teammate fall. We all stumble when we see our first. But you're made of sterner stuff than that. Your father—"

"Don't talk to me about my father." I couldn't bear hearing the news from Silken of all people.

Silken nodded. He had the nerve to give me a small smile. "No one else realizes you're here, Larson. Because of what your father has done for me, I'll tell the others you've been in Florian custody this whole time. It's the only explanation. Then, we'll go back to winning this war. We need people like you on our side."

I stared, trying to figure out Silken's angle. There was no way a Bellovian commander could be uttering these words. It went against all I knew about them. "Why?"

"We'll give you some better training. Convince you of our cause. A day in the Squalor should be enough to show you the Florians have wronged us. Then, when you're back with us, we'll shape that gift of yours and make you a powerful force against the Florians. With your Bellovian training and warped Bellovian strength, you will make all the difference."

So they told him I could skip. Another pang of betrayal knowing it was likely Oken who had. And they thought it was a Bellovian gift. Pride reared within me and the words coated my tongue. *I won't fight for you. I'm Trish.* But I couldn't say them. Not when I didn't know for sure. Silken eyed me like a new shiny gun and the possibilities played out in his mind.

When I didn't respond he continued. "I can see you need a bit more time to think. I understand you went through something traumatic. I'm sure your time with the enemy wasn't easy. Let me help handle the situation downstairs while you collect yourself. Look forward to seeing your team again if anything else." He paused. "They really haven't been a cohesive group since losing their leader... it may be time for them to test their skills at the Front." Silken watched his words sink in before turning to leave.

I didn't want to let them but sink in they did. Beneath the chill his threat left, hope rose just a fraction. What if my parents *were* alive? I could go back to them, follow this ache in my chest for Vichi. No one else got this opportunity. To come back after desertion. Our army must truly be desperate. Silken must really think they could mold me and my gift into the perfect weapon. The thought made my fists tighten on the knife, reminding me of its presence.

Silken opened the door and I braced myself to see Oken again. Instead, Nico walked into the room. He only looked slightly sickened by the blood covering my face from the fight downstairs. "Where is Sars?" Silken demanded.

"There was a disruption with the slaves. The girl, Jaspers I think, was sent to collect Sars. Commander Adkins told me to take his place. He wants her taken to the cells downstairs." Nico nodded in my direction.

"I told him I needed to question her first."

"He needs your help and would rather she be watched with the other prisoners."

I held my breath. Ten seconds ticked by.

"Very well." I sagged back in my seat. "Take her down to the cells with the rest. She shouldn't be much trouble. Just go for the nose if you must. What was the name again?"

"Travs, sir."

Silken nodded. "Think about what I said, Larson."

We sighed in relief once he was gone. Nico gave me that look he had. *Fisha grens.* Tears flooded my eyes as he came to a stop in front of me. "Would you be able to hear if someone approached?"

I nodded.

"Ready?" I squeezed my eyes shut, ignoring how it forced the tears free. I nodded again. With a crack Nico yanked my nose back into place. I bit back a shout and pulled in deep breaths until the pain faded.

When I opened my eyes again Nico was untying me from the chair. He kept my ankles and wrists bound together, but made a noise of approval when he saw the knife.

"What's going on, Nico?" I whispered. "Since when are you..."

"I've been in the rebellion for years. Dad too." Nico looked up, apology burning in his gaze. "He would portion out funds for them. I listen to commanders at events and feed the information to the rebels and the Florians."

It made complete and total sense, yet I sat stunned. How could I not have known? "You're the rebel Londe talks to?"

"Yes." Nico's voice went soft on the syllable.

"So you got there in time to help Mom and Dad?" Hope bloomed in my chest. Nico's hands stilled and he lowered his eyes. The hope died, leaving a gaping hole in its place.

"I got there as fast as I could, Finny." He swallowed. "The house was empty, but... there was a lot of blood." He ended on a strained whisper. "I've heard since that someone jumped the gun, they were supposed to wait for further orders, but..."

We fell into a heavy silence. Nico's nimble fingers finished untying me from the chair. He straightened, but I couldn't find the strength to stand. "Why didn't you tell me? Why didn't anyone tell me? I had to find out about the rebellion from the Florians!" The rebellion was so much easier to focus on than what might have happened before Nico got home that day.

"We don't have time to get into the details, but Mom didn't want you getting distracted."

"Distracted? From what? Becoming just like the commanders? From shooting Florians when they send me to the Front?" *From becoming a monster?*

"From your duty. Your Trish abilities are coming in, yes?"

"Yes..."

"Tell me you know where she is," Nico said, suddenly urgent. "That's the most important thing."

"Where Mom is?" I was lost in this conversation, my brain unable to sort through the anger at the secrets, grief for my parents, fear for my brother surrounding himself with commanders.

"Not Mom. The queen, Finny. The Trish queen."

"But she wasn't here. How am I supposed to—"

"You're the *resa magsai*. You're the only one who can find her."

I shook my head, ignoring the pain of the motion. "That's impossible. I was born in Bellovi..."

"No, Finny. Mom already had you when she met Dad. He smuggled you both out of Traesha. She was a *magsai* and knew you were *resa*. She had to keep you safe. Protecting you ensured someone would be there to help the queen when she needed it. When she was ready. You're the only hope we have at finding her."

"But... Dad?"

Nico helped me to my feet and pulled me into his chest. I fell against him, unable to catch myself with the ropes blocking my steps. I was momentarily comforted. My brother's hug was a balm for any hurt. The pressure of his arms brought more tears. Or maybe I hadn't stopped crying.

"He's still your dad. Just like Mom is my mom. And I'm still your brother. This changes nothing about our family. But it changes everything for you. Nothing is more important now than saving the queen." He stepped back, holding me at arm's length. "Do you think you can break out of here on your own?"

I nodded, repositioning Oken's knife behind my back.

"Good. First chance you get, go to the queen."

"But how will I know where she is?"

Nico's mouth quirked. "Your heart will lead you true, *resa*." He touched his fingers to my sternum, right above the pull begging me to go to home for days now. I frowned until it suddenly came to me. The draw toward Vichi wasn't homesickness. It was the queen calling to me. No wonder it had grown so consuming since arriving in Traesha.

Nico saw understanding in my eyes and nodded in satisfaction. "You can do this."

"I can't leave everyone behind." My team. My friends. I let them all down today; to just abandon them in the mess I'd made was cruel.

"You can. You must. The Florians will understand once you find the queen."

I took a breath and reshuffled my thoughts. "Okay, yes, I can leave them. But, Nico, I can't leave you again." My voice broke. I was shaking just from the thought. Nico pulled me in for another hug, hands rubbing my back. I'd missed him so much. This one conversation wasn't nearly enough.

The hug felt like goodbye.

"I have to stay, Finley. Your role in all of this is to find the queen. Mine is behind the piano, reporting to the rebellion. When the time comes and you need us, I'll be ready."

"No. Come with me."

"Finley, this war is about to explode. Everyone keeps hinting at some big alliance and the Florians are on the brink of sending in their elites. Both countries want Traesha. The only way this country will be left standing when the ash settles is if they have their queen. And the queen needs her *resa magsai*. She needs an army. Finding her is your priority."

"She's in Vichi." I was still amazed I knew. The bond pulsed in response to finally being acknowledged.

"Perfect. You can go to the rebels first. Ask them for help. I can't guarantee the committee will... but you can at least hide out there while you think of a plan."

"And how am I supposed to find this rebellion? You all did a damn good job keeping it a secret from me."

Nico grimaced. "They mostly have contacts in the Squalor."

"Why didn't you tell me? Any of this?"

"I'm sorry, Finny. I really am. I would have told you, but Mom thought knowing about the queen would awaken your powers sooner and put you at risk and she didn't want you involved with the rebellion when your loyalty would be to the queen."

I took a breath and willed the budding anger to cool. I heard voices down the hall and angled my head, listening to check if they were coming our way.

Nico caught the movement. "We should go. I'll take you to the cells, but leave the first chance you get, okay?" He gave me one last hug and I accepted it quietly. "I know you can do this," he whispered in my hair.

I nodded against his chest. He bent and lifted me up and over his shoulder. I groaned when all the blood rushed to my aching face.

"Sorry. Have to make it believable."

"Yeah, yeah, yeah."

Nico carried me down the stairs, halls, and to the very depths of the castle. With little ceremony he dumped me in a cell. I sat up and watched his back as he went back up the stairs and exchanged words with the guards that made them laugh. He was a good spy. And all I ever thought he was meant for was making music. My heart broke.

CHAPTER 20

"Finley?" I tore my eyes from the top of the stairs. The narrow cells were dug from the ground, damp dirt creating three walls and bars gleaming like the blade of a *magsai* sword providing a door. The cells were arranged in a circle and I was directly across from the stairs. I could see Lilah in her cell to the left of their base. Brea on the other side. I could make out Sam sitting uncomfortably in the cell next to Brea. Silken's throw must have hurt if he'd allowed himself to get captured. I longed to talk to him about what Nico had just told me, but something kept me silent. This had been my family's secret for so long, secret even from me. It was precious knowledge I didn't feel I could share yet. "Finley? Are you hurt?"

"Hinze? How did they get you?"

His voice came from the cell next to me. "I used too much on the wall. We can leave soon, though. I just need to gather my strength. What happened to you?"

"I got caught while fighting in the ballroom." Though my capture had been surprisingly painless, my face must look a mess.

"Are you hurt?" Hinze asked again, but he didn't wait for an answer, just came in through the side of my cell. He stumbled from the effort, catching himself against the wall.

"I'm fine. It'll heal. I'm so sorry. This is all my fault. Silken knew I was interested in the celebration. He found out I was looking for the queen. She isn't even here. I'm so sorry."

Hinze knelt in front of me. He didn't look mad. I tucked my ankles in and away from him when he reached for the ropes at my feet.

"Bitch." I knew that was Mesa and only felt relief. She was still alive. Let her hate me. "How could you not have figured this into your *brilliant* plan?"

I sagged against the wall. Hinze was pale and his hands shook. "Who all...?" I couldn't voice the question.

Hinze's eyes dimmed further. "Garris is dead. I sent Savha and Fisher with the slaves to help them organize. The rest of us are down here." Garris was dead because of me. All my fault. My stupid fault. The queen wasn't even here and if I'd paid attention to my instincts, I would have known it. The answer was with me all along.

Why hadn't my mother told me I was *resa*?

"No thanks to you," Brea said, reinforcing my thoughts. The bars to her cell frosted over and the temperature in the dungeon dropped.

Hinze reached again to untie my feet. I shifted away. "Not yet. Don't give yourself away until you can get everyone else out."

"Wait, are you in her cell? Hinze! She betrayed us! Garris is dead because of her!" I winced at Mesa's shout, wishing she'd keep her voice down so the guards wouldn't be tempted to investigate.

"No." Hinze shook his head. The trust in his eyes made

my breath hitch. "She wants to find the queen more than any of us. She couldn't have known her commander would figure out so much."

He lifted a hand but hesitated before touching my face. "When I saw them take you..."

"I'm fine, really."

He shook his head again. "You don't have to be, Finley."

I raised an eyebrow, but it was over my right eye, so the look turned into a wince of pain. Hinze took a sharp breath and then put his hand on my cheek. I had to admit his cold skin felt nice.

"I am, though. What happens next?" If he already had a plan to break out, it would save me a few steps. I would leave them knowing they were going to be okay.

"We get out of here when I recover. Go back to Floria. I'll ask my father for help. We'll find the queen, wherever she is."

"Will he send troops to help the Trish? That boy was right, it'll be worse for them here now."

"I'm sure he will once we have the queen. And there's still a chance Savha and Fisher can rally them. My father can't claim to be her ally and not send help." I didn't like the way he said "*have the queen.*" And the Trish needed help now. I remembered Nico's warning. Who was to say the Florians wouldn't just claim control if they sent help without the queen to lead? I found myself doubting the validity of the Florian alliance. I doubted Hinze. Nico was right. Finding the queen was my task. My burden alone.

Hinze's hand was still on my cheek. I felt the first stirrings of caution when he lifted his other one, both hands gently framing my face. I met Lilah's eyes over his shoulder and she frowned. But she didn't look angry, more so puzzled. She was covered in blood, her hair loose from its holder and dangling around her face. I'd never seen her so unkempt. I begged her with my eyes to say something to break the moment. Her eyebrows only knotted closer together.

"I was so worried when they didn't bring you down here with us. I was sure you were dead too," Hinze whispered.

"Not dead." My voice came out a little squeak.

Hinze leaned closer. I could see every fleck of color in his hazel eyes. His head began to lower and my brain sputtered. Was he serious? My wild thoughts focused on the blood covering my face. Who would want to kiss blood-covered lips? I didn't want this. I jerked back, unable to turn my face while his hands held it in place. His eyes flashed with hurt before he caught himself. Horror drained the color from his face. "Finley, I'm so sorry. I'm just so..."

"No. Um, it's okay. Just not..." *Now* is what I meant to say, but I couldn't promise him a later either. My cheeks burned; my heart was beating like a wild thing in my chest. "I've... I've never kissed anyone before." ... and he wasn't the one I'd always dreamed of sharing this moment with. I hated the thought for forming, but it was the truth. Would I ever want to kiss anyone else? A prince knelt before me, beautiful and kind, but my thoughts were still upstairs with Oken. I could feel the ghost of his warmth at my back, the genuine, unguarded emotions in his golden eyes. My hand still clutching the knife he gave me, stubbornly waiting for the moment to free myself with it even when Hinze could so easily untie me.

"Never?" Hinze shook his head. "I can't believe they were so horrible to you."

I bristled before I caught myself. "They weren't all bad." Why was I even defending them? Even if he gave me the knife, Oken was the reason the queen was still missing. She would be here, already with me, if not for him mentioning my interest in her... Right?

"No one should have to live in fear like you did."

"Says the guy who probably hasn't felt fear since his powers set in."

"I feel fear. I fear I'll fail. I fear my friends will die... more of my friends will die. I fear for you. Every time you straighten your back in the face of a challenge, I'm afraid." His hand came up again, solid and soft. I swallowed, worried he was going to try and kiss me again, but he let his hand rest on my cheek.

Footsteps approached the top of the stairs. "Go back!" I hissed. With a look of regret, Hinze slipped through the wall. I heard his exhausted grunt on the other side.

A commander clomped down the stairs. Her face was the embodiment of Bellovian fury.

"Silken didn't give clearance—" one of the men guarding the door started.

The woman raised a hand and he stopped talking. She marched to the front of my cell. "You Teo Larson's daughter?"

Apparently not. "What do you care?"

Her lip curled and I knew exactly what was about to happen. I pushed all thoughts of pain away. I braced myself, spinning the knife around my fingers with nervous energy.

"You're a damn deserter." She produced a key ring and unlocked the door of my cell. "I'm going to show you what we do to deserters. Silken is going too soft."

I made my voice sweet as honey. "But did he give you permission?"

She jabbed at the stripes on her shoulder. Four. "Silken doesn't give me orders."

The guards watched from the top of the stairs, smiling at the promise of violence despite their previous reservations. The commander bent to lift me by the front of my dress. I erupted, throwing my weight forward fast enough to get to my feet and ram my forehead into her nose. She stumbled back with a roar and I hopped from my cell, awkwardly angling the knife and slicing through the bonds at my wrist.

"Thanks for the knife," I said, hoping to clear any suspicion from Nico or Oken. Her eyes flickered with confusion. I heard Hinze throw himself against the bars of his cell, too weak to get through them to rescue me.

I freed my hands but didn't have time for my ankles before the commander recovered enough to tackle me to the ground in the middle of the cells. I heard the guards running down the stairs toward us. My breath left me when her shoulder connected with my diaphragm. I forced myself not to panic as I struggled to pull in air. I focused on the pain when she landed a punch, going for the nose. I caught her wrist when she lifted it for another blow and let the ease of energy Traesha provided fill me. I snapped her wrist toward the ground, then forced her face to follow the momentum into the dirt. I spun around behind and forced her arm up her back until I heard the pop of her shoulder and she screamed in pain.

I shifted my weight and brought my elbow down on her temple. She stilled beneath me. My movements blindingly fast, I sat up and cut through the ropes at my ankles. The guards cocked their guns. I lunged off the ground and ran at the first one. I stepped in front of him and shifted to the side as I passed, thinking to feint the other way. I shouldn't have bothered; I moved too quickly for him to follow. I jammed my knife into his side before he knew I was even next to him.

When his partner fell, the other guard turned to me and fired. I heard Hinze cry out and my heart plummeted. I spared him the quickest glance and saw him grab hold of his arm. Not fatal. Relief rushed my head.

I grabbed the first guard's gun before he could shoot again. I couldn't resist a last look around the cells at the shocked faces. Hinze, Lilah, Brea, Mesa, Londe. Sam's face unreadable. I turned and skipped up the stairs, abandoning them to the Bellovians.

I SKIPPED out of the castle, the Bellovians a blur in the hallways I avoided as easily as the trees in the forest. I burst out into Shalta's streets and drew up short at the scene that greeted me. The bright backdrop of Trish buildings was diluted by the black uniforms of commanders swarming outside. Yelling, laughing, whooping. A celebration that turned my stomach to lead. Slaves screamed and ran. Some lay bloodied on the ground. Others were resigned, watching everything take place from doorways, stepping forward to tie up their own people when the commanders ordered it. I forced myself to press on, taking any abandoned street I could find as I left my mother's people in the aftermath of my failed plans. Bellovians patrolled, looking eagerly for rebelling slaves. I took a few of them out on my way but skidded to a stop once again when I saw Oken riding a cycle in my direction in the narrow alley.

Oken braked when our eyes met, tires screeching. He took the time to look me up and down, gaze focusing on my face. I was a bloody, hectic mess. Oken swung his leg over the cycle, never breaking eye contact as he kicked down the stand. He stepped close. I desperately wished my face was clean of blood. That it wasn't swollen and bruised.

Then he reached up and pressed his earpiece. My mouth went dry.

"All clear," he said. And he smiled. He stepped around me, sweeping an arm to gesture at his idling cycle. I turned with him and he abruptly leaned in, bringing our faces inches apart. "You should probably hit me or something if you want to take it. Maybe use the knife, make it look convincing."

I looked down at the blade in my hand.

"C'mon, princess. I don't want to ask Jaspers. She'd enjoy it way too much."

"I really would." I jumped and turned to see Rennie step out of the shadows with a smile. She took in the two of us with a knowing look. "It's good to see you, Finley." I tensed as she stepped into my space, but in a second her arms were around me. As she squeezed gently, she whispered in my ear, "Not everyone in the rebellion will help you, but look for Levi."

I barely had time to hug her back before she was stepping away and waving over her shoulder. "I'm going to watch the entrance. Keep it quick you two."

"Seriously, you do have to make it look convincing," Oken said. I looked back to him, head spinning. I'd seen hints Rennie didn't believe in the Bellovian cause but hadn't seriously thought her part of the rebellion. The evidence of the movement kept growing and I didn't know what to think of the hope growing alongside it for the people of Bellovi. Even the one standing before me with his perfect smile in place. I shook my head at him, unable to

257

fully keep the smile from my own lips. I swung my hand holding the knife but kept the blade from his face when I punched his cheekbone. He stumbled back at the impact.

"You get two minutes, then I'm reporting it stolen," he said, holding his cheek.

I bit my lip. I tried to hold on to my anger over him telling Silken about the queen but looking at the bruise already forming from my hit, I couldn't.

"Oken—"

"Just get out of here," he tried to make the words light, but his smile wasn't right.

I rose onto my tiptoes and swept a kiss over the bruise. I never thought the boy capable of stillness, but he sucked in a breath and held it, his entire being frozen in place.

"Thank you." I stepped back, watching him with a turning stomach. What if I was wrong? What if he really was just being kind? What if he didn't like the kiss and that was why he wasn't moving?

Then he smiled, hand going to his cheek. He opened his mouth, but Rennie made a warning sound from the other side of the alley. Without another word, Oken winked, spun on his heels and walked away. My hands fluttered and I took a step to follow him. But my chest squeezed, tugging me in the opposite direction.

I watched his back a second longer and turned for the cycle. My black dress ripped as I swung a leg over the seat. Cranking the engine and wrenching my thoughts away from Oken and Rennie, I drove at top speed to the edge of the city and to the house we'd stayed in the night before.

I dumped the cycle on the lawn and ran inside. Taking the stairs three at a time, I stopped in the room I'd shared with Mesa. I ripped off the horrible dress and swapped it for a pair of leggings, a sweater, my hat, and my boots. I scrubbed the blood from my face in the bathroom, smearing the liner around my eyes. I almost smiled at my swollen, discolored face. I felt like myself for the first time in days. I was centered. I had purpose.

I pressed my lips together, holding in the echo of Oken's warmth.

Before leaving the room, I snatched one of Mesa's spare knives from the nightstand and tucked it into my waistband. I paused to look at Oken's. It was tiny, but the blade was wicked sharp. The handle used to be black but had faded to gray with use where his hand had gripped it. I wondered how many years he'd carried it before giving it to me. Why had he done it? Why had he given me the cycle? Why did he tell Silken I was interested in the queen if he was just going to turn around and help me? I spun the blade through my fingers, amazed by how quickly I could do it with Traesha's energy aiding me. I tucked it into my boot.

I found a pack and filled it with food and one of our water-purifying bottles. Right before I left the house, I grabbed one of the blankets off the couch. It wouldn't be enough, but it fit in the pack and was better than nothing. Shouldering the pack, I jumped back on the cycle and took off toward the forest.

I stopped at the entrance of the single road cut through the Trish trees leading back to Bellovi. It was lined with a high, thick fence separating those who drove it from the forest and its wildlife. I hated the sight of the cleared dirt. The road was dark and haunted, the spirits of whispering trees lingered. A cold breeze rustled the branches that hung over the fence. I opted to go around and take my chances with roots and branches rather than step on the cursed Bellovian path. I remembered the tree's whispers when I

thought about the Bellovians: *unwelcome, unwelcome*. I shivered and banked the cycle, entering the forest further down
and weaving painstakingly through the trees.

The sky was nearly black by the time I reached the edge
of Traesha's forest. The trees beyond grew shorter, the bark
a faded, lifeless brown and the leaves thirsty and sparse. I
paused under the comforting canopy of Traesha's trees and
closed my eyes to enjoy the warmth and kinetic life satu-
rating the forest air. I wasn't ready to lose this to the
Bellovian climate. The leaves rustled.

Tell them nisashan.

I tilted my head, sure I misheard. It came again. *Tell
them* nisashan.

I thanked the trees even though I didn't recognize the
Trish word. Nor could I imagine who *them* might refer to.

I leaned over on the idling cycle and placed a hand on
the nearest tree. The bark was soft to the touch, the
humidity from the ocean keeping it conditioned. But the
tree was solid and strong beneath the damp. A buzz of
energy radiated into my palm.

With regret, I straightened and twisted the grip of the
cycle toward me once more, calling on the engine and flying
out of the whispering trees. I found the road and drove
through the night and into the next morning.

As I traveled deeper into Bellovi, the land sloped
upwards into mountains and the leaves condensed into
sharp needles of pine trees. The road twisted back and forth
as it climbed, breaking into tunnels often or running
against the sharp edges of rivers. The temperature began its
steady decline. The cold felt unnatural.

It soon became clear I would have to stop in the small
village of Trent and get a coat. *Steal* a coat. When I finally
stopped a couple of hours before sunrise, I shivered under

the light blanket the entire time. I barely slept before putting my socks on my hands for mittens, wrapping myself in the blanket as securely as I could and continuing. I searched anxiously for the lights of Trent at every switchback. My father had grown up there, but seldom spoke of the mountain village. The last time he visited was when his mother died. He said when he volunteered he had been excited to leave, but I knew he grew to miss the quiet life.

The village lights finally came into view and I let out a relieved laugh. Coaxing more speed from the engine, I flew down the mountainside and stashed the cycle at the edge of the village. I was so cold and excited by the thought of a coat I accidentally skipped to the nearest cabin. The quick movement gave me a flush of warmth. I paused to consider leaving the cycle and trying to run the rest of the way to Vichi, just to stay so warm. But that would take more endurance than anyone possessed. I shook off the thought and walked around the small home.

I crept window to window. There was only one bedroom and the man snoring inside was huge. I moved to the next home, hoping to find someone closer to my size within. It took three cabins to find someone: a woman sleeping soundly next to her husband. The door was locked. I stood on the sagging porch for a time wondering what to do. I didn't know how to pick locks, and even if I did, I had nothing to pick it with. I could kick the door in, but that would be loud and wake them immediately, possibly wake the whole village, and I'd had enough of angry mobs to last a lifetime.

I moved to the windows and cleared dirt from the glass to see how it was latched. It seemed simple enough. I brought out Oken's slim knife. It took a couple of tries, but by sliding the blade under the window, I managed to unhook the latch. And Rennie made breaking and entering sound like such a skill. I felt myself grinning. My cheeks were stiff with cold and my bottom lip split, it was so chapped. Sucking at the blood, I levered the knife to open the window enough to get my fingers under it.

The window squealed when I pulled it up, but no sounds came from the bedroom save a rumbling snore. I breathed a sigh of relief and slipped inside. I quickly found the closet and pulled out the warmest, smallest coat. I grabbed the mittens on the shelf. I wanted to stay and take more, maybe a better hat and a thicker pair of socks, but the bed creaked as someone shifted. I panicked and ran for the window, but I moved too fast and my Trish speed kicked in. I hit the wall with a loud thud, grunting when my bruised stomach slammed into the window ledge. The wind whooshed from my lungs.

"Who's there?" the woman called. The bedroom door opened. I dove out the window, dropping one of the mittens I had just stolen. I bent to pick it up right when a bullet connected with the porch rail above my head. I froze in my crouched position for a beat too long. The second shot shattered the glass in the window and icy pain sliced across my cheekbone. That was all I needed to get over the shock and move. I took off toward my cycle, slipping into a skip.

The village behind me came alive. I reached the cycle and hastily donned the coat, shoved my socks into the pocket, and pulled on the mittens, swearing when I dropped another one into the dirt on the first try. Finally dressed in layers, I mounted the cycle. I tore off into the nearest cluster of rocks, cutting around them and hoping they would give me some cover. A valley opened before me and I groaned. I twisted the grips, asking for more speed from the whining engine. I leaned forward over the handle-bars. This felt painfully slow after skipping.

Familiar with the landscape, the villagers quickly found me in the beam of their cycle headlights. A few were newer models than my own and gained on me in little time. Bullets pattered the ground around me, one pinging off the cycle near my right foot. I swore and swerved. With no choice and a tug of regret, I leaped off the cycle and ran, tapping fully into the speed that landed me in this trouble in the first place.

The miles passed in a blur under my feet. The tight panic in my chest loosened, the villagers far behind. The mountain angled steeply uphill, but still I barely slowed, my feet moved in silent accuracy. Every cell in my body rang with energy and excitement and *rightness*. My eyes missed nothing despite my speed. I couldn't hold back a loud whoop when I jumped over a wide, rushing river with ease. The wind stung my cheeks, especially the cut on my right one, but I didn't slow. I didn't dare. I had never felt so alive or such a satisfying burn in my muscles. No sparring match had ever compared to this. Well, that wasn't quite true, but I was trying not to think about Oken.

After running maybe an hour, my breath grew ragged and it started to snow. I found a cave and decided to hide there for the rest of the night. I sat down and slumped against the wall. I didn't have another thought until I woke.

CHAPTER 21

I'd heard people complaining about sore muscles before, but upon waking it was my first time experiencing the pain. I groaned and reached for my pack. After I ate my fill, which was half the food I brought, I used the wall of the cave to climb to my feet. I winced every step it took to get outside and relieve myself. I drank everything in my purifying bottle, using only a tiny bit to clean my cheek. I pulled my pack onto my shoulders and began walking in the direction the *magsai* bond pulled me. It was easier to focus on the strange feeling there rather than the ache of my legs or the itch of the healing cut on my cheek or how the cold made my nose throb. The bond was like an invisible string tied to my sternum. I imagined the other side of it was connected to the queen, her tugging and reeling in.

My mother always spoke of the royal family with such intense sadness; I realized now it was because she knew them personally. She was raised in the castle as a *magsai*. She must have felt she failed them. Why hadn't she been with the royal family and other *magsai* during the invasion? Were she and Sam the only two *magsai* left? She must have known the baby princess escaped or she wouldn't have guarded the secret of our bond so tight. Did she guess the new queen would end up in Bellovi? What if she allowed my father to take her to Vichi with the hope of finding the queen someday?

The thought stopped me short. My father was not my father. I didn't even know who my father was.

I flushed with sudden anger and kicked at a rock, sending it flying through the trees and clattering down the mountain slope. Why hadn't they told me any of this? I was already hiding who I was from the world, why didn't they trust me with this too?

I remembered Nico's words. She hadn't wanted me to start looking or to trigger my abilities early. The excuses felt hollow and rekindled the frustration in my gut. A small part of me knew these spiraling, angered thoughts were simpler than the worry. I was good at distracting myself from certain pains. I just needed to move forward. I needed to find the queen.

It was easy to redirect my attention back to the bond. I found a sense of sadness there and the anxious boredom that came with waiting. I let these feelings become my own, numbing me as I found a stream and filled my water then straightened to run. I was still immersed in the bond as I forced my sore legs to move. I ran toward Vichi, the world blurring with my thoughts.

It took me the night, a few hours of rest, and a few more hours of painful skipping until the boulders of Vichi came into view. It was only then I pulled fully back into my own mind, though the bond throbbed stronger than ever. I stood at the edge of the boulders and took quick stock of myself. The miles of running were wearing through my boots faster than I'd considered possible, leaving my feet cold and wet. I was tired and had a dull headache from lack of water and food. But the bond was so strong, I felt almost as alive as I had standing in the forest of Traesha. I could go on. I was so close.

As I began navigating the boulders, climbing with numb fingers and shaking legs, I was weighed with memories of my father. I couldn't remember the last time I laughed and smiled freely like we did here. The perfect and clear image of his crinkled eyes over his scarf momentarily robbed me of breath.

I grew a little more energized when the city finally came into view in the early hours of the morning. City Center stood tall, full of concrete buildings, and tallest of them all, exactly in the middle, bulky and rectangular, shining for me like a beacon, was Command Hall. I stared at it and goose-bumps that had nothing to do with the cold rose on my arms and neck.

I'm close. I'm coming.

BY THE TIME I reached the end of the boulders, not even the queen's energizing proximity kept me from stumbling. I wouldn't be pulling any daring rescues tonight. I wanted nothing more than to go to my old home and pull my over-stuffed comforter over my head like I used to. I found myself dreaming about hot showers. Tea steaming just out of the kettle. Fresh bread. My mother's warmth. My father's hugs.

Not my father. I was so tired I was hollow to the reminder.

I looked up from the last jutting rock as I carefully stepped around it. My neck was stiff from staring at the ground, trying to avoid rolled ankles or stubbed toes. My stomach sank as I stepped into the Squalor. Right in front of me was a tarp strung up against the side of a crumbling building. A white hand stuck out from underneath, fingers curled gently and tipped an ashy gray color. A dog growled nearby, letting me know who had been there first. I swallowed and forced my legs to walk, hugging my coat closer around my middle.

The Squalor stretched on and on. The houses slanted in one direction or another, often leaning into each other for support and missing windows, doors, or complete walls. The streets were mud and slush that sucked at my boots with every step. Eyes peeked around corners and pale faces stared through cracked, brown windows. I passed even more dead bodies on the streets, their frozen gazes following me even when I looked away.

I asked Mags to bless me with enough strength if it came to a fight. I clutched both knives in the pockets of my coat and listened hard as I walked deeper into the Squalor. I only had to bring them out once, and the woman who approached fell back with a hiss. I avoided sounds of fighting, people snoring, and even once a volley of gunshots. A baby cried a few houses to my right. Every noise made my chest heavier. The commanders did nothing to help these people. Change had to happen. This was so wrong. So incredibly wrong.

I looked in the frosted windows, trying to find a place to sleep. I should have asked Rennie more about this place and how she survived it. Through one spiderwebbed window I saw a dead woman rotting on a worn-out couch. In the next house, two skinny children stared defiantly back at me. When I finally found an empty one, there were so many rats, I passed it up. I went back to the house with the children. One was coughing now, the sound coming from so deep in the boy's small chest that I cringed. I paused for a second, then pushed open the door.

The kids were obviously siblings. I couldn't help but think of Rennie again as I watched the rail-thin girl hold her coughing brother. They moved away from me when I came in, but I held out my hands, a sign of peace. I pulled off my pack and offered them the blanket inside. It was the cleanest thing in this place.

"If you let me sleep here too, you can have this."

The girl looked from my blanket to her shivering brother. His wide eyes were pleading and his red, chapped hand clutched hers. She sighed and aged five years from one moment to the next when she nodded and held out the hand he didn't cling to. I gave them the blanket, relieved when they draped it over their small bodies.

"I'm Finley."

"I'm Leigh. This is Jon. You stay in that corner."

She pointed away from them and pulled the blanket over their heads. I went to the corner, hidden from view of the window by the couch covered with rat droppings and revealed springs.

"What happened to your face?" the boy asked. His sister shushed him loudly and I decided that meant I didn't have to answer. I pulled my hood low over my hat and slid down the wall, curling up on the floor. Sleep came quickly.

"Finley?" I opened my eyes to Jon standing over me. I couldn't believe how small he was. Sunlight streamed in through the window. "Leigh won't wake up. Did I get her sick?"

My heart went solid and plummeted. I hurried to Leigh's still body, Jon trembling behind me. As I approached, her chest rose and fell. I let out the breath I'd been holding and crouched to see what was wrong. When I reached to shake her shoulder, Leigh sprang to life. She grabbed my arm and raised a rusted kitchen knife to my throat.

"Give us the pack and coat!" she barked.

I couldn't stop my laugh. I jerked back my head and jabbed her wrist upwards. The knife flew from her grip and toward the ceiling. I stood and caught it on its descent. It was a knife like the one my mom used to cut bread, with serrated edges too dull to be much of a threat. I twirled it in the air and caught it again, never moving my gaze from Leigh's wide eyes. Jon whimpered and tucked himself into her side.

"Nice trick," I said, holding the blade and offering the knife back to her.

After a moment of hesitation, Leigh dejectedly took the handle and tucked it behind her. "Thanks."

"I have an empty water purifier in here, but that's it. If you show me where I can refill, I'll let you have a turn with it. I bet you two know this place pretty well."

Jon nodded enthusiastically. He opened his mouth to reply but went into a fit of coughing instead.

"We know things," Leigh said for him. "Like don't go by the old church. Madam Stilly likes girls and kids, but they're not happy living there. They sell guns under the bridge on the Thirdday but won't take kitchen knives for them. They give out rations closer to City Center, but people will jump you if you take them back into the

Squalor. Most of the water will make you sick, but the house next door has a sink that drips all the time and still runs because the son is at the Front, you just have to hold your breath when you go in because the woman smells bad."

Jon shuddered. "I won't go in. She used to be fine, but now she's scary since she started to rot."

I stared at the two of them and regretted every moment of my childhood I ever felt sorry for myself.

"Okay, stay here. I'll be back with water." Leigh looked wary about letting me go, but Jon asked her for more of the blanket and took up her attention.

"The back door is broken," she called right before I slipped outside. I went around to the back of the house. There was a single hinge holding the door, so I had to lift it to push it open. The smell hit me right away. Even the heat was still running, and I gagged at the warm, sticky, too sweet odor. Holding my breath, I ran to the sink and filled the bottle. I hurried outside and drank its contents. I did this until I tricked my stomach into thinking it was full and then filled it for the kids. I walked back to the house, thinking about Jon's horrible cough. The one and only time I had gotten sick from Brea was still fresh. I let them drink from the bottle anyway.

"Do you guys know where the people are who didn't want to go to war?"

"Is that why you're here? You ran from the commanders?" Leigh's eyes narrowed.

I took the empty bottle from Jon and stood up. "I should go," I said.

"Wait!" Jon shouted. I paused. Were these kids smart enough to know how much they'd be rewarded for finding a deserter?

"The people who don't go to war sometimes feed us," Leigh conceded. "They don't want us telling people, though. They can't feed every kid in the Squalor."

"How far are they?"

"They're closer to the city, where people shoot more and fight for rations," Leigh said. "If you go to the big statue with the missing arm, sometimes Levi is there. He has a red mid gun."

Levi. The rebel Rennie told me to find. It seemed too lucky a coincidence after all I'd been through the last few weeks. "Is Levi going to shoot me with this red gun?"

"The girl, the old man, and the big one sometimes shoot. Levi is nice. He gives us oat bars. Wait for him," Jon said.

We waited for his next coughing fit to finish. "Why are you guys helping me?"

They shared a look. "Because usually we need help," Leigh said with a shrug.

Jon gave me a sweet smile. How was he still able to smile? I knelt and pulled out Mesa's knife. I held it in the air; forearm parallel to the floor and elbow bent ninety degrees.

"Next time you go to stab someone's throat and they're facing you, hold it with the sharp side of the blade to you. Slide it in the side and pull toward yourself." I pointed to where the blade should enter on my throat. "If you're standing behind them, push it out away from their spine. You'll have more strength that way than trying to slice. It'll do more damage." I mimed the motions and Leigh nodded, tucking the knowledge away. I pressed the hilt of the knife into her small hand. The sight made my throat tight.

I handed Jon the pack with the purifying bottle. I

thought about Oken's knife, but I couldn't stand the thought of parting with it.

"Which direction am I going?" I asked.

"Stay on Fonners Street and head toward Command Hall." Leigh's knuckles were white clutching the knife.

"You two take care of each other. Stay strong." They both nodded. Jon gave me another smile before I slipped from the house. I hadn't done enough for them.

AS THE HOUSES grew into compact and rugged apartments, the people grew rowdier. Men and women stood guard at building entrances. The crack of gunfire rang out at regular intervals. Some of the streets were so thick with mud and slush they had to be avoided entirely. Dogs with shaggy, matted coats slunk around corners. One woman threw out a bone, cackling while she watched three dogs snarl, claw, and snap for it. When one was left behind, weakened, a man darted forward, slit its throat, and collected the body. The hunger in his eyes left no doubt as to what he intended to do with it.

Eyes followed me everywhere I went. I knew they mostly saw my thick coat and its promised warmth, but I still pulled up the hood and lowered my hat as much as I could. When I had to take the second man out with a quick punch to the jaw for drunkenly reaching for me, I decided the streets weren't worth the risk. I grabbed the nearest drainpipe and climbed to the roofs. They were slippery from ice and snow, and some sagged worryingly beneath me, but my bones were light and with deliberate steps I went from building to building with no problems.

When the statue came into view, it was settled directly

in the middle of a busy square. Just as Leigh said, it was a large man missing an arm. And a nose. This man's statue was all over the city. I remembered Hinze naming Florent Bellovi as the Bellovian who started the rebellion. I was willing to bet these statues were made in his likeness.

Men and women called out to the stream of people hustling by, offering to perform magic tricks, selling knitted hats or lucky trinkets, drinks to increase strength or eyesight for aiming. Some men and women stood in too little clothing, trying to make the dark corners or doorways they waited in seem welcoming to anyone who caught their eyes.

I settled down on my stomach to watch the activity, ignoring how the snow on the roof melted and seeped into my clothes. Someone was passing out fliers for a gambling din. It caused a bit of a stir when a rival gang came to stop him. People rushed by with small bundles of what must be rations under their arms, eyes down and makeshift weapons clutched in their hands.

My eyes rested on the statue for a long moment. A girl stood leaning against one of its legs. She wore her black hair in two braids down her chest, rebelling even from the traditional Bellovian hairstyle. Her hand rested on the short gun tucked in her belt and her eyes constantly swept back and forth over the crowd. She *did* look trigger-happy.

I moved from the roof edge and sat down near the chimney, pretending the wisp of smoke was warming my clothes. Every so often I crept back to see if the girl had left. A few times someone stopped to speak with her, heads ducked and lips barely moving. I tried to imagine what rebellion secrets they could be sharing. Did they already know what had happened in Traesha? New offers to join the cause? I couldn't imagine a girl my age would be privy to very much information. But then a city official, the first one I'd seen in the Squalor, walked by. Everyone in the square scattered. Everyone except that girl. Her expression never shifted. She didn't even push off the statue to stand up straight. My mouth dropped when the official glanced around, then walked over to her. They shared a conversation just like everyone else had with her. In the end, she pressed something into his palm and he kept walking. The square gradually filled again.

The sun was setting when the girl straightened and brushed off her jacket. A boy approached, hands in his pockets, steps unbothered. Even from here it was easy to see the shiny red barrel of his mid gun tucked in his belt. I hurried to the other side of the roof so I could descend into the alley unnoticed. Without a drainpipe on this side, I used the crumbling bricks and window ledges to find hand- and footholds. My body was still exhausted, my arms and legs trembling, but I dropped the last several feet to the ground and landed in one piece.

I turned the corner to leave the alley and was pushed into the side of the building by a tall Bellovian man. I swallowed a startled yelp. His forearm pressed against my throat, pinning me to the wall. Two others were behind him, plus the girl who had been standing guard at the fountain. Her gun never wavered as she aimed at my face. One of the men stepped forward to search me while I choked against the first man's forearm. I squirmed away from his fingers, worried about Oken's knife hidden in my boot. Levi appeared, stepping out of the building's shadow, his eyes bright with amusement.

"Well, now, the little bird came down from her nest. What can we do for you?"

"I need help from the reb—" The man pressed harder on my windpipe and cut me off.

"Another one of the commanders' spies," one man said.

The one holding me pushed harder, digging my head into the building. Black began to crowd my vision. Frustration welled, hot and furious and unfamiliar. I hadn't come this far to be stopped now. I brought my knee up hard. The man grunted when I made contact but held tight, lifting me higher so my toes barely touched the ground. I jabbed the pressure point inside the bicep of the arm holding me up, hitting with my knuckles quick enough to deaden the spot. The pressure let off just enough for me to draw in a breath, then I grabbed his forearm on either side of my throat, planted my feet on the wall and kicked off. We fell heavily to the ground. From my place on his chest I took advantage of his shock and drew back my arm. My fist connected with his nose and his head slammed back into the rocky street. I couldn't stop a wince at the pain of a broken nose we now undoubtedly shared. He went limp. I jumped off him.

I heard the girl's gun cock and turned to continue the fight, but Levi stepped forward and put his hand on the barrel, pointing it down and away from me. She sent him a chilling glare but didn't point the gun at me again.

"You certainly don't look like you need our help," Levi said.

I lifted my chin. "Maybe I don't. But my brother said you would."

"And your brother is..."

"Nico Larson." I had Rennie's name ready too, but it quickly became clear Nico was enough. Levi's eyebrows rose, but the expression came off more theatrical. He really didn't seem surprised. The girl fully lowered her gun with a disappointed frown.

The man I'd taken out began to stir, rolling to his side and coughing past the blood streaming from his broken nose.

"Well, he did say you weren't one to go down without a fight," Levi muttered. "Nol, get Melvin out of here and cleaned up. Audrey, put the gun away. You can come with us, Finley." I started at his use of my name. He turned and left the alley without another word.

CHAPTER 22

Levi led me through the square. The girl, Audrey, followed silently. Levi kept a casual pace, his manner completely at ease and opposite that of the people I'd been watching all day. Yet everyone ducked quickly out of our way. He whistled tunelessly while we walked through a series of alleys, taking hard turns and even cutting through abandoned buildings, sending rats scurrying.

We stopped at a sewer grate. Aubrey crouched to lift it easily and I couldn't stop myself from taking a step back. The Squalor sewers were infamous. I knew better than to fear actual sewage when very few could afford plumbing this far from City Center. Here, the underground tunnels were filled with vicious rodents. Diseased packs of dogs that hadn't seen sunlight in years. Feral cats. Homeless people gone insane breathing in the mold. Their rotting corpses after said mold finished them off. Most of the entrances were impossible to get into, bolted to the ground to prevent injury.

Those rumors in my head, I hesitated slightly when,

with a glance over his shoulder to make sure we weren't being watched, Levi jumped inside. I sucked in a breath and followed, landing in a crouch.

"You certainly are light on your feet for a pampered city princess," Levi said. Now I really felt like I was back in Bellovi. We moved to make way for Aubrey. She somehow managed to pull the sewer grate back into place above her before dropping to the ground with us.

"Of course. You know, after all those fancy dancing lessons."

Levi laughed. "Oh, I know all about those dancing lessons." He pitched his voice lower, "'C'mon, Levi, my daughter was doing this combination at age seven.'"

"You know my father? He trained you?" It hurt to talk about him, but I couldn't help but press the bruise.

"I don't know where we'd be without him."

"Have you seen him? Recently?"

Levi stopped. He didn't need to answer. His face said it all. The bubbling hope stilled once again. When would it stop rising entirely?

The two rebels pulled out flashlights from Levi's pack as we walked deeper into the tunnels. The air wasn't quite stale, it was too cold for that, but it hung lifeless. The curved ground made our steps slow and careful. Our pace dragged compared to the speed at which I'd traveled the last two days. It set my teeth on edge. My bond had shifted to internal compass, letting me know as we followed the turns and dips that we were in fact getting closer to City Center. Every once in a while the air warmed precariously with the smell of sewage, but we always remained a level above it or a turn in the opposite direction.

"We're close," Levi told me when the air was humid and nearly unbreathable.

"Your base is under the city?"

"We'll go up in a second. We don't really have a base per-say, but some of us stay in the house we're going to and the rebellion leaders meet there. We live throughout the city and meet in places like the statue when we have news. Aubrey and I are messengers, so we have access to the main house and the committee. I'll try to get you a meeting with them."

Eventually Levi stopped at the base of a ladder. It hadn't felt like we were going down, but we were much further from this sewer grate than the one we originally entered. I followed Levi's lead and stepped back against the wall to let Aubrey go up first. She climbed quickly and used her shoulder to move the grate enough to poke a head out into the night. It must have been clear, because she pushed it the rest of the way and climbed out. I was only too happy to hurry up behind Levi, fresh air beckoning sweetly.

We emerged on a quiet street. The houses were old and in varying states of disrepair. Just down the street, the first rows of apartments jutted into the sky. Beyond that I knew was my old neighborhood, then City Center. We were right on the edge of the Squalor. Levi made a sound, drawing my attention as I tried to fully place myself. "We can't stay exposed long."

I followed them into a home three houses down. The windows were barred, the door padlocked shut. When the Squalor spread closer to town, many houses put up similar defenses. Some were even bordered by fences that had long since fallen in sections and been rendered useless. Levi made quick work of picking the padlock and forced open the thick door. We ducked inside.

The room we entered had a fire burning strong against the far wall. Piled beside it looked like pieces of wood from the rundown houses and fences we'd passed on our way here. The room was scattered with armchairs, rocking chairs, and creaking dining chairs and pieces. About fifteen rebels sat around eating, an obviously recent silence filling the space between them. Most were young, about mine and Levi's age. A few were older, faces tired and lined. They watched me warily. They had a similar scrawniness to those in the Squalor, but a determination in the set of their shoulders.

The energy in the air was different than any I had felt. At school and the training base, everyone was young and focused. Raw power marked out commander hopefuls at every turn. Thirst for war made for easy smiles and simplicity of thoughts.

In Florian, Hinze and his team were surrounded by the calm of a group who knew they had support coming. Assurance there was a way out. None of the fierce spirit of those ready to die. Even in the cells beneath the castle, they remained sure of themselves. They'd never been in danger like that before, but it was only a matter of time before Hinze was rested.

Here, determination was a quiet ambiance. Behind the wary glances I could see minds that were sharp, quick, calculating. These were people who learned to think for themselves. Everyone was focused, but there was an underlying desperation. Those eating shoveled food like it was their last meal. Whatever resources the rebellion had for bribing city patrol hadn't gone into the base's upkeep.

My stomach sank. These people were different. Maybe more like me. But they weren't supported. They were self-sacrificing. They were tired of the commanders and saw through the propaganda, but the grand resistance I built in my head wasn't what I looked at now.

As my toes slowly began to thaw, Levi gave me a tour. He took me through the kitchen, where he served us both from the pot of stew on the stove. As we ate, he explained a commander held ownership of the house. She'd let the outside grow rundown but spent a good deal on the upkeep inside. Thus, the kitchen held a relatively new stove and enough utensils to feed the rebels living here and any guests. Next, we walked into an office space with binders full of notes connected to a sparsely shelved library. I leaned over one of the desks and found a map scribbled with notes on movements along the Front. There was a half-covered page on "Red Uniform Command." Another paper was labeled with "Detono Updates" and filled with etchings of guns and some strange winged vehicle I'd never seen before. I wasn't given a chance to figure out how it would run before Levi moved on. He explained as we went upstairs that the bedrooms of those who lived here were on the upper level.

"What about the leaders of the rebellion?"

"Most the committee still hold important jobs throughout the city. They have homes and families that don't know they're in the rebellion."

"Sounds familiar."

Levi shot me a wince over his shoulder. "Your father thought it was for the best. They gather in the basement and we share our notes and they make the big decisions." Did I detect an edge of resentment in Levi's tone? "Anyway, they won't be here until tomorrow. I could show you around more, but you seem tired. I thought you'd want to rest up."

He opened the door to one of the bedrooms at the end of the hall. It was separated into three sections by blankets and sheets, giving the occupants some privacy. He led me to the section on the left, lifting the sheet to reveal a small mattress and a dresser only slightly bigger than the nightstand I grew up with.

"I still don't understand how I never knew about this. Any of it. Why did they hide it from me and not Nico?"

"Nico is valuable to the rebellion because of his piano playing. He's probably safer playing at events than he ever would be at the Front. He's good at what he does, blending in and listening. He can remember everything the commanders talk about. I'm sure you could have done the same, but Nico may have mentioned once or twice how little interest you had in playing the piano." Levi smiled at me.

My piano skills were a family joke. It hurt to realize Nico had a different set of friends, a different family, he joked with about me in the same way. All those years Nico was the only person near my age I could talk to. My one friend. And he'd hid this from me the entire time. He might have been my only friend, but I wasn't his. He had an entire set of people working toward his same goal, while I thought I was alone on my path. I was figuring it all out on my own and here Nico knew exactly where to go to play an important role, to find people of similar values and forget the bullying we faced at school. Here Nico was liked and befriended away from me.

He wasn't even my real brother.

Levi must have sensed something of my thoughts in my silence. "I'll help you, Finley. Even if the committee is difficult. I don't know if I completely understand Trish culture, even after what Nico told me about it, but I understand your people could change the tide in this war. And from everything he's told me, you're going to play a huge role in that."

"What did Nico tell you?"

"Not so much, just bits and pieces," Levi said. "The last thing he said about you was when your Trish abilities started to mature, you'd be looking for something that would help the Trish people gain their strength back. He hoped he could give you a head start looking for it in Traesha when he took the job at the Conquering Celebration."

"I saw him there."

"You were at the ball?" Audrey asked. She'd been so quiet thus far, I'd forgotten she was with us. Disbelief colored her tone.

"But... you got here so quickly," Levi said.

His words reminded me of my journey here and the soreness of my body. I shrugged and glanced toward the mattress on the floor. When Levi saw I wasn't going to elaborate, he turned to leave. "Before we go, I have to ask, can you find what Nico was looking for?"

"Yes."

"But not alone. Otherwise you wouldn't have come here."

I hated to do it, but I nodded.

"And then what?"

I hesitated. "I need to sleep before I can think up any kind of plan."

He eyed me for a second before he shrugged. "Fair enough."

Audrey rolled her eyes and left the small space.

"Audrey sleeps right next door," Levi said, laughing at the clear lack of a door.

I dropped my voice, though her boots already clomped further down the hall. "What's her deal anyway?"

Levi grinned. "Let's just say she isn't easily impressed. But we're good friends. I trust her. I think Nico liked her, too. She doesn't open her mouth enough to give away information and she's intimidating enough that no one bothers us."

He rocked back on his heels and looked around the space. His grin died a slow death. "The girl who used to live here got caught. They sent her to the war." Levi sighed. He lifted a brush twisted with black hair from the small dresser, but set it down a second later. "I'm sure she wouldn't have minded you staying here." I noted the pessimistic past tense.

Without thinking, I gave him a small smile and gripped his arm in thanks. He looked down at my hand in surprise.

"Nico did stuff like that too." He patted my hand and turned for the doorway, promising to come wake me in the morning.

I settled into the mattress and was struck by a familiar scent I couldn't place. As I willed my body to relax, I focused on the insistent pull in my chest. I'd felt the queen there for so long, I wanted to see her. The thought was only half formed and tired, but it was enough to spur my mind along the bond as I slipped into sleep.

I was in the dark, but I could hear someone breathing. I reached forward, my hands meeting the bars of a cell. My eyes adjusted a bit and made out some shadows. The girl inside looked up. My dream shadow. The one person whose company was constant and reassuring during the nights when darker thoughts struck. All these years, I had felt her there but been unable to see her. Her presence was as familiar as Nico's. She was grimy and dressed in rags. Her Trish features were shadowed, but I could still see enough to make out her white hair.

I knelt to her level. "I'm coming, my queen."

She nodded and attempted a smile. I put my hand on the bar and she crawled closer. She lifted a hand and gently placed it on my own. There was a flash of white. A burst of energy.

I jolted awake. I stared up at the ceiling, power tingling along my fingers. Energy crackling under my skin. It felt so right.

MOVEMENT on the other side of the sheet barrier woke me. I waited until Levi came to get up, though. My body was still so stiff and exhausted from the run here. I had no idea how I would go about breaking into Command Hall. When Levi opened the door and called my name, I forced myself to roll off the mattress.

"I brought you some toast." He offered the bread, already slightly hard from his trip up the stairs.

"Will the committee meet with me?" Levi grimaced but nodded. His throat bobbed with a swallow. "What? You think they won't help me?"

"I'm worried you won't agree with their politics. Did Nico tell you to go for them for help? Or people like me in the resistance?"

Rennie had been the one to give me Levi's name, but Nico hadn't sounded certain about the committee. Had I made the wrong choice in coming here? In wanting to meet with them? "Why? What's the committee like?"

"Let's just say they don't entirely share your family's beliefs. Your father and them argued often. He believed a true alliance with Traesha and Floria was the only way to save our country, even if it meant falling back under Florian rule. The committee thinks that would be giving up; they still want independence from Floria. They think we need to distribute the wealth Traesha provides more evenly and focus on holding the border while we regain our strength as a country. That in time we could be formidable enough to discuss a truce with Floria or go to war in full."

"They want to continue to rule Traesha as the commanders do?"

Levi fiddled with the button on the cuff of his sleeve. "I believe so. Well, they'd likely be less cruel and I think they plan to send Bellovians up there to work the land too. But they want to remain in charge."

"You don't think I could convince them otherwise?"

"How could you? Your father tried for years."

"The reason I'm here... I think it could help persuade them. I could give the Trish people some of their power back."

"The rumors of their abilities are true?"

"Yes. I can return their strength and the life of the land."

Levi looked truly confused now. The secrets of Traesha were at the tip of my tongue, but as always, I was reluctant to share. All these warnings left me shaken. Who was to say he felt all that differently than the committee downstairs if he was still here working for them? What if he was sent here to learn my mission? Spying on me like they did commanders throughout the city?

Only Rennie's trust in Levi made me want to believe in him.

"Finley, Nico was very vague about what he hoped to find in Traesha when he convinced the committee to send our members there. The fact that he seems to have failed won't go over well. They're going to want to know even more than I do what it is you're here for..."

"My only goal is to free Traesha." I hesitated and Levi waited, looking at me closely. He was a fan of eye contact and it made me uncomfortable. I realized suddenly how often I looked away first from the Bellovians in vain hopes of hiding the blue of my eyes. "I think I can do that when I rescue—"

"Levi," Aubrey's voice at the door interrupted me. We both started. "The committee is ready to see her now."

Levi nodded and we stood. I ignored the pain in my stiff legs and followed Levi through the old house to the basement. There was a door at the top of the stairs and Levi paused before opening it. But there wasn't time to say anything else. We descended.

CHAPTER 23

The basement was warmer than the rest of the home. Thick rugs covered the concrete floor and held the heat of the earth in the other side of the walls. A furnace roared. Before it stood a long table containing four Bellovians all facing me. A boy about my age sat in a stool by the door, gun held limply in his hands. I couldn't help but imagine how much that must have gotten on my father's nerves when he was down here.

"Finley Larson!" I nearly jumped at the familiar voice and turned to see Commander Gale smiling from the table. She looked much as she did during war meetings, her stripes proud on her shoulder and braid immaculate. The other table occupants would not have fit in so well. Loose and unbound hair. Unshaved chins. Wrinkles proving a strong will to live in a world that makes it too difficult.

I did my best to return Commander Gale's smile despite the stony looks I was receiving from the others. "Have you heard anything about my parents?"

As quick as that her smile died. Her face turned guarded. "We have not. We owe a lot to your father. It's

288

been a hard loss." Metal chairs protested down the table as their occupants shifted awkwardly. Levi was tense at my side. It surprised me how grateful I was for his presence.

Commander Gale pressed past the moment. "So, the secret is out now. You've discovered your family's rebellion. Or at least your father and brother's. This is my family home; I've donated it to our cause."

"It's... nice." I wasn't sure what Commander Gale wanted from me. Just then, the bond tugged, a sense of hunger washing over me. We needed to move.

"I like to be helpful. Unfortunately, your brother isn't here."

"I know. He was still in Traesha."

A man with a jagged scar down his face leaned forward. His voice shook with age. "How do you know that?"

"I saw him there. He sent me back to... complete his mission. We discovered what he was looking for is here in Vichi. He thought the rebellion might help me get it."

"You saw your brother that recently?" The woman next to Commander Gale had a loose braid and a downturned mouth. My skin pricked at the shift around the table. I'd already said something wrong, but I didn't know what. I just nodded.

"How did you get back so quickly? We weren't expecting our rebels for a few days more."

Oh. "I... um. I can't tell you." Even Commander Gale looked confused, proving to me my father hadn't shared our Trish ties. I wouldn't let the secret go so quickly.

A long, tense pause. The old man broke it. "It's just as we feared."

"What is? I need your help. When I complete what I came here to do, I can restore Traesha's strength. We can create an alliance with the rebellion. Help the land and—"

"And what stake do you have in Traesha's welfare? Or the rebellion for that matter? Why did your family not tell you about us?" Commander Gale asked.

"I don't—"

"We believe it is because they didn't trust you, Commander Larson," the younger man who had thus far been silent spoke.

A chill crept over my skin. The same worry had nagged me since discovering all my family's secrets. "Please. I can help. I don't know why they never told me, but I always hoped to succeed in the army in order to take down the commanders from within. I have never supported the war."

"We find that difficult to believe. After how adamantly Commander Silken defended you to the lead commanders, trying to persuade them you were a valuable asset despite desertion, we began to have our doubts about the younger Larson child. Silken knows how to weed through his trainees. He must have sensed great loyalty in you. Great potential to serve the Bellovian cause. He promised you'd come back with enough information from Floria to make the trouble worthwhile."

"No, I—"

"And then to return to us so quickly. Only the commanders have access to vehicles capable of traveling so fast. Silken returned you to Vichi as a 'deserter' in order to gain our confidence next. We know you saw him there. Tell us, is the trap you intend to lead us into here similar to the one you led the Florian prince into?"

"No. That wasn't my intention. I'd never—"

"Your family has served us and our cause well. That is the only reason we ask that you leave and don't take further measures. Have no contact with our cause." A significant look at Levi. "Just know, if you betray us, it is your brother who will suffer."

Faces of stone stared back as I struggled to take in the words. Only Commander Gale looked slightly doubtful, but when I met her eyes she only shook her head. I wasn't truly surprised. The familiar sensation of being adrift swept over me. Here was the one place I may have felt belonging. I never felt it among the Bellovians who raised me with battle cries and savagery. I didn't feel it among my team. I got the sense of it among the Trish trees but was still too influenced by Bellovi to truly feel it with the Trish. But I was a rebel to my core. Had always considered myself one. I dreamed of taking down the commanders even as a child. And yet I wasn't enough.

I debated telling them who I was. Showing them what I could do and pleading the queen's case. But I couldn't trust them, not when they so clearly didn't trust me.

"One day, you'll want my help. Just remember how quickly you turned me away when you ask for it. You better make it worth my time." I turned to leave, overwhelm creeping in as I finally confronted the fact that I was on my own. How would I do this?

"Your father would be ashamed of you." The old man's parting words echoed in my ears as I climbed the stairs, dread washing over me. If I failed in this, my parents had every right to be.

I BARELY STOPPED to check if the street was clear before pushing my way out of the house. The city was gray and cold and unchanged. I could hear Levi yelling after me, but even without skipping I'd always been faster than Bellovians. I ran into the crisp morning air, squinting in the light reflecting off the snow. These streets were quiet. In short time I'd reached the apartments and the sound of the city. Vichi's familiarity at once comforted me and stole the air from my lungs. The apartments made me wish Nico was here to visit and demand answers from. To ask for advice. As I cleared their shadowed streets to the homes of my neighborhood, longing for my parents stung my eyes.

I caught a glimpse of Command Hall standing tall in the center of the city and sighed. My dreams of a Bellovian rebellion aiding its overthrow crumpled around me. I walked with my head down, ignoring the bond. Losing myself in the city of my childhood. For once, my clothing was shabby enough, my boots so worn, that no one paid me any attention. I passed through the streets just like any other citizen of Vichi. Hungry, cold, miserable. I needed a plan, but every train of thought shattered with all that could go wrong. I knew how to get to my father's office in Command Hall. I also knew they had low-ranking commanders guarding the entrances and every level. I could follow the bond with relative accuracy to the queen's location. Maybe I could skip to her and avoid guards entirely, but I lacked control and wouldn't know where to go from there. It wasn't as if I could carry her and keep up the same speed. Not to mention the locked door that was sure to hold her in. If I managed to get a gun, maybe I could shoot the lock...

I froze in my steps, breath catching painfully in my chest. Without thought, my feet had led me home. It was insane to think I'd lived here only weeks ago. The gray facade and undisturbed layers of snow looked too quiet. Dark windows empty and unwelcoming. My instincts screamed for me to leave. Skip away before anyone saw me.

I pushed them to the back of my mind, next to the pull in my chest.

I walked where I knew the path to be under the snow. My feet sank heavy through the soft layers. It was my favorite snow. The kind that cushioned sound like a soft blanket. That refused to clump together, even when you used a bare hand to melt and force it into shape. How many times had I stood here, throwing handfuls of this sparkling snow into the air and creating my own, gentle storms? I used to cup it in my gloves and blow it at my father. When we came back inside, I'd shake my scarf out on my mother. She'd push me away laughing and trying to look angry before going to make us all steaming cups of tea.

At this point, I couldn't even feel the cold.

The front door was unlocked. No heat rushed out when I opened it. The air was abandoned. I stepped in and closed the door without bothering to reach for the lights. I gave my eyes the time they needed to adjust after the blinding snow. I knelt to undo my laces; a habit born from years of my mother fuming over tracked mud.

On the carpet where I knelt was a dark brown stain. I stilled. Then clamped a hand over my mouth so quickly I felt back against the door. I held my face so tight my bruises ached, but I contained my scream. I pressed as far from the stain as I could. The image of the Florian guard, blood pooling out from his dead body filled my mind. The spread of blood this same shape. The same amount. The story told in this bloodstain was the same. Death.

The hand over my mouth didn't help. I turned my head and wretched, the food my body desperately needed to recover from my run leaving me in a rush. Tears blurred my vision. Gasping, I clutched my stomach. My parents. My parents were dead. I didn't need to see the rest of the house to confirm it.

I had tried to accept it, but no one had been able to tell me flat out they were gone. Part of me held on to hope this whole time. Only seeing the stain, feeling the death in the air, confirmed what I had been avoiding.

My parents were dead.

I used the doorknob to pull myself to my feet. I shook and swallowed hard, not wanting to be sick again. I was so stupid. So ridiculously stupid. I ran outside, not bothering to shut the door to the empty house behind me. I stumbled into the street, slipping into a skip to get away like I should have initially.

I had nowhere to go but Nico's apartment. I skipped all the way to his door and twisted the nob so quick and sharp I didn't even need a key. I froze when I stepped inside, taking in the piles of canvas bags. The smell of home that had been missing at the house. Somehow Nico had saved our things. Through the tears, I found a bag of my mother's things and carried it into the bedroom. I stripped from my winter layers and wet leggings. I upturned the bag of my mother's clothing onto Nico's bed and fell into the mess, burrowing down for warmth. My hands found my mother's softest sweater and pulled it up close to my nose.

I fell asleep drowning in my mother's scent, my brain too desperate for escape and my eyes too heavy from tears to fight the darkness.

I sighed, opening my eyes to Command Hall. Snow fell in swirls around me. The bond was an incessant tug. I squared my shoulders, buried another sigh, and started up the steps. I would still come for her. I had to. But I might as well warn her things aren't going to plan.

I stepped up to the doors and waited for them to open. They didn't. I pulled at them, but they were jammed somehow. I yanked and yanked. The snow was falling so thick now I could barely even see my hands where they tugged at the handles.

"Don't you see, Larson? You've gotten yourself into a corner this time," Silken spoke from behind me.

The doors weren't going to open. I let my head fall against the metal.

"You know what to do. What your parents would want. They knew your limits. Just take my hand, we can save Bellovi on the simple, easier path they planned." The words cut.

"No," my protest was just a whisper.

My father's gentle admonishment from so long ago filled my head. The dream shifted so I was there, watching myself on the first day of school.

"She's so small!" Laughter. "She's going to cry!" A push sent me to the ground. I watched it all, numb and at a distance as my child self was bullied. "My dad said your dad isn't wanted at the war anymore, because he kept shitting himself during battle." The loudest round of laughter yet. My tiny fists curled in rage. Someone kicked snow and dirt at my face. I screamed and tried to get up to fight back, but children's feet surrounded me, kicking snow, kicking me, laughing and shouting. Teachers finally came, speaking in bored voices. "Time to go back in."

A hand in front of me. I remembered so clearly how it felt to look up into those light brown eyes, impossibly large in his small face, the color of honey on my favorite Trish bread. I let him help me to my feet and watched as he turned and ran back inside. He would barely look at me in years to come. In that moment, he probably just thought I was his cousin. Mayze and I were the same size back then. Still, as I watched now I smiled at his back and the look of complete bewilderment on my small face, eyes so wide and helpless with emotion under the dirt, blood, and melting snow. My small hand clenched into a fist as if I could capture the warmth from his grip.

I came home from school crying. I sat on the couch, a parent holding me on either side. Nico sat in front of us on the rug, crying his own tears of sympathy. He never liked to see anyone hurting. I sank to the floor, where I watched and drank in the sight. All of us together.

"Don't make her go back, Teo."

"She has to, Elise. It's too late to pull her out now. Not without looking suspicious. Without looking weak."

"I don't mind looking weak," I mumbled.

My father slid off the couch. Nico leaned into his side as my father knelt in front of me. His hand was big enough to hold both my own at once, his other hand went under my chin, lifting it and holding it high. "You listen, Finny, and you listen good. My daughter is not weak. It doesn't matter what anyone else says. Nothing they say means anything. All that matters is how you react. That's all you can control. You don't give them the satisfaction of your tears. You don't let them see they've hurt you. And you fight back. I'll teach you," my father finished, ignoring my mother's sounds of protest.

I watched my little chin lift.

"Fight for him. For his people." I was ripped back to the initial dream. I turned from the doors and barely made out Silken's dark outline where he lounged on the steps. The snow was nearly suffocating. Some panic began to build in my chest. If I reached out to Silken, I could work my way up again. Maybe, eventually gain access to the queen...

But that wasn't what my father would want.

I lifted my chin. I let the panic crowd in, knowing it would wake me.

I struggled out from under Nico's blanket and my mother's clothing. My head was pounding. I needed to figure out a plan. But I would take this day one step at a time. I found a change of clothes in the living room and went to shower. I tried to concentrate under the low-pressure water, but panic kept shifting in my chest. I could barely think past the tug there. It was like half my consciousness was below Command Hall with the queen. I felt disjointed and torn.

I was dressed and braiding my hair when I heard the door hinge creak in the main room. I pressed my ear to the bathroom door, listening close.

"Damn, what did she do to this knob?"

I threw my hat on and pushed out of the bathroom. "Levi? Audrey? What's this?"

Levi entered Nico's apartment grinning. Audrey was close on his heels, looking bored. Then—

"Commander Gale?"

A boy entered behind her, confusing me further. He was probably fifteen and took in the room slowly.

"Where did the bags come from?" he asked.

I answered automatically. "My parents' home." He nodded and went to sit at the piano bench. I stared after him. Levi was still playing with the doorknob, trying to get the latch to take. Eventually he shrugged and kicked a bag in front of it to keep it shut like I had.

"What's going on?" I asked. I eyed Commander Gale, still wary after her unwillingness to help just yesterday with the committee.

Levi grinned. He walked to the kitchen counter and pulled himself up to sit. His familiarity with Nico's apartment rubbed my nerves. Another reminder of their friendship. Here I always thought I was Nico's only visitor.

"We're here to help you get the thing!" He spread his arms. I must not have looked very excited. One of his hands went to scratch the back of his neck. "Well, I mean, it isn't a lot. But we can help. If you still want to get it. Gale has to play her role with the committee, so we know what they're thinking, but we all trust Nico and your dad and therefore you. If this mission is as important as you say, we'll do what we can to make it successful."

"But..." I didn't even know which question to ask out of the many filling my head. I finally settled on the most pressing. "Why?"

Levi rubbed his palms together. "Nico thinks this is the best shot for Traesha. And Traesha is our best shot for ending the war. I don't trust the committee. Their focus has twisted and now they just want power... Your dad made it sound like there were ways to help everyone. I want to do the level of good he imagined."

I looked around the room. Audrey gave me a curt nod. The boy at the piano wasn't paying attention. He cautiously struck a key and tilted his head to listen to the note that rang out. Commander Gale was watching me intently. I couldn't shake the way she'd spoken with the committee or even the image of her standing as a commander before the Bellovians. Which side was she truly on? How did she keep all the deceptions straight?

"You'll really help me?" I asked her.

"Yes. Your father is a persuasive man. He convinced me to join the rebellion all those years ago. Neither of us liked the direction it began to take when the committee formed, but we thought joining it would be best to stay close to them. I knew before we met with you they would never back you after Traesha failed and Silken pushed for your pardon, so I stood with them to keep my place, but you must know I want to help."

She would know the layout of Command Hall. Maybe even have keys. She was too valuable an ally to turn away.

"A lot of the commanders who went to Traesha are scheduled to return tomorrow. We should get it tonight," the boy said, matter-of-fact like the task in front of him was as daunting as a trip to the market. He looked up suddenly. "Where is it?"

"*What* is it?" Audrey asked.

I hesitated. The boy saw my doubts. "You don't trust us. That's okay. My name is Hue Adkins. My father is a five-striped commander. Lead Commander of Vichi. When I go out, he thinks I'm training with friends, but really I'm telling Levi about the things I've read in his office. Sometimes Gale gives me lessons, though, and your father used to as well, so it looks like I'm improving. My mom was a Squalor prostitute, but he says I'm legitimate from the wife he had at the time. I still go see my mom. I sneak her money. That's how I found out about the rebellion. You can trust me."

I blinked at the influx of information. Looking into his wide eyes, I believed him. I wasn't in a position to turn away help. "I'm here to save the queen of Traesha."

Stunned silence. Even collected Gale's mouth dropped open.

Hue processed the information first. "How do you know where she is?"

"I..." Again, I hesitated. Nico hadn't told them I was half Trish. But at Levi's encouraging nod and thinking about the condemning information Hue had just shared, I pressed on, "My mother is from Traesha. My dad snuck us both out of the country during the invasion. The royal family there always had a guard; the strongest and quickest of the Trish were trained at the castle from the time they were children to be part of it. Those who developed Trish speed—"

"You have it right? That's how you got here so fast from Traesha?"

"Hue, don't interrupt," Gale said, but the chastise was half-hearted.

"Yes, I just developed the ability. It comes when we reach adulthood. Those who could skip were recruited into the *magsai* guard. And every queen also has a *resa magsai*. They come into this world at the same moment and share a bond for life. This bond tells the *resa magsai* when the queen is in trouble, if she's hurt, where she is... things like that."

"And you're the queen's *resa magsai*?" I was impressed by Hue's accent. I nodded.

"Okay. Will you tell us where she is now?"

"Command Hall."

Audrey swore. I jumped when she spoke up so suddenly. Gale frowned. I felt for her, the only person in the room over twenty planning to infiltrate the commanders' main headquarters.

"How are we going to get in there?" Levi asked. He walked to the window. The imposing form of Command Hall was visible in the distance.

"It's the most heavily guarded building in Vichi." Audrey sounded angry at us for even considering it.

"It's not so bad. I'll be right back." We watched Hue jump up and leave the apartment. I could hear him running down the stairs. I laughed a bit over his abrupt departure in the silence that followed. Levi shrugged and went to Nico's cabinets in search of food. Apparently, this wasn't unusual behavior for Hue.

"Do you think it's not so bad?" I asked Gale.

She shrugged. "My office is on the second floor. I've been to the upper levels, but, besides guards at the entrances of each hall, I suppose it isn't so locked down where the higher-ups stay."

"What about the basement?"

"That I don't know. I haven't been." Something in her voice hinted at knowing more.

I turned to Levi. "How did you know I'd be here?"

"Where else would you go?"

"But the committee didn't want you to help me."

Audrey muttered the committee could do something fairly impractically and highly inappropriate that made me like her much more. Dread still coiled in my stomach, but, surrounded by allies in my brother's apartment, I was beginning to feel slightly more hopeful.

But only slightly. What if this new team ended as poorly as the last two? What if nothing ever worked out for me in a group because I was meant to work alone? I was too violent for the Trish. Too conflicted to be a Bellovian. Too willing to see the good of this country to fit with the Florians... I was too hopeful even for the damn rebellion. I never expected they had formed just to create more of the same. I had envisioned an organization in search for peace capable of lifting everyone, not just those in power. Could Levi, Gale, Audrey, and Hue really share my vision?

And, more importantly, would the queen? Could I follow her if she didn't? For the first time I felt a flutter of fear. What if I didn't have a choice? What if this bond was stronger than my own will?

"I'm glad you survived getting sent to war," Gale said. "You did as well as we expected. What prompted you to desert?"

I didn't want to talk about tripping over Dani's body or

the Florians and Trish I'd abandoned in Traesha. "Feels like I'm still in it."

"Still, you must have done well. Especially for Silken to be so impressed."

I dropped my eyes and shrugged. Silken's approval hadn't gotten me anywhere. It hadn't saved my father despite his claims of their friendship and it had dug me deeper into holes at every turn.

Gale must have seen the defeat in my eyes. "The worst has happened, Fin. It can only get better."

I shook my head. Didn't she see I still had so much to lose?

CHAPTER 24

Hue came back in short time, breathing hard and cheeks red from the cold. We sat in a circle on the floor. Hue spread out the blueprints he'd taken from his father's office of Command Hall in the middle of us, muttering a hasty apology when he nearly knocked over Audrey's mug of hot water. The rolled paper was old and faded. We had to use random items from around the room to hold down the curling edges, including the mug, a music book, Levi's gun, and, without any hesitation on his part, Hue's left boot. He sat there in one shoe as we leaned over the map.

I pointed to the bottom right corner. I had gotten lost so many times in the halls during my dream, I felt oddly satisfied to finally be able to orientate myself. Like I had finally beaten the nightmare.

"The queen is down there."

"There are cells down there. But other stuff too. My dad has only mentioned the basement briefly; what happens down there is confidential," Hue said. He bent closer to the map, taking in the section I pointed to, his nose much too close to his shoe.

I caught Audrey and Levi sharing a look. "And how are we supposed to get down there?" she asked. Did I imagine the tremble in her voice?

Hue shrugged. "There's never even been an attempted break-in. I've only ever heard about people trying to get out, but even then, not for the last couple of years. Security can't be too tight."

"Commander Silken might have warned them I'm coming…" I wasn't about to put a second team in jeopardy because he knew my plans.

Hue shook his head. "Even if he has warned them, they won't even expect you for a couple more days at least."

"I can get us in probably," Levi said. "Locked doors shouldn't be a problem."

"Why can't you just run, skip, whatever, in and out?" Audrey asked me.

"I could skip to her, yes. But I don't know if she can skip out with me. I don't think I'd be able to carry her and skip. And I probably couldn't get her out of the cell. I don't know how to pick a lock."

Audrey glanced at the broken knob on Nico's door and didn't argue.

"How are guards posted inside?" Levi asked Gale. He found a pen in Nico's drawers and began dotting the map with little x's where Gale told him of the guards she knew were stationed.

We fell quiet, staring at the blueprints as though they held the answer.

"We need to get to her quickly," I finally said. "I think the element of surprise will be all the advantage we need. I can do a lot of damage in a fight. I could at least get us down there."

"But that still leaves getting out!" Audrey said.

"If we get to here," Hue pointed to the set of stairs, "I can blow up a hole in the wall without bringing the whole building down. The supports are here and here, so this point is safe. And it's the closest we can get to the cells that is level with the ground."

"What makes you think you're going in with us? You're fifteen! I'm not letting you get shot at, Hue." Hue didn't seem to hear Levi's protest.

"Where will that bring us out in the city?" I asked.

"The east side of the building." Levi pulled around his backpack and brought out a map of Vichi. We unfolded it on top of the blueprints. Levi pointed to the street the wall aligned with.

"That's the closest wall to this apartment. Ten blocks, a straight shot," I said.

"I don't know if coming back here will be a good idea. We should get out of Vichi as soon as possible. Get a head start on the commanders," Levi said.

"We?"

"Oh, I have no plans to stick around. The city is too cold for my liking." Levi forced lightness into his tone.

"And?"

Levi considered me. "The rebellion can only do so much from within the city. And I don't agree with the little they *have* been doing. I work mostly with recruiting people from the Squalor, getting them comfortable, giving them missions. Even they find the rebellion lacking. At the end of the day, I'm not doing enough. I grew up hungry in the Squalor and I know the people here. I want to do more to help them." Levi took a deep breath and shared a look with Audrey. "The Florian abilities aren't just rumors?"

The question caught me off guard. "No, they're not just rumors. I only met a few of them, but it was enough to know the stories are not exaggerated by any means."

Levi nodded. "My sister had them. Abilities, I mean." I started. I'd never heard of a Bellovian with a gift that wasn't strength. "She used to be able to make people feel better, to give them more energy and even help if they got sick. I have an ability too, but it doesn't present often. Even so, the commanders dislike any sort of threat. I'm not like the Bellovians. I'm not Florian. Just like I don't think you're just Trish. I think you and Nico and this queen will change this war. I want to be a part of it, not hiding here until the time is right or we starve."

"I feel... similarly," Audrey said. "If you'll take my help, I want out." She looked down and picked up her mug of water, ignoring how the edge of the blueprints curled back up. She did not like asking me for this.

I knew what it meant to live in fear in Vichi. I nodded slowly to both of them. "I'm not in a position to turn down help. And I don't think this war will ever end if people can't come together." I said the words and accepted I was part of a team yet again. Hopefully the queen would approve of her newest followers. Hopefully I wouldn't fail them too. "I have to warn you, though, so far my journey has been quite the ride. I can't promise anything will go remotely as planned or how the queen will react once we find her."

"If you just help us out of this damn country, that'll be enough for me," Audrey said. The determination in her eyes was a hard glint.

"It's not like we really have that much of a plan to go by anyway," Levi said with a shrug.

"I can't go, Finley," Gale said. "I mean out of Vichi or into Command Hall. I'm sorry. My stations within the commanders and the committee are too valuable. But maybe I could cause a distraction to lure some of the guards away?"

Hue's pointer finger trailed over the city map while he thought.

"I understand." I wasn't eager to lose an ally in those positions either.

"Here," Hue said. I knew the square he pointed to. It held a statue of his father in the center and was a block from the west side of Command Hall. "You can set off an explosion on the statue. They'll send guards to check out the blast and it'll distract everyone. You can blend into the people walking around. If we time it for when the workday ends, everyone will be going home. Some people might get hurt, but I can control it enough not to kill anyone. Then the sun will be set by the time we get out of the cells and we can sneak out more easily."

"That sounds like the best plan we've come up with yet," I said.

"You should go with Gale, though, Hue," Audrey put in. "I can get us out of the cells, but Gale will probably need help with the explosives. We can't afford for them to go wrong and people to get hurt."

Hue considered this and nodded once. "Go fourteen stairs up when you break through the wall. That's ground level." Hue collected the blueprint and stomped his boot back on. "I'll go make the bombs. Meet me at my house, Gale? And the rest of you be ready to go in right at closing."

Hue left. Gale soon followed, shaking my hand and smiling encouragingly. It was hard to watch her leave. I wanted to cling to every bit of home I had left.

"So, how exactly do we plan to get out of Vichi? And where do we go after?" Audrey asked, pulling my attention away from the sound of Gale descending the stairs.

"Not Traesha. Unless we want to plow fields the rest of our lives," Levi muttered. He looked up in time to see my scowl. "Sorry, just thinking out loud."

I let my glare linger just a little longer. "Traesha's out. And I think we should leave Bellovi completely. I might have friends in Floria, if they don't hate me for leaving them behind. Either way, I think the queen will need to start talking alliance with the king. And there are Trish people in Floria, refugees and ambassadors. I'm counting on them to flock to the queen. With their help and through negotiations with the king we might come up with a way to get Traesha back into our own hands."

"And if the queen disagrees? What if she doesn't want to go to Floria?"

I paused for a moment. "I guess I'll have to do what she says."

"Somehow I don't think you'll be one to play the obedient servant gracefully," Levi said. I couldn't tell if his bluntness was refreshing or annoyingly unnecessary. "Plus, you'll have to figure out how to get past the Front to cross into Floria. I don't suppose you made any friends in the army that might help?"

"I think so." Unless Oken felt he'd done enough after the knife and the cycle.

"Hue could check the records for us, see where they're stationed. You'd probably have to chase the kid down before he gets home, though. Think you could catch him?"

I rolled my eyes and started to stand. "Yes."

"Wait, you sure they'd help?" Audrey asked. "What makes you think so? What's their name?"

It was a good thing Rennie knew them as I couldn't bring myself to say Oken's name out loud. "Rennie Jaspers."

Audrey and Levi both gasped and I fought a smile. Somehow, I knew this conversation was playing out in a way that Rennie would have enjoyed immensely.

A slow smile crept up the corners of Levi's lips. "She *is* on her way to the Front. Hue told me where she was being stationed just yesterday. Rennie's room was the one you slept in back at base."

I returned Levi's smile, the pieces clicking so effortlessly into place. Thank the gods.

"They didn't just send her to the Front?" Audrey asked. She was smiling too now, small and unpracticed, but a smile all the same.

"No. She did well in training. She was on my team."

"What are the odds?" Levi laughed.

"So we have a place to cross. How do we get there?"

"You get me to a lot, I can get us transportation," Levi said. He grinned and rubbed his hands together. It was such a slip of a plan I could barely grasp it. Yet still, I felt the fluttering of anticipation in my stomach. I hoped the queen could feel it too.

WE PACKED OUR BAGS, Audrey taking most of the food from Nico's cabinets. I went to my mother's clothes on Nico's bed. I inhaled her scent and ran my hands over the soft fabric before stuffing things in my pack for the queen.

"You sure those will fit her?" Audrey asked when I returned to the main room and found a pair of my mother's boots. I shoved them in with the clothes.

"They'll probably be too big..." I muttered, finding the

thickest pair of socks. Audrey arched an eyebrow, but she and Levi were beyond questioning me. Thinking about the queen's white hair, I packed my mother's shawl on top.

Levi had come prepared. He handed me a rusted short gun with an apologetic smile over the shape it was in. He and Audrey carried an array of weapons, all fastened close to their bodies. I was surprised to spot a hammer easily accessible on Audrey's left hip and wanted to ask about the choice, but I'd moved beyond questioning them too.

I returned to the bag of my clothes and dug out my spare pair of boots. They were a dark brown and less warm than the ones I'd worn through. I hadn't liked them when my father gave them to me. They sat untouched in my closet for months. I cringed from the memory and pulled them on.

Our bags loaded and the plan fresh in our minds, we made to leave. I spared one last glance, breathing in the smell of home and my family's belongings. A sudden thought struck me.

"I'll catch up!" I called down the hall. Slipping back inside, I shifted through the bags, opening some, folding others, feeling around. I frowned when I had to accept my mother's *magsai* sword was nowhere in the apartment. Then I realized, with the blood draining from my face, it must have been taken by the commanders who killed them. It was probably hanging from someone's hip or strapped to their back. The closest thing Bellovians had to jewelry. My fists clenched and I blinked away a rush of tears. I hurried to catch up before the emotions fully claimed me.

The streets were still relatively free of people. It was snowing lightly. I hoped it would snow harder for cover. I hoped it would stop snowing so the way out of the city would be clear. I watched the dark shape of Command Hall emerge out of the white swirls and felt it wouldn't matter either way. How could we possibly hope to get in and out of there alive?

Levi took us off the main road and into a narrow alley. The buildings surrounding Command Hall contained factories, gyms, specialized schools for those recruited for weapons building, technology, or keen minds for strategy, and other like buildings. I honestly didn't know what went on behind many of these doors and windows. But Levi knew his way around them as well as he knew the Squalor. It seemed he'd memorized the Vichi map he carried.

Eventually he stopped us in an alley that provided a view of Command Hall's east entrance. We could barely see the statue of Commander Adkins in the square and there was no sign of Gale or Hue. We huddled up in a padlocked doorway, pressing into the shadows to wait.

"So, what do we think this queen of Traesha is like?" Levi asked, his breath drifting up between us in a white cloud. I stomped my feet a few times, thinking about my answer. Audrey didn't seem interested in conversation and kept watch, facing away with her head peeking out from the doorway. Her fingers strayed often to the hammer at her hip.

"I'm not sure, but she's supposed to be the embodiment of Traesha. My mother said the queens were always kind, fair, intelligent, and giving. They valued peace in their lands more than anything."

"Always queens?"

"Always queens."

"A queen like that is supposed to end this war?" Audrey scoffed, but I could see the interest in her dark eyes when she turned to look back at us.

"Sometimes peace comes at a price. A price I'm sure

she'll be willing to pay," I said, reaching a bit. I wasn't even sure how the Trish could help the war efforts to begin with.

"And as her res magsy you'll be in charge of the fighting?" Levi asked.

I smiled despite myself. "*Resa magsai*. And I guess so, yeah."

"Good thing you grew up in Bellovi."

I started a bit. So far I had only considered my childhood to be something that set me apart from the queen and the people we were supposed to save. "Maybe it does put me at a bit of an advantage."

Audrey checked her watch and quickly returned her hands to her pockets and out of the cold. "Hue and Gale should be setting off the bomb right about now," she whispered. Five more minutes passed. We exchanged nervous looks. More people were spilling into the streets, the workday over. It was only a matter of time before someone noticed us lurking. We stomped and jumped in place, using quick, restrained movements in an effort to stay warm. The air bit at the inside of my nose, making it run, but wiping it was agony. I tucked it carefully into my scarf and breathed in the humid air caught inside.

My link to the queen was yanking at me now that I was so close. An urge in need of satisfaction, like an intense itch I had to scratch. It set my nerves completely on edge. After ten minutes I was ready to go in myself, explosion or no.

"Calm down, Finley. They're probably waiting for a break in the crowd or something. I'm sure they're fine." Levi's words flooded me with guilt. I was so concentrated on the queen I hadn't even thought to worry about Gale and Hue.

The air shuddered with the sound of Hue's explosion. Finally.

"There it is! Move!" Audrey took off. I barely glimpsed the damage Hue's bomb caused. I saw flames, thick black smoke, and people running in every direction amid screams. More than one person pulled a knife and looked for who was to blame, as trained as the guards standing at the east entrance who shouted and took off toward the sound. They rounded the corner right as we reached the doors. Within the next breath, Levi's steady hands had it open.

"Hue wasn't kidding about lax security. These locks have to be at least twenty years old."

The heated hall instantly made me feel compressed inside my heavy coat. I longed to dump it, but I needed to keep it close if we were going to get across the city and to a transport lot. Audrey and I took our positions looking down the hall on either side of the door while Levi swept our tracks off the stairs outside and relocked it. There was distant shouting, but no alarms or approaching footsteps.

The bond tugged and my body jerked with it, stepping deeper into the building before I fully realized what I was doing. My adrenaline sparked with energy, boiling at the surface of my skin. I was so close. Everyone who suspected the queen capable of giving her people strength was right. Hope blossomed as I imagined how much she could do for the downtrodden I'd seen in Traesha.

I waved Audrey and Levi forward with two fingers. They kept low and quiet, the Bellovian war signals known even to those who grew up in the Squalor. I led them down the hall to the right. Unlike my nightmares, I could tell exactly where to turn and which doors to tell Levi to unlock. It was hard not to tap into my Trish speed and just get there already. The buzz of power made my body hum. My senses heightened overwhelmingly. I could barely focus on all the input. I almost failed to stop us in time to wait for two commanders to walk by before we turned the corner. I heard them so early I couldn't judge when their footsteps were close. They were rushing to go see the aftermath of the explosion, speaking into earpieces. Levi smirked with satisfaction from the panic-tinged chatter.

The air chilled as we neared the basement. Audrey was now clutching her hammer, her forehead furrowed. Levi kept looking at her, concern in his eyes. She returned his looks with a glare. I wanted to ask, but now wasn't the time for questions.

We came to a corner. Keeping low and glancing around it quickly, I saw a set of stairs leading to the basement guarded by two soldiers, just like Gale said. They were talking to each other, guns held slack at their sides.

"Probably just another idiot over in explosives. They're almost more trouble than they're worth these days."

"You hear about the new one they're building, though? Could be—" We didn't learn what it could be. I signaled for Audrey to take the left and was at the right guard in a heartbeat, snaking behind and catching him in a headlock. His companion's eyes widened in shock, but it took her just long enough to react for Audrey to get her in a similar position. They twitched, tried to shout, and fought until they lost consciousness. We lowered them to the floor.

"Over here!" Levi open a closet nearby. He pulled some thin ropes out of his bag while Audrey and I dragged the guards over. Audrey easily maneuvered the woman's considerable bulk.

Levi tied their hands, ankles, and mouths before closing the door on them. "I'm fairly sure this is the staircase Hue said we needed to leave through."

"There are probably guards stationed at the bottom,"

Audrey said. None of us liked the thought of going down blind, knowing they'd see us before we saw them. No corners to hide behind.

But I felt the queen. So close in the charged air. When I clenched my fists and flexed, the pulling of my muscles was foreign. Saturated. The strength so present and primed I wanted to test my limits. I looked at my companions. Levi's return gaze didn't falter. Audrey swallowed and grabbed my arm. "Whatever happens, don't let the commanders take us," she said, her voice strained.

I nodded. We descended cautiously, our steps whispers on the concrete, but the guards saw our feet before we saw them. They shouted and shots rang out. I flew down the stairs, misjudged with this new coursing energy, doubled back, and stopped behind them. I was still amazed by my own speed. They hadn't even seen me pass between them.

"Excuse me," I said. They whirled; guns raised. I grabbed the nearest guard and threw him into his companion. They sailed through the air, landing in a heap, and I fought a smile. Trish people weren't supposed to enjoy this violence or power. A couple of well-placed blows just to be sure, and these guards were unconscious too.

I turned, my feet no longer my own, my mind in a daze, pulled forward by the intoxicating promise of more power. The strength of Traesha's queen. I went further into the halls, barely hearing Audrey when she said they were behind me. I skipped the short distance. It didn't even feel like my feet were moving, more like I was yanked forward by the bond. I stumbled to a halt in front of a large cell with a rumpled bed and walls covered in scratched letters and artwork. A small, skinny girl with silver hair so light it was a shimmering white stood in front of me. Her eyes were a blueish green that stood out stark against her red-rimmed eyes. She was beautiful despite being covered in grime and ripped clothing.

"You're the one then," she said, Trish words floating like music.

"I'm sorry. I'm sorry it took me so long."

We stared at each other, just feeling the bond and the relief of being together. The relief of being whole and centered. I came out of my thoughts and gave an awkward bow.

"My queen."

She let out a soft laugh, her cheeks dimpling. "Just call me Natasha and get me out of here."

CHAPTER 25

I slipped off my backpack. Natasha bounced on her toes as she checked down the hall for more guards. Her eyes were wide under a dramatic widow's peak.

"Levi will be able to get the door unlocked. Hurry and change."

The queen moved at lightning speed, changing into the leggings I pushed through the bars and the thick sweater. The sleeves hung halfway down her small hands and she set to work rolling the leggings to free her feet. She'd just slipped into the boots I'd shoved roughly through the bars when Audrey caught up, supporting most of Levi's weight.

"Couldn't have taken them out a little faster there, Finny?" he asked, voice strained. His ashen face and use of my family nickname made my heart stop. Audrey gently set him against the bars of Natasha's cell. Panic crowded my vision. Audrey opened his coat to reveal the hooded shirt beneath glistening with blood. I stumbled, catching myself on the bars.

"No…" Another person dead. My brother's friend. Rennie's friend. The boy who fed starving children in the

Squalor. My doing. I swallowed, but my throat wasn't working. I stared at him, waiting for his eyes to dim. For death to claim his gaze and follow me forever.

Natasha watched closely. In my periphery, I saw her eyes flicking between me and the Bellovians. She knelt behind Levi and reached between the bars.

Audrey shot me a confused glance when Natasha took Levi's hand and closed her eyes. I shrugged in response, a strange calm settling over me, driving away the panic. I realized it was coming from Natasha. The calm was hers, traveling over our bond to reassure me. When Levi's breath came out in a sigh, I was certain it was his last. But instead, he drew in a gasp and his eyes flew open. He whirled on the ground, keeping his hand in the queen's. She looked as shocked as he did.

"I've never done that before," she said in Trish. Levi lifted his shirt, revealing a pale, skinny, and bloody chest. But... no sign of where the blood came from.

He ran a hand over where the hole used to be. Not even a scar. She was stronger than Garris even. My excitement dimmed at the thought. It seemed every moment of happiness these days was quickly chased by death.

"We're stronger together," I whispered. I thought about how easily I'd thrown the large guard just moments ago. Natasha stood and reached through the bars to put a hand on my cheek. The throbbing of my nose and bruises, throbbing I hadn't even noticed with everything else happening, eased away. I curled my fist and felt a flush of relief that the scabs on my palm from Oken's knife were still there. I stepped away before she could cover the scars. Natasha stared at her hand and let out a giggle, the unexpected sound making Audrey and me jump. Levi looked up, staring at the queen like she was the sun bursting through the winter clouds.

"This is amazing," Natasha whispered, her dimples still out in full force. With the widow's peak and contrast between her white hair and dark skin, she'd appeared fierce. Regal. Striking.

The dimples definitely ruined the look.

Audrey raised her eyebrows at me. *Is she serious?* But I couldn't stop myself from smiling back at Natasha, the rush of emotion coming from her side of the bond intoxicating.

Shouting at the top of the stairs broke the moment.

"*Shit.*" Levi pulled out his lock picks. I finished feeding Natasha my mother's coat through the bars as he worked. We'd worry about the rest once we had a second to breathe. The door of her cell sprang open right as footsteps thundered on the stairs. Lots of footsteps.

"Looks like those stairs are out," Levi muttered. We turned and ran in the opposite direction.

"This way!" Audrey waved us on, her face nearly as pale as Levi's had been moments ago bleeding out in front of Natasha's cell.

The door we came up to had a strange lock sporting a series of buttons on it, a number in white on each one. "It's electronic!" Levi was completely bewildered by the sight, picks useless in his hands.

"Just get back!" Audrey pulled him away, positioning us all at a safe distance. I checked over my shoulder, trying to judge how long she had before the guards reached us while their shouts and pounding steps echoed in the hall. I waited for her to pull out the explosives Hue must have given her to get us through the stair wall. Instead, she swung her hammer down on the lock, leaving nothing but sparking wires. She shouldered open the door and gestured for us to follow.

The hall was newer. No concrete or rusted bars. The floor gleamed white. The cells were solid metal doors with window slots through which narrowed eyes watched us. Fans whirled and each cell was equipped with a similar electronic lock blinking a red light. A woman in a lab coat turned the corner and yelped when she saw us. I was so thrown by this new pristine setting, I hesitated. This gave her ample time to pull the alarm on the wall next to her.

"Defend m—"

I skipped to her and knocked her unconscious before she could finish, but I went cold as the wailing filled the air. I turned to Audrey. "What is this place?"

"Trainees," she mumbled, looking dazed. I looked to Levi, but he just shook his head. Right. We weren't asking questions.

With a clank, doors at the end of the hall opened on either side. A man and a woman stepped out. I paused, taking in their strange uniforms. The same as any other Bellovian commander's, except opposite in coloring. Blood red and the single stripe on their shoulder black.

"Finley..." Levi's voice was a low warning behind me. I saw two more of the strange commanders had stepped out behind him, Audrey, and Natasha. The blaring of the alarm was nearly loud enough to drown my thoughts. I skipped back to them. Levi had his gun out, pointed at the two Bellovians behind us. Audrey flexed her grip on her hammer. I stood at their backs, Natasha between us.

"Just let us through," I said as firmly as I could to the pair I faced.

Some of those still trapped began whooping and pounding on the doors. Some of them pounded so hard their doors were denting outward. At this point I couldn't even hear if the initial guards were still following us. The alarm would bring them here, no doubt. We had to keep moving.

The man laughed at my words. The girl next to him smirked and raised her hands. I waited, my mind flashing to all the Florian abilities I had seen. But nothing happened. I glanced behind my shoulder. Natasha was puzzled; Levi wore a grimace; Audrey's face drained of color and she sagged into Natasha.

"Take them out!" she groaned.

I skipped forward. A quick punch to the jaw took out the girl, but as I spun to deal with the man, he rammed his shoulder into my stomach. He had to bend nearly double to get his shoulder there. The air whooshed from my lungs as he pushed me up the wall. Stars danced in my vision when we hit harder than I dreamed possible. My feet dangled and I struggled to breathe. With all the speed I could muster but no room for momentum, I braced my hands on his shoulders and pushed myself up, scraping my back against the wall and hitting my head on the ceiling. I gritted my teeth against the newest shock of pain. I was still misjudging my abilities but I was past being able to afford mistakes like that.

He scrambled to keep hold of me, but I grunted and managed to free a leg, swinging it up around his neck so I was riding his shoulders. He roared and grabbed my calves, ready to throw me. I could feel his strength just from his grip. I wouldn't be able to maintain this position for long. I wrapped a hand under his chin and braced the other on top of his head. I paused. He froze. I couldn't draw in a full breath of air.

I chanced a glance at Natasha, my gut churning. Her

face was stone save for the fury in her eyes, burning through the fear. She nodded once, fast. I jerked my arms and the man crumpled underneath me.

The crack of his neck snapping momentarily drowned out the sound of the alarms and pounding at the doors. I heard gunshots and then Levi was pushing Natasha toward me.

I turned to run with them but made the mistake of looking down. The man's head was turned unnaturally, looking back at me. I groaned, bracing myself against the wall as I swallowed hard. The feel of the man's neck snapping still tingled in my palms. So much worse than a deliriously aimed kick. So much worse than pulling a trigger.

I straightened and wiped my hands on my pants, gathering myself and forcing in deep breaths. "Which way?" I asked Levi, my voice rough. The world was tilting suspiciously.

"Through here. Quick!"

The guards were catching up to us. The world felt strangely sped up and slowed at the same time the more I used my abilities. All of that seemed to take so long, but in reality, it must have been seconds. My hands felt dirty, heavy. But I drew my gun from my belt and started shooting at the approaching guards, motioning for everyone else to keep going. Every time the gun kicked, I felt something inside me fracture further. But I couldn't stop. The queen needed me now and the instinct to back her overshadowed every other thought. Levi fired off a couple of rounds as he ran, each one a direct hit.

I aimed to slow them. I heard Audrey break the lock on another door ahead and the ensuing fight as she took out the four guards who had gathered. I skipped to catch up.

The halls split off in front of us. My head spun, back in

my nightmare as I stepped over the prone guards. Natasha reached and squeezed my arm, her presence grounding me enough to breathe.

"They'll be blocking the entrances!" Audrey shouted over the chaos. Now that we were clear of the pristine hall, her voice was strong again, her gaze returned to normal. Steady and remote.

"This way," Levi said, turning to the right. We came across a set of stairs. I skipped up them to check if the coast was clear. More guards coming, led by a three-striped commander. Guns drawn. But only six of them. I didn't pause and in seconds I was skidding to a stop on the other side of their group, six unconscious bodies in my wake. I doubled back and impatiently waved everyone else forward. They were only halfway up the stairs. Levi let out a low whistle when they reached the top.

I smirked, but it died quickly, the feeling of cracking a man's neck stuck in my palms. My stomach twisted again, but I swallowed down the bile. Natasha reached and squeezed my hand. Her soft fingers replaced the sensation of a spine breaking.

We continued down the winding corridors. Levi muttered to himself, talking through his memory of the blueprints. I realized after a bit that the halls were familiar. Sure enough, we passed the closet where we'd stashed the guards and the staircase we'd initially come down appeared, guards shouting in the halls at the base. Levi's blood was still wet on the chipped concrete steps and spattered up the wall where he'd been shot. Even knowing he was fine now, the sight turned my stomach.

Audrey took the lead. I waited for her to pull out the explosives Hue had given her to blow through the wall. Instead, she positioned herself fourteen stairs up, backed against the opposite rail and pushed off in a powerful lunge. I should be used to seeing the incredible by now, but when Audrey smashed through the wall in a shower of dust and concrete bricks, my mouth dropped open.

The shouting downstairs shifted and focused on the sound of the crash, but by then we had followed Audrey outside. The cold night air was a welcome bite in my lungs. Levi let out a tentative whoop.

We ran for the nearest alley. I couldn't remember the details of our plan past this point. I hadn't actually expected us to get this far. It was too surreal. Levi took the lead again. A slight amount of pressure lifted from my shoulders. I had done my role, now I just had to keep Natasha safe. Levi knew the next part of the journey. He'd get us out of Vichi. I focused on that lightness rather than the memory of death held in my palms. Every hopeful thought was a distraction. I had Natasha. No one with me was dead. I might see Rennie and Oken soon.

We had just slipped into the shadows of the alley when a sleek black transport screeched around the corner. I'd never seen anything like it. Small and compact. A subtle plow attached to the front that snow steamed off. The tire treads were glowing orange, sizzling into the sheet of ice when the transport parked. I drew to a halt and watched. I knew who was behind the tinted windows. Still, my breath caught when Silken got out of the driver's seat on the other side. The disappointment in his eyes carried across the distance between us. A woman got out of the backseat, the same lady who had tried to attack me in Traesha's dungeon. Her eyes burned with fury and found me quickly. She raised her gun and pulled the trigger. Silken protested and Natasha shouted behind me. The bullet hit the concrete where my head had been, but I'd already skipped two steps away.

"Go! I'll catch up!" This was business I wanted behind me. My last nightmare and my own doubts needed resolved once and for all.

Frowning, Audrey grabbed hold of Levi and Natasha and pulled them deeper in the alley.

"Back away, Commander Silken! We need to deal with this traitor as we have all the others!" the woman was shouting. "Show yourself! You've made an enemy of the Bellovian army!"

I skipped, stopping directly across the vehicle from her. I looked at the building behind them, the disorganized shouting, the hole in the wall. "That wasn't at all our intention." I let the sarcasm drip heavily in my voice. The disrespect felt amazing. It tasted like freedom.

I looked down when Yike started to open the passenger door, but I slammed it shut so quickly the metal crunched. My old teammate settled back into his seat. A smirk played at his lips but I had bigger problems than wondering why.

I pulled my gaze back to Silken. The conflict was heavy on his face. He wasn't a threat, at least not now. The woman's gun was aimed between my eyes.

"I will kill you," she promised as her gun kicked.

I skipped, stopping behind her. I rose on tiptoes and whispered in her ear. "You won't be fast enough." She whirled, firing her gun uselessly. The bullet hit a lamp post with a harmless *ping*.

I snorted, back across the transport from her now. She spun to face me, her gun taking longer this time to steady. I was rewarded with the sight of doubt creeping into her eyes. Power thrummed in my veins. I wanted to say more. I wanted her to be afraid. I wanted her to regret her cruelty.

Then Silken hit the back of her head with the butt of his gun and she crumpled to the ground. "Enough games. This is serious, Larson. Your last chance. Please, just listen to me."

I stilled at his tone. The kindness in his eyes wasn't genuine, the cadence of his voice wasn't his normal way of speaking. He was mimicking my father. I knew it wasn't true, wasn't the familiar I longed for, but still my chest cracked.

"You were made to lead the Bellovians. You aren't a follower of some peace-driven and inexperienced queen. You're stronger than that and we all know it. Your father knew it, that's why he trained you so diligently. Did you know he used to pull me aside at events to ask for advice on how to train you? He would pester me for details about how the first week changed from year to year so he could prepare you. He wanted your success, Larson. He thought that you were the key to ending this war. I believed him. So should you. Stop this nonsense. Stop fighting your instincts and the lessons he taught you. Join me and we can achieve what our great country was meant for."

Natasha tugged on the bond, urging me to her side.

"What was that downstairs? The cells?"

"Our most gifted. They need more advanced training, and they need someone gifted to lead them. They need you. Bring back the queen and you can help me decide how to help her reunite with her people in a way that benefits us all."

"No."

Silken cocked his head, feigned patience in his dark eyes. It had to be feigned. This wasn't a man who liked losing. "Larson, you won't get a better offer."

I felt Natasha tugging. I'd gone through so much to get

326

to her. The thought crept into the back of my mind that I didn't know her. That to return to her would be a pledge to follow her, maybe blindly.

But that was what Silken was asking too. I already knew how the commanders led. It was time to give someone else a chance.

"I won't fight for the commanders. You're cruel and power hungry and only cause destruction."

"I'll return your team, your stripe, and when we win, you'll share in our glory. I know my people. I know *you*. Power hungry is the right term, but it's not the negative you paint it in. Power is the only thing worth fighting for. Power means freedom. It means security. It means *never going hungry*."

"It means a fight that never ends."

Silken's smile brightened. He didn't look like my father anymore and it made my head swim with relief. "*Exactly!* And if the fighting doesn't end, neither will our victories. We will stay strong and fed."

"You can't possibly expect to win. Not really. Floria is massive. Their powers are unbeatable. You'll be crushed."

"Floria overestimates its strength. The king doesn't want to fight. He is content. He is weak. The only time he stirred was when we killed his queen. Now he gathers his forces, but what's come of it? Nothing. We're prepared. We know where and when to strike. He won't know what hit him. And then, he'll regret spurning all those who would ally with him. Because I warn you now, he is a sorry friend to have."

Natasha was getting desperate. I urged her to go, sending assurance. My understanding of the bond was instinctual. I knew exactly how to send my wordless message across and how to read the ones she sent.

"Bring me the queen, Commander Larson. Two girls fighting alone can't free a people. But, maybe, you could convince the Trish to fight for us. Then we could talk peace. We can talk about more freedom. You could save their people and ours. We honor our alliances much better than the Florians. You won't get a better offer."

I had already turned from the compassion and peace of my mother's people. It was possible I didn't deserve my position as *resa magsai*. Death loomed in my future, brought on by me. Sightless eyes in limp bodies scattered across my path. I knew that was coming as sure as I knew I belonged at the queen's side. Joining with the Bellovians would mean accepting the inevitable.

But I remembered Dani's body blocking my path. I remembered the unfamiliar kindness shining in the glint of Hinze's eyes. I remembered the blood stain on the floor of my cold home.

"I already have a better offer." I turned to answer Natasha's call.

Silken sighed behind me. "So it begins then. I have completed my duty to Teo's memory. From this moment on, you and I will be enemies."

I laughed. "We have been since the moment my father began training me to take down everything you stand for."

I skipped to my queen's side.

CHAPTER 26

Following Levi, we lost Silken's strange transport easily. After running down a series of side streets, he took us to an abandoned building. He didn't even have to pick the lock, just opened the door to a rundown lobby.

"An old hotel. Hasn't been used much since we don't get guests from Floria anymore."

We settled to catch our breath, leaning against pillars and sitting in window ledges. "Well... that went better than I thought it would," Audrey said between gasps.

"Please tell me you have a plan to get out of here," Natasha said, her eyes on the rat rustling in the corner.

"We just have to stay here long enough to lose anyone following us." Levi stood at the window, watching the dark streets for headlights.

Alarms broke out. At first, I thought our hiding place had a system but soon realized it was coming in from the streets outside. I hadn't even known citywide alarms existed.

"Excellent," Levi said. I thought it was sarcastic, but

when I turned, he was genuinely smiling while he looked up at the ceiling.

"How is that excellent?" I asked. I slipped out of the straps of my backpack.

"The streets will be packed. Everyone will want to know what's happening and try to help. No way they'll be able to chase us with that transport. I've never even seen anything one like that."

"Must be how he got here so quickly."

"That was the commander you saw in Traesha?" Levi asked.

Natasha started. "You were in Traesha? How is it? What's happening? Are they..."

I shook my head. We didn't have time to get into this. "One thing at a time." I pulled out my mother's favorite shawl and draped it over Natasha's head, knotting it loosely under her chin and pulling the rest to cover her shoulders. I pushed back the image of my mother huddled under it, clutching it to her chest and sipping tea. I untucked a few wisps of Natasha's white hair. "When we get out, walk like this." I demonstrated, hunching over and nearly gasping at the pain in my ribs. Natasha rolled her shoulders forward to mimic me. It was then I noticed how impeccably straight her posture had been so far.

"One of our few esteemed elders. Clever," Levi said.

I straightened and Natasha winced like she too felt the stabbing pain in my ribs. She put a hand on my arm and within seconds it had faded away. Natasha swayed.

"You need to take it easy," I said, grabbing her arm so she didn't fall.

"I'm fine. Just haven't eaten and that took more effort than I thought it would," she said, breathless.

Levi fished out his map and flashlight while I handed

330

Natasha a pair of mittens. "They have mechanic shops closer to City Center, but there's one a bit further out with a lot where they keep repaired vehicles ready to go to war. I think that will be our best bet. The fewer people we have to avoid driving the streets, the better."

My heart lurched when he pointed at the shop we were going to target on his map. Of course, it was where Oken had worked. How many times had I gone out of my way walking to Nico's just to pass by hoping to see him working? Very out of my way. The lot was nearly in the Squalor.

"You think we can get there?"

"It won't be easy, but hopefully the crowds will hide us. We'll go through Nico's neighborhood, then it's just a few blocks. We get a transport truck and it's straight on to Floria."

"Floria? What about Traesha?" Natasha pursed her lips, and I felt a flash of frustration through the bond.

"We need help if we're going to get Traesha back," I spoke carefully.

She nodded and took a breath, the anger easing. Its force left me a bit winded. "So, we're going to talk to the king," she said. "My grandfather hoped to one day meet with him."

"And the Trish refugees in Helsa."

Her face relaxed fully hearing that. "Good. Let's go."

With the streets full and our breathing normal, we had no reason to wait. We slipped back into the crowd. I kept Natasha's arm tucked in my own as much to keep her close as to keep up the pretense. The people were shouting about an attack on Command Hall, but nothing about Natasha yet. They didn't know what the alarms meant. I prayed word wouldn't spread quickly. That no one would be looking for us.

Even in the excitement, people made room for us. Respect for the elderly was a prominent aspect of Bellovian culture. There were so few people who lived to that age. Natasha kept her head down and let her white hair disguise her as much as her shuffling walk. The night sky was thick with clouds. Snow continued to fall in gentle puffs, making it just that much harder to see through the crowd. The dust covering us streaked, until we looked as grimy and sodden as everyone else. I couldn't wrap my head around how well it was working. Natasha kept squeezing my arm in her excitement.

Word inevitably spread. People began shouting about Trish in the city and my stomach clutched in fear. I checked my hat. Natasha kept her head ducked. People trickled into City Center from the Squalor to join in the excitement, leaving the streets clear as we neared the outskirts, but also making us more noticeable moving in the opposite direction of the stragglers.

"You two should go ahead," I told Levi. "We'll attract less attention in smaller groups. Try to get the truck hot-wired by the time we get to you."

Levi frowned, but didn't hesitate for long. With a nod, he turned down the next alley, Audrey on his heels. They took a longer route, but at their faster pace they'd still make it before the queen and me. I could feel Natasha's concentration as she forced herself to hobble along. It was torture to pace ourselves so slowly. I kept glancing over our shoulders, looking for small black transports, red uniforms, or commanders.

We were nearing the lot when a woman stepped out of the shadows. Her hollow features etched in lines. The face of the Squalor. She licked her lips, bulging eyes betraying her hunger. She crept closer and I tensed.

"Those are some rich folk coats there, grandma," she said, her smile twitching. She pulled out a knife.

Natasha glanced up in surprise. Of course we were directly beneath one of the few functioning streetlights. The woman took in the youth in Natasha's face. The silver sheen in her hair.

"The Trish!" the woman shrieked, jumping wildly. "I found them! I found them!" Yells answered her from the street over. I quickly silenced her with a jab to the throat. She slid down the wall croaking.

"Skip! I can do it!" Natasha shouted. I thought about how she swayed in the hotel and prayed to Mags she was right.

I took off down the alley, the brick buildings a blur. I didn't even have to look to check if Natasha was matching my pace, I could just tell she was there. The skip didn't help us much in the end—we had already been so close to the lot when the woman saw us. Audrey and Levi were inside working on one of the transport trucks. Natasha and I quickly scaled the fence, Natasha losing the shawl when it caught in joined links on top. My heart lurched when we were forced to leave it behind. Another piece of home, gone.

The jangling of our climb drew the attention of the woman's friends. The shawl, waving like a flag, marked our location. Audrey's eyes widened as she stood guard. Levi's legs were hanging out the driver's side as he worked under the dash.

"Thank the gods," Natasha said over the sound of the engine roaring to life. Audrey jumped over the hood and into the passenger side while Natasha and I scrambled into the back seat.

"Hold tight!" Levi shouted. Our pursuers were already at the fence. Audrey rolled down her window and pulled herself out to sit on the door, gun drawn. Wind and snow swirled inside the truck. She fired a few warning shots over the roof of the truck and they scattered, but only for a moment before firing back. Levi swore and revved the engine. We took off down the line of serviced cargo trucks, transport vehicles, and army grade cycles.

Levi cringed into his seat as we neared the fence. Audrey slid back inside and rolled up her window just before we made impact. The windshield cracked but held as the truck forced the chain-link fence up and over us. It scraped the hood and roof, caught on the lip of the bed for a heart-stopping second, and then we were tearing out of Vichi.

I sagged against the seat and Natasha took my hand. She was trembling, but her dimples were out in full force. Eyes shining as she watched the distance between us and Vichi grow.

We didn't talk for a long time. Each of us working to calm our racing hearts. Adrenaline still rushed my veins, and a flutter of anticipation warmed my stomach. We were on our way to the Front. I would see Oken and Rennie again. Dread threatened knowing I would have to contact the Florians after I'd abandoned them in Traesha's dungeon, but Natasha's presence made me confident that they would want to help no matter their feelings about me. Worry gnawed for Nico, Gale, and Hue. So many people in danger from this war.

I looked over at the queen of Traesha, dumbfounded by the sight of her. I had finally found her. I found a purpose and a possible path toward ending the war that didn't mean killing Florians and giving into the Bellovian commanders. A path my mother had followed and protected for me. I could embrace my Trish heritage, my wildest fantasies, as we made our way forward. Natasha was already brightening the world around me, laughing breathlessly and clutching my hand. Not a shadow at the edge of my dream. Not an incessant pull in my chest. Not dead from the Bellovian attack so long ago. She was here. We were together.

Natasha turned and smiled at me. "Thank you. I just can't believe this. It's perfect. It feels like..."

"Belonging."

ACKNOWLEDGMENTS

It feels like this book has consumed my adult life thus far. Since graduating college, it has been the one thing I have constantly returned to and so many amazing people have been there every step of the way to make it a finished product.

First, thank you to Ben and Allison who kept asking for chapters of the very rough first draft. It was a motivation that likely solidified my writing habits. Every time I get in the chair thinking there might be someone interested in what I have to type, I think of you two.

A huge thanks to Sarah. *Huge.* You made the first suggestions that got this book to where it is and your constant encouragement, willingness to answer texts as I made every decision in this process, and knowledge of the trade has been too helpful to describe.

Thank you to Anna and Kaitlyn for being the target audience and loving it enough to make me feel I'm on the right path. Your excitement and smiles made every minute of work worth it.

Thank you to my editor, Emily Morris, and copy editor, Clem Flanagan, for working with me as a first-time writer. Despite my overwhelm and the length of time it took me to get to your edits, this book wouldn't be what it is without you both.

Thank you Mom for always asking for updates and

making me feel I'm doing the right thing when I could have gotten a "real job."

Thank you to every person who got excited for me while I talked about self-publishing. Your enthusiasm and interest made me believe this was possible. To everyone that read an early draft, thank you for all the kind words and the time you took. Every encouragement went right to my heart and some days I only keep writing because you've asked for more.

Love you all!

About the Author

Kelly Cole graduated with a major in English from the University of Wyoming. She lives in Wyoming with her dog, Maya. They exist in a constant struggle of trying to find enough time to write, read, and play fetch. Visit her website at www.kellycolebooks.com for more information.

CPSIA information can be obtained
at www.ICGtesting.com
Printed in the USA
LVHW050859160422
715845LV00002B/16